Marie Sophie Schwartz

THE

SON OF THE ORGAN-GRINDER.

MARIE SOPHIE SCHWARTZ,

AUTHORESS OF

"GOLD AND NAME," "BIRTH AND EDUCATION," "GUILT AND INNOCENCE," "THE WIFE OF A VAIN MAN," "THE RIGHT ONE," "TWO FAMILY MOTHERS," ETC., ETC.

TRANSLATED FROM THE SWEDISH

BY

SELMA BORG AND MARIE A. BROWN,

THE TRANSLATORS OF "THE SCHWARTZ," "BLANCHE" AND "TOPELIUS" NOVELS, AND OF "NORTHERN LIGHTS."

PHILADELPHIA:

PORTER & COATES.

822 CHESTNUT STREET.

WESTCOTT & THOMSON,
Stereotypers, Philada.

HENRY B. ASHMEAD,
Printer, Philada.

MADAME MARIE SOPHIE SCHWARTZ.

THE introduction of a new author is always an era in the history of a country. As the reception of a stranger into a family may turn the whole tide of that family's destiny, laying a train of causes whose results may reach many generations into the future, so a new mental personality may exert an untold influence upon the thought and character of a nation, moulding it, imperceptibly, until all the old outlines are changed and an entire transformation effected. All progress is due to this interior assimilation of fresh elements. Everything starts in a thought; even the most material operation. A book is the most perfect vehicle of thought, one that can travel everywhere, over all roads, to any and every destination. If that book is freighted with sound and healthy thought, clothed in the attractive garb of fiction,—which only means objective style,—it is a condensed force, capable of effecting in a flash what years of experience, long knowledge of the world and constant observation may fail to do. The reason of this is, that it takes us entirely out of ourself, beyond our own realm of sensation, and strikes chords of feeling that have never been touched before. It elaborates unimagined ways, untried lines of conduct, illustrates the tendency and ultimate of all action, and is, in a word, a panorama of life scenes.

A book's power is in proportion to its worth: if it is trashy or pernicious, it fails of assimilation and is soon rejected, for human nature, in spite of its ignorance and perversion, ever seeks the good, and will not cleave to anything else after it finds out the deception.

The value of the literature of any nation may be estimated by its permanence in other lands: if an author is broad and far-reaching in his sympathies and perceptions, he writes to and for the world; if he is walled in by his nationality, he can never attain more than a local interest. Because he is selfish and isolated, other people become selfish and isolated and exclude him.

He may be received at first, out of curiosity, but he can never become a member of the family.

This transplanting upon foreign soil is the hardest test that can be applied to an author. If he grows and thrives in the new condition, he is numbered with the great; if he droops and withers, it only hastens his decline elsewhere.

Madame Marie Sophie Schwartz was subjected to this test three years ago, and was one of the happy exceptions, as indeed Swedish writers ever have been, for they seem to have an "open sesame" to the hearts and homes of the world. The Scandinavian literature enriches every land into which it enters, and is *always* pronounced worthy.

This fact is our sole excuse, our sole motive, for introducing it in the United States, through one of its ablest representative novelists. That she had become standard in several European nations entitled her to acquaintance here; that this acquaintance has ripened into sincere love and appreciation, justifies us in reproducing all her works.

The following sketch of Madame Schwartz's life is interesting as coming from one who met her personally, besides having an æsthetic knowledge of her as a writer. It appeared in the *Gartenlaube*, 1869, and is from the pen of von Robert Byr, the celebrated German novelist and critic:

". . . After the appearance of her first books Mme. Schwartz showed uncommon diligence, and several volumes appeared annually from her pen. The incentive to this must have been in the unabated enthusiasm of the public, or perhaps in her pecuniary condition. She is the only Swedish novelist now writing, and whatever may be brought up against female authors, even the sharpest opponent must concede that she understands how to combine and weave together the affairs of the heart in a manner never equalled by any man. The life of the emotions is a field in which she is the prominent leader, and seldom has an author been able with so small means and within so narrow confines to evoke such a healthful agitation of thought without transcending due limits. Long strides and abrupt movements do not become ladies. Swedish female novelists especially exhibit this natural tact, this indisputably womanly quality of impressive delineation. But where Mme. Schwartz surpasses her predecessors is in the clear and admirable moral tendency which forms the basis of all her works. In every book she tries, with an honest purpose and a clear spirit, to solve some social or ethical question, and the result is a healthy vigor, which cannot be said of all writers. Every mother can put the novels of Mme. Schwartz, without hesitation, into the hands of her daughters. Life in them is not presented through a prism that bends the rays of truth, but spirit and character are portrayed for the world as it is instead of for a perverted ideal.

"And now we ring the bell, soon to meet face to face the lady of whom we have spoken so much.

"A fine-looking and elegant young man opened the door for us and showed us into a reception-room, where he left us alone in order to apprise his mother, as I believed, of our visit. I felt abashed when Mme. Schwartz entered at having ascribed to her such a full-grown son, so little did she make on me the impression of an elderly lady. In her simple house dress, with her plainly arranged hair and her expressive but not exactly beautiful features, she seemed to me scarcely forty, yet she is past that age.

"Marie Sophie Birath was born in Boraes, West Goethland, in 1819. She was left an orphan at an early age. Her uncle who had taken care of her also died and left his widow with their adopted child in great poverty. As it was necessary to prepare the young girl for a vocation, she herself chose the art of painting, for which her fine talent qualified her and the assistance of a friend of the family enabled her to pursue. She painted landscapes, and the art-loving king of Sweden himself purchased one of her productions, which is now placed in the small north gallery in the royal palace. But before this, however, when the young artiste only numbered seventeen years, a wonderful change of mind occurred with her in consequence of a severe illness. The maiden, before so serene, became melancholy and dreamy, and in order to lighten her oppressed soul the scarcely-matured girl seized the pen and wrote, but all alone in quiet and seclusion.

"Married in the year 1839, the young woman was for a time obliged to abstain from her usual occupation, as her husband, Professor Gustaf Magnus Schwartz, cherished, in spite of his great learning and intellectual culture, a peculiar aversion to the beautiful arts, and especially toward a public pursuit of the same by women. It caused the active spirit a hard struggle, until the prejudice was so far put aside that after eleven years the first novel of Mme. Marie Sophie Schwartz appeared in print, and as this one gained public recognition her husband no longer placed any obstacle in her path. Still these works were published with merely the initials of her name. Not until after the death of the Professor, when her prominent position as a writer made it necessary, did she appear openly under her full name. From that period her works have appeared in rapid succession. By her assiduity she obtained a comfortable income, of which the beautiful but unostentatious apartments bore evidence. At the time of our visit she was preparing for a journey. She told us that she was about starting for Norway, where she hoped to find rich material for future stories. Her eyes, deep and full of soul, spoke of unusual gifts. The mild glance softened the otherwise too stern and somewhat masculine features, and gave beautiful testimony of the richly endowed mind, while the prominent chin indicated firmness of will and strength of character.

"After the usual inquiries which followed the first introduction the conversation turned upon Fraulein Marlitt, whose 'Gold Elsie' was published by Mme. Schwartz in a Swedish translation shortly after its appearance in the *Gartenlaube,* thus finding an audience also in Sweden.

"Madame Schwartz heartily and unreservedly praised Madame Marlitt, and she spoke with enthusiasm of the literary excellence of her work. An amiable smile lighted her countenance, and the loveliest look, the frankest joy and recognition illumined the shy eyes. It was no artificial praise, it was the happy outburst of a noble soul at finding a sister, to understand whom nothing was wanting but a common mother tongue.

"I went away feeling that I had, that day, become acquainted with an authoress who writes, not from vanity, but from a high and sincere purpose, not forgetting that she is a woman, and maintaining the most beautiful of all things—a true womanhood."

It is due to Mme. Nilsson-Rousaud to state that her glowing testimony to her countrywoman's fame at home prepared the way for Mme. Schwartz here, in a manner which no other could have done. Her letter will be prized by all who love and admire these two gifted women of Sweden.

To MISS SELMA BORG.

NEW YORK a 28 Novembre 1870.

MADEMOISELLE,

C'est avec grand plaisir que j'ai appris que vous, en collaboration avec Miss Marie A. Brown, avez entrepris de traduire en Anglais les magnifiques œuvres de Madame Marie Sophie Schwartz.

Permettez moi donc, chère Mademoiselle, en fervente admiratrice du talent de Madame Schwartz, de vous offrir ainsi qu'à Miss Brown, mes vîves félicitations d'avoir choisi un Auteur d'un si immense mérite afin de faire connaitre au public Américain un écrivain qui a contribué à faire la gloire de notre Pays.

Je vous souhaite tant le succès que vous méritez et vous prie de vouloir bien m'envoyer un exemplaire de l'ouvrage aussitôt qu'il sera publié.

Veuillez agréer, Mademoiselle, pour vous et Miss Brown, l'expression de ma vive sympathie et l'assurance de ma parfaite considération.

CHRISTINE NILSSON.

[*Translation.*]

NEW YORK, November 28, 1870.

MADEMOISELLE,

It is with great pleasure that I have learned that you, in conjunction with Miss Marie A. Brown, have undertaken to translate into English the magnificent works of Madame Schwartz.

Allow me then, dear Mademoiselle, as a fervent admirer of Madame Schwartz, to offer you and Miss Brown my liveliest felicitations for having chosen an author of so immense merit to introduce to the American public, a writer who has contributed to make the glory of our country.

I wish you all the success you deserve, and beg you to be so kind as to send me a copy of the work as soon as it is published.

Accept, Mademoiselle, as well as Miss Brown, my warmest sympathy and the assurance of my perfect consideration.

CHRISTINE NILSSON.

And lastly, we append Madame Schwartz's letters to us, the translators, as indicative of the feelings with which she received the tidings of her new success across the ocean. These also contain an account of her literary career and the order in which her works appeared. Out of the list she sent us we have published six books: "Gold and Name," "Birth and Education," "Guilt and Innocence," "The Wife of a Vain Man," "The Right One," and "Two Family Mothers." These novels differ widely from each other, and were selected in this order to exhibit the various phases of her exceedingly versatile talent. The first one, "Gold and Name," published December 17th, 1870, established her success, and the five that succeeded it only served to elaborate the remarkable powers which, although they make themselves felt in one book, need all her productions to exhibit the marvellous scope and originality of her genius.

SELMA BORG,
MARIE A. BROWN.

[*Translation.*]

STOCKHOLM, April 28, 1871.
Majors Gatan, No. 9.

HIGHLY ESTEEMED FRÖKEN SELMA BORG:

Your letter of the 28th December, 1870, I have had the honor to receive. I would also have replied immediately, had not a severe affection of the eyes placed a hindrance in the way. The physicians have now given me permission to begin work a little, and the first use I make of this permission is to reply to your dear letter.

Receive my heart's sincere thanks for the interest you have shown my efforts as an author, as well as for the gift of my work, which you have translated in America. It is to me more dear than I can in words express to know that in the New World also, attention is devoted to my productions. That Europe has encouraged them is something which has constituted, not only my joy but also my surprise; for I considered myself undeserving of the favor the public has lavished upon me. Warm and fervent is my gratitude to God for this unmerited success. If I should also succeed in gaining a large number of readers in America, who interest themselves in what a Swedish woman has dreamed and written, it will be you to whom I shall stand in obligation; and be assured that I shall always preserve this debt in grateful remembrance.

You desire to receive some information with regard to my literary career. Ah! my Fröken, this account would be too long, as circumstances have forced me to an incredible productivity. You will therefore allow me to mention only my larger works, as the lesser could scarcely be of any other interest than that which they had for the moment.

My first attempt as an author was published in the year 1852, and was entitled "Slander." I believe that it betrayed all the lacks of a new beginner, and also some of the merits of an overflowing fancy. It was well received, and was followed the same year by the little romance "The Unprotected." The public also received with much kindness this over-wrought sketch of the illegitimate children's sad fate, which was perhaps written too much in the French style, then fashionable. I will leave the romances and novels which followed during the course of several years, and pass on to my first "*tendance*" work, published in 1858 under the title "Two Family Mothers." It was succeeded by "The Man of Birth, and Woman of the People;" the tendency of which was against birth, aristocracy. It had a greater success than any of my preceding works. I became fashionable in my native land, and I wrote with increased zeal and with all the joy success bestows. Then followed "Work Ennobles Man," "Guilt and Innocence," "Is Man's Character his Destiny?" "The Nobleman's Daughter," "Birth and Education," "The Right One," "Gold and Name," and "The Children of Work." All of these, as well as some not mentioned, are translated into Danish, German and Hollandish languages, some in French ("The Man of Birth"), in English and Polish.

Since "The Children of Work," no larger work of mine has been published in Swedish *with my name.* In 1865 I entered into a contract with Otto Janke, in Berlin, which authorized him to publish my works in German, with the reserved right that they would not be printed in Swedish until one year after they had appeared in Berlin, and then only under a pseudonym. The children of my pen had been so well received in Germany, that Janke was able to offer me a larger "honorarium" than the Swedish publishers. After this contract, I published here "The Son of the Organ-Grinder," without the author's name, and then "Souvenirs of Youth," "My Life's Changes," and "David Waldner," all by the author of "The Son of the Organ-Grinder." Then a new contract was made with Janke, in which he increased the "honorarium," on the condition that some of my works should not be published in Sweden at all until three years after they were issued in Germany. Upon these conditions were published "Aunt Gabriella," "To be, or Not to be," "The Linnet," "The Sisters-in-Law," "The Step-Daughter," and "The Two Comrades;" the latter this year.

Now I have fatigued you, Fröken Borg, with these accounts, but I have considered it my duty to give them to you, as you desired to have a complete knowledge of all my works.

Warmly did my heart beat for the ideas I tried to vindicate during the time I made the "*tendance*" novels my aim; but I felt that I, alas, was not up to the problems I wished to solve, the abuses I wished to point at, or the truths I wished to defend; and this feeling of incapacity in accomplishment has often cost me bitter pangs. Deeply and sincerely do I love the good and the true, and from my inmost heart have I tried to work for their promotion; but a woman remains a woman, whether she wields the needle or the pen; and I have felt deeply that the clearness in rendering, and that deep knowledge of human nature which is required to carry through what I, presumptuously enough, made the main object of my writings, is lacking in me. That I, in spite of these deficiencies, have had a success far greater than I dared to hope for even in my boldest dreams, shall always be regarded by me as something for which I have God's goodness alone to thank.

If you have read "The Man of Birth, and Woman of the People," you will also find that I have loved and admired America, and regarded that continent as the cradle of the highest ideas. You can then understand how great is my joy and gratitude when I, through you, see a possibility that this fresh America's people shall become interested in Swedish literature. Once more my heart's warm thanks for this joy.

Have the great kindness to present my thanks to the publishers of my works, for their politeness in sending me the translation of "Gold and Name;" and give your friend Miss Brown my most obliging thanks for her co-operation in rendering my works into the English language.

Dear will it be to me to continue the correspondence now begun, and I hope you will soon gladden me with some lines from your hand.

With utmost esteem,

MARIE SOPHIE SCHWARTZ.

STOCKHOLM, May 8, 1871.

HONORED FRÖKEN SELMA BORG:

Your letter of April 19, I have had the honor to receive through Herr Sigfrid Flodin, and permit me to thank you most heartily for it. The sympathy you have there expressed for my works is to me very flattering. It is also a dear duty to openly acknowledge that the translation of "Gold and Name" has been accomplished with all the care and accuracy an author can desire. One sees from it that the translators have put themselves completely into the author's thoughts and ideas, something which places all translation on a level with the original. It would also be a fervent desire of mine that you, my Fröken, and Miss Brown, were the only ones who translated Swedish authors in America, because they would then be introduced in a worthy manner.

You have desired a list of all my works, and I enclose it together with a portrait of the undersigned.

What I may be able to do for you, I shall do with true pleasure and interest, if you only turn to me; I beg you to be assured of this.

Present to Miss Brown my most obliging greetings, and thanks for the courtesy which has been shown me.

With the utmost esteem,

MARIE SOPHIE SCHWARTZ.

LIST OF M. S. SCHWARTZ'S WRITINGS.

1852. Slander.
" The Unprotected.
1853. Marriage.
" Self-Interest.
" The Passions.
1854. Family Life.
" Mathilda.
1855. Where there is a Will there is a Way.
" Leaves from Woman's Life.
1856. The Widow and her Children.
" Ellen.
" The Emancipation Mania.
1857. A Double Purpose in Life.
" The Wife of a Vain Man.

1858. Alma.
" Two Family Mothers.
" The Man of Birth, and Woman of the People.
1859. Work Ennobles Man.
" Viola.
" A Victim of Vengeance.
1860. Guilt and Innocence.
1861. Is Man's Character his Destiny?
" The Nobleman's Daughter.
1862. Birth and Education.
" The Girl from Corsica.
1863. The Right One.
" Gold and Name.
" The Children of Work.
" The Son of the Organ-Grinder.
" The Daughter of Poland.
1864. Recollections of Youth.
1865. My Life's Changes.
1866. David Waldner.
1871. The Linnet.

The following are not yet published in Sweden:

To Be, or Not To Be.
The Sisters-in-Law.
The Step-Daughter.
Two Comrades.
Aunt Gabriella.

A collection of short stories under the following titles published in Sweden:

Turn the Leaf.
Once More.
Historical Tales.
Novellettes.
Images from Reality.
For the Moment.
Episodes from the Lives of E. Tegner,
F. Bremer, C. G. Nicander, etc.

THE

SON OF THE ORGAN-GRINDER.

FIRST PERIOD.

CHAPTER I.

THE first recollection I have of my father is that he taught me to stand on my head, turn somersaults, roll like a wheel and jump through hoops.

I was quite a little fellow when these exercises took their beginning. My strong physique and natural agility had probably given my father the idea of making me an acrobat.

To become an "artist" in the noble art of putting myself into repulsive and grotesque positions was the aim which was set before my ambition, in case nature had endowed me with any such thing.

I had to learn to eat while standing on my head, walk on my hands with my feet crossed over my neck, scratch myself behind the ear with my foot, etc.

My career was to begin with performing these feats to the music of my father's hand-organ before the gaping street-boys of the town, and in the country before the astonished peasantry, afterward collecting in my cap a few coppers in reward for my efforts.

When I had thus acquired the habit of appearing in public, I might in the happiest event be raised to the rank, honor and dignity of circus-rider, and in this capacity accompany some travelling troop of "artists."

Whether I was by nature called to this career is hard to decide. It certainly looked so, when I, at four years of age, began my practice, for I learned very easily, and cannot remember that my father a single time at these lessons used the whip he constantly held in his hand. If I had been dull of comprehension, it is pretty certain that the rod would have spurred it up. As it was, he quite frequently, after the lesson was over, patted me on the head, and said proudly:

"It is plain to be seen, Conny, that you are blood of my blood, that something can be made of you in time. You have no peasant nature, but an artistic bent which will some day make you a fine gentleman."

It is true I was quite contented with the praise, but especially because I entertained a high degree of fear for my father. My contentment did not have its ground in any pride over the prospect that I might in time become a "gentleman," but proceeded merely from the selfish satisfaction that I for that day had been spared from tasting the whip.

Even at the very first lessons I felt an inner dislike to them. I thought, as children often think, that it was unnecessary to learn these arts, and that my father, in his artistic career, had not gained particular success.

The first good luck which he had enjoyed was, according to my understanding, that he obtained my mother for a wife. Still, this was a blessing which I afterward discovered that he did not value very highly; for it often happened that father, when he came home after being away for a length of time, committed such abuses toward his wife that it was only with the greatest difficulty that my elder brother, Paul, was able to save her from his violence.

To me there was no gladder sight than when my father, accompanied by Paul and his hand-organ, started off on a long tramp.

Mother and I then remained in our humble home, where poverty, it is true, was a constant guest, but yet where a quiet peace prevailed during father's absence.

My mother worked, spun and sewed all day long, while I, sitting beside her on a stool, learned to read. The catechism and biblical history were the works which occupied my time and my thoughts. When I was not reading, I made large, straight characters on a slate which mother had received from the sheriff's wife.

As a general thing I liked to learn, with the exception of the acrobatic exercises; but when father returned home, the book and the slate were laid aside, and my arms, legs and joints were set in motion, to accustom them to do service in a way that stood in direct opposition to their natural function.

My life appeared to me as the ideal of heaven and hell. I found myself in heaven when father was away; hell began when he blessed us with his presence.

I had formed a peculiar conception of the former as well as the latter.

I imagined the prince of darkness as a large, heavily-built man, something like the one who gave me life, armed with a whip, and engaged in teaching a lot of little boys to stand on their heads, etc. His whole kingdom was peopled with beings who, day in and day out, performed all sorts of acrobatic feats. I could not get any other idea into my head than that these were invented by the evil one.

The kingdom of heaven I peopled with mild, pale and beautiful women resembling my mother, who worked and had beside them children of my age, who felt happy in being allowed to read the catechism.

This proves that human beings, even in the years of childhood, imagine eternal compensation or retribution in accordance with the ideas of joy and torment which experience has conveyed to them.

Of my parents' earlier life I only know that my father was a German by birth. He had when quite young accompanied an organ-grinder to Sweden. The latter paid him a certain amount for performing juggler tricks in the street to the music of the hand-organ. Afterward he had fallen in with some circus company and married one of the female artistes; by this wife he had a son, my brother Paul.

My father's first wife broke her neck in a performance, and left the two-year-old Paul motherless—a serious obstacle to my father's artistic career.

The circus company were at that time staying in Lindköping.

Father and his wife lived with an old woman who kept a tavern. When the accident occurred, and my father was puzzled about finding a place for Paul, the old tavern-keeper offered to take the boy for a certain price.

My father scraped together all the farthings he could get and gave them to the woman, after which he left Lindköping and his son, promising to return in two years. He came back according to agreement, yet not after two, but four years.

He had now ceased his "artistic" exhibitions, and was an organ-grinder instead.

The former acrobat looked up the old tavern-keeper and his child.

Paul was at that period six years old, and had been very ill. The tavern-keeper had not been especially wicked to him, but she had left the boy entirely to himself. If she gave him food when he asked for it, and a thrashing when he pilfered, it seemed to her that she had done all that could be expected of her; that the boy was scarcely clothed, and besides covered with eruptions and vermin, were such trifles that his foster-mother did not take them into consideration.

Paul would undoubtedly have perished from neglect, had it not been for a chambermaid who lived with a lady of rank a few houses from his home.

The chambermaid had conceived a compassionate interest for the pretty but abandoned boy. She gave him clothes when he was without them; and when her mistress was away, she took the boy to the house, combed his hair, washed him and put clean linen on him.

Whether my father was touched by his son's situation I leave to conjecture, yet he seemed to be too much of an "artist" to pay attention to such trifles. He was struck by something quite different—namely, Paul's beautiful voice; when the boy sang some of his street songs, the child's tones awakened in my father great hopes for the future, and Paul was taken from his foster-mother to accompany him as street-singer.

From the beginning the intention had been to only stay in Lindköping long enough to earn sufficient to be able to go to another place, and for Paul to learn some new songs; but fate had ordained otherwise.

Chance brought father in connection with Paul's protectress, the pretty and good Annette.

An organ-grinder can also have an eye for the beautiful, and this was just the case with my father. He himself was a stately, fine-looking man, who, with his velvet blouse, his little cap on one side over the dark curly hair, and the most seductive black moustaches, must of a necessity have been dangerous to a chambermaid's heart. This was actually the case.

He fell in love with Annette, and was loved in return.

Six months after my father's arrival at Lindköping they became a pair.

Father had done an excellent business while he remained there. My mother, besides, had a few hundred thalers in inheritance from her parents. This money was drawn immediately after the wedding, and the newly-married couple left the place to go to my mother's native province, Uppland, where they were to buy a cottage.

Mother had at their marriage made the condition that they should purchase a piece of land with her money, and that father should settle down in peace with his wife and child, working for their support, and no longer stroll around with his hand-organ.

My father might have left his "artistic career" and lived easy, cultivating the soil, but he had no inclination for private life; he loved the public one too well. He was too much accustomed to his nomad existence to thrive in one spot. He liked the bustle of the streets, the racket of the taverns, and found it more to his taste to grind the hand-organ than to dig in the earth.

They established their abode in a village called Skärparby. My father bought a house there, with the accompanying potato-patch, but without any other land. He continually postponed getting any, notwithstanding he promised my mother from day to day that he would do it. Time passed, and one fine day it was found that the money was all gone, so that he no longer had anything to purchase with.

This sad discovery was made when they had been married a little over a year.

Father had spent this year in doing nothing; he lived well, and at night frequented the tavern, gambling and drinking with the peasants.

When the purse was now found empty, he took the matter quite philosophically, drew out the dusty hand-organ, took Paul with him and left his home and wife, perfectly contented at having a chance to get rid of both.

All that my mother possessed when he went away from her was two rix-thalers in money, a little herring and milk, and the potatoes that grew in the yard.

It was at the end of summer that my father entered upon his first "artistic journey" since he married my mother.

In the winter I was born, and in the spring my father and brother returned, bringing with them some money. As long as this lasted they stayed at home; but when it was consumed, they went away again, leaving my poor mother to take care of herself and child as best she could.

During the very first months of their marriage, my mother had every reason to repent the step she had taken, for a life of suffering and privation stared her in the face.

To repent a folly is indeed very commendable, but generally avails nothing. All the tears in the world cannot make it undone. Accordingly, my mother chose that which was much wiser than to mourn over it—namely, she tried to make her fate as endurable as possible.

She was good at all sorts of handiwork, and soon became the seamstress and assistant of the village in everything that demanded a little more knowledge than the peasant-women in general possess.

In this way she succeeded in closing her door to want, and would even have been able to live a life free from care, if father had not spent five or six months at home, and then used up, not only what he himself had earned, but also the small savings which mother had made during his absence.

It often happened that he came home without a single

farthing, and then it was mother who had to provide for the whole household. The result was that she never, with all her work, could get farther than to keep hunger banished from her dwelling.

The first bitter sorrow that befell my mother was when father took Paul with him to sing to his hand-organ.

Paul was dear to her, and it pained her that the boy should not have a chance to go to school or learn anything except to stroll around as a street-singer, but what father wished she knew it would be vain to strive against.

He did not intend to make his son a peasant or mechanic, but Paul should become a "singer," and earn his bread as his father and grandfather had done—that is to say, in the street.

If Paul could have become an acrobat or juggler, father would certainly have trained him to it; but Paul's body had through neglect become misshapen. He walked with his knees bent and so close together that his legs formed a sort of angle. In addition, they were so thin that it seemed as if they were not able to support his body. He was, besides, lean and spindling, with long arms and a stooping posture. It looked as though he, from his earliest childhood, had obtained the stamp which is always found with those who go around with hand-organs.

If the rest of Paul's body was in complete harmony with his capacity of street-singer, his face was not. Nature had through one of her strange caprices endowed him with such beautiful and regular features that it made a sad impression upon a lover of beauty to see this well-shaped head on a long and crooked neck, which raised itself above a pair of round shoulders.

There was, however, in the expression of the face, a mixture of careless unconcern, good-natured cheerfulness and a certain sadness. The large dark eyes had occasionally something melancholy, which was in sharp contrast with the nonchalant smile around the well-formed mouth.

His voice was as clear, pure, ringing and fresh as his face was handsome.

I have heard my mother say that every time he returned from his "artistic" journey, as my father called their perambulations, his voice had developed in strength and clearness. When Paul became older, he brought home entirely new songs, and also various pieces of music. How he learned these he did not say, and was particularly anxious to conceal this knowledge from father. He had also procured books, although my mother could not comprehend how he had learned to read them.

When father and he were at home, Paul would spend whole days sitting in a corner reading the books he had bought. To my mother's question, how he had acquired the knowledge of reading them, he answered:

"Mother, have you not told me that I ought to learn something? I have learned to read and write, and I shall certainly learn more than that in-course of time. When father sits drinking in the taverns, then I get a little learning in my head instead, in order to give you joy, mother, and, when I grow older, help Conny."

Paul's disposition was cheerful, gentle and quiet; but when his will was set on anything, he appeared unbending.

If father, in an intoxicated condition, forgot himself toward mother, Paul was like a lion, and let father beat him as much as he chose, but kept him from ill-treating her.

Paul loved me so deeply that he knew no greater delight than to afford me a joy. Even if he sometimes returned to us covered with rags, he nevertheless had a plaything or picture-book for me.

When my father made me, at four years of age, begin my training as an acrobat, my mother came near sinking under the sorrow it gave her that I too should be formed into a "vagabond," as *she* called highway and street "artists."

She vehemently opposed my father's intermeddling in the direction of my life, and asserted that she had resolved to educate me for a regular trade. Father's whip, however, settled the dispute. After this termination I began my gymnastics.

It was early in the spring. I was just six years old. As father had been away the whole winter, I scarcely thought that he would return, but played quite unconcerned with some other children from the village, as mother had gone out with a piece of work she had finished.

Apropos of the village, I will say something about this remarkable place, where my cradle stood.

It was one of those ugly places surrounded by wide-stretched plains, where a mass of crooked and sunken wooden cabins, some red and some bleached in the sun, had been brought together in wild order, with barn-yards and dung-hills for an embellishment.

Most of the houses in Skärparby had no potato-patch and no tree near them, but were destitute of everything that could please the eye. In the whole village there were only two trees, and these stood on the rich Pehr Pehrson's place.

Below the village went the high road which leads from U—— to G——. The village street ended at the main road, where the sheriff's house lay to the right.

This, with its little well-kept terrace under the windows, and its large garden on the other side of the road, resembled a flowery gem thrown in the midst of these ugly, bare flats.

When you came from G—— and passed by the sheriff's

place, you had directly after it three cabins, which lay separated from the village by the street on the other side of them.

This little row of dwellings was called "the grove," because there were a few trees, which before each one of the cabins formed, as it were, a little kitchen-garden.

The last of these cabins was my paternal home. The scrap of earth which surrounded it was carefully cultivated. In every available spot my mother's industrious hands had planted peas, beans and potatoes. The crooked windows of the cabin were clean, and inside were a few blooming geraniums, balsams and fuchsias, and a fine myrtle. There were also little snow-white window-curtains, all of which gave to the organ-grinder's cabin an orderly and unusually trim appearance.

The well-raked path which led from the gate to the cabin door, the freshly-scoured stoop, all contrasted sharply with the two neighboring houses, with their untidy entrances and yards filled with weeds, sweepings and refuse.

These two miserable cabins had as bad a reputation as their exterior was repulsive.

In the one which lay nearest our cabin lived a peasant by the name of Fransson, who had been in prison for theft. His wife had been accused of hiding stolen goods, and the children were known over the whole village for their pilfering.

At the time when I reached my seventh year, Fransson's term of imprisonment had expired, and he returned to his family.

In the cabin nearest the sheriff's house lived the widow of a soldier by the name of Barsk, who, as a murderer and felon, had been executed.

Mother Barsk was generally called Black Stina. She was large and gross in form, broad-shouldered as a man, and with arms and hands so muscular that they denoted an unusual strength. She had black hair, a dark complexion, a low, broad brow, and a pair of small black eyes which were piercing as knives when she looked at one. Her whole appearance had something defiant, sinister and secretive.

It was said that she was of Tartar origin, and knew things which no one else had any knowledge of.

All the children of the village were afraid of Black Stina; and when they saw her from afar, they took to their heels and began to run as fast as they could.

Among those with whom she inspired the greatest terror, I was included.

My mother also seemed to fear her, for she often said to me:

"When you see Black Stina, get out of her way; but greet her politely, and take care not to provoke her and her Janne."

Janne was Black Stina's son, and of the same age as Paul—that is to say, several years older than I. He resembled his mother as one berry resembles another. The children of the village were as much afraid of Janne as of Black Stina. He scarcely ever associated with any children but the Franssons.

Only in passing had Janne devoted any attention to me, and that was a couple of times when mother had gone to the village and not taken me with her; then he watched his chance, and quite kindly gave me a drubbing, in order, as he asserted, to make me limber in the joints.

When this happened for the second time, my mother considered it advisable to take me along when she was obliged to leave home, and thus I came in no further contact with Janne.

Black Stina was only twenty when her husband was

executed, and Janne only two. Still, she continued after this event to live in the same cabin where Barsk had been taken, and supported herself, after his death, by spinning wool. Her especial means of gaining a livelihood, however, was to tell fortunes, pronounce incantations over sick-beds—or "cast spells," as it is also called—and to cure animals. She was the help of the village and the country round about in everything where superstition was in the performance; and we all know what an important rôle it plays among the peasantry.

Black Stina made the most of this fact; she was well aware that people at once feared and abhorred her, but yet solicited her aid, because they ascribed to her the honor of having knowledge of things which were inexplicable to others.

Taciturn, hard and shy of humanity, she had all that was needed to overawe the superstitious and to inspire the credulous with the thought that she stood in alliance with the under-world.

Ever since her husband's death, Stina was clad in a black skirt and jacket. On her head she was accustomed to wear, in winter, a black woollen handkerchief resembling a pall.

Her skirt was, at the end of the year, an incomprehensible hanging mass of tatters, which had lost their color and passed over to gray, so covered with dirt were they. Every New Year's day one saw her in a new costume, which was then worn steadily for a whole year, while no needle ever did anything to mend the slits it received.

If I except the fear of my father, there was no one who gave me such a panic as Black Stina. There was nothing that could have induced me to enter her gate.

In my imagination this abode constituted something terrible. There, inside the broken windows stopped up with rags, were any number of small naked children, who performed acrobatic feats all the day long. The beholders consisted of a lot of owls, crows, cats and frogs, which sat around the walls, looking at the poor little creatures, who stood on their heads, while Black Stina beat them.

How this absurd notion ever entered my head I cannot explain, unless from the fact that I had heard all the children say that Stina had owls, crows and frogs, as well as two large yellow cats, which never showed themselves outside her cabin door. That there were little children whom she tormented was a product of my own imagination.

The amount of the matter was that Black Stina was my dread and horror. When I saw her step out of her cabin, I ran with all my might until I had gained security in ours. If I met her on the road and could not avoid encountering the object of my fear, I took off my cap and bowed as deeply as if I had seen a royal person, well recollecting my mother's words to be polite.

This woman and the Franssons were thus our nearest neighbors. It must be admitted that they were not of the kind that people like to have in their vicinity. Truth demands, however, that I give them the credit of never occasioning my mother any harm or disturbing her in the slightest way.

The Franssons' young ones pilfered from everybody in the village, even from the sheriff, but they did not take as much as a bean or pea from my mother. Their parents now and then entertained suspicious persons, but without our having any knowledge of it, except that the sheriff made frequent visits to them and generally gave these uninvited guests free passage to U——.

It was, as I have said, early in the spring, when I and a few other children were playing outside our cabin. We amused ourselves by throwing snow-balls. The sun shone mildly down upon the soft snow, and dissolved it into water.

We had been bombarding each other without either side gaining the victory. The two parties we had formed had been treated equally, and the battle continued in tumultuous glee, when all at once Janne jumped over the fence and stood in the midst of us, shouting:

"What numbskulls! what rabbits! who are not able to wallop each other, so that it tells. I will give it to you for being such weaklings;" and with this he seized hold of the boy who stood nearest to him, and began, with mauling and blows, to bury him in the snow.

The little crowd of bantlings, of the same age as I, scattered instantly and took to their heels; they all scampered off at the top of their speed, leaving one of their comrades in Janne's power, to be abused by him as much as he pleased. I also had beaten a retreat to the front stoop, but there I stopped, checked by the poor little boy's cries of lamentation.

Although only six years old, I was both strong and agile, but, alas! entirely destitute of courage. Still, it seemed to me that I had not done right in running away from one who had fallen a victim to Janne's wickedness. There was something within me which said that I ought to help the abandoned. After a moment's struggle between my cowardice and my sense of right, the latter conquered.

With an acrobatic leap I was back at the place of conflict, but came so that I literally fell upon Janne's back like a bombshell, and that with so violent a shock that he was obliged to release the hold he had in his victim's tow-colored hair.

For a second Janne and I rolled over each other in the snow. I had thrown my feet around his neck and my arms around his legs; thus we tumbled about, until we struck against the gate-post.

In the meantime the little maltreated boy had taken to flight, screaming and bawling at the top of his lungs, leaving me to extricate myself as best I could.

At the instant we knocked against the gate-post I let go my grasp of Janne's neck and legs, turned a somersault and was again on my feet, firmly resolved to make for our cabin and lock the door behind me; but this intention of mine was never realized. Before I got there Janne had caught up with me, and now began a chase around the little yard.

I, who never made any use of my gymnastic skill except when father was home, now employed it to save myself from Janne's ill-treatment, which I foresaw would be pretty thorough if he got hold of me, as our collision with the gate-post had given him a bruise across the face, so that the blood flowed from his nose.

To a beholder it ought to have been a very peculiar sight to see how I vaulted back and forth over the fence, or made a spring and jumped over my pursuer when he bent down to seize hold of me.

This chase could not last long, however, before my strength became exhausted. After we had continued about half an hour, I fell down at my last leap over the fence, completely wearied out, without being able to get up.

My heart throbbed from exertion and fright. I closed my eyes and expected Janne's clutch. A pair of hands did indeed seize me. They resembled a vice, so tight was their grasp, and a bass voice cried out:

"You imp, if you have beaten Janne so that the blood runs, you will now get your pay for it, that I promise!"

My heart's violent beating stopped, my blood became cold from horror. I found myself in the hands of Black Stina.

The thought of blows and abuse disappeared when I opened my eyes and saw her dark physiognomy grinning at me.

My terror was so great that I did not feel how she squeezed me, when she held me high up in the air and shook me like a glove. The only thing clear to my mind was that my time had now come. I took it for granted that I would the next minute be changed from a human being into a lizard, frog, or some other ugly creature.

After she had held me in the air for a little while, and shaken me so that I fancied my father's cabin stood with the chimney downward, she threw me to the ground and seized me by the neck. I now expected my transformation, but, instead, the pain which I experienced, when a heavy stick fell with a powerful blow on my neck, taught me that I was not yet any frog, but a little urchin who was punished with a sound thrashing. If I had been treated to many such strokes, I fear that my back would have been broken. I did not receive more than two, however, for just as the second reached me, a voice cried to my tormentor:

"What the d——l, Stina! do not destroy the boy for me; you certainly understand what a capital that chap can become. He is nimble as a cat."

Black Stina flung me from her into the nearest snowdrift, where I remained lying motionless.

I had recognized my father's voice, and the impression it made could be compared to that which one would experience if he, from being suffocated with smoke and believing himself saved, had quite unexpectedly been thrown into the flames.

For a long while I neither heard nor saw. Fright had to that extent overpowered me. Suddenly I felt a cold hand, which stroked my brow, and a kind voice whispered:

"How is it with the liliput? Have they beaten him very badly? Mercy sakes! can you not move, not look at Paul, not speak?"

And now I felt the flutter of a warm breath on my cheek, after which some one lifted me up quite carefully and carried me into the house.

I had full consciousness of all this; I could very well have responded to Paul's words and also opened my eyes, but I lacked courage. It seemed to me so comforting to rest on Paul's breast, to avoid meeting my father's eyes or answering his questions.

Paul laid me down on the bench in the cabin. He kissed me, and some tears fell down on my brow.

This touched me; I threw my arms around his neck and began to weep aloud.

My mother found us clasped in each other's arms when she returned from the village.

At the sight of Paul she understood that her husband was home. The poor woman sighed.

Paul related to her in brief that when father and he came near the grove they had seen me in conflict with Janne. Paul had wished to hasten forward to assist me, but father's strong hand had held him to the spot. They witnessed how I, through my agility, for a long time kept my assailant at a distance. Not until Black Stina meddled in the affair did father advance and hinder her from injuring me for life.

My mother had taken me in her lap, caressed and petted me, while the tears ran down her cheeks.

She wept, but silently, without sighs or sobs. It was the mute outpouring of bitter grief.

I twined my arms around her neck and tried to console her by saying that it did not pain me so dreadfully when Black Stina beat me. Of course I took it for granted that she wept over the beating I had received.

My mother finally dried her tears, and said, turning to Paul:

"Where is your father?"

"He went in to Black Stina's," answered Paul.

At these words I began to scream frantically, for I had no idea that father's visit to Stina could signify anything but that I should be sent to her to stand on my head with the other children whom I imagined to be there.

Only with difficulty were Paul and mother able to calm me. When they at last succeeded, Paul mentioned that father and he did not come home alone, but that they had company with them.

"What do you mean by that?" asked mother.

"Oh, I mean that father has gone into partnership with a man who has monkeys, a little trained horse and some dogs. It is an Italian by the name of Alphonso. Father and he have already given exhibitions. Father has taught Alphonso's daughter to dance on the horse; and besides, father has appeared as a clown. I have ground the hand-organ and sung between the parts. We have earned considerable money for the last few weeks, so that I have bought a good many books for Conny, which we will enjoy together; and then I have treated myself to a violin, and I can play some little tunes on it."

Mother sat silent.—My curiosity had been excited to see the monkeys and dogs that could dance. I forgot all that had troubled me, to ask some questions about these interesting objects.

"Where are the monkeys and dogs?" I asked.

"They are on the way," answered Paul. "Alphonso wished to let the horses rest a couple of hours in T——; therefore we are here before them."

"Oh how amusing it must be to see dogs dance!" exclaimed I.

"Ah! you may perhaps see more than you wish, dear

Conny," replied Paul. "Father and Alphonso intend to give exhibitions here, and then you will have to help; you can be sure of that, poor young one!"

"Paul, it cannot be, that—" interrupted my mother.

"That Conny shall make his appearance? Yes, mother. It is just so, and it is no use to object," added Paul, passing his long thin hand over my mother's; "it will only irritate father, who has lately been real cruel when he could not immediately have his will."

The conversation was here interrupted by my father, who stepped into the cabin. He was obliged to stoop in order to get in the low door, and after he had muttered a string of oaths over the miserable shanty, he turned to mother:

"Good day, Annette; where the d——l do you keep yourself, not to have an eye on the boy there? If I hadn't come, Stina would certainly have so pickled him that by this time there would have been nothing but shreds left of the whole creature. Black Stina is a woman who is not easily got rid of. Such a wife would have suited me. There, now! out of the way; I need to rest myself."

This latter utterance was accompanied with a motion of the foot, as if father intended in this way to clear the bench where we sat.

We were instantly a long distance from the place upon which he wished to lie down. After he had stretched himself out to his full length, with his dripping boots on the clean seat, he plunged his hands in the pocket of his velvet blouse, originally black, but now a grayish brown. When he again drew up one hand, it was full of coins. He laid these on the table, saying:

"Here is some money, Annette; go and get some brandy right away, and see to it that I have good living while I am at home, else you may go to the d——l, the whole of you. Bring out what you have immediately, and let the boy there run to the tavern. I need food and drink, after walking twelve miles. Do you understand that, you creature? Well, be lively."

Paul had already grabbed a few of the coins, and was the next instant on his way for the brandy, so as to spare me, who was completely battered up, the necessity of using my limbs.

Paul had walked as far as father, but with the difference that, while the latter had nothing to carry but the stand for the hand-organ, the fourteen-year-old Paul carried the hand-organ on his back, and yet he forgot his weariness, his hunger and his aching legs to save me from the hardship of going for the brandy.

I did not reflect then upon this trait in him, but I have done so since, when I considered how Paul, in the least things as well as the greatest, always forgot himself to avert a torment from me.

CHAPTER II.

ALPHONSO, with his little trained horse, his monkeys, dogs and daughter, had in due season arrived at the grove and been lodged with us. The horse had his stall in the shed where my mother kept her wood; the monkeys, dogs, men, children and my poor mother occupied the cabin.

The very next day after he came home my father resumed his instruction with me. I had now a companion in this torture, and this companion was Alphonso's ten-year-old daughter.

We learned wonderful things, Antonia—or rather Tonia—and I.

How many stifled sighs of pain these lessons cost us, poor children that we were, how many suppressed lamentations we kept within us, it would be hard to tell. We dared not cry or complain when we were taught to contort our bodies in a painful way, because the least sound from our lips would have put us in connection with father's whip.

My mother's cosy little cabin, where she and I had lived so quietly and peacefully when we were alone, was now changed into a dirty hole, in which, while father gave Antonia and me lessons, Alphonso drilled his dogs and monkeys.

At the end of April it was decided that the first performance should be given. There were to be three of them.

A large barn was changed into a circus, and there Tonia and I were to appear before the peasants and notables of the place, Tonia on horseback and I as an acrobat.

The memory of that day stands vividly before my soul.

Shortly before the performance my father delivered the following speech to me:

"See here, Conny, if you fail this evening, and do not perform your feats as you should, you will get such a dressing down that you can have the good of it for your whole life. You will then make acquaintance with the lash, and that in such a way that the d——l may take your hide!"

I shuddered at the thought of being skinned in that style.

Rigged up in old, patched-up flesh-colored tights, a tunic of red odds and ends embroidered with tarnished spangles, and my teeth chattering with cold and fright, I awaited the moment when Tonia had finished and I should go in.

My mother held me, wrapped up in a shawl, and was so pale that she looked as though she had not a drop of blood left in her veins.

Tonia and the little trained horse left the ring, and now my father took me by the hand.

At the moment when I stepped in on the scene of action I had forgotten all the fine things I had to perform. Everything whirled before me, and for a few seconds it appeared as if the front bench, upon which the sheriff with his family and the rest of the gentry were sitting, hopped up and down, and as if the peasants standing behind them turned somersaults over them. I held tight to my father's hand, afraid of falling on my nose myself.

Father said something; what it was I did not hear, but that his hand let go of mine I felt to my horror.

At the same instant a voice which came from the gaping crowd of peasants cried out:

"Just see there! the organ-grinder's boy! He is going to do great things, I suppose. No, thank you prettily; it will be a perfect bosh. Pay money to see such an object as that!"

I had recognized Janne's hateful voice.

Although I had no ambition as an "artist," his words piqued my childish vanity, and without waiting for my father's order I threw myself on my head, rolled like a wheel, walked on my hands, and God knows what I did not do. I went on with all my might to dumfound Janne with my skill.

Since our last encounter I had a thorough grudge against him. I neither heard nor saw. I thought no more of father's whip. I gave no heed to his words. I performed one exploit after the other, panting and blowing from exertion, until I had gone through the whole list. They applauded me, and I was to put the crown to the work through the last and most difficult of my feats, when just at that moment something was flung in my face from which I received so violent a blow that I tumbled backward, screaming loudly, with the blood running from my mouth and nose. My father took me up and carried me off from the scene of my triumphs.

Two of my front teeth had been knocked out and my upper lip cut in two by the stone which had been thrown at me.

I screamed desperately, fully convinced that my last hour had come.

Among the beholders there was a terrible commotion. They swore, wrangled, shouted, and in the midst of this tumult was heard the sheriff's thundering voice. Janne's and Black Stina's names were mentioned with threats by the excited peasants. This much I caught in spite of my agony.

As soon as father had placed me in my mother's care he went back to the barn again to find out who threw the stone.

So began—and I can gladly say so ended—my artistic career.

CHAPTER III.

FOR three days I lay there with my swollen, aching face. Fru Wrikter, the sheriff's wife, came to us the same evening that the misfortune occurred, and gave mother some advice through which my pain would be relieved.

Janne seemed to have had the sheriff to thank that he was not badly beaten by the peasants, who had been perfectly enraged at him for throwing the stone in my face; but if he was saved from the violence of the peasants, he received, on the other hand, a private castigation from the sheriff, who took him home with him.

Paul told me of this.

Black Stina met Paul the day afterward, and then she clenched her fist at him, saying, with venom:

"You may be sure, you pack of vagabonds, that you will have back the beating that the sheriff has given Janne, and that in a way that you will also have him to deal with, I promise you."

In the meantime, father and Alphonso gave a new performance two days afterward, from which they had very good receipts.

That night, when it was over and the partners had gone to the tavern to have a gay time, Tonia sat crouched up by the hearth, where a cheerful fire was burning.

Mother was engaged in preparing our evening meal. Paul had thrown himself down on the hand-organ, and sang a merry song to me, who was lying down.

When Paul finished his song, he said, turning to Tonia:

"What is the matter with you, dear child? You are so silent—you, who are usually in such good spirits."

"Oh, I was thinking that we are going to leave you to-morrow, and go to that black woman's," answered Tonia; "then I will have a very different time from what I have had lately. You have been very kind to me—you, mother."

"Nonsense!" replied my mother; "why should you remove to Black Stina's?"

"I ought not to speak of that, for, you see, if father learns that I have let it out, I will get a whipping. He is awful when he gets mad."

The girl glanced, frightened, at the door, and continued, in a low voice:

"Now they are at the tavern. How horrid it is at the taverns!" She drew up the little faded and ragged handkerchief which covered her shoulders, and stared again at the fire.

"You must tell me, Tonia, how you learned that you were going to move," said mother, after a while, patting the girl. "Perhaps I can manage it so that *you* are allowed to stay here."

"That is impossible, mother. But it is all the same; I can certainly speak of what I have heard. You will know it, any way, to-morrow."

Tonia took hold of my mother's arm and drew her down closer, saying in a low voice:

"Last night, when father and I were down there in the barn, Black Stina came stealing in to us. She wanted to talk to father, she said, and I was sent out. But, you see, I stopped and listened at the back part of the barn, I did. At first I could not hear what they said, but finally I made out that the organ-grinder, Fredrik, your husband, cheated my father out of money, that he stuffed all of it into his own pocket, when father ought to have had the most. Father became very angry, and then they talked the matter over, after father had promised to separate from Fredrik, and instead take up quarters with that black, hideous woman. To-morrow father will go there. But first father and Fredrik have to share the money they have earned, and Stina advised father to do it at the tavern. Mercy! how afraid I am!" added Tonia, looking anxiously around the room.

One of the dogs came and licked the little hand, as if he wished to calm her.

"Afraid? and of what?" said Paul, merrily. "You, Tonia, must certainly have seen enough of tavern brawls not to be afraid of them, and so much can I tell you—that Alphonso cannot get as much as a farthing more than he ought to have from my father. If they drink and quarrel to-night, they will be all the better friends in the morning. Separate they will not. I would just like to know how your father would have any music without our hand-organ, and who would teach you to make curvets on horseback if he had not father? Perhaps Black Stina would do it? No, there would be a stop to the whole thing. She does not know as much as that about such things," declared Paul as he passed the palm of one hand over the other. "To be sure, she might instruct him in some other tricks, but not those which he knows. Throw away all such thoughts; and if you promise to look happy, I will sing you a song."

Paul sang a song while the supper-table was being set. Mother looked uneasy, something which did not hinder Tonia and Paul from eating her porridge with a good appetite.

When they had finished, they crept to bed, and soon I

slept the deep sleep of childhood, notwithstanding my face still ached.

The darkness of night was spread over the earth, when we were quite suddenly awakened by a violent knocking at the front door.

I opened my eyes in affright. The light was still burning in our cabin. Mother had not gone to bed. She hastened to draw the bolt with which the outer door was fastened.

Paul had started up from his bed, and stood at her side; at the same moment the door opened. Tonia and I sat up in our beds. Indistinctly I heard some one outside utter the words "fight," "dagger-thrust," "mortally wounded." My mother gave a piercing shriek, and rushed out into the dark night.

I, who generally lacked all courage and was scared by the least thing, began to cry for help. But no one paid any attention to me.

Paul and mother had gone off, leaving the door open behind them, so that a cold stream of air rushed into the cabin and extinguished the burnt-down tallow dip. We were thus left in darkness. Tonia and I crept to each other; and as I did not succeed in calling back either mother or Paul with my outcry, I ceased abruptly and clasped my arms around Tonia, who was all of four years older than I.

"They have been fighting about money, and that with knives!" exclaimed Tonia, suddenly. "Oh how terrible, Conny! One of them is dead. Oh dear! how I shiver! If it were father! I feel such a pain in my heart. But perhaps it is your father. I am so frightened, Conny."

"And I too," stammered I.

We began to cry.

The short spring night was succeeded by the dawn. All continued to be so quiet, so grave-like, around us; neither

Paul nor mother came back, and not a living being appeared.

We sat huddled up on our straw bed, and neither of us dared to leave it to close the door. The cold spring air had cooled the cabin and stiffened our limbs, but yet we remained motionless. The sun stood high in the heavens, when steps approached. They were heavy and slow. They stopped an instant on the stoop, and then the weary wanderer entered. It was my mother, and yet not my mother. Her look was so strange and her whole appearance so changed that she frightened me.

She closed the door after her, and then, without casting her eyes upon us, went to the fireplace, murmuring to herself:

"A murderer's wife! A murderer! a murderer!"

Neither Tonia nor I had courage to address her, she stared so strangely before her. A few minutes elapsed in this way, then the door again opened, and Fru Wrikter entered, accompanied by Paul.

What afterward transpired is not clear to my memory. That my mother was sick in some way, that they opened a vein and put her to bed, are all that I vaguely remember.

The same day my mother came home both Tonia and I were taken ill, probably in consequence of the chill we received.

Tonia was only sick a few days, but I lay ill several weeks, a prey to a malignant fever, and without any consciousness of what was passing around me.

When I at last became better and could understand what had happened, there was no one in the cabin but Paul and I. My first question was for mother. Paul answered in a sorrowful tone that she was gone, and that I never would see her again. She was dead.

Dead! When Paul uttered that word, I could not

realize it. I did not understand how it was possible that I would never see my mother again, and yet fate soon taught me that it was so. She did not come back. She was gone for ever.

Some time elapsed, after which I again asked a question. It concerned my father.

"Dear Conny," answered Paul, "it has gone as it generally goes with people of his sort; he has had a bad end."

"Is he dead, too?" said I, remembering that awful night.

"Ah! if he were only dead, it would be well enough, but it is something much, much worse. He has been in prison. I suppose you remember, poor liliput, that night when they came and knocked us up. Father and Alphonso got into a quarrel about the sharing of the money. Alphonso only wished to give father a quarter part of the profits. From a quarrel they soon came to blows. Father seized a knife and stabbed Alphonso— "

"And then, then?" I exclaimed.

"Then came the sheriff, and father was arrested. The trial took place the next week, and he was sentenced and taken to the county jail."

"Was he sentenced to imprisonment?" I asked.

"Ah, no! he was condemned to death; but the day before he was to be transported to U.——, he was found dead in his cell. He had hung himself to avoid all punishment."

I did not understand much about this, but sufficient to know that father, if he had lived, would have been like Fransson or Black Stina's executed husband.

Again days elapsed of which I have no recollection; one was like the other, without any change or break. Paul and I did not say many words. He sat silent and read, and I lay quite still in my bed. At noon the sheriff's servant-girl or Pehr Pehrson's wife came to us with food. Once or twice there was also a messenger from the pastor's who brought food. Otherwise we saw no one. Paul never went out. In the evening he played on his violin, and in the daytime he read. Once I inquired after Tonia.

"Pehr Pehrson has adopted her."

"And Black Stina is just as ugly as ever?"

"I have not seen her since the night mother and I ran to the tavern where the fight took place. When she saw mother, she cried to her:

"'You have now been paid up for the beating that Janne got; your husband shall lose his head just like Barsk, and then you will have to content yourself with seeing the people of the village point their fingers at the murderer's wife.'

"From the sheriff," continued Paul, "I heard that she and Janne had gone to G——."

I breathed easier. The thought of Janne and Black Stina had disturbed me very much.

When I became well, Paul still kept me shut up, and would not allow me to go outside the cabin door, although I was completely recovered. One day he said to me:

"Conny, we cannot stay here. People do not like murderers' children, but they point their fingers at them. We will therefore leave the place, and try to earn our living, so that you can have a chance to learn something, as mother desired. The cottage here we cannot sell, for mother said on her deathbed that we should keep it. Perhaps we will come back some fine day, and then it will be nice to have it. Now, we will start to-morrow, and that quite early, for Black Stina came home last night, and she has no good eye for either you or me."

At the intelligence that Stina had returned, I lacked all desire to wait until morning, but began to beg Paul that we should begin our journey that very day. He did not allow himself to be entreated long, but immediately gathered together the things we were to take with us, stuffed his pockets full with the little stock of food we possessed, ran over to the sheriff's, and when he returned he took the hand-organ on his back, his violin under his arm, and gave to me the little bundle of clothes to carry, after which the organ-grinder's two sons started out in the world to earn their bread.

It was at noon and at the end of summer when we bade farewell to Skärparby. The sun shone brightly down on our heads, as if it wished to inspire us with hope and trust in the Father there above.

I was only six years and a half, and the fourteen-year-old Paul constituted my sole support in life. I was happy in mind—so happy as I had not been for a long time. It seemed to me that everything had changed form and aspect since I was allowed to turn my back on Skärparby and go out in the world to all the places that Paul had so often described. I thought with delight of all the glorious things I would see.

To me the future seemed so bright, and the new, the unknown, smiled at me so temptingly, that I entirely forgot the sad events which concerned me so closely.

Happy age, when sorrow pales before the slightest sunlight!

When we had walked about two miles and come to a pretty hillside, Paul set down his hand-organ. Here we would rest.

"We have now gone a quarter of the distance we must walk to-day," said Paul. "Are you tired?"

"How silly you talk!" answered I. "Ah, no! I could go ten times as far."

"That is big talk, you little liliput!" Paul smiled quite sadly, just as he had smiled after the murder of Alphonso.

"Do you know, Conny, it looks as if our journey would be successful? The sun shines so bright, and it is a good sign; but now you must listen to a wise word from me, you little banty, and that is, that it is best for us to leave sorrow behind us on this hill. That which has been we will think of no more. It has happened once for all, and cannot be changed. What boots it, then, to mourn?"

Paul began to dig a hole as large as the palm of his hand, and put the key of our cabin in it; then he filled it up again so carefully that no one could discover it. When this was done, he said, with a peculiar mixture of jest and earnest:

"Lie there in peace, and with you all the sad things that have occurred. You will not leave your grave in a hurry, you key to our parents' sorrowful abode."

We rested a while, and then continued our way. Paul hummed a song and I prattled, as children are wont to do when they are in good spirits.

Toward evening we arrived at T——'s station. Here we were to spend the night. Outside the house several idle peasants stood talking. When they caught sight of us, as we were about to pass them, they drew aside, and one of them said:

"There comes Fredriksson's Paul. Where the deuce can that rascal of a boy be going? I suppose they couldn't stand it to see the pack of murderers there at Skärparby, and so they have driven the young ones away."

Paul pretended not to hear what the tall boor said, but took off his cap as he went by him, saying:

"Good-evening, Anders."

I had looked up at Paul, and perceived that he was pale.

The peasants did not answer Paul's greeting, but they

went their way, and we entered the waiting-room. It was empty. Before the desk sat a large, fleshy woman with an appearance just like all other Uppland women. She threw a quick glance at us, and exclaimed:

"Good gracious! I believe it is Paul. Well, how does the world wag with you, now that your father has hung himself? He was a regular jail-bird. I always said that he never would end like an honest man. Yes, you are real scoundrels down there at Skärparby, and your father, he was the very worst of them; for, you see, to be both a thief and a murderer is enough, in all conscience, to make one afraid of such a set of vagabonds as you. It was an eternal shame that your father escaped the gallows, for he was ripe for them, and—"

"Now there is an end to that tune, I tell you," interrupted Paul, striking his clenched fist on the desk. "You may slander father as much as you choose, but not so that I hear it, for, you see, I will not stand it. Now give me a room for the boy here, and I will have some food and beer for us both."

"Will you?" screamed the woman, looking angrily at Paul. "But I will not give any room or food to such murderer's young ones without having money in advance, I can tell you. Perhaps you have nothing to pay with, and I don't give credit to such as you, for of devil eggs come devil young ones."

"How much shall you have for a room over-night and food this evening?" asked Paul, and looked the woman steadily in the eyes.

What Paul's face expressed I could not tell, as I stood there frightened and trembling behind him, holding him by his coat-tails, but the fact of the matter was that the woman turned away her head and answered in an entirely changed tone:

"Eat and sleep here over-night; then I will tell you

afterward what it costs. I only wanted to know whether you had any money or not."

"It is all the same what you wanted, mother," replied Paul, "as I now wish to pay first, else we will go a piece farther."

The woman named the price, and Paul took out an old red silk handkerchief with several silver coins tied up in one corner, out of which he paid her what she asked.

Then we were conducted to a little side room.

Once alone, Paul seated himsef on his hand-organ, and his head sank down on his breast. It appeared as though he wept.

I climbed up on a chair, and with my elbows on the table and my chin resting in my hands I regarded Paul.

The landlady's words about our father had made a painful impression on me, although I was not able to define it. The appellation "murderer's young ones" re-echoed dismally in my ears, and drove away all the joy which had filled my soul during the walk. I felt instinctively that some of our father's guilt clung to us, and that this was what made people look with contempt upon his children.

The consciousness of being as good as branded for lifetime awoke confusedly in my soul. I felt that the inheritance my father left me was that of a malefactor, and that his disgrace would follow me as faithfully as the nobleman's former achievements cast their reflection upon his descendants. I was a child of ill-repute.

All know how sensitive children are to everything that resembles contempt. The instinct is wounded as deeply by it as the clear consciousness of humiliation in riper years. It was to me a bitter moment, and so much the more so as what I experienced was vague, and thus could not be reasoned away. I had no palliative for my grief in understanding, no consolation in the thought of being able to wash away the guilt I had inherited through my own work; I had only the knowledge of the shame which the words "murderer's young ones" contained.

Taken up with our own emotions, Paul and I sat silent. I was a child, and consequently an egotist. What I myself experienced thus occupied my whole soul, without my devoting any attention to Paul.

After a while the landlady entered with our supper. She set it on the table and looked in passing at Paul, who remained in an unchanged position.

"See here, Paul," said she; "you took my words too hard. You ought to know that I have always liked you and considered you a good and well-behaved boy, but, you see, you also know that—"

"Hush, mother; I know much which you need not prate about," interrupted Paul, hastily. "Now, go your way; you have done enough mischief for to-day. There, now! march!"

Paul rose and the landlady went out, muttering a whole string of words which did not denote any particularly great friendliness, but showed that she found Paul's behavior improper in the highest degree—something to which the latter, however, did not seem at all sensitive.

He took the key from the outside and locked the door after her. When he then turned toward me, his features had regained their original unconcerned expression, and he said, with an encouraging smile:

"What now, Conny? Do you sit there and hang your head? No, liliput, that will not do. Away with all stupid thoughts, for now we are going to eat, and after we have slept here over-night we will go hence. The world is large—we are young; and if things do not always go crosswise, it will surely be well with us in time."

He stroked the hair away from my brow and smiled so kindly; but notwithstanding this smile I had no mind for anything but my own despondency. My answer was a pettish refusal of his invitation to take supper. I was not hungry; I wished to sit just as I was, etc.

"How is this," said Paul; "is liliput bad? Then I will go out in the waiting-room and leave him alone, for you must be good, else I will not like you."

"I am not bad, Paul," I answered, and began to cry. My tears had always been something that Paul could not endure. He took me on his knee, caressed and played with me; but I only cried.

God knows whether there was not as much anger as grief in the feeling the landlady's words had excited.

"Conny, what is the matter with you?" said Paul, finally. "Have the old woman's words made you feel bad? Don't mind them, boy; they are only owl-hootings, and we mustn't be so sensitive—we poor folks' children. We will have to bear more than that, you better believe, and this you will experience in added measure when you become as old as I. Now away with tears. It does not trouble me, what they say. I am only sorry that you shall hear it; I did not wish you to learn so soon what evil words could do. But now there is enough said on that subject, and we will think no more about it. We have nothing, it is true; let us therefore preserve our cheerful dispositions and our innocent hearts. Away with everything that causes trouble," sang Paul, and filled a glass of beer for me.

"Now the liliput must eat and drink," added he, and then chatted about all the fine things I would see, and how pleasant we would have it, until I found it good to go to work and taste the food. When I was once under way, it went of itself to consume the landlady's viands. My lost appetite returned, and with it my cheerfulness. Children's sorrows are for the most part fleeting clouds, which disappear as quickly as they come.

When we finished our meal, the impression of the land-

4

lady's words was effaced, and I fell asleep, dreaming of large cities, grand buildings, etc.

Early in the morning Paul awoke me, and before any one was yet in motion on the place we left it.

Two days afterward we marched into U——. It was the first city I had ever seen.

Staring quite dumfounded at the large houses, stopping, struck with amazement, at the store-windows, and screaming with delight at the sight of the church, I drew attention to us unavoidably.

Some street-boys who went by cried to Paul:

"Hallo, singer Paul! what have you done with your papa? I guess he has gone and shaved himself."

These more or less edifying greetings slipped by my ears, so engrossed was I by all the wonderful things I saw.

Paul quickened his pace, however, notwithstanding my resistance, and turned off abruptly from the large street into a smaller one, as he happened to hear the tones of another hand-organ. We continued our way until we came to one of the most remote streets in town, where we stopped before a little red house. Here Paul knocked at the door, which was soon opened by a girl of ten or eleven, neatly but extremely humbly clad. Her cheeks were rosy, her eyes blue and her hair golden. It was one of those fresh, childish faces which delight the soul and please the eye.

"Good gracious! if it isn't Paul!" she exclaimed. "How glad grandma will be when she sees you! We have cried so bitterly over you, and we supposed that we would never meet you again. But who is it that you have with you?"

"My brother, dear Hanna. Well, how are you getting along these days?"

"First rate; but come in quick to grandmother."

Hanna led us into a large, tidy but very simply furnished room. It reminded me of our cabin the time when mother and I were alone there. When I entered, my thoughts fell involuntarily upon the beloved dead, and I would probably have begun to cry if Hanna had not at that moment taken hold of me and dragged me forward to an elderly woman who stood ironing.

"Grandma, Paul is here; he has this boy with him, and it is his brother," exclaimed Hanna. "Just see what a pretty boy his brother is!"

The woman turned her face toward us. It was mild as a spring day. She looked down at me with friendly eyes, patted me on the head and said a few words; I do not remember them, but only that they made me feel good. She gave Paul a hearty welcome.

Hanna took me entirely under her charge. Grandmother—or rather Aunt—Grönqvist, as Paul called her, had much to say to my brother.

We stayed a few days in this poor but tranquil home. Aunt Grönqvist supported herself with washing, and was closely occupied the whole day through. Hanna was thus commissioned to go around town with me, so that I should see its remarkable features.

Paul also walked out with his hand-organ. He sang on all the streets and squares; but he did not wish to have me with him, something which offended me very much. I consoled myself, however, with Hanna's company, and the time we stayed in U—— was to me very happy.

But the day approached when we were to take the steamboat for Stockholm.

The evening before—it was a Sunday—we sat with Aunt Grönqvist eating supper.

During the meal Aunt Grönqvist said:

"Now is the time to say a wise word. Let me hear, Paul, how you think of managing for this little chap."

She patted me on the cheek. "I cannot think that you intend to let him go and grind the hand-organ."

"Ah, no! that is not my purpose; I shall try to get him in school up there in Stockholm," answered Paul.

"And then you will look up Pastor J——, I suppose? That is right. Now to another matter: where are you going to live?"

"With Jungfru Lovisa, I think," said Paul.

"With my sister," rejoined Aunt Grönqvist, and pondered a moment. "Ah, yes! that will do. To be sure, Lovisa is rather brusque, and not particularly tender-hearted, but she is a trustworthy and orderly person, and will keep Conny nice and clean; that is beyond all question. Now to come to the most important thing: how will you earn your living?"

"With my hand-organ and my throat, dear aunt," answered Paul, laughing. "They think a great deal of me in the streets of Stockholm; and as there is nobody now to drink up the income, it will be sufficient, and besides— "

Paul ceased, and looked smiling at Aunt Grönqvist.

"Besides what? Speak out. Perhaps you have some one who will provide for Conny?"

"Not at all—he will have to content himself with having me do it; but when mother lay on her deathbed, she told me that she had saved up a little money for Conny, which would be a help, so that he could learn something. She died without having time to communicate where the money was concealed, and I was obliged to search through the whole cabin to find it. Finally I came across this silk handkerchief sewed up in one of the pillows."

Paul took out the handkerchief.

"The sum which it contained was certainly not large—

it amounted to twenty rixthalers; but still, it was something. Besides the money, it also contained these things."

He took out a broad gold ring. It was my mother's wedding-ring, which she probably concealed in order that father should not take it from her; a pair of old-fashioned gold earrings and a large silver watch such as are now called "turnips."

"Ah! was that all?" said Aunt Grönqvist. "Well, well! better that than nothing. The ring you must keep, for, you know, it isn't just the thing to sell such rings. It is pleasant to know that you don't go empty-handed to Stockholm."

"Far from it. I have, besides, during the days we have been here, gained so much through my singing that it will cover the expense of our journey; and it will be all right with us after we get in running order."

"And you yourself intend to remain a street-singer?"

"Yes, certainly."

"Yet you had other thoughts at one time?"

"Then I was a child, and did not know what I now know—that what one is, one ought to remain. Amen!"

"What will become of your violin, then?"

"We will take it with us. Now, we will say no more about that matter, but we will wind up with a song."

Paul began to sing:

"What boots it to mourn, what boots it to worry," etc.

The next morning Hanna and Aunt Grönqvist stood on the dock waving their handkerchiefs when the steamer left the shore.

Seven hours later we were in the capital.

CHAPTER IV.

MY head was dizzy during the first days of our stay in Stockholm. It seemed to me that everything I saw was a dream.

For two whole days Paul's hand-organ was allowed to rest, and he went around only to show me everything that was worthy of notice. On the third day I was given over to Jungfru Lova, with whom we were lodging, and she did not wish to hear of any "running around the streets," but I had to content myself with looking at a brick wall which rose straight and high right before our window.

One day, after I had been thoroughly scrubbed, combed and fixed up by Jungfru Lova, I was taken to a minister with whom my brother seemed to stand very well. He and Jungfru Lova talked together a long time, and the result was that Pastor J—— would get me into a charity school.

Such schools are very useful institutions, but the one that I went to was not according to my taste—that is certain. I got along there about as well as a snake in an ant-hill. The catechism and biblical history, two books which I had formerly considered it a pleasure to read, now constituted my torment. The zeal I showed when my mother was my teacher was no longer found in me, but I was a pattern of listlessness and laziness.

Everything has its cause, and so was it with my lack of zeal. From the first day of my entrance in the school, I had been the scape-goat upon which the other children exercised their malice, and they always greeted me with derisive words. As the teacher, besides, was not particularly well disposed toward new-comers, but regarded me as a safety-valve for his impatience, I lost from the very beginning all interest in learning, and met these persecutions with indifference and inattention.

An organ-grinder has also his reputation and his public, by whom he is known and discussed.

My father, who had sojourned in the capital year after year, was known by the people of the streets.

Paul's beautiful voice had too often amused chambermaids, journeymen, errand-boys and soldiers for my brother, as the son of Fredrik the organ-grinder, not to be known.

Those who had known Paul and father were also aware of the latter's crime and unhappy end.

The natural result was that it was generally known in the school that I was the son of the organ-grinder and murderer, and for such a child neither teacher nor pupils considered it necessary to put themselves out. Before long they had inspired me with an absolute horror of the school. Half a year had not elapsed before I roamed around the streets instead of going to school. Once, when I, after such a diversion, which, this time, lasted two days, presented myself at school, driven there solely by the fear that Jungfru Lova might find out that I had not been there, I was greeted with a sound flogging. I returned home in a deplorable condition, and firmly resolved not to continue my schooling.

In the liveliest colors I pictured to Jungfru Lova how I had been treated, showed her the marks the rod had left in my flesh, and actually succeeded in moving the rather unsympathetic woman. She declared positively that my visits to the school were over. The rod, according to her opinion, had never improved any human being, and after she had expressed this truth, my bruises were bathed with brandy, and I was put *nolens volens* to bed, to sleep away the physical pain.

Like all other children, I had lamented and complained far more than there was any reason for, merely to excite compassion, and now nothing remained to me but to patiently comply with Jungfru Lova's regulations, although I found it rather unpleasant to go to bed in the middle of the day.

Paul came home late that evening. I pretended to be asleep, so as to have a chance to hear what Jungfru Lova said. It was not many words.

"Conny has had a whipping again at school," said she.

"Has he had one before?" asked Paul.

"Yes, and on this account I will no longer hear of his going there, but he shall be sent to the madam next door. She charges twelve shillings* a week, and he will then have the right kind of instruction without flogging."

Paul made no reply, but came to the bed. He bent down over me, and kissed my brow softly.

The next day I was taken to the "madam's" school by Jungfru Lova herself, who now took my education in hand.

I was now obliged to recite my lessons aloud to Lova, and there was no longer any possibility for me to be lazy. I found it advisable to abjure indolence and make it my business to be diligent. It went right well. I received good praise from my teacher, but the scholars could not endure me. At recess they overwhelmed me with nicknames. I was called the street-singer's brother, organ-grinder Paul's little banty, loafer, etc. If we were all in the yard during play-hours, it was:

"Look out for that fellow! his father was a murderer, his brother is a vagabond." Or else: "Look at the patches on his jacket; Paul has put them there, and behind them

* Swedish pennies.

the beggar young one peeps out. Say, do you know such a chap as that, whose father has hung himself? He will some time be food for the gallows."

At first I complained to my teacher, and those who had molested me were punished. But the next day they were only much worse. Finally they so irritated me that my anger overcame my natural cowardice, and I began to pitch into the crowd. After that day there was a little amnesty. They had conceived respect for my uncommonly strong fists.

Winter and summer had flown. We were now in the beginning of fall. It was five o'clock in the afternoon, and school was over for the day. The little troop, which consisted only of poor children, were collected in the yard to play. Our teacher had gone to make some calls. I was just on the point of leaving, when some of the scholars took hold of me, crying:

"Now you shall stay and play with us. Yes, you shall, for we have made up our minds to have you."

My assailants were some of the largest children, among whom was an unusually tall red-haired girl, who distinguished herself through her wickedness. I had several times been obliged to defend myself in a forcible way from her attacks. She was generally called Rora.

In answer to their command that I should stay, I declared that I was not inclined to play with them; but then Rora and two of the boys took such a firm hold of my coat collar that I, in spite of a violent kicking and beating about me, could not get loose. They dragged me to the lower part of the yard, while the other children followed, hurrahing and screaming. Here, behind some sheds, they had erected something, but I could not understand what it was for.

A cutting log lay at the bottom, and at each side rose a pair of poles, which were joined at the top by means of a smaller one. When they had got me to this place, Rora screamed:

"I suppose you understand, you rascal, that this represents a gallows, and that you are the murderer who is going to be executed. Calle will be the executioner, and we who are holding you the guard."

A violent shiver went through my frame. I looked, frightened, at Calle, who stood by the log with an axe in his hand.

I was instantly seized with the thought that they really intended to cut my head off, and I began to cry for help with all my might.

At my screams they all laughed, and Rora began to thump my head as hard as she could.

"Will you hush, you little villain! Do you think it is proper to yell in that way when one goes to the place of execution? It is plain to be seen that your father was a miserable coward, and hung himself; but, you see, you shall not gain anything by your screeching. Your head must off; that is decided."

In a twinkling several hands were placed over my mouth, my cries were stifled, and they actually got me as far as the log; but at that instant a fresh voice exclaimed:

"Why do you abuse the boy there? What horrid game are you up to? Let go of him immediately, or you shall all have a taste of my riding-whip, I promise you."

In a minute I was free. My little tormentors tried to save themselves through flight, but now the same voice was again heard:

"That won't do; stay here on the spot, and let the boy come to me, so that I can hear why you have been so wicked to him."

Rora and those who had tried to drag me to the log

were obliged to remain; but the rest of the crowd drew back, in order to have the retreat free.

Before me stood a young officer clad in the uniform of the guard. He was so young that he seemed to belong more to youth than to manhood. He was tall and slender, with noble, handsome and regular features. At a few steps from him stood another officer, somewhat older.

"Step forward," said the first-described to me, "and tell me why they have chosen you as delinquent. Have you done them any harm?"

"Yes, indeed, he has!" screamed Rora and her followers. "He tells tales all the time and gets us punished, and then he fights, and is just as ugly as he can be."

"I have told tales and beaten them, that is true," answered I, quite bravely, and looked up in the young officer's clear blue eyes, "but I have done it because they would not let me alone, but—but—called me—"

I ceased. I could not get the words "murderer's young one" over my lips. The bitter humiliation my childish heart experienced was such that the tears streamed down my cheeks, and I bent my head.

"What the deuce, boy? I verily believe you are sniffling," said the officer, sportively. "Do you think that befits a boy? Speak out manfully, and tell us the reason why your schoolmates and you cannot get along together."

"I will tell you, sir," joined in a little girl who had been among the spectators, and who had always, when the others did not see it, shown herself kind to me. "Conny has complained to the teacher because they call him murderer's young one and jail-bird. His papa has committed murder, they say, and after he did it he hung himself. That is why they do not like Conny."

While she was speaking my tears ceased to flow. I raised my head again and looked up in my protector's face. It had an expression of compassion and goodness.

"Poor child!" murmured he, patting me on the head; "you have received a sad inheritance."

He said some forcible words to my assailants, and promised them a sound flogging if they dared to give me any nick-names or lay hold of my person. The lecture was finished with the command to the little crowd:

"There, now! march home!"

The little torments did not wait to be told twice, but scudded away at such speed that they raised a dust after them. When they were gone, he turned to me.

"Where do you live?" he asked.

"Next door, with Jungfru Lova, in the little red house," was my answer.

"What is your name?"

"Conny Fredriksson."

"All right; now go home to Jungfru Lova. We will meet again some time," added he, giving me a silver thaler.

I took off my cap and passed by my protector and his companion. As I did so I heard the latter say:

"It is easily perceived that you have quite recently become an officer, else you would have more respect for your uniform than to appear as the defender of criminals' offspring. Do you think that it behooves Count Sten Mauritz Strålkrans to deliver sermons to a lot of beggar young ones?"

"Hush, and don't talk nonsense!" replied the count, laughing. "I have defended innocence, and I should think that was as much of an honor to my uniform as for you, Baron Fabian Lodstein, to have been witness to my laudable deed."

I heard nothing further, but what I did hear remained faithfully in my memory.

When I stepped into Lova's large room, Paul sat at the window with his arms crossed on the table and his head sunk down on them. Before him stood Lova.

It was something very singular for Paul to be home at that time of day, and this led me to stop just inside the door, so as to listen to what was said.

Neither Lova nor Paul observed my entrance. Lova had just finished speaking, and Paul uttered, in answer to what she had said:

"It does not matter that I am completely innocent of my father's crime; they still call me a criminal. I have for a whole year endured the taunts and jeers of the street-boys and other organ-grinders on account of father's deed—I have borne it for Conny's sake; but now it is all up, as the 'madam' has spoken to me and said that she could not have Conny in the school because the other scholars could not tolerate him."

"Won't she have Conny in the school?" interrupted Lova, excitedly. "Well, then, there are certainly other schools, I should think; and I will tell you what it is, Paul: you are not going to drag the boy around the world and make him a vagabond. No; I have once for all taken the child in hand, and I will surely make a man of him. Besides, I would like to know what place you could find where they did not know your father's history through the newspapers. So you had better stay in Stockholm; that is my advice."

"But I cannot obey it."

"Where, then, do you intend to travel off with your brother?" screamed Jungfru Lova angrily.

"I intend to take him with me to Denmark and Germany, that is my decision," answered Paul, throwing his head back.

Lova had no time to answer. I hurried forward and threw myself on Paul's neck, crying:

"Yes, let us go far, far away. All are so wicked here, all hate us on account of our father."

With vehemence Lova tried to oppose Paul's resolution; but it was no use. He was firm in it, in spite of all that Lova said.

Two days afterward we were on our way to Copenhagen.

How Paul managed to defray the expense of the journey, I do not know. I can only say that when we arrived at the capital of Denmark, we did not have enough to buy bread. It was toward evening when we landed there, and we would probably have had to spend the night in the streets, if one of the sailors had not directed us to a lodging-house and lent us a few shillings.

CHAPTER V.

A STREET-SINGER'S and organ-grinder's life is also distinguished by its triumphs and defeats.

He has his competitors, his listeners and those who envy him. The one who has the best hand-organ, sings the newest, not the prettiest songs, can be sure of having the other organ-grinders and street-singers for enemies, and that they will try in all conceivable ways to injure the individual who has gained the preference.

This was an experience which Paul had already had in his native land, and which was still more confirmed during his stay in Copenhagen.

The first days were those of triumph. Around our hand-organ were gathered a large number of listeners, lured there by Paul's beautiful clear voice and well chosen songs, as well as the unusually good hand-organ.

They were liberal with coin, and we earned a good deal, but in the course of a week there was a downright persecution from the organ-grinders and their friends among the street-boys and the rabble, who made us all possible trouble, so that we were finally compelled to leave Copenhagen.

For a year's time we wandered from one German town to another. During the winter we stayed first in Hamburg and then in Berlin. Our income was very irregular, but yet such that we never suffered need nor were obliged to hunger; still it was not sufficient to procure Paul a new coat or a pair of whole pantaloons. That which did not go for food was used to buy shoes and clothes for me. He forgot himself in order to get me what I required. Finally he wore a pair of boots without soles. Not until we went away from Berlin did he succeed in gaining money enough from his singing to buy himself a pair of shoes; but his coat was on the point of falling to pieces, so that he had to sew it up every evening, to avoid presenting himself before the public too poorly covered.

We had travelled from town to town, sometimes riding a little distance on the rail-road, sometimes going on foot. The whole of this period forms a variegated and indistinct recollection of many cities, of many exertions and innumerable proofs of love from Paul's side.

He and I always spent the mornings in our humble lodgings, when he studied with me a couple of hours every day. Then he practiced some new songs, learned some little tunes on the violin, and toward noon we wandered out to let the populace enjoy Paul's performances. Toward evening we returned home with a larger or smaller profit, or perhaps none at all. Paul never went into any tavern with me. He very seldom visited such places himself, and then only when he needed to buy some food. Every time we started out he used to say:

"Patience, Conny, in a year or two you will not be obliged to go with me and the hand-organ. For then I shall have earned so much, that you can learn something."

And with this hope as a guiding star, I was glad and happy.

Never did I hear an unkind word from Paul, never did any murmur pass his lips, never did his cheerfulness desert him, and he was always able to jest over adversity. That he subjected himself to a thousand deprivations, in order that I should lack nothing, was something which he never let me perceive and which I did not realize until I grew older.

In the spring we bent our course to the Rhine and Coblentz, as these regions during this time of the year were much visited by travellers. How we went, what places we visited, have passed from my memory; only one thing stands clear to me, that we finally arrived at one of the large German watering-places. Which one, I must refrain from mentioning. The events which occurred there compel me to maintain silence in this respect.

We had, during the last few months, done a very good business. Paul had bought himself a new coat and pantaloons, so that he might appear with a certain elegance in this scene of luxury and folly.

After two days' stay in * * *, one morning when I woke up I found Paul standing before me, dressed in his new clothes. Of course it seemed to me that he looked very grand, although the coat, which he had purchased in some second-hand clothes store, was entirely too large, as it had been made for a tall, stout man; but this escaped my attention. I had never seen Paul in anything else but large coats, and it was consequently something which I deemed fully in accordance with his personality. Besides, the trousers were so long that they formed a mass of folds around the ankle. This was also something that had always characterized Paul's costume. The vest of black velvet on the contrary was entirely too short, and the green neck-tie was so extremely long that it ended far below the vest. Over his abundant dark curls he wore a nice little straw hat, which, together with the head itself, formed the best part of his appearance, as the latter was the prettiest part of his body. How Paul's twisted, knock-kneed and stooping frame was clad seemed to trouble him very little as a general thing; but on the other hand he was always careful to have a nice-looking covering for his head.

Still, I considered my brother extremely genteel, and my

joy was raised to its greatest pitch when he showed what he had bought for me.

I sprang out of bed to hastily put on a pair of blue pantaloons, a black velvet blouse and a little straw hat. It appeared to me, when I saw myself in the scrap of looking-glass that was bestowed in our garret, that I looked like a prince.

Paul rubbed his long thin hands with delight, and declared that there was not a prettier boy to be found in the world.

Thus attired and as happy as if we had possessed millions, we set out with the hand-organ. Paul sang that day with a voice clearer than ever. Even I, who was used to hearing him, was surprised at his singing, and fancied that his tones had never sounded so before. I stared at my brother, as I ground the hand-organ, and thought:

"What has come over Paul, to sing so splendidly?"

We had stationed ourselves in front of a theatre. Right before us lay the spring-house with its two galleries and magnificent fountains.

Paul's singing gathered around us a ring of listeners; not of the usual street public, however, but of elegant ladies and gentlemen.

When he finished they threw a quantity of silver coin to the singer, and an old gentleman came to him asking what country he was from and how long he had been in * * *, etc., questions which Paul could only answer incompletely, as he spoke very poor German and could barely make himself understood.

Days passed during which it rained silver coins. The *haute volée* were amused in listening to the street-singer, who sang such pretty melodies in so fine a voice. Paul had also before his appearance in * * * learned our most beautiful Swedish people-songs. One day when he had sung "*Necken's Song*" and accompanied himself on the violin, the same old gentleman, who had addressed him the first day, came up, saying:

"Be in the park to-morrow evening at seven o'clock, and wait for me at the music-stand. I wish to give you an opportunity to earn money."

Paul's eyes shone, and when the strange gentleman left us, he swung his hat in the air, exclaiming with delight:

"Hurrah, Conny, now I will get lots of money, and then —then we will make a gentleman of you."

"If I am to become a gentleman, then you shall become one too, dear Paul."

"Scarcely, I will remain what I am and nothing else."

"But, Paul, if you had very, very much money, then you surely wouldn't go around the streets and sing?"

"If I had money, I would give every bit of it to you, you little liliput; as for myself, I would keep my violin and my itinerant life. I have never known any other. It is dear to me and I cannot change it; but you, you, Conny, of you must be made an able man, for I promised mother that, when she died. But away with all worry about the future. I shall now buy some fruit and a little Rhine wine, and then we will go home and have a treat."

After we had drank our wine and eaten the fruit, came night, slumber and dreams. It seemed to me that I saw my mother. She stood by my bed, leaned over me and stroked my brow with her hand. "Mamma," I tried to cry; but then she laid her hand on my lips, whispering:

"Hush, my child, and listen to what I have to say. You will never see me more, therefore give good heed to my words: Beware of everything black. The black color will be your misfortune. Remember this and all will go well with you."

She pressed her lips to my brow and disappeared. Then I awoke, or rather, it appeared to me as though I had not been asleep, but as if this had occurred in a waking condition. I again fell asleep and dreamed that Black Stina's Janne was pursuing me, and that some invisible voice incessantly repeated:

"Beware of everything black! Beware of everything black!" But in spite of this I could not escape Janne's black eyes, which were fastened upon me, and his black hair, which fluttered in the wind, so that it blew right in my face.

My agony was so great, that I gave a shrill cry. At the same instant Paul called me by name. I looked up. Paul stood leaning over my bed. Quite agitated by the dream, I threw myself on his breast and he tried to calm me with his caresses. But when I was dressing, it was impossible to get me to put on the black blouse, and Paul was obliged to buy me one of the same color as my pantaloons.

At the appointed time we presented ourselves at the music-stand, Paul holding his violin under his arm, and I going into ecstasies over the children's fine clothes. We were not obliged to wait long, for the elderly gentleman soon showed himself. He told Paul to follow him, saying, as he pointed to me:

"Let the boy stay here."

But this was something that Paul did not by any means agree to. The fine old gentleman was obliged to comply with the street-singer's will, and I was allowed to accompany my brother.

We were conducted to a large company that had congregated in front of the house, just outside the windows. The old gentleman said a few words, which I did not understand, and then he asked Paul to sing.

All Paul's songs were well known to me; I therefore paid no attention to them, but looked around me at the fine ladies, who, when Paul finished his song, said something expressive of their satisfaction. Just as Paul began to sing "*Necken*" my ear caught a sound which resembled the jingling of coin. It came from the open window behind me. I turned my head quickly and looked into the room. It was a large and handsome saloon. In the middle of the floor stood an extension table of unusual length, and around it sat, quite close to each other, a number of persons; behind them stood a large crowd of spectators. At the middle of the table sat two well dressed gentlemen, one on each side. Their chairs were higher than the others. These gentlemen had in their hands something that looked like large spoons with long handles. With these they continually scraped toward them the gold and silver coin that lay on the table.

I had stepped up on one of the benches outside the window, in order to see better into the room. Just as I succeeded in getting a good view of it, a young man rose hastily from his place at the table and came directly toward me. My first impulse was to hurry down from my elevated position. When he stopped before the open window, I found myself beneath it. I looked up at the young man, to ascertain whether he had observed that I stood peeping in.

His face was pale and looked disturbed; but it seemed familiar to me. I fancied that I had seen those fine features before, but then they were smiling and blooming. Just as I was wondering where and when I had seen him, his eyes fell on me. The disturbed expression disappeared and a joyful smile played around his lips. Now I recognized him. It was my protector in the school-yard, it was Count Sten Mauritz Strålkrans.

He nodded to me to come nearer. I stepped up to the window, saying in Swedish:

"Do you wish anything, count?"

"I declare, do you speak Swedish?" exclaimed he.

"That means that we are countrymen and have perhaps seen each other before, as you know who I am. What are you doing here?"

"I am with my brother, who is singing there."

I pointed to Paul.

"Thus you are obliged to earn money?"

I took off my cap, fully convinced that he intended to give me a piece of money; but instead he seized me quite suddenly by the collar and before I knew it transferred me into the large saloon. When I found myself inside, the young man took two gold coins out of his pocket.

"These two I will give you," said he, "but on the condition that you risk one of them at the gambling-table there."

"Gambling-table," that was an entirely new word to me, so I stared at the count with my mouth wide open.

"You do not seem to understand what it is," said he, laughing. "It is all the same, however. You must go with me to the table there, and you will expose yourself to either losing the gold coin or getting more. Do you comprehend now? I wish to see if you cannot take revenge upon the person who has won all my money."

It began to be clear to my mind. I remembered that I had seen the boys in the village and also in Stockholm play heads and tails, and I took it for granted that the count meant something of this kind. He took me by the hand and went to the table. One of the players rose from his seat. The count took it and made me stand beside him.

"Do you wish me to stake this coin on red or black?" asked he.

My dream appeared vividly, and I cried involuntarily: "Not on black! no, not on black!"

"Well then, on red; but take care, you will certainly lose it; I have lost all I possessed on red."

My answer was:

"Not on black!"

"Here goes for red. Do you see that red square there? put your coin on it."

The roulette was set in motion. It stopped again. The red had won.

"Try it again," whispered Strålkrans.

Again red won.

An hour, two hours, three hours and several hours elapsed. Red won constantly. The gas in the large chandeliers had been lighted. The chink of gold, the intensely anxious faces around the table, the marker's monotonous repetition of what numbers or what colors had won, my protector's continual injunction: "Try it again,"—all seemed to me like a dream, and the strangest thing of all was the heap of gold I had before me, and which during the last few hours had grown and become larger and larger. The clock struck twelve.

"Now stop," whispered Strålkrans.

Thereupon he had me gather together the gold, and when it was put in two bags which he had got from God knows where, he said:

"There, now, my boy, I will take you to your home, since I have made you a rich man. This is certainly the first time one has done a good deed through gambling," added he, speaking more to himself than to me.

He took me by the hand and we left the saloon. On coming out into the darkness I remembered Paul, and then for the first time it occurred to me that he had possibly been impatient over my disappearance; but I had no sooner begun to think of it than Paul, to my great surprise, stood before me. He had risen from one of the steps at the entrance to the house.

"Have you been anxious about me?" I asked.

"Somewhat," answered he; "but I knew that you were in there."

"Is that your brother?" inquired Strålkrans.

I answered the question in the affirmative.

"No matter," resumed Strålkrans, "I will go home with you anyhow. So march on!"

We had not gone farther than to the theatre, when some one came walking after us with rapid steps, calling to our companion.

Strålkrans stopped.

"What do you want, Lodstein?" asked he in a tone entirely unlike the one with which he addressed me.

"To tell you something, of course." Lodstein stood at Strålkrans' side, and the light from one of the street lamps fell on his face. It looked wild and distracted.

"You have won about forty thousand gulden," resumed he, turning to Strålkrans, and without paying any attention to us, "and you have won them from me," continued he in an excited voice.

"In the first place I have not won this money, and in the second, you have in the space of two days won from me about one hundred thousand Swedish thalers," answered Strålkrans.

"So you do not intend to return to the gambling saloon and give me my revenge?"

"No, I neither will nor can do it. I no longer have any gold to gamble away. The forty thousand gulden you spoke of belong to the boy here. He, and not I, has won them." Strålkrans pointed to me.

"What a silly joke!" exclaimed Lodstein, impatiently.

"It is no joke at all, but earnest."

"You certainly cannot mean to let the boy keep the money?"

"Yes, by my honor. It belongs to him. He has

won it, and I have no right to deprive him of his property. Even if I had, I would not take a single gulden of it. I have gambled away my fortune, but notwithstanding that, I will not have it again, if I must obtain it by gambling. And now good-night. You have taught me the curse of gambling, chance has allowed me to change this curse into a blessing. I will remember the lesson. Farewell, our ways are now separated."

"One word before you go!" exclaimed Lodstein violently, and seized Strålkrans' arm. "What joy can it give you to throw this gold to a pair of strolling German beggars? Give them a few hundred gulden and let us share the gain. We have both been unlucky. What I have gained from you is gone, so also with the rest of my money. We do not know either of us how we shall get the means to return home. Let us use this gain to depart from here. Let—"

"Hush! and say no further words which degrade you," interrupted Strålkrans with anger. "Although you have made me a gambler, you will not succeed in changing me into a scoundrel."

Strålkrans left Lodstein, taking me with him.

An oath, a threat, which I did not catch, were muttered in a low tone by the latter; but the sound of both was drowned by a swarm of gamblers that approached.

We walked silently and with swift steps to our remote abode. On arriving there Strålkrans counted over the money. It actually amounted to a little more than forty thousand gulden. Neither Paul nor I could realize that this money belonged to us, and I had only a very dim understanding of Strålkrans' words, when he spoke to Paul and gave him some instructions. All that I could make out was, that we should leave the place without delay, that Paul should take good care of the money, and that Strålkrans wrote down the name and address of the pastor at Skärparby and promised to write to him. Then he took leave of us and promised to return early the next day, which he also did. He had the gold changed into bills in the greatest haste, wrote a letter to the pastor in Skärparby and added a testimony to the honest acquisition of the money, with his own seal attached, in case any one should question it. When this was done he said:

"See to it that you are away from here before noon, and you, my boy," added he, turning to me, "preserve the warning in your memory, never to put as much as a gulden at stake. What you have now won, you would lose, if you tried to tempt fortune once more."

The noon sun shone warm and bright upon * * * when we departed with the train. Paul had sewed the money in his clothes together with the letter to the pastor.

The rich harvest he had reaped in * * * as a singer was put in a bag, to be used for travelling expenses, and so we started off, taking our places in the third-class car.

We passed the first two stations without anything remarkable occurring. At the third there was a longer stop.

The passengers rushed out of the cars to get some air and drink lemonade, but we sat still. Paul was not willing to leave his place.

In the meantime my attention was fastened upon an elegantly dressed gentleman, who promenaded slowly the whole length of the train, casting searching glances into each of the cars, as if he was looking for some one. Finally he came to ours. His eyes stopped at me, after they had slipped by Paul. I had only seen this face once by daylight, but nevertheless I recognized it.

The elegant gentleman was no other than Baron Lodstein.

He checked his steps an instant when he saw me, but then continued his way.

I turned to Paul, saying:

"Did you see Baron Lodstein; he who talked with the count last evening? There he goes."

"I was then not mistaken, when I fancied that it was he," muttered Paul.

The bell now rang. It was time to start. The passengers came streaming into the cars, and, to our no slight surprise, the elegant Lodstein stepped into ours, which belonged to the third class. The conductor blew his whistle. The doors were closed again; but just as he was going to close our door, Paul seized me by the arm and jumped out, and the next minute the train glided away.

I comprehended nothing of all this, but stared after the retreating train and then gaped at my brother in blank amazement.

"Why did you do that?" said I finally.

"Simply because the count said: 'if you meet Baron Lodstein, avoid him.'"

Without any further adventures we arrived at the capital of Sweden. Paul gave himself no time to remain there, but the very same day we arrived we went on board a steamer which was going to G——, from whence we were to continue the journey to our native place.

Paul had no peace until he had placed the money in the pastor's hands. Pastor Wenner had already at our parents' death invested himself with the rôle of guardian to us, and although we had left the village without his permission or knowledge, Paul was sure that he would take a kind interest in our welfare.

During the twelve hours we were on board the steamer it appeared to me, in the night, when we sat curled up on the forward deck, that I had caught a glimpse of Baron Lodstein, but I was not quite sure.

CHAPTER VI.

IT was with a very peculiar feeling that I, after three years' absence, again stood before my parents' cabin. I was now ten years old.

The memory of my deceased mother forced itself involuntarily upon me, and so overpowered my soul that I burst into tears.

The little patch of earth outside our cabin, which had formerly been so nicely kept and so carefully cultivated, was now overgrown with weeds, and the cabin itself with its barred windows looked more crooked and dilapidated than ever. When we stepped out of the buggy, which brought us to our home, Paul remembered that he had buried the key. We could thus not get in without forcing the door.

It was late in the summer evening, and in the two neighboring houses they had retired to rest.

Paul went round the cabin and tried the shutters; they were securely fastened. He looked uneasy, as had been the case ever since he came to carry so much money about him.

"I do not know any other way than to start off again," said Paul. "We will have to walk to the parsonage. It is only a short five miles there."

"But I am so tired," objected I, who was not particularly disposed to such a promenade.

"Then I will have to try to break open the door," said Paul.

"Oh no, I can go down through the chimney, if the damper is not closed," I suggested.

Said and done. I climbed up in a tree that stood by the cabin, and from there I came on the roof and so to the chimney. Just as I was about to glide down through it, I happened to see on the high-road a carriage, which stopped before the sheriff's. From it alighted a gentleman. He went up to the house.

I attached no importance to this at the time, but was the next instant down in the cabin, the door of which I immediately opened. The air in there was musty, and it seemed to me as though it smelt of corpses.

The shutters were opened, and the light of the summer evening, or rather night, filled this abode, where my mother had silently and patiently borne life's trials and worked for her children, under a thousand privations and countless tears.

The remembrance of her, which had of late been paled, stood vividly before my soul, and from my childish heart went a sigh of inexpressible regret.

Paul had entered without uttering a word. I seated myself on the same stool upon which I used to sit at mother's feet.

I wept now quite silently. Paul had thrown himself down on the bench muttering:

"It would have been better, Conny, if we, tired as we were, had continued our way to the parsonage. I don't feel right here, I wish we never had entered under this roof."

I too felt anxious. After the memory of my mother came the thought of Black Stina and Janne. I now repented that I had persuaded Paul to rest here, and I exclaimed eagerly:

"Yes, let us go away."

"No, Conny, you said that you were tired, that your head ached. We will stay here through the night."

Paul shook up the old straw mattress and made a bed

for me, the best he could under the circumstances. He lay down on the bench himself, without taking off his clothes, in which he had the bank-notes sewed up. On the table, before one of the windows, he threw the bag with the remainder of the cash.

Weariness soon closed my eyes, so that I fell into a heavy slumber. I had slept several hours when I caught, in my sleep, a confused murmur of voices. I tried to awake; but I was unable, and yet it seemed to me that I heard Paul speak in an agitated tone. Finally my will overcame the trance in which I was sunk, and I opened my eyes.

In the cabin were three persons; the sheriff, my brother and Baron Lodstein.

The sheriff had spoken earnestly, but without hardness, to Paul, who on his side solemnly declared that the accusation was false, and that the baron, pointing to Lodstein, was well aware of it, as he had talked with Count Strålkrans the same evening the event occurred.

I did not immediately comprehend what it was all about; but looked frightened at the sheriff, who said:

"My dear Paul, you have hitherto been known in your native village as a good and honest boy, but if you have now, as the baron asserts, made yourself guilty of a crime and appropriated the money in question, the fault committed can only be righted through your confessing it and immediately returning the stolen property. The baron promises to make no further charge against you, if you only give him back what you have taken. In any other case I will be obliged to treat you as one suspected and denounced for theft."

"No, it is not true, Paul has not stolen; Paul is innocent, for it is I who won the money," screamed I, rushing up from the bed.

They had probably entirely forgotten that I existed, for my appearance produced a no slight sensation. The baron met me with a contemptuous glance, and the sheriff looked at me with an air as if my words had made a certain impression upon him.

"If you would be so good, sir, as to go with me and Conny to the pastor," said Paul, wiping his eyes with the sleeve of his jacket, "then I would deliver both the money and the testimony that it is not stolen; but I cannot do it to any one but the pastor. If it can afterward be proven that I am a thief, you have me anyway in your power."

"Why can you not just as well give me the proof of your innocence as the pastor?" asked the sheriff.

"Because I have a letter to him from Count Strålkrans and the express order not to give the money to any one else."

A moment's hesitation arose in the sheriff's mind. The baron put an abrupt end to it, however, as he said:

"You seem inclined to concede to that rascal's demand. If so I consider your behavior very singular. I have pursued the thief from * * * here, and when I meet and inform against him, I cannot believe that the sheriff himself would try to hinder me from regaining that which has been stolen from me. Thus I insist that the boys should be searched in order to ascertain, in the first place, whether they have the sum of money I have lost in their possession. After that they can prove how they obtained it."

The sheriff was obliged to comply with this exaction of the baron's. It was soon found that Paul had just the sum mentioned.

At this discovery the sheriff's face changed and assumed a stern expression. Paul and I were required to appear before court that same day.

All our assurances and tears availed nothing. The affair had to be brought before the bar.

"Well, so be it," said Paul finally, and took out a sealed letter which he carried in a bag that he wore around his neck; "but," added he, "you ought to be so good, Herr sheriff, as to give this letter yourself to the pastor. When he gets it, I shall be freed."

The sheriff took the letter, and then we were ordered to follow him.

The baron's eyes at that instant fell on the bag that lay on the table. He pointed to it, saying:

"Shall not that be searched too?"

The sheriff opened it in silence and emptied the contents on the table. They consisted of a small number of silver coins, but among these was a costly signet ring with the Lodstein coat of arms. At the sight of it the baron cried, surprised:

"What do I see! Have the little villains appropriated this too, which I missed a few days before I lost the money!"

Paul staggered a few steps backward and exclaimed in despair:

"Herr sheriff, by the Eternal God! I know nothing about that ring, it has not been in my possession before, it has been put there."

The sheriff did not answer, but commanded us to go with him.

When we stepped out of the cabin, I came near falling over; for on the stoop stood—Janne.

He grinned at us, when we went by him.

"Aha! the murderer's young ones have become a pair of strolling thieves!" shouted he, but drew back and took to his heels when the sheriff came. Still he continued, as he ran, to shower abusive epithets upon us.

The sheriff took us to his house, where he locked us up

in one of the rooms, after which we heard him give orders to have the horses harnessed.

At ten o'clock in the forenoon he came back, accompanied by Pastor Wenner.

Not only was the honest acquisition of the money proven through the letter which Paul had begged the sheriff to give the pastor, but the latter had besides, a few days before our arrival, received a communication from Strålkrans, in which the count related the whole occurrence and confided us to the pastor's care and protection. Now remained the ring.

Baron Lodstein could not be induced to withdraw the charge. It became a court affair, and Paul must be tried for the theft.

The whole village, and in fact the whole parish, soon knew that the organ-grinder's Paul had stolen a ring, and although Paul, at the end of the trial, for lack of full evidence, was acquitted, there was no one but the pastor and sheriff who considered him innocent, and he was generally regarded as the one who had committed the theft.

I had stayed at the sheriff's during the trial, but when Paul again became free, we were both taken to the parsonage.

The fortune of forty thousand rixthalers, which had so unexpectedly become mine, was taken charge of by the pastor, as our guardian.

CHAPTER VII.

WHAT a revolution in a person's life is produced through being suddenly changed from an itinerant child to the owner of a considerable fortune!

We, a pair of strollers, who had lived on the income from the streets, with an inheritance of disgrace and despised as belonging to the dregs of the rabble, were now rich.

I say we, for when I came to the parsonage, I did not comprehend how one of us could possess property without the other.

Paul, however, soon taught me the contrary.

Pastor Wenner, a man of honor and a minister in the finest significance of these words, was the one who took upon himself the arrangement of our future, with the assistance of Sheriff Wrikter.

Both of them were to be our guardians, but before this was settled, a very strange scene had occurred between them and us.

Of course all this property was regarded as something of which we would both come into possession, and this so much the more as Strålkrans, in his letter to the pastor, had mentioned the brothers Fredriksson, although in describing the gambling night, he had only spoken of me as the one who had won the money.

He regarded us, however, as joint owners of my gains, but this was what Paul would not agree to.

The money was mine, he said, and not a single farthing of it belonged to him. There was no power on earth that could make him receive any of it.

When the pastor and sheriff, in spite of this, wished to divide the property in two equal parts, he declared that they through such a division would only drive him from his fatherland, and for ever separate him from me. He cited Strålkrans' account, where it was expressly stated that Conny Fredriksson had won forty thousand gulden at roulette in * * *.

I was too young to realize the true nobility of Paul's conduct. It seemed to me simply that he was foolish; for that which was mine must be his too.

Finally, after much talking and arguing about the matter, Paul gained the victory, and I remained sole owner of the whole amount.

When the money had been securely placed, etc., they proceeded to the consideration of my education.

I was to be sent to the high school in Lund. There nothing was known about my father's sad end, or the grievous trial for the theft of the ring. I was simply to be Pastor Wenner's ward, who was to board with his brother, Professor Wenner.

Paul was to stay in Skärparby parsonage through the winter, in order to be confirmed.

We would thus be separated from each other. This was for Paul a very hard trial, yes, almost as hard as the accusation for theft had been. When they told me of this decision, I begged and prayed to be allowed to stay with Paul. I twined my arms around his neck; I wept and declared that I could not live without him, but although Paul's own eyes were full of tears, he said with his gentle smile:

"Conny, it must be. You will now become what I have always predicted, a gentleman. You shall study and become an able man. We must separate—it is for your welfare."

"If I become a gentleman, Paul," I replied, "then you must also become one."

Paul shook his head and said half sadly, half in jest:

"No, Conny, I have already told you several times that I will remain what I am, a street-singer. A person is not fit to be a gentleman who is known by all as an organ-grinder, and in addition has been pointed out as a thief, whom they have released for lack of proof. I have no desire to learn any profession, but will support myself by my singing; but you, Conny, you shall learn many other things."

The days we spent together before my departure will never pass from my memory.

A kind mother could not have treated me with greater tenderness and more complete forgetfulness of self than Paul did, although his pale face and his red eyes told that he lay awake the night through.

At last the day came when I was to leave. They were obliged to tear me away from Paul by force. I cried and screamed with all my might, and struggled violently when they carried me to the carriage. Through the mist of my tears I saw how Paul, when the carriage rolled away with me, ran after it a long distance; then he stopped abruptly and I heard him call my name, but in a tone that sounded like a heart-rending scream.

I tried to throw myself from the carriage. Magister Wenner, the pastor's oldest son and my conductor, held me fast.

The next minute Paul had disappeared from my sight. I neither saw nor heard him more.

How the journey went, I do not remember. I had no mind for anything but my sorrow at being separated from Paul.

It had once seemed to me inconceivable that I should never see my mother again, when they told me that she was dead; but still harder and more bitter did it now seem to me that I should live apart from the only being on earth I loved.

We arrived in Lund one evening at the end of August.

The impression the city made on my smarting soul resembled that which a captive must experience when they lead him to the place where he is to undergo his punishment. It was here that I should drag out interminable years, far away from Paul.

All the friendliness of Professorskan* Wenner was thrown away upon me. I sat sulky and cross in the corner of the room, completely engrossed by my trouble.

The first night in my new home I cried myself to sleep, and when I woke up I cried, until the professorskan came to take me down to breakfast. I was now to be presented to the professor, whom I had not seen the evening before.

The professor was a man of medium height, with a stern face. His greeting was cold. He informed me in a few words, that I in two days would begin to study with the teacher that he had engaged on my account, so that I could enter school by the first of September.

The following day Magister Wenner returned home, and now it seemed to me that I was really abandoned by the whole world.

It would take too much space to describe the first part of my stay in Professor Wenner's house. This period stands before my memory so cold and desolate, that it scarcely possesses a single ray of joy. Paul's letters alone sustained my courage.

The first letter I received was long, and although it was written with characters half an inch high, and in a Swedish which was not Swedish, I have faithfully, and under all changes, preserved it. The spirit of love which

* Wife of a professor.

pervaded it gave evidence of the highest degree of human devotion. When the devastating storms of fate have passed over my life, when my joy has been turned to worm-wood, when I have fancied myself abandoned by God and humanity, I have taken out this letter, read it and then bowed humbly before the Supreme Being, and acknowledged that the person who possessed such a brother-love had no right to complain of destiny.

For me, the child, it was, however, not sufficient. I was consumed with an inner longing.

My naturally happy, although somewhat effeminate disposition, became dull and insensible. I was indifferent to everything, praise or blame, scolding or kindliness; I had only two things clear to me: first, to be allowed to see Paul again, and then to be diligent in order to get through with my school time. I considered that it comprised our term of separation. Besides, Paul wrote in his letter that if I worked well, we should soon meet.

I never associated with any of the other scholars, took no part in their plays and received the name of "plug."

Silent and inaccessible, I went to and from school without having any frolics. Zealous and assiduous with my lessons, I became the favorite of the teachers; but this gave me no joy.

I, who had hitherto not been accustomed to think for myself, was now obliged to be sufficient for myself, as I had an inner repugnance to approaching anybody. All that was peevish and fretful in my disposition disappeared. I thought of my position in life, the events that had occurred, yet without telling any one about my past life. Through this, I developed my powers of reflection and my character to an independence which I would perhaps never have attained under other conditions.

Being severed from all other connection with my fellow-beings than that of pupil with teacher, my school-mates and those around me exerted no influence upon me. My vanity was not excited by my school-mates; my self-love was not wounded, and consequently I formed no false ideas of what one ought, or ought not, to be ashamed of.

It is true, I never spoke of my parents or my brother; but it was simply because I did not speak of anything that concerned myself.

Professorskan Wenner, a talkative and inquisitive woman, had at first asked me various questions concerning my family relations, but soon got tired, as she never received any answer but "yes" and "no."

The professor, as blunt and close-mouthed as his wife was garrulous, never made any inquiries. His whole interest for me was limited to that which pertained to my instruction. Over this he watched with the greatest conscientiousness; but how it stood with me in other respects, whether I was consumed with longing and sorrow, or whether I rejoiced at life, was a matter of which he did not take cognizance.

With all this he was, however, the only one to whom I devoted any attention, probably because my instruction was so closely allied with him, and I considered his judgment of my progress as the gauge of my diligence.

The whole first winter Paul's letters came from Skärparby parsonage; but after he was confirmed, he resumed his itinerant life. I then received them from different parts of Sweden.

One thing which in nowise escaped me was, that Paul's handwriting had become better and better, as well as his spelling.

It was evident that he had employed the time, while preparing for his confirmation, in improving himself in other ways.

Five years elapsed without my seeing Paul. I was

now fifteen, and was to leave school and enter the gymnasium.

Not once during this long and joyless period had I lost the hope of being allowed to see Paul when I left school.

I had frequently written to him about it, but yet he had not given me any decided answer. I was no longer a child. My will had ripened, my understanding was considerably in advance of my age, and I knew very well what I wanted. My decision was consequently taken, that if Paul did not answer me definitely, when and where we could meet, I intended to leave Lund and go to G——g, where he told me to address my letters.

I passed my examination with the highest honors.

It was a mild and beautiful summer day when I, at the close of the examination, returned home with Professor Wenner, who had been present.

Fate ordained that it was the same date as when Paul and I, then a pair of lonely orphan children, started out in the world to seek our fortune. He was at that time of the same age as I then was.

Eight years lay between that day and the one when I finished my course at school.

I had a vivid recollection of how glad I felt when I walked by Paul's side, and how kindly he looked at me while I prattled.

I now went along without any happy dreams, in company with my cold and silent instructor, but with the firm resolution to inform the professor, on my return home, that I intended to go and see my brother.

While my thoughts dwelt upon my bright hopes eight years ago, the recollection came up of the accusation of theft, Paul's trial and the shadow of suspicion which clung to my poor brother. The bitter grief I then experienced again pierced my heart, and with a feeling of deep despondency I remembered, in connection with it, the sad inheritance my father had left us.

Whatever I became, I was stamped as a malefactor's son. I had come thus far in my reflections, when the professor quite unexpectedly addressed me:

"You have gone through your studies like a brave boy," said he, turning his face to me. "If you continue as well as you have begun, you may become something in time."

I took off my cap, so honored did I feel by this praise from the usually taciturn lips.

The professor continued to look at me, and that with an expression as if he had seen me for the first time.

"I cannot remember to have heard what your parents were," resumed the learned man. "That they are dead, I recollect that my brother mentioned in one of his letters. Well, what was your father?"

For an instant I hesitated to utter the truth. The pastor's words resounded in my mind, when he on taking leave said to me:

"Avoid mentioning your father's vocation and whom he was. I have to my brother only alleged that you are the son of a German, who resided in Sweden and married a Swede."

As I made no reply, the professor resumed:

"Did you not hear what I asked? Why do you not answer?"

At his first question I had dropped my eyes. At the renewal of it, I looked up in the old man's face and answered quite undisguisedly:

"My father was an organ-grinder."

I had expected that the professor through some gesture would have indicated his surprise, but I was mistaken. He did not seem astonished in the least. His harsh features lighted up. I cannot say that they changed expression, but it was as if an inner satisfaction shone from his eyes when he said:

"That's right. I thought that you might have been infected with a miserable vanity, and that this would tempt you not to acknowledge that you were a child of the masses. I can tell you that I knew both this and a little more still, but I wished to test what spirit you were of."

When the professor said "and a little more still," I felt that my cheeks burned, and I bent down my head, humiliated at the thought of this "little more."

The professor probably perceived the effect of these words, for he added in a firm voice:

"Fredriksson need not bow his head for what his father has done. Bear it like a man, and remember that 'the misdeeds of the parents only pass in inheritance to one who treads in their footsteps.' You are diligent, have good ambition and an excellent power of comprehension; with these qualities it will be easy for you to wash away the stains your father has left after him—and now we will say nothing more about that matter. In the autumn you will become a gymnast, and if you work as hitherto, you will in three years be a student at the University."

The professor turned away his head and added:

"It is just as well for you to continue to maintain the same silence toward the women folks about your family affairs, as you have done during the time you have been with me. There is no harm in keeping still, but it is a shameful cowardice of one who intends to become a man, to deny the truth when he is asked about it."

We continued our way in silence. I was deliberating whether the moment was not at hand to come out with my resolution to go and visit Paul. After considering a while I said:

"There is something that I desire to say to you, Herr professor."

"Let me hear it."

"I intended to ask permission to go and see my brother."

"Where does he live?"

"He is staying for the present in G——g."

"Ah! and what is he doing there?"

The professor again looked at me.

"He goes around with his hand-organ," answered I, fearlessly.

It did not enter my mind to be ashamed because Paul was a street-singer and organ-grinder.

"We will think of the matter, yes, that we will, there is no hurry about it."

"Yes, but there is though!" cried I daringly, entirely forgetting the respect I usually showed the professor.

"What did you say?" The old man now gave me a penetrating look.

I had taken the first step, and to shrink back was not to be thought of. Sink or swim I must make the attempt. It concerned my heart's most burning desire, my five years' longing after my brother, the realization of the hope which had impelled me to zeal and good habits; in short, it concerned everything.

In what words I clothed my feelings I do not remember; but I know that I, for the first time since Paul and I separated, spoke out all the grief, all the longing and all the suffering my soul had concealed.

The shyness, diffidence and reserve with which I had surrounded myself during these years, now resembled a dam which had broken way, and the long pent-up stream of feeling rushed unimpeded over my lips. I declared boldly, that if I was not allowed to see my brother and be with him for a little time, my zeal and ability to work would die out, like my happy, light-hearted disposition.

The professor walked straight ahead, notwithstanding we had passed his abode. Not a word escaped him. He did not even turn his head to look at me, he only stepped a little faster than usual. At length I ceased, stifled by my emotion and rapid talking. When he no longer heard my voice, the professor stopped, and that so abruptly, that I, who had kept pace with him, rushed several feet ahead before I observed that he had halted. I turned round hastily, and in this way we found ourselves standing opposite each other.

"Hm, ah, hm, hm!" were the first sounds he uttered. Then he turned to me and said gruffly:

"The deuce how you talk, when your tongue is once let loose. If you are silent between times, you make up for it afterward."

And with this he swung to the left, to find his residence.

I rushed after him, completely beside myself with anxiety, and, height of presumption, I seized one of his hands, stammering:

"Herr professor, I may go, may I not? Isn't it so, I may go and see my brother?"

"What are you doing? What do you take me for, to seize hold of me in that style? Perhaps you think that I don't know what I ought to do?"

"Yes, Herr professor, but—"

"There is no but in the case,—you may" . . . the professor was interrupted by a sneeze, and my heart stood still . . . "see your brother," added he.

He now went like a streak through the gate and up the steps, so that I could with difficulty follow him. On reaching the entry I faltered some words to express my gratitude. But he hastily flung open the door and said in a huffy tone:

"Go to your room and leave me in peace."

CHAPTER VIII.

HOW strange life is! How completely ignorant we are of what the next moment may bring forth! We stop outside a door, we lay our hand on the knob, and we do not know until the door opens what we shall find within.

So it was with me. The professor had disappeared in the saloon, and I hastened to my door, fully convinced that my little chamber would be as empty and desolate as when I left it. I turned the knob and stood for a few seconds as if petrified, but exclaimed the next moment, with a cry of joy:

"Paul!" and then rested on the breast of the so long missed, so intensely longed for brother.

What is there to say about such a meeting? Nothing. Any one with feeling realizes it. The heart's beatitudes are not to be described.

Of the first moments of our reunion there is therefore not much to say. We were both so exclusively absorbed by the happiness we experienced, that we were like a pair of children delirious with joy.

Dinner had been brought in to us. Whether we ate any of it or not, I cannot recollect. Not until evening, when we had for several hours talked about how we had missed and longed for each other, did we begin to ask questions.

I noticed that Paul had changed considerably. His handsome head was, if possible, handsomer than before, but the expression of his face was no longer the same. The careless unconcern had disappeared, and over it rested something that resembled a light veil of melancholy, behind which the natural sprightliness sometimes glimpsed forth. His long arms had grown fuller; his back was not so bent, his shoulders not so round; his legs had become somewhat straighter and his neck had lost its crane-like appearance. His attire, however, was characterized by the same peculiarities as before. He had now, as when he used to present himself to the public in great style, a neat brown coat, but too large; a pair of black pantaloons, too long; a pair of boots with low heels and singularly turned up at the toes; a vest of velvet, somewhat too short; a very long scarf, over which a broad but dazzlingly white shirt collar was turned down. On the table lay an almost elegant straw hat, and beside it—Paul's violin.

If Paul had been dressed according to the latest fashion journal and been the most exquisite young man in the world, I could not have been prouder and happier at seeing him again than I now was. All the depression which had tormented me these five years had fled, and I was again the same light-hearted boy as when Paul and I wandered around with our hand-organ.

Paul, again, could not wonder enough, that his little Conny had become such a large youth. He regarded me with looks of the most undisguised admiration, when I related about my success in school, that I had obtained the premium in all the classes, and that I would become a gymnast in the fall. Paul's eyes shone with delight, and he exclaimed every little while:

"It is just as I have always said, you will become something uncommon. God bless you, Conny, for being such a splendid boy! When you are as old as I, that is to say, twenty-one, then you will have been a student in the University a whole year. Gracious, how delightful that will be!"

Our conversation was interrupted toward evening by

the professor, who came in very unexpectedly. He said in his usual brusque voice:

"I will tell you, Fredriksson, that you and your brother can go with me out to Torparbo (this was the professor's summer residence) and stay there while your brother is with you. My wife and I are going up to Stockholm. I shall leave for Torparbo in an hour, and you must be ready by that time."

Without waiting for any answer, he went out again.

I now asked how Paul had happened to come to Lund.

Paul informed me that he had written to the professor and asked whether I could come and see him in G——g. In reply the professor had given Paul to understand that he considered it better for us to stay together at his country-place during the summer.

Paul accepted the invitation, and arrived at the professor's home a half hour after I had gone to the examination. The professor had spoken to him a whole hour, praised me very much and asked Paul to await my return in my room, after which the old man had gone up to the school to hear how the examination went.

At the time appointed we started for Torparbo, which was twelve miles from Lund.

There Paul and I spent the summer entirely alone.

The affection which bound me to my brother became still firmer and stronger.

Although our life careers, our tastes and our aspirations for the future were entirely different, there was yet heart sympathy between us, and that is always stronger than all else. It was also impossible to live with Paul every day and not become attached to this richly endowed child of nature.

When little, I had loved him from instinct, because he loved me, but now that years had ripened my understanding, and separation increased my affection, my attachment became something which would defy time, and like a vein of gold go through my soul, however full of dross it might be. During our stay together, I tried several times to persuade Paul to give up his itinerant life and share with me the property which had fallen to me so entirely without my merit.

His answer to all my urging was always a refusal to share anything with me, but together with an injunction to me to be grateful for being able to obtain through it a good education, and to become something else than a strolling adventurer.

"But if this is really a blessing, which I willingly acknowledge," said I, "why then will you not leave your wandering life and become something different? You can surely never mean to assert in earnest that you would do wrong if you shared this money with me and through it procured the knowledge which you yourself admit to be so essential?"

Paul leaned his head in his hand and said in reply:

"Wrong, oh no, not precisely that, but I would not be happy if I were obliged to change my way of life. As long as I can remember, I have led an irregular life, sung for bread and been contented when it was not lacking. Singing was dear to me from my tenderest childhood, and habit has unfitted me to earn my bread through work. When I was at Skärparby parsonage, I thought of devoting myself to some trade and ceasing to go around with the hand-organ; but when I had been there a while, the longing seized me to roam about and sing free and without constraint. My mind became heavy and troubled, my thoughts dark and gloomy, during the time I stayed in the parsonage, where one day was just like the other, and where my eyes always met the same sights. I studied and I worked, but my cheerfulness was gone; work was irksome, and I compared myself to a sparrow that has been put in a cage; the sparrow is happy and contented when it is free, and sends up its twitter as joyously from the streets of the town as from the woods, but put him in prison, and he dies, even if you surround him with all possible abundance. I should die if I were forced to live quiet in one and the same spot, even if it were a paradise. No, Conny, my singing and my freedom are my happiness. I would not have it otherwise. I love to wander around and sing for the children of the people. They understand me and I understand them. We are suited to each other."

"You are thus perfectly contented and happy?"

"I would be if—" he passed his hand over his curly head, and added abruptly: "but it is not worth while to speak of it."

"Yes, Paul, you shall speak out. Say that you are not happy because we are obliged to live apart."

"Conny, that we do it, is for the sake of your future welfare, and can thus not contain any unhappiness for me. It is an evil which I gladly submit to, because I know that it will bring joy with it to you. Dear Conny, when it is a question of you and your welfare, my own must be put aside. It is something entirely different that disturbs my happiness and places itself between me and my peace."

"And that is?" I looked at Paul and thought of our father involuntarily.

"It is that ring which was found in my bag and which fastened the suspicion upon me that I had stolen."

"But, Paul, you were acquitted," said I.

"Acquitted for lack of proof," answered Paul, smiling sadly. In this smile I found the explanation of the shade of melancholy which sometimes rested upon his face. Paul continued after a moment's pause:

"It is as if I could not look folks in the face, until I had found out how the ring came in my bag. When I now sing, and my mind feels free and glad as before, then the recollection suddenly comes that I have stood before the bar as a thief, and away goes my joy and contentment. I finish my song abruptly and continue my course with sorrow in my heart."

On hearing this my mind was seized with a deep animosity toward Baron Lodstein. I felt that if there was any person whom I with heart and soul detested, it was this man, who although fully conscious that we had not stolen the money, still accused us of it. That he, in some inexplicable way, had placed the ring in Paul's bag, in order to make him still more suspected, was my full conviction. How much harm had he not thereby occasioned my poor brother?

Paul, who knew by the expression of my face what was passing within me, now began to speak of other things, my future and the career I had before me, which, according to his opinion, was brilliant in the highest degree.

While Paul painted my coming life in the brightest colors, I sat quite silent and followed him in thought to all the eminence and distinction which he predicted that I would attain.

It had never before been clear to me what I wished to become. But now, when Paul spoke of what a rich choice I had, my thought stopped at the calling of judge. It may be that it was led there by the bitterness with which I thought of the injustice which my brother had suffered.

The reminder of it thus decided my choice of a profession. With the usual inexperience and presumption of youth I considered it the judge's fault that Paul was not acquitted on other conditions. I would now devote my energies to becoming a stern and incorruptible judge, who might one day proclaim my brother's innocence and Baron Lodstein's baseness.

Time passed quickly, and we were soon at the end of August.

One beautiful day, when Paul and I had been speaking of our fast approaching separation, and agreed to meet every year, no matter how far we were apart, we saw the professor's chaise drive up in the yard. I experienced at the sight of it a very disagreeable feeling, for I knew this was the signal for Paul's and my departure from Torparbo.

Two days afterward we were separated.

Paul had gone off with his violin, to continue his nomad life; I returned to Lund to begin my studies anew.

My former room in the professor's house, on the second floor, I was now allowed to exchange for a larger one, which was situated two flights up and next to the professor's library. It was separated from it only by a thin door, which gave him free access to me whenever he pleased.

The day after I had become located in my new apartment, which was considerably more cheerful and comfortable than the former, I returned toward night from a long walk, which I had taken to dispel the regret for Paul.

As I was about ascending the second flight, a man came running down, and we met in the middle of the stairs.

I stopped abruptly at sight of him and stared at him. He also looked at me with an air that expressed the greatest surprise, but without either of us clothing our feelings in words we hastened by each other.

I thought:

"Is it possible, can it really be he?"

The following day was the first time since our return to Lund that we assembled for dinner. The first days we had been in town each and all had taken their meals in their rooms.

When I entered the dining-room, I found the same man whom I had met on the stairs, standing with a waiter in his hand. I now understood that he was installed as servant at the professor's, in place of the old man who had died shortly before the journey to Stockholm.

The professor could not endure female domestics, but the attendance and care of his rooms had always been performed by a man-servant.

During the meal I had time to examine the new-comer more closely.

There was no longer any doubt. I had not been mistaken, when I, at the meeting on the stairs, believed that I knew this face. It was none other than—Black Stina's Janne.

The glance he cast on me, while waiting on the table, said that he had recognized the organ-grinder's son. It is true, I did not experience any of my old fear of him, but I had a presentiment that Janne would make me pay up for having a seat at the table on which he was waiting.

I no longer feared his misdeeds nor his fists, but so much the more his tongue. There was something of malicious exultation in the look he fixed upon me. He seemed to say with it:

"Just wait, my fine gentleman; my old grudge has not disappeared, although I have grown up from a boy to a youth. I have by no means forgotten the flogging the sheriff gave me on your account, and this you will have to pay up for."

When I after the meal again found myself alone in my room, I reflected upon this singular meeting.

I went through in my memory the persecutions I had endured from the scholars during my school-days in Stockholm, and I asked myself whether I was disposed to stand a repetition of them. The answer was "no." I had received too much praise in school not to realize that work and knowledge ought to possess the power to obliterate inherited disgrace.

The intercourse with Paul had strengthened my affection, stilled my longing and diffused peace in my soul. The despondency which had filled my being was gone. Paul's portrayal of my future had awakened my self-consciousness and my energy. Although young, I felt that I ought not to let any difficulties or reverses keep me from attaining the aim to which I had resolved to come.

Whatever the consequences might be of my meeting with Janne, my resolution was taken that I would not allow them to depress my courage.

The meeting with my childhood's enemy thus roused my slumbering powers, and taught me to realize that every attempt to escape the humiliations my origin occasioned would only magnify them.

The only way in which I could overcome the prejudice was to stand erect, and never, from false pride and a childish vanity, attempt to deny my birth.

The hours which elapsed between dinner and supper were very decisive in the direction of my character.

The next day the preliminary examination for the gymnasium was to take place.

A week had elapsed since Janne and I first met in the professor's house. I saw him daily, he brushed my clothes, waited on me at table, etc., but as yet not a word had been exchanged between us. I avoided addressing him. He attended to his duties, but said nothing.

If there was anything I desired or needed I turned to the chamber-maid, but never to Janne.

In short, when a week had passed without my hearing anything which showed that Janne had related my father's fate, I ceased to think of him.

Besides, my attention since I had begun at the gymnasium, was so taken up by study, that I had no time left for other things.

One day in the middle of September, I returned home from the gymnasium in exceedingly good spirits.

I had really distinguished myself in mathematics.

Quite joyfully I entered my room, but stopped, checked by voices which spoke with great vehemence in the professor's library.

It was usually so quiet there that no sound was to be heard but the creaking of the learned man's boots, when he paced the floor.

Surprised that anything resembling a dispute could take place there, I listened. I then overheard these words, which Fru Wenner screamed with unrestrained violence:

"It cannot be helped, you must hear me, and I tell you what it is, Wenner, I will not allow myself to be ruled to such a degree as to have in my own house so disreputable a person as that scamp. Yes, it is just a nice story. Professor Wenner has for five years had the son of a murderer for his pupil, and placed such a child at his table, allowed his wife to take the same care of him as of a child of honest parents. It is such a disgrace, that—that—"

"You forget yourself entirely," interrupted the professor.

"No, I do not forget myself! I should think that it was you who had forgotten yourself, and if I did right I would tell everybody how you treat your wife, what a tyrant you are, in forcing her to associate with the lowest rabble. I tell you what, if he does not leave the house immediately, I will not stay another day in this home, where I was born and for which you have me alone to thank." The voice now assumed a querulous accent. "In consideration of that," she continued, "I ought to have been secured against its being polluted by disreputable people. Yes, so much respect my husband ought surely to show me, but you have always been ungrateful, heartless and despotic."

"How long do you intend to keep on in this way?"

asked the professor, yet all the while speaking in his usual cold tone.

"Until that boy is out of the house."

"In that case it is best for you to remove immediately, as you just said. Fredriksson is going to stay until he becomes a student. You have now heard my words, and can consequently take your departure."

"So you drive me away for the sake of that wretch!" burst out the professorskan.

"Yes, if you cannot get along under the same roof with him."

"But do you know what sort of a fellow he is?"

"Yes, I know that his father was an organ-grinder," replied the professor, in a somewhat harsher tone than before; "furthermore, that the father during a quarrel stuck a knife in an Italian, and that he then, when he was doomed to death, hung himself. You thus perceive that I know all about Fredriksson's family, and that you cannot say anything that is new to me. I knew all that before Fredriksson came to my house, but it did not hinder me from taking him, or from having him remain until his education is finished. Therefore I do not advise anybody, whoever it may be, to behave ill toward him. His board is paid, and he has a right to demand good treatment of those who receive his money, especially as he in his whole conduct has shown himself to be an exemplary boy."

"It is thus for the paltry gain that you keep him? It is from avarice?"

"Woman, weigh your words," warned the professor.

"I need not weigh them, and I must tell you that your behavior is—is—very singular. You make common cause with a thief. The money which is paid you is stolen. The father as well as his children have been accused of the theft of it, but were acquitted for lack of proof. The brother has besides suffered punishment for stealing a ring. These two unmitigated scamps have been living at Torparbo. They have probably helped themselves while there. And yet you, you who are so puffed up over your learning, that you set yourself above other people, and believe yourself inaccessible to scandal, will through this disgrace yourself and your poor wife. There is not a single teacher or scholar in the whole gymnasium who will have anything to do with such a pupil and school-mate. He will be turned out of the institution of learning, in spite of your protection, and people will point their fingers at us."

"Now not a word more!" exclaimed the professor, in such thundering tones that they made me jump. He struck his hand in an energetic way on the table, adding: "If you dare to say another word against Fredriksson, I will never, mark, Anna Maria, I say never, forgive it. You know that I hold to what I promise. You ought also to know how impossible it is to change my resolution. If you cannot live with my pupil, then move to Torparbo, but do not dare to utter a prejudicial word about him, for then we will be separated, and that for ever."

"And that, Wenner, *you* say to me," stammered the professorskan.

"Yes, and if you irritate me, I may say still more. Be on your guard therefore, you know that I am not to be played with."

"You will thus force your poor wife to continue to have a thief in her house?" rejoined the worthy dame.

"I force her to nothing. She can leave this house, if she cannot behave in the way which I demand of the woman who bears my name. Fredriksson is an uncommonly proper and richly endowed boy, of whom there is nothing bad to be said. His behavior during these five years has been such, that it leaves nothing to desire. Besides, he interests me as if he were my own son. When you hear this, you also know how you are expected to treat him."

"But yet, he has been accused of theft," the professorskan ventured to object.

"It is an untruth; who said it?" roared the professor.

"Wenner, you frighten the life out of me," exclaimed the professorskan.

"Who said that Fredriksson had stolen? Do you hear, I wish to know," cried the professor with unbridled rage.

"Our new servant, Janne; he is from the same place as Fredriksson."

"Ah!" I heard the professor cross the floor and ring a hand-bell.

"What do you intend to do?" sobbed the professorskan.

"Call Janne here and give him his dismissal," answered the professor.

In a few minutes Janne entered.

The professor informed him in few, but forcible words, that he must leave his service immediately. He paid Janne his wages for the time he had engaged him, but he would not have in his house a person who spread calumnious and lying reports about other people. One who was in his employ should in the first place possess the virtue of being able to keep silent, and would not be allowed to gossip.

Janne tried to excuse himself, but was cut short by the professor, who told him to absent himself and within an hour be ready to quit the house.

After Janne was gone, the professor uttered some sharp and stern injunctions to his better half.

She wept and begged for forgiveness, confessing that she

had forgotten herself, etc. But the professor's only answer was a command that she should leave the room.

When it again became silent in there, I threw myself on the sofa, as if stunned by what I had heard. It appeared to me, on one hand, as if I ought to leave this abode immediately, but on the other, as if I must stay. Janne had thus branded me too as a thief. This was something that I had not calculated beforehand.

Just as my pride and my whole soul rose up against this new attack, the library door opened, and the professor stood on the threshold with his eyes fixed upon me.

"Have you been here long, Fredriksson?" asked he.

"About an hour," answered I, rising. My agitated face enlightened him about all the wounds my soul had during this hour received.

"Have you heard what has occurred?"

"Yes, I have. I also intend to ask your permission to leave Lund," said I, entirely obeying the impulse of the moment.

"And wherefore?"

"I cannot remain in your house, professor, and I will not stay in Lund when I cannot be with you."

"And what hinders you from being with me?"

"Why, because — because the professorskan does not wish to have me here, and — and — because I would be a cause of — of — trouble," stammered I, scarcely able to restrain my tears.

"Very good, very correct; but unnecessary. You need not busy yourself about what occurs between me and my wife, that is a matter which does not concern you. You will stay just where you are; this is your guardian's will and also mine. Now not a word more on the subject. Have you understood me?"

"I have, but—"

"There isn't any but,—you understand. If you are not

contented here, then write to your guardian. Until the latter says you must move, you remain. And now to another matter. How do you intend to act in case these stories come to the ears of your school-mates at the gymnasium?"

For a moment I remained silent. The new humiliating blow that had reached me had entirely destroyed the self-confidence my first meeting with Janne had called forth; something resembling anguish overpowered me, but only for a few seconds; then I lifted up my head and looked the professor in the eye, as I answered with firmness:

"I intend to acknowledge that which is true, but to contradict that which is false."

"Good, I am satisfied; you really begin to do credit to yourself."

The professor turned to go into his room; but I rushed after him, seized his hand and exclaimed with the uncontrollable pain of wounded pride:

"Herr professor, send me away, I cannot remain in a house where they regard me as a thief, where they will show me contempt as such, notwithstanding I am completely innocent. I cannot endure the consciousness that—"

Here I was choked by my tears.

All the resentment I had experienced during the last hour now gave itself vent in spasmodic weeping, that consolation which women and children alone possess. I had let go of the professor's hand, and buried my face in my own, completely overpowered by my emotions.

For a few minutes no sound was heard but my sobs; finally the professor said in a tone which seemed quite mild:

"You are still a child, Fredriksson, and therefore talk and act like one.—Come in here with me, and I will say a few sensible words to you."

A hand patted me on the head. I looked up hastily; anything like an affectionate caress I had not received from any one but Paul, since my mother's death, and least of all did I expect any such proof of sympathy from the gruff professor.

When I glanced up in his face, my tears ceased to flow. He looked at me so kindly and compassionately that it was like balm on a wound.—Without saying anything further, I accompanied him.

He spoke long and seriously, but if the words were somewhat stern, the tone, on the contrary, was gentle.

He told me that his wife had not at all regarded me as a thief, that her words had been an expression of her then prevailing feeling, but that her naturally good heart had probably already caused her to repent them. He then proved to me that if I now left Lund, I would, in case Janne's story became circulated, only give credibility to it. The surest way of refuting it was to remain, and through continued good conduct silence every derogatory report; "only the guilty flee," said he.

The result of this conversation was that I within myself acknowledged the professor to be right, and when I a while afterward followed him down to the dining-room, all my trust and reliance in my own innocence had returned.

The professorskan was not visible at dinner, and a female domestic waited on the table.

CHAPTER IX.

A YEAR went by without my being reminded by my school-mates, or anybody else, of Janne's story.

The professorskan had a few days after Janne's departure from Lund again showed herself at the dinner-table, and then treated me just as before, with the only difference that she was colder and no longer entered into any conversation.

I studied more diligently than ever, and lacked interest for everything else. With every progress I made my trust grew, and hope, youth's glad companion, was rich in promises to me. I felt proud and satisfied with myself, because I stood in advance of my comrades in knowledge and application. At sixteen years of age my mind was filled with vanity over my intellectual gifts, a vanity to which the teachers, through holding me up as something unusual, gave all possible nourishment.

In the measure my self-conceit grew I showed myself more accessible to my school-mates, and condescended now and then to help them with their lessons. I became a sort of oracle to them, a model which the teachers cited, and a piece of perfection to myself as well as one of the wonders of the world in Paul's eyes.

Every letter from him contained the most enthusiastic admiration over my success, which I by no means refrained from relating to him. When the summer vacation again came, the professor and I went to Torparbo, where Paul arrived a little later and remained a week. The professorskan had gone to Malmö to visit through the summer with her relatives.

I knew that Paul would be with me but a very short time, but I consoled myself with the thought that I would, after his departure, plunge into my studies, which the professor now directed entirely.

The summer, like the rest of the year, was to me only a period of continued work. I gave myself no time for rest or recreation. I was driven as by a fever, in order to soon enter the University. When I had got so far, I would amuse myself, then I would enjoy all the pleasure I now voluntarily renounced.

When the fall term again began I passed my examination for the third class in the gymnasium, and thus took a leap over the second.

The same day I gained this, as I fancied, brilliant success, the professor had some company.

The guests consisted of the professors and pupils of the gymnasium and school. I was still of the age when one prefers to behold strange people at a distance and is, as it were, a little shy of contact with them. I had accordingly taken my place in a corner of the parlor, listening to what was said and making silent comments to myself.

Two professors stood conversing with each other, when the rector of the gymnasium came to them, saying:

"Well, brother K——, have you heard who has moved to Lindesfors?"

Professor K—— had heard nothing.

"Young Baron Casper Lodstein has inherited the estate from Count D——," said the other professor, turning to the rector.

"Yes, it fell to him as fidéi-commis at the count's death last spring; and now Casper Lodstein's uncle and guardian, Baron Fabian, has moved there in order to be nearer his ward. The young heir has to-day passed his examination at the gymnasium. His uncle and guardian has had the first floor of Count D——'s house, here in Lund, fitted up for their use. The baron's family intend to spend the winter months in Lund and the summer at Lindesfors. Fabian Lodstein is, as you know, married to the sister of the late Count D——, and has with her obtained a very fine fortune, which he will probably, during the time he takes care of his nephew's, increase considerably."

"Fabian Lodstein seems to have been as economical for the last few years as he was extravagant before," said Professor K——.

"That is very often the case. After one, like the baron, has squandered all that he possessed, reason awakes, and he turns abruptly from the road which would lead to poverty and misery."

What was further said, I did not hear, so engrossed was I by the thought that this Lodstein would again cross my path.

My blood boiled at the thought that I could not be revenged; that I was still too young and impotent to do anything to one who had caused my brother and me so much harm.

Two or three weeks after this, as I was coming from the gymnasium, I met an elegant carriage, in which sat a solitary gentleman. My attention was not fastened on the latter, however, but on the servant who stood behind. I did not know myself through what accident my eyes fell on him; but at the first glance I had recognized the dark physiognomy.

The carriage drove rapidly by. I had seen Janne again in the liveried servant, and Fabian Lodstein in the gentleman who rode in the carriage.

In the gentleman and the servant I had thus regained my bitterest enemies.

That Janne would now do everything to injure me was

clear; but with a certain youthful presumption I thought, that neither he nor his master would be able to do me any harm, as I had made myself deserving of so much praise.

One morning, a short time afterward, when I came to the gymnasium, I found some pupils belonging to the first class standing outside the entrance. When I passed by, one of them said:

"Was that Fredriksson?"

I turned round involuntarily and cast an inquiring glance at the questioner, whom I, after looking at him, guessed to be Casper Lodstein, as he belonged to the new-comers in the first class, and besides had a striking likeness to his uncle. Without paying any attention to the answer he received to his question, I continued my way.

Two days later, when I entered the third class, I noticed that my school-mates looked at me with a singular expression.

We had that day mathematics, a study in which I was ahead of all the others and which particularly interested me.

My whole thought was fastened upon the coming lesson, in which I was so absorbed that I gave no heed to my school-mates.

The lesson was over and I prepared to go. On reaching the door, the tallest and largest in the class, Arvid Ahlgren, stepped between it and me, saying:

"Ah no, Herr Mathematicus, you shall not stir from the spot until you have solved a problem which I will give you, and which will be more intricate than the one which you have just received praise for."

I turned a proud glance upon my assailant, who was the feeblest in knowledge, but the strongest in physical powers, of the whole class.

"I believe I am able to solve whatever problem you wish to give me," answered I.

"All right, come, I will draw up one."

We went to the black-board.

The rest of the scholars gathered around us. Ahlgren took the chalk and wrote:

"If one who steals is equal to a thief, what is then one who has been accused of theft?"

"One suspected of theft," was my answer, which I gave with perfect calmness, although every drop of blood boiled with anger.

"No, he is a thief, and do you know what honest people do with such a person, when he comes in among them?"

"They drive him out," said I, still maintaining my self-command.

"Good, you have now shown us what we ought to do with you."

Ahlgren had not fairly got these words over his lips before he received from me a powerful blow right in the face, and that so energetically, that he gave an enraged shriek. Instantly the whole class was up in arms. They had immediately divided into two parties, one for and one against me.

Ahlgren and I fought as ferocious boys are accustomed to fight.

He was considerably stronger than I, but I on the other hand possessed unusual agility. Benches, tables and books were used as weapons of attack and defence. It was a stormy scene and a terrible tumult. The strife continued without either side gaining the victory; we gave and received black eyes, flattened noses and swollen lips. It is uncertain how it would have ended, had not the rector suddenly appeared in the midst of us. At the sight of him most of the scholars rushed to the door, in order to escape all reprimand.

A short investigation was held as to the cause of the battle, and who had begun it.

I acknowledged immediately that I had dealt the first blow. Ahlgren and I were ordered to present ourselves to the rector the following day.

When I went home I was firmly resolved to mention what had occurred to the professor, but to my regret, he had gone away, and would not return for two or three days. How I would clear myself seemed a little perplexing, for I feared nothing more nor less than expulsion from the gymnasium.

The following day I appeared before the rector, and both Ahlgren and I gave a true explanation of the affray.

Ahlgren acknowledged that he had begun the quarrel, led to it by a story that Lodstein had related, or in which it was asserted that I and my brother had been arrested on the suspicion of having stolen a large sum of money from his uncle, and that we had only been acquitted from lack of evidence, and because his uncle did not care to pursue the matter.

Ahlgren, as he quite openly declared, had availed himself of this story to humble my pride.

The rector listened to us in silence, and first gave Ahlgren a serious rebuke for the meanness of using a scandalous report to attack a person. Then he turned to me and gave me a setting down for the way in which I tried to refute such an accusation. He concluded with the words:

"The fist is a poor advocate when our honor is concerned, and one does wrong to employ such a defender."

Ahlgren and I were warned not to engage in any further quarrels or strifes, if we wished to remain at the gymnasium.

After receiving these injunctions, we went in to the lesson. As we were about to enter the hall, Ahlgren said:

"Before we appear among our school-mates, we ought to know whether we are friends or enemies."

"It is best to decide, that matter at the close of the lesson," answered I, and opened the door.

The lesson was again ended, and again were we each and all to return home; but this time it was I who asked the scholars to stay.

"Lodstein, who is in the first class," I began, when they had complied with my request and gathered around me, "has said that I and my brother have been accused of theft; is it not so?"

"Yes, it is," answered they.

"I will explain that matter to you."

I then gave a faithful account of the circumstances, beginning by acknowledging to them all that I was the son of a poor organ-grinder, that I myself had gone around with a hand-organ, and that during our wanderings in Germany, I had come to a watering-place, where chance changed me from a poor boy into a rich one; further, I mentioned how Baron Lodstein, probably through mistake, had accused Paul and me of the theft of the money, and how we had succeeded in proving that we had come by it honestly.

I finished my account with these words:

"If there is any one among you who does not wish to have me for a school-mate, then say so. I will in that case never enter these doors again. I leave it to you to decide whether you wish me to remain or not."

Youth is the age of enthusiasm. We are then easily carried away.

It was easy to foresee that my words would impress their uncorrupted hearts. Ahlgren, my assailant, was the first of all to cry that Fredriksson was a brave fellow, something in which the others joined unanimously.

Thus I had, without any advice save that which my

own reason gave me, met and conquered the first attack against my honor.

I also considered myself to have put an end to these attacks for ever, but I was mistaken. Although my class-mates held together and defended me, I was nevertheless constantly exposed to insults and stings from those who belonged to the same class as Lodstein. Notwithstanding the latter had been twice thoroughly thrashed by me, he could not refrain from flinging some opprobrious words at me whenever we met.

The two remaining years of my gymnasium time were consequently a continuous chain of daily attacks from Lodstein's side. In the meantime I saw plainly that the people in the town, in general, were not particularly well-disposed toward me. I was no longer invited by the scholars' parents to their homes, as had been the case before, when the sons needed my help. The professorskan had also become more distant, but the only effect of this was that her husband showed himself still more friendly toward me than he had before considered necessary.

I felt deeply wounded by all this dislike, but it only made me redouble my zeal, and through this secure the favor of my teachers.

During these two years Paul and I did not meet. He had written that he would not come to Lund, as Janne was employed there, but he proposed that we should postpone our meeting until I had finished at the gymnasium.

In the spring, when I passed my final examination, the professor informed me that he intended to visit his brother, my guardian, Pastor Wenner. The latter had moved from Skärparby, and was now settled in R—tuna, in one of the northern provinces of Sweden.

CHAPTER X.

IT was in the beginning of June that the professor and I started on our journey from the south to the north.

Eight years had elapsed since I came to Lund. It seemed to me that a weight had been lifted from my breast when I turned my back on the learned city.

I was now a large, strong and healthy youth of eighteen, with great self-love and great hopes; but without experience and with much desire to know more of life.

The professor was during the journey less spare of words than he was accustomed to be, and I, who seemed to myself like a bird that had escaped from the cage, felt a great need of being communicative. The deep respect that I entertained for the professor kept me within the bounds of propriety, but did not hinder me from breaking the silence every little while.

We remained two days in the capital.

I was only a little boy when I left Stockholm. I now saw the beautiful city as a youth, and what was more, as a rich youth, whom his guardian had supplied with plenty of money for the journey.

My head turned when I thought of how much pleasure was in store for me. I had a burning desire to enjoy everything; but as this was not easy to be done, I contented myself with visiting Jungfru Lova. She screamed and wept with joy when I made myself known to her. I presented her with a ring, which I had purchased on her account.

After this duty was accomplished, I drove around to

Haga and *Djurgarden*, and then the professor and I went on board a steamer, which was to carry us northward.

By Professor Wenner and his family I was received as if I had been one of them. There Paul and I met.

My stay with my guardian was like a single sunny day. The inmates of the parsonage were for the most part young people. My guardian had no less than four sprightly, fresh and artless daughters at home, together with two sons, who were "students," and one, who was an adjunct.

The whole family were characterized by the fact that each and all in their own way tried to work for the right, and had thus acquired cheerful and sound views of life. They loved pleasure, but they did not neglect the useful for it. One felt happy in living with them.

All the liveliness, which had been kept prisoner within me by my passion for study, now had loose reins. I became as gay and wild as I had been silent and reserved in Lund.

The circumstance that all here had known me from childhood and were as well aware of what had happened to me as I myself, contributed very essentially to this condition. Their friendliness was not assumed, accidental or a matter of reason, but it was what it appeared to be: an expression from the heart.

Even Paul was in the beginning merriment itself. He sang with a glad mind, rambled about with me and was more light-hearted than ever; but after a few weeks the shadows were seen on his brow, and it was as if an undefined uneasiness had seized his soul.

Finally he declared one morning that—"the cottage was to him too narrow."—He longed for his nomad life, and intended this time to take a long journey; it should extend to Denmark, and from thence to Germany.

It pained me that he wished to abandon me before we were *compelled* to separate, but still I said nothing, and we took leave of each other one day in July, after I had gone with him a little distance.

When I returned to the parsonage the pastor sent word to me to come up to his room. When I entered I found the pastor and the professor sitting one in each corner of the black leather sofa. My guardian looked uncommonly serious, and took several strong puffs from his large meerschaum pipe. The professor, on the other hand, was just the same as usual with his cold, stern mien.

"You are to take your student examination in the fall, is it not so?" began the pastor without any introduction.

"Yes, so I have supposed," was my answer.

"Good; I have spoken to my brother about the matter, and he is of the opinion, as I, that you ought not to continue your studies in Lund, but in Upsala."

I looked at the professor somewhat surprised.

He had always before said that he did not wish me to leave him until my studies were finished. Could it be that I had displeased him in some way, or was it the professorskan who had occasioned this change?

Probably the professor divined my thoughts; for he broke in abruptly:

"The reasons why I have gone over to my brother's opinion are, first that I consider the Upsala University better than the one at Lund, and second, I intend to resign my position in Lund and seek one in Upsala. You now know all about it. Consequently you are to have your name entered as student in Upsala. Next year we will meet. You understand?"

The pastor again took the lead and spoke a long while about my student time, etc.

I listened in silence to what was said; but my thoughts were fixed upon the circumstance that the professor intended to move away from Lund, and that his words were in complete conflict with what he had before said, when he asserted that the University at Lund was the best.

A voice within me said that this change of view had some cause, which neither the professor nor the pastor wished to impart to me, and I thought involuntarily of Lodstein and the thousand annoyances and persecutions to which I had been subjected during the last year.

It was very natural to suppose that the professor, in consequence of his many vexations, now denied all that he had said about the advantage for me to continue my studies in Lund.

When I left my guardian's room, the cheerfulness, which during my stay at the parsonage had filled my soul, was gone. It was succeeded by extreme heaviness of heart. It pained me that I should have to separate from the only friend, besides Paul, that I possessed.

However undemonstrative the professor's manner was, he had still given me so many proofs of good will and interest, that they showed that he cherished friendship and sympathy for me.

With a clouded mind I took a long walk, in order to avoid meeting any of the young people, who would probably have asked me a thousand questions about the cause of my changed demeanor.

The thought of my sad paternal inheritance and the stain which the accusation of theft had placed upon my life, haunted me continually. I asked myself the question whether I would actually succeed in the future in removing this shadow, or whether it would still follow me, and over the bright days of success spread sorrow and gloom.

During these reflections I had gone far into the woods. The summer breeze sighed through the tops of the pine trees, and it appeared to me as though this mighty sigh was an echo of the sigh of depression which issued from my breast.

When I had gone a little way farther I threw myself down on the soft moss, tired from my walk and my monotonous train of thought, took off my hat and let the breeze fan my temples.

One who has never known how disgrace burns, what pangs it engenders, especially in a young mind which revolts against the undeserved shame, will find it difficult to place himself in my position, or realize how sensitive I was to everything which had any connection with it.

Youth feels humiliation, more deeply than manhood, because self-love is generally more active; for neither experience nor circumstances have taught us to tone it down.

I was very conceited. I was proud of my mental attainments and the way in which I had pursued my studies; but just because my self-conceit had grown and was fully developed, I suffered so much the more from every humiliation. It seemed to me bitter that I, with all my uncommon qualities, should yet be pursued by a dishonor in which I had not the slightest part. In my bitterness it seemed to me that I never could forgive my father for the inheritance he had left me. I even felt indignant toward Strålkrans for making me rich, and I fancied, as I lay there, that it would have been far better if I had been allowed to remain a poor organ-grinder, who never came to the consciousness that he possessed any unusual talents. I felt a sort of grudge against the mine of gold, through which I gained the opportunity of having an education, but which at the same time was the cause of Paul and I being accused of theft.

Just as I lay there and in my ingratitude cursed Mauritz Strålkrans' passion for gambling, which had had such fortunate results for me, I was roused by the voices of two speakers, who approached. I started up like a deer driven from its hiding-place and withdrew behind the bushes, supposing that it was some of the people from the parsonage, who had come out to look for me.

The voices came nearer. It was a man and a woman who conversed. At that moment they turned a bend in the path, so that I had them right before my eyes.

It was a tall and slender man, clad in a hunting suit, with his gun on his shoulder. He had his face turned from me, but his whole bearing had something so noble, that it chained the eye. At his side walked a young girl. She seemed to be of about my age. Her features were regular and fine. Her face was somewhat pale, her hair deep black and her form slight and supple, but not above medium height.

When they reached the place where I had concealed myself, I heard the gentleman say:

"Bertha, you are cruel! How can you try to repel, with such icy coldness, an affection whose strength and faithfulness you ought to realize?"

As he uttered these words, I started.

If there had been a whole century between the time I first heard this man speak and the present moment, I would still have recognized the voice. Yet it was only nine years.

The bitterness in my soul disappeared and something resembling repentance seized my heart, when I was now suddenly reminded of the two occasions he had spoken to me.

How friendly had his voice sounded, when he, at our first meeting said: "Poor child, what a sad inheritance you have received," and then the second time fate brought our ways together, when he at the gaming-table whispered to me, "try it again," and at this "try it again," the gold before me had constantly doubled. The events of which this voice reminded me were so full of significance to me, and had exerted such an important influence upon the direction of my life, that for several minutes I did not know what was passing around me, so overpowered was I by the recollections of the past.

When I recovered from my surprise, I heard the young girl say these words:

"Let us rest here, and try to listen to me with calmness."

"I will listen to you, Bertha, but certainly not with calmness. I know that you will not say anything that can still the disquietude in my soul, but only excite and torment me yet more. What a strange girl you are!"

"I am less strange than you believe, and in order to prove to you the truth of this, I have to-day agreed to meet you. I hope that when we separate, I shall have made it clear to you that you ought not to remain longer in the place. Ah! count, you ought to have realized it long ago, and not have forced me to tell you."

The young girl took off her straw hat, and I now had a good chance to see her. Her face expressed mildness and earnestness. She continued, after drawing a light sigh:

"It is perhaps my fault that you have become attached to me, but that is something which I dare not decide. I am still too young to be able to judge how I ought to have acted when fate brought you and me together. That your friendliness would then make an impression upon my fifteen-year-old heart, I consider at this moment so natural, that the contrary would seem to me incomprehensible."

"Bertha," interrupted the count with animation, and tried to seize her hand, but she drew it away, saying:

"I beg of you, do not interrupt me, but let me speak to the end. You were so kind, I so lonely, and it was so sweet to cling to you, as one clings to the good. Still,

I was too much of a child for my friendship for you to have anything of—of—"

Bertha ceased abruptly and a dark flush covered her cheeks and neck.

"Of love, you mean to say," completed Stralkrans.

"And I believe," resumed Bertha, "that I am not yet old enough to realize what is comprised in that word. When you, at our next meeting, said that you loved me, I did not understand you, I regarded your attachment as friendship, and I was happy." Again Bertha ceased.

"But I forced you to realize that my feeling for you was one of the mightiest the human breast can contain, then your happiness fled and you drew back, became capricious, cold and cruel," said Strålkrans in a bitter tone.

While he was speaking, Bertha had bent down her head, as if his accusation pressed upon her brain. When he finished, she said sadly:

"Yes, you are right, I have felt very, very unhappy." She raised her head quickly and added with a certain energy: "But this unhappiness must have an end. It must not continue. Count, my heart cannot love you. A sister's affection is all that I can give. Let us therefore part. In a week my betrothal will be celebrated. I beg of you—go, go far away. It would be bitter to me if I knew that you were near me, if I were obliged to think that you suffered, while—"

"You revelled in felicity!" exclaimed Strålkrans, seizing hold of the young girl's arm. "You then love this old fool, whose wife you mean to become?"

"I do not love him, you know it very well; but he is the man whom my father has destined for me, the one whom I from childhood have regarded as my future husband."

"Bertha, now hear me; I have patiently listened to

you. That you do not love me, that you recklessly cast away my love, my peace and the future I offered you at my side, I may perhaps be able to forget and forgive; but that you increase your cruelty by becoming the wife of a man that you can neither respect nor have affection for, is something which it will be hard for me to pardon. If you can marry without love, why not give me your hand, me, whom you have friendship for, and who, you ought to realize, would do everything for your happiness; while, on the contrary, you know beforehand that this slave to his vanity and egotism will draw untold suffering upon your head."

"Stop, count, and let us finish," interrupted the young girl, pale as a marble statue. "Mark my words; if I followed the voice of my heart, I would become neither your wife nor Lagerskog's. That I give the latter my hand is because my father so wills. Even if I were ever so sure of being unhappy, this certainly would not affect my resolution. And now, count, we have spoken to the end. Every word further is wasted. Let us therefore bid each other farewell, and not prolong a mutual torment."

She offered her hand to Strålkrans, adding in a milder tone:

"Go, I entreat you; you do not know what a torture your presence is to me."

"It has then gone so far that I am a torture to you," exclaimed Strålkrans, springing up.

"Yes," answered Bertha, but without looking at him.

"Then you are right, Bertha, that for me remains only a hasty departure. Farewell, Mamsell Engberg. You have caused me to forget that you told me two months ago that my presence was your only joy, and you have besides effaced the remembrance from my mind that I but a few seconds ago loved you with my whole soul. Whenever or wherever we may meet in the future you will be to me a stranger, and I promise you, so far as it stands in my power, to try to prevent our ways from coming together. A man does not care to see the woman again he has once adored as if she had been an angel, but was forced to despise as a being without heart."

Strålkrans strode rapidly away. I followed him with my eyes. His appearance was disordered, and so agitated that it made on me a painful impression.

Wonderful play of chance, which brought me in his way just when ill-luck visited him! The former time he had gambled away his money, now the stake had been the heart's most beautiful dreams, and he had again lost.

A long moment I looked after him, then the sound of a faint cry of grief met my ear. I turned my head hastily. Bertha lay stretched on the ground, to all appearance lifeless.

Without hesitating an instant, I hastened to the young girl, feeling sure that she needed my assistance.

At the noise I made, she raised up quickly and looked at me in alarm. Her face was suffused with tears.

I felt very much embarrassed at having rushed forward so heedlessly. The instinct of delicacy whispered that I ought to act as if I had not heard any of their conversation.

Although I was extremely confused at finding myself alone with a young and beautiful girl, who was weeping, I took a bold resolution to save us both from embarrassment through a little untruth.

"Beg your pardon," stammered I, and became just as hot about my ears as though some one had been boxing them soundly, "but I have lost my way—and—now—I do not know where I—am."

Mamsell Bertha Engberg rose.

"You are at Engsgård's woods," answered she. "If you

will tell me where you are going, I may be able to inform you about the way."

"To the parsonage."

"It will be a little difficult to show you to the high-road," resumed she, passing her handkerchief hastily over her eyes to efface the traces of her tears, "but as I am also going there, you may accompany me."

Without waiting for any further words from me, she began to walk down the path. I followed her in silence. Not a word was exchanged between us. I was right glad to get rid of talking, for verily I knew not what to say. At the large forest road we stopped. She pointed to the left, saying:

"Go straight ahead until you come to a path that turns to the right, then follow it, and you will come to a rye-field. On the other side of it is a church. When you see that, you will surely find the parsonage."

She bowed her head and turned in the opposite direction. I had scarcely time to falter my thanks before she was gone.

This little episode gave me much to ponder on. Hitherto I had not devoted a thought to anything that could be called love. All such conditions were to me completely unknown.

I had been in little, or rather, no connection with girls, and consequently had not occupied my fancy with the rôle in life Herr Amor plays.

During my visit at the parsonage, I was for the first time in daily intercourse with girls of my own age. The pastor's daughters were lively and pleasant girls, but as homely, prosaic and material as any pastor's daughters could be, and not dangerous in the least to a youth's heart. They had also taken me in charge like kind, elder sisters, who did everything to make life cheerful to their brother.

Fate now ordained that I should be thrown headlong into a love story. I had listened to words which denoted warm feelings, bitter grief and burning resentment. I had witnessed how a woman repelled a man's tenderness; I had in his face read the pangs he experienced. I had afterward heard a cry of grief from her, seen a beautiful woman-face bathed in tears, and finally come in direct contact with this same girl, who through her beauty must unavoidably have struck a youth. Everything that had disquieted and tormented me was thrust aside. My whole thought was fastened exclusively upon her, who in my eyes resembled an angel from heaven.

When I came home to the parsonage it was dinner-time, and we seated ourselves immediately at the table.

My place was beside the youngest daughter, Lotta. It was not long before I came out with the question, whether there was any family in the neighborhood by the name of Engberg.

Lotta looked at me with an air as if I had asked whether the sun gave light by day, or any other silly thing.

"Gracious! what a question!" exclaimed Lotta. "Engberg is the owner of Engsgård, didn't you know that?"

"No, dear Lotta, I have never heard you mention him, and cannot remember to have seen that family when the other neighbors have been invited here," answered I.

"Neither have you, for old man Engberg never goes out. He has the gout and is very decrepit. He is not particularly sociable either, and the people of the parish do not like him very well."

"Well, but his wife and children then, I suppose that he has both?" said I.

"Yes, he has a daughter, but his wife died many years ago."

"Has the daughter gout too?" asked I, smiling at

Lotta, who began to laugh, so that she showed all her large white teeth.

"Ah no, Bertha Engberg is a fine girl, who has been educated abroad. She has only been home twice since her mother's death; once when she was twelve years old, and last summer. Both times she has only stayed six weeks with her father and then went away again. They say she has great talents and a tremendous amount of knowledge."

"Do you know whether she is home now?" asked I.

"No, I do not. But why do you ask so many questions about Engberg's daughter?"

At these words I colored and could not at once find any suitable answer. I did not feel at all disposed to mention the truth. Luckily, in my great confusion, there was at the table a person who always had her ears open when her neighbors were spoken of, and was always ready to answer questions. This person was no other than Fru Wenner's unmarried sister, Mamsell Juliana Grön.

When I began my inquiries about the owner of Engsgård, she had pricked her ears. At Lotta's last answer, it became utterly impossible for Mamsell Juliana to maintain silence any longer. She therefore broke in abruptly, before I had time to recover myself:

"Bertha has already been at Engsgård three weeks, and I am surprised that Lotta did not know it. She is going to be married, God preserve us, and the wedding will probably take place at Engsgård; but right curious are the stories which go about her; they say—"

"Pass the potatoes, Juliana," sounded the pastor's voice, with such sharpness, that Juliana jumped, snatched the dish and gave it to her brother-in-law, who then said:

"Let the folks at Engsgård alone, dear sister-in-law; you know that I do not like to have any one in my house relate stories about the neighbors."

Juliana became red as a turkey-cock, and swallowed, in

her vexation, a piece of bread rather too large for the long and narrow passage through her throat, so that it threatened to cost the worthy dame her life.

Lotta flew up and began to thump her dear aunt on the back with no light hand, while she whispered to me that papa's words were not particularly digestible.

Dinner was over. We rose from the table.

The girls tripped out in the yard, where they seated themselves under a pair of large trees with their work. I was just going to follow them, when Aunt Juliana came and seated herself beside me, on the stoop where I stood.

"Have you seen Bertha Engberg, Conny?" began she, knitting at a great rate on a coarse woollen stocking.

"Yes," was my simple answer.

"An exceedingly beautiful and fine girl, is she not?" The worthy mamsell now bent a pair of small, sharp gray eyes on me.

I made an affirmative bow of the head and a motion to depart; but this did not enter into Mamsell Juliana's plan; therefore she hastily stretched out a thin bony hand and seized hold of my arm, saying:

"Come and sit here a while, Conny, and I will tell you a wise word. So you think that Bertha is beautiful? There are several besides you who think the same. They say there was an aristocratic gentleman residing at Glastorp, who came here only for her sake, and drives over to Engsgård every day. Her lover has not yet arrived, and she tries in the meantime to console herself as best she can with the nobleman."

"It is not true," exclaimed I, impetuously.

"Isn't it?" said Juliana; "how do you know that? I guess the amount of it is, Conny, that you are more closely acquainted with Bertha than one believes. How has that acquaintance been made, it would be interesting to know?"

Juliana's mien was such, that it would have enlightened

the stupidest creature in the world about all the conclusions she came to in the twinkling of an eye. I saw that I had committed an indiscretion, and therefore answered immediately, that I had lost my way in the woods and happened to meet a young lady, who gave me the right direction.

Far from remedying the matter as I supposed, it seemed as if I had only made it worse.

Juliana considered it singular that Bertha was in the woods, she had probably gone there to meet somebody. Moreover, she could not comprehend how I, after such a meeting, could know whether it was the truth or not that Bertha liked that high-born gentleman, etc. In short, I became utterly bewildered and felt an inexpressible desire to beat a retreat, but was kept prisoner by Juliana, who suspected something was wrong, and whose long bony hand clasped my arm tighter and tighter.

The old virgin seldom had an opportunity to express herself, as the pastor, Fru Wenner and the girls were decided enemies to gossip, and as soon as she began anything of the kind, they shut her mouth. When she therefore got hold of any stranger, to whom she had an opportunity to convey her opinions, observations or biographical notices of her neighbors, she was not willing to let go of her prey.

After she had poured forth a whole deluge of words over the strangeness of my meeting Bertha, and so perplexed me with it, that I did not know how to extricate myself, she continued, without noticing what impression she made on me:

"But so much I will tell you, that you ought to beware of those people." Her voice now sank, she cast a searching glance around her and continued: "There are some very strange reports about the old man, and it is not gout alone that keeps him prisoner at Engsgård, but the detestation of the neighbors. They speak of some trick that he committed in younger years, and it is now asserted that he has sat on the *thief-stool*,* at least they say it is very certain that the law has declared him *void of honor*. In consequence of this, people cannot abide him here in the place, and that is the reason the girl was educated abroad, where no one knew of her father's misdeeds. She would probably never have got an honest man for a husband, if that Lagerskog had not stood in some relation to her, which made Engberg give him his beautiful daughter for a wife. I will therefore give you a friendly piece of advice, Conny, and that is, to avoid those people. Bear it in mind that honest folks do not associate with impostors and dishonest adventurers. Their children and relatives are also shunned by those who care for their own reputation. You ought not to follow the example of my crazy brother-in-law, who constantly gathers persons of ill repute around him, and really seems to have a predilection for them."

Whether Juliana knew anything about my parents or my early life, I cannot tell.

During the years the pastor was settled in Skarparby, Juliana had not once visited her sister, but lived in Calmar with her mother. This was the first time during the last three years that she visited at the pastor's. Be this as it may, her words touched a painful chord in me. My patience gave out; I jerked myself free from her, said in a loud voice that it was unworthy to talk so, and rushed away as if I feared that she would pursue me. Without calculating where I went, I ran down into the garden and directly into an arbor, where I threw myself down on a bench.

It can easily be seen what increased interest my new

* A high stool in church, where a delinquent is obliged to sit before the whole congregation, as a public disgrace.

acquaintance acquired through Juliana's story. The young girl's father had prejudice against him, just like mine, and she would thus receive as sad a paternal inheritance as I had.

If she was beautiful in my eyes before Juliana's story, she became still more enchanting after it. She stood before my imagination as a revelation from a better world.

I was not allowed to abandon myself long to these dreams, however, for a merry voice called me. It was Lotta.

Not to obey the call was to me impossible.

I therefore rose immediately to go and meet her, but got no farther than the entrance of the arbor, where she stood before me.

"What in the world did Aunt Juliana do, to put you to flight? I hope she did not propose!" exclaimed Lotta, laughing heartily. "Well, you dear boy, answer, what tender things did the old woman say?"

"She was talking about the Engbergs," answered I, and could not refrain from joining in Lotta's merriment.

"That's it; she probably related the family's history, although she doesn't know the least thing about it, but Juliana finds it very pleasant to make up yarns about her neighbors. Well, what did she say, the good soul, that could put wings to your feet?"

"Ah! she said that—why, it is no matter what she said. Tell me, is it true that Bertha's father is—disgraced?"

Instead of answering, Lotta laughed still more, so that she irritated me a little.

"That is something bran new, which she did not invent herself," said Lotta, when she had finished laughing. "Some one else must have given her that idea. Yes, old man Engberg is disgraced, it is too bad. Well, he has probably undergone church-penance too?"

"Yes, Aunt Juliana was sure that he had."

"And therefore you ran away?"

"I ran, because it made me feel uncomfortable to hear her talk so."

"I do not wonder at it," said Lotta. "Ah, that aunt, that aunt, she is too ridiculous; her tongue is a power in the land."

"Perhaps the whole thing is a fabrication?"

"Stories, which foolish people repeat, who do not know the true facts of the case. The old man has had strange experiences; what, no one knows, and just on this account have gossipping old women and idle people calculated that he has done something wrong.—He has lived here twelve years, and during this time has shown himself kind to all the poor, but inaccessible to those who have what they need. Since he became a widower he has preferred to live by himself, plough his fields and take care of his dependents, by whom he is loved; but does not associate with the neighbors. For the last few years he has been sickly and entirely unable to leave home.—He has had his daughter educated abroad, because he could not have her cultivated enough.—The only thing one can say against him, is, that he is very stern in his demands upon the girl. This probably comes from the fact that he wishes to have her as distinguished a woman as her mother was. But now I stand and talk just like Aunt Juliana. One thing I must know, however, before we leave the subject, why are you now so much interested in the Engbergs? You have been here seven weeks, and never spoken of them before."

"Because I learned to-day, for the first time, that they existed."

I told Lotta about my meeting with Bertha, but I avoided saying anything that had reference to her and Strålkrans' conversation.

Lotta praised Bertha, and after we had talked a while

about her, Lotta proposed that I should accompany her to Engsgård. She was going there that afternoon, as she had an errand to the gardener. She invited me to drive for her.

Of course I embraced the opportunity with delight. But as my joy was but too plainly revealed in my face, Lotta burst out:

"Do not rejoice so much at the trip! The visit only concerns the gardener, and I can assure you beforehand, that you will not see as much as the tip of Bertha's nose."

"It is all the same, I will be your coachman anyway."

It was just as Lotta said, we did not catch a glimpse of any one but the gardener and a couple of laborers.

Several days passed, in which I walked six miles every morning to look at the buildings and surroundings of Engsgård.

All the buildings, the dwelling as well as the out-houses, were new, and the whole place looked as if it had been erected that year. It had something extremely trim and attractive.

At length one Sunday morning, when I took my long promenade a little later than usual, fate favored me, so that I actually met Bertha.

At the sight of her I was on the point of turning round, so excessively embarrassed did I feel; but summoning all my self-confidence, I walked on and greeted her, as well as took courage to thank her in a few words for the service she had done me at our last meeting.

Bertha looked at me with an air that was extremely wounding to my self-love. It showed that she had entirely forgotten my features and was surprised that I addressed and thanked her.

When I added that she a week ago had shown me the right way, a hasty flush passed over her cheeks. She smiled and said in a friendly tone that there was nothing to thank her for, after which it was plain to be seen that she expected me to leave her; but however dear it would otherwise have been to fulfil her slightest desire, this was not in accordance with mine, therefore I paid no regard to it, continued to walk at her side, and opened a very stupid conversation about the weather and wind.

She was going to visit a sick cottager; I went with her there, and also home again, after which we separated. Notwithstanding I roamed around Engsgård for several days, I did not have the good fortune to see her.

Bertha occupied my thoughts day and night. I forgot my studies, my future and everything else, and abandoned myself without resistance to the delight of thinking and dreaming about a beautiful girl. Finally, those at the parsonage had begun to notice my long walks. The girls joked about it, and the professor said one Sunday morning at breakfast:

"I should think you had forgotten, Fredriksson, that you are to take your student examination in three weeks! I cannot remember that I have seen you look in a book for a long time."

To conceal my confusion I drank two glasses of milk, and rose so hastily that I came near upsetting the whole breakfast table when the pastor said, turning to his better half:

"Well, are you going to Engsgård this afternoon? The bans are to be read to-day for the first time for August Lagerskog and Bertha Engberg. The wedding will take place on the third Sunday."

While I was taking repeated walks in order to have a peep at Bertha's home, I had completely forgotten that she was going to be married. With a youth of my age the feelings can be said to be childish, and as a child only strives for that which satisfies the desires of the moment, so does he. Youth's feelings have no future, they live and die in the present.

The pastor's words about the bans and wedding came upon me like a thunder-bolt. What I experienced was rather consternation than grief, although I considered myself to endure one of the cruellest sufferings that could befall any human being. I would be at the church; I would hear the bans read with my own ears, and at the same time drain the bitter cup to the last drop, I thought, and regarded myself as the most unhappy of all unhappy beings who had bound their hearts to a young and beautiful girl.

It was now a decided thing, that I for the first and *only* time in my life was seized with love, and that I would bewail the loss of the beloved object until my death.

Lotta made all manner of fun of me for jumping so and almost knocking the table over, because the pastor spoke of Bertha's wedding. Her raillery made me feel so out of sorts, that I would have been tempted to weep, if pride had not restrained my tears.

When breakfast was finally over, Lotta asked me to drive the chaise, in which she was going to ride to church. In spite of all her gabble about my "dreadful" appearance, I accepted the invitation.

I heard the bans read, without dying; but persuaded myself, however, that I was now as miserable as I could be.

Henceforth, I would not allow myself to be infatuated with any woman; I would instead keep away from them.

All these dismal resolutions in the forenoon did not hinder me from laughing right heartily with the young people, after the pastor and his wife had gone to Engsgård that afternoon.

A few days subsequent it was the pastor's birth-day. All his parishioners came to congratulate him, and neither sorrow nor my unhappy love prevented me from participating in the games.

We were playing tag on the large lawn, when a handsome droschka drove up and in it sat—Bertha.

I was just trying, with the aid of my long limbs, to contest the right of a pretty little maiden to reach the goal first, when the droschka came like a disturber of our pleasure.

"Bertha and her betrothed," whispered the girls. The pastor's daughters hastened to welcome the new guests.

Bertha brought a bouquet of exquisite flowers and a basket of delicious fruit to the pastor. She smiled so sweetly and was so beautiful, when she congratulated him, that my heart whirled and I was again seized with my enchantment and the sense of my misfortune.

The lover, Herr August Lagerskog, looked like an old coxcomb. His attire, his curled peruke, his ringed fingers, and his stereotyped smile, all showed that the man stood in open conflict with age and did not wish to acknowledge that he was approaching *fifty*. He was dressed in the newest style, just as if he had been cut out of a fashion-plate. Of course I immediately took a decided antipathy to him.

It seemed to me that I could not endure the sight of him, so I betook myself to my chamber, where I began to march to and fro; but when I stopped for a moment, I found that this was no longer pleasant, and then determined to observe what was going on down below.

I intended to appear with such a mien as to inspire fright in the intended bridegroom and show Bertha how deeply she was loved.

The rôle I proposed to play was entirely forgotten when I again found myself among the young people, who were playing "*widower*."

Herr Lagerskog was among them. When I saw him, the boy in me asserted itself and I resolved to play him some trick through which I might get the laugh on my side.

I waited, however, until I became "widower," and Bertha and her betrothed should run outside the lines.

Bertha ran with the greatest fleetness, but yet it would not have been hard for me to catch her, if this had lain in my plan. As it was, I merely tried to hinder the betrothed pair from meeting; then I suddenly slackened my speed, but just as they were going to take each other's hands, I rushed with such violence against Lagerskog that he lost his balance and tumbled over. His hat, followed by his peruke, flew away across the lawn, so that the youthfully rigged out bridegroom lay there with a bare pate and his heels in the air.

An involuntary burst of merriment was heard from the young crowd, and two of the laughing youths hurried forward to pick up the hat and peruke, but I prevented them, as I snatched hold of the latter and with many excuses, which I could not utter with a perfectly sober voice, I handed him the handsome head ornament.

Herr Lagerskog flung an enraged glance at me and covered his baldness. The elegant dandy looked as if he had been annihilated, but still tried to make the best of it. I was declared to have acted so unskilfully, that I must remain "widower" as a punishment.

At this doom, which was pronounced by all present, I looked at Bertha. I had not dared to glance at her during the merriment which her lover's somersault occasioned. I now met her gaze.

My boyish malice was punished, for in her eyes I seemed to read, that if I had succeeded in ridiculing her betrothed, I had at the same time placed her in a ludicrous and painful position. The expression of reproach and grief in the dark eyes pierced my heart, and brought me to the consciousness of the wrong I had done. I then felt that it is generally a poor way to console one's self through doing harm to some one else.

I almost blushed over my behavior, and as soon as I could, I withdrew from the play, without approaching Bertha for the remainder of the afternoon.

Three weeks after that, Bertha stood at the altar. I, with the rest of the pastor's family, had attended the wedding and been in the ring, when they danced the wreath off the bride.

Bertha's appearance on the wedding day was so peculiar, that I cannot give any name to it. She smiled, she talked, she was friendly to all, tender to her father, who from his easy-chair followed her with anxious looks; but yet, there was something in all this friendliness, in this calmness, this smile, which made one freeze. Perhaps it was her extreme paleness.

I could not tell why, but when my eyes followed Bertha it cut me to the heart and I remembered Strålkrans' words to her:

"You will be terribly unhappy."

Three days after the wedding I bade farewell to the pastor's family, and in company with the professor travelled to Upsala.

In this city of learning our ways were to part.

Gloomy and silent as it befits a youth who has become the victim of an unhappy love, I commenced and continued the journey.

That I was enamored, was certain, and that I ought to be in the depths of despair, was equally certain.

In Upsala the professor introduced me to a family, where I was to live.

The leave-taking from the one whom I had respected and revered as my teacher and father, was short but painful. Neither the professor nor I uttered a single word of regret, nor anything of the kind. He merely said:

"See that you continue to do me honor, Fredriksson, and now farewell till next year."

"Herr professor, I will endeavor to study so that you will be satisfied," was my answer, as I pressed the hand which had guided my first steps on the road of knowledge.

CHAPTER XI.

I AGAIN stood alone among entire strangers; again felt inclined to live an isolated life, engrossed by study.

What a fever one is in, when he is to pass his examination and does not yet know the result of it! At length the ordeal was over. I had gone through successfully and was now a regular student.

Away were all dark thoughts, all melancholy feelings, all doleful reflections. I was a student, hurrah! College-life with its pleasures and excitements lay before me, and filled my breast with delight. I felt my heart beat and my blood flow more swiftly in my veins; in a word, I was overjoyed in the consciousness of having taken the first grand step in life. I was young, I was rich, I had a future and a fine aim to aspire to. What more was needed to enable me to enjoy my existence?

Long live Upsala! It is there that one first learns the value of life and the happiness of being young.

I abandoned myself entirely to the delights of my new condition, I no longer sat nailed to my book, inaccessible to the joys and errors of youth, but I threw myself into pleasure, and tasted the allowed as well as the forbidden fruit.

It is true I studied my six or seven hours a day, but amused myself eight or nine and slept as little as possible, so as to have time for both recreation and work.

I was sometimes out with my comrades until three o'clock in the morning, drank as bravely as anybody and sometimes more than I could stand. But notwithstanding I plunged into such dissipation with the recklessness of youth, I can say to my own praise, that it never occurred at the expense of my studies.

If I as a school-boy had been retiring, and as a gymnast proud, I was as a student the most approachable, the merriest and the richest in friends.

That such was the case proceeded probably from two circumstances: first, I had plenty of money, was always ready to lend, and never refused to take part in singing, amusements and entertainments; but yet, did not give the professors any cause for displeasure.

The first year passed like a hilarious festival. Between the terms I made a visit to my guardian.

Bertha was forgotten. I had had so many flames during this year, better and worse, that I had entirely forgotten my first one.

When I saw the parsonage again it reminded me of her, and I then made a few inquiries.

The newly married pair were residing in the capital, and that was all they knew about them.

One great fault that could be laid to my charge, during the first year of my student life, was, that my affection for Paul was pushed aside, and it seemed to me almost disagreeable, when I was forced to think of him, because I was then reminded of the past, which I desired to forget. It is true I wrote answers to his letters, but it often happened that the reply was postponed. In spite of this neglect of mine, Paul never reproached me for my behavior with a single word. His letters were always full of love and spiced with little piquant and humorous descriptions of his wanderings in Germany, the success he met with, etc. But never did he speak of the deprivations or reverses he endured, and I was frivolous enough not to think about them, but took it for granted that he always had good-luck, forgetting how changeable a street-singer's life is, where want so often follows the singer's steps.

My two visits to the parsonage were not calculated to awaken my reflection. I had amused myself to my heart's content, been made much of, and through my self-confidence, acquired greater ease in the society of my fellow-beings.

It was in the spring-time of my second year in Upsala, when I was one morning awakened by the tones of a hand-organ. I rushed out of bed. The melody which was played was well known to me since the time when I ground our hand-organ. When the first measures were played, a clear childish voice was heard singing a song that Paul had often sung.

The veil of oblivion, in which I had enveloped the past in order to enjoy the present unrestrained, was swept away. It seemed to me that I was suddenly transported back to the time when Paul and I wandered around the streets, singing and playing.

I stood erect and listened a few moments, then I went to the window. In the yard stood two boys, one larger than the other. They seemed to be of the same age as Paul and I, when we for the first time visited Upsala. Just as I was carried back to this moment in my life, two beings whom I had hitherto entirely forgotten appeared before my memory, namely Aunt Grönqvist and Hanna. The old woman's kindness and sympathy toward Paul and me I now remembered vividly, and also that Paul had said:

"If you ever come to Upsala, Conny, you must promise me to go and see Aunt Grönqvist."

I had promised him, but forgotten my promise when I came here. Paul had not reminded me of it in any of his letters. I now found this very strange when I came to think of it, and I accused Paul, in order to be able to excuse myself; but it did not work very well. I was provoked at my forgetfulness, at the organ-grinder who had made me think of past times, because I was thus surprised with a certain disapproval of my own conduct.

Completely out of humor, I went away from the window; but the voice which sang down there in the yard in the cold spring morning sounded so plaintive, like a tone from my own conscience. I turned back, raised the window and threw down some silver coins to the little organ-grinder, after which I dressed myself in the greatest haste and went out.

When I came out in the street, the sun shone clear and the white snow glittered under its rays. Enlivened by the fresh air, I walked ahead and soon came in sight of Aunt Grönqvist's little abode.

I knocked at the door, which after a few moments was opened by a young girl, golden-haired and pretty, with eyes like forget-me-nots, and cheeks blooming as roses and lilies.

"Hanna!" exclaimed I, fully assured that it could not be any one else. In that mild way had the child's eyes smiled at me.

The young girl changed color and looked at me with wonder.

"Do you not recognize Paul's brother?" asked I, trying to take one of her hands; but she prevented it, and stammered:

"Good Gracious, it is Con—Herr Fredriksson, I mean. Be so good as to step in, grandmother will surely be glad to see Con—Herr Fredriksson."

She drew back still more, in order to let me enter. I stalked boldly in and at the same time caught hold of Hanna's hand, saying with all the gallantry a student can throw into his words:

"Call me Conny, as before, and do not be so strange, dear Hanna."

"That wouldn't do," answered she timidly and drew away her hand, as she tripped across the little hall, and the next instant we entered the large neat room.

Aunt Grönqvist stood ironing, just as when I first saw her. Everything, from the least to the greatest, was precisely the same, and if Hanna had not stood before me as a full-grown maiden, I would decidedly have believed that time had stood still.

"Grandma!" exclaimed Hanna with the same cheerful voice as nine years ago, "do you know whom I have with me? no more and no less than Paul's brother—Herr Fredriksson!"

The old woman put down her iron and turned round abruptly. She had grown considerably older.

"Well, it is true and certain that it is a joy to see you again, and it was very honorable of you to look us up. You have become a fine gentleman, Paul says. God bless you," and with this she offered me her hand.

I spent the whole forenoon with Aunt Grönqvist, and for the first time missed a lecture.

After forgetting Aunt Grönqvist and Hanna for a year's time, I now became an almost daily guest with them.

Not to make myself appear any better than I was, I must confess that my visits especially concerned Hanna.

Her unusually pretty face had made a lively impression upon my susceptible heart, so that after two or three visits I was head and ears in love.

I presented her with flowers, confectionery and books. I waited upon her when she went out, so as to have a chance to say some pretty phrases, and I went there by preference when I knew that her grandmother was away. Besides I made presents to the old woman, so as to keep myself in her favor.

The good old lady smiled at me so kindly and saw in my actions only an effort to recompense her for the good-will she had shown Paul and me.

The proofs of gratitude of a student toward an old woman who has a pretty grand-daughter are always dubious and ought to excite distrust, yet they failed to do this with Aunt Grönqvist.

Hanna, however, was more clear-sighted. She feared my politeness and became colder and more inaccessible. This piqued me and increased my fancy. I could not comprehend why she should be so distant, and it cruelly wounded my self-love that she could not be induced to treat me with the friendliness I considered myself entitled to receive. My fancy for Hanna became through this more violent than any I had had before, as they did not usually last more than a week, but this lasted three whole months, and that in constant crescendo.

I thought of Hanna by night and by day, I wrote verses, I went on sprees to console myself, when Hanna had been entirely too ungracious toward me.

It had not been particularly hard for my comrades to find out that I went to washer-woman Grönqvist's every day. They knew that the old woman had a pretty grand-daughter, and they believed that they saw through the whole thing. They made fun of me for my "washer-woman idyl." I responded to these allusions with a flippant laugh and the assurance that Hanna was the prettiest girl in Upsala. I thus exposed her name to the frivolous jokes of a lot of young men.

One evening, when we had had a large supper and been drinking considerably, some of the most hilarious proposed to give a serenade to "Fredriksson's pretty Hanna."

The wine had affected my head a little too much, so that I thanked them and accepted the proposal. We marched off. I, who belonged to the singers and was the most interested in the matter, was to lead the serenade.

On reaching Aunt Grönqvist's little low cottage, we sang one song after the other. Many a night-cap in the adjoining houses peeped out of the windows, to see who the happy one was that was treated to such a fine serenade.

Whether *she*, to whom we sang, heard it or not, we did not know. The shade before the single little gable window, which overlooked the street, remained untouched.

When I returned home, it seemed to me that Hanna ought to feel very much honored by the serenade, and that she would unavoidably appear grateful to me the next day. I made up my mind to go to her as soon as I came from the lecture, in order to get an encouraging smile at least, as a reward for the singing.

But in carrying out my resolution I was hindered by some of my comrades, who came to tell me that they repented the serenade to Hanna. People had got wind of it and the whole town were making a great ado, because the students had sung to washer-woman Grönqvist's granddaughter. We must make amends in some way for the foolish act, said my comrades, and it is resolved that we will each one of us mention wherever we go, that we stopped before old woman Grönqvist's house by accident, as we were going around singing, but that we had no intention to give a serenade.

It was not one of my natural traits to deny the truth or to conceal my faults behind a falsehood. I was entirely too proud and conceited for that. The deed I had committed I considered it a cowardice not to acknowledge, no matter whether it was good or bad. Consequently I would not agree to their proposition, but declared that we could sing to Hanna just as well as to any one else.

In reply to this one of them said:

"How the deuce, Fredriksson, can you talk so silly?

Your connection with Hanna is not one of the kind that one openly acknowledges, and if you wish to let the whole world know that you have sung to Hanna, we do not care to have people say that we assisted you, and thus be compromised ourselves. So we demand of you, that you think of us in the first place and do not let your connection with Hanna lead you into any further folly."

"All I can do is to keep silent," answered I, "but I will not condescend to lie. Besides, it was you and not I who proposed the serenade."

A little debate followed. They were not satisfied with my answer, but it could not be helped. We separated less pleased with each other than we were accustomed to be; the tension would probably have been still greater, if it had not been decided before that all the students were to sing in the park that afternoon. We assembled after dinner, and our little quarrel was forgotten during the music, dissolved as it were in the harmonious tones.

The next day I was invited to Professor X——'s, together with some comrades of the same province, and it was thus two days before I could visit Hanna, in spite of my longing to see her.

On the third day toward evening I walked with light and rapid steps to the little red house. I had my pockets full of oranges. I was perfectly sure of having overcome Hanna's coldness, and I was considering how I should make it clear to her that I loved her. To be sure I had told her so many times, but I was now going to say it in other words, and in such a way that she would be forced to confess that I was dear to her; I took it for granted that this was the case, although she had not been willing to show it.

When I knocked at the gate, I had to wait quite a while before it opened, and when it did so, it was not Hanna's mild and pretty face that met my gaze, but an ugly old woman, who used to help Aunt Grönqvist to wash. I asked if Aunt Grönqvist was at home, and received the answer:

"No, the old woman is away; but Hanna is in there, and I suppose it is she, sir, that you prefer to see?"

I was too impatient to meet Hanna, and too delighted at the intelligence that she was home alone, to attach any importance to an old woman's words. I went by her and the next instant stood in the room, which for three months had contained the object of my passion.

I got no farther than the door, however, and remained standing on the same spot several seconds, so painfully surprised was I by the sight before me.

Hanna lay face downward on the bed, sobbing aloud.

Hanna wept. Hanna was plunged in grief! What could have happened?

Dear reader, if you remember the time when you were nineteen and in love, then you can realize what I experienced. It seemed to me that the heavens ought to fall, when anything so terrible could occur as for Hanna to weep. To spring to her and tell her this, and something still more foolish, was what I did the next minute.

Words dictated by compassion for her grief, by my own over-wrought feelings and senseless passion, passed my lips.

At the first sound of my voice, Hanna had risen. She tried to interrupt me and go away, but I detained her. I talked until I myself lost all connection of what I said, when I ceased quite abruptly. Hanna snatched away her hands, exclaiming in a voice almost choked by tears:

"Have you not done me sufficient harm through making me the talk of the whole town, without increasing it by going on as you do? Good God, why is Paul so long away? He would defend me, he would tell grandmother and everybody that I am innocent, that I have not done anything wrong, that—that—"

Here her sobs suffocated her, but after a few moments she told me that all the neighbors spoke ill of her, that they had said to her grandmother that she had appointed meetings with me, that I came to see her when the old woman was out, and that the serenade was a regular scandal. Her grandmother had been very angry, and as Hanna could not deny that I sometimes met her in the street, and also, in spite of her prohibition, called on her when the old woman was away, she had believed that the neighbors were right, and that Hanna had committed acts which she could not answer for.

The neighbors had so pictured the matter, that the poor girl through me was hopelessly compromised. Aunt Grönqvist had now gone out to buy a steamboat ticket. Hanna was going to be sent to Stockholm, so that she should no longer be a cause of trouble.

At the thought that she should separate from her grandmother, she again burst out weeping and exclaimed in a tone of despair:

"Herr Fredriksson, you can never atone for the evil you have done me. You are the cause of my being separated from grandmother, whom I love so dearly. Perhaps you will also be the cause of Paul's doubting my love and my faithfulness. Oh, my God, how unhappy you have made me!"

At these accusations I felt very wretched.

She was the first being to whom I had occasioned any harm, the first upon whom I had drawn suffering. I, who, with youth's blind faith in myself, considered it impossible for me to act culpably, or in such a way that any one would have reason to upbraid me, now stood humiliated before myself, burdened with the consciousness of having been the source of so much grief.

We representatives of the male sex generally acquire a hasty experience of life and evil; I had in one year gained more knowledge of it than a woman gains during a whole lifetime. Consequently I realized immediately that if my importunity toward Hanna had excited scandal, her sudden departure from Upsala would only give more impetus to it. Therefore I tried to console her. I said that I felt unhappy over the harm I had done, but I would remedy it. I promised to speak to her grandmother and to persuade her not to send Hanna away. My words had the effect of calming her somewhat. She dried her tears and offered me her hand, but at that instant the door opened and in came Aunt Grönqvist with a stormy step. Her mien was stern, and she exclaimed vehemently:

"It is just as they said, that you manage to come here when I am out, but I tell you what it is, that performance is now ended. You ought to be ashamed to behave as you have done, and to heap disgrace and misery upon honest people."

The old woman turned to Hanna and ordered her to leave the room immediately.

I was then treated to the sharpest and bitterest reproaches.

In vain did I endeavor to calm the old woman, assuring her that neither I nor Hanna had done anything wrong, but it was like talking to the wall. She did not listen to my justification, she paid no regard either to my assurances or my persuasions not to send Hanna to the capital.

It was with the old woman as it often is with credulous people. From not distrusting anything or anybody they begin to distrust everybody and everything; in the hope of being able to repair their former short-sightedness they pass over to blindness, and in the fear of again being deceived, they will not even see the truth.

After I had implored and expostulated in vain, I was shown the door, and that with the following words:

"We have talked enough and you had better go, else you might make me so enraged at the girl that she would have to pay up for it in a still harder way. But you leave this house as a thorough scoundrel, who has put a dark stain on a girl's reputation, and this you have done to Hanna, whom Paul has loved for so many years and whom he intended to marry. When one like you, Herr Fredriksson, has been elevated to the upper classes, he considers it an honor to destroy a poor girl's reputation. Yes indeed, it is something to boast of before his comrades, when a man drinks like a beast with them at night, and then in that condition goes to sing before a poor girl's window, to let the whole town know of his fine deeds. You have rewarded your brother in a splendid way, and I tell you what it is, never put your nose inside my door if you want to keep it."

I went, but in what a state of mind compared to the one in which I had come!

Shut up in my room, I spent the evening and night in reviewing my life during my academy time. I was then surprised by the discovery that I had recklessly abandoned myself to all kinds of pleasure, degrading ones as well. The frivolousness with which I had spoken about Hanna to my comrades, the way in which I had made known my fancy for her, the reputation which I had acquired of not being scrupulous when it concerned love intrigues, all appeared to me contemptible and unworthy. Yes, so much the more so, as my dissipations and my boasts of success as a general thing had not derived their impulse from others, but had proceeded entirely from myself and my vanity. In addition to this, I found at my self-examination, that I did not love Hanna so much that I was disposed to make any great sacrifices for her.

I had thus exposed her without being actuated by any stronger motive than a paltry and fleeting boyish fancy.

Then came the thought that I had injured Paul through the one he held dear.

The following morning I went down to the wharf, and mixing in the crowd that collected there, I saw Hanna with her eyes red from weeping go on board, accompanied by Aunt Grönqvist.

I did not wait until the boat started, but hastened away, to avoid my comrades' jokes and taunts.

The next day I received a letter from Professor Wenner, in which he informed me that he hoped to be in Upsala by fall, as he in all probability would obtain the professorship he sought there.

The event with Hanna and the letter from the professor roused me from the intoxication in which I had lived. I left pleasure and banquets and plunged into my studies in good earnest. I no longer participated in serenades, masquerades or midnight revels. I went to and from the lectures and spent the rest of my time with my books, shut up in my room.

The term approached a close. The trees began to bud, the birds twittered and wild flowers adorned the fields; but still this did not tempt me to leave the University and go to my guardian, as I had done between the other terms. I stayed in Upsala to study and thereby hasten the end of my course.

My mind was heavy, I was pursued by an incessant dissatisfaction with myself, and therefore tried to regain my lost peace through diligence and zeal.

Another circumstance which troubled me very much, was, that I had written to Paul shortly after the occurrence with Hanna and given him a truthful account of what had taken place; but weeks and months had elapsed without my receiving any answer. Was Paul angry with me?

I was, alas, but too well aware of the degrading conclusions which people had formed with regard to Hanna's departure. I know that she was generally regarded as one of the many who had fallen a victim to—students' love. I also knew that Aunt Grönqvist had returned from the journey to Stockholm and that she desired to sell the place, as she did not wish to remain in Upsala after it had gone so ill with the girl.

Her house, however, was not sold, and at the beginning of the fall term, the third year I was in Upsala, my landlady told me that washer-woman Grönqvist, the grandmother of the pretty Hanna, lay so ill, that the girl had to come home again.

Through my landlady I sent the old woman some money, for I knew that she could no longer depend upon the labor of her hands. Still she did not need my assistance long, for in the course of two weeks she had left the poor Hanna behind her.

I dared not go there. It made me feel, when my landlady mentioned that Aunt Grönqvist was dead, as if I had had some share in her decease.

CHAPTER XII.

IT was a rainy and windy October afternoon, the day after Aunt Grönqvist died. A fire burned on the hearth in my outer room. I sat before it, reflecting upon the sad events that had occurred. I had just sent my landlady to the house of mourning and asked her to offer Hanna all the assistance she needed, as if it came from herself, and I was now awaiting the good woman's return, to learn how it was with the poor girl.

At last I heard the stairs creak. Some one was coming up. "It is Fru Sjöberg," thought I. A hand seized the knob. It turned and the door opened. In the room stepped—Paul.

Yes, it was indeed he, and yet not he, so pale and wasted looked the figure which stopped on the threshold and cast a searching glance around the room. Finally his eyes fell upon me, who rushed up, exclaiming with undisguised joy:

"Paul!—God be praised that you are here!"

He had remained still, but at my cry he stretched out his arms to me, and I threw myself upon his breast, in which beat a heart so warmly attached to me.

It was two years since we last saw each other. Two years—and how much had not changed since then.

How completely unacquainted with temptation and evil had I not been when we parted, and what a short, but varied experience had I not gained within this time!

I felt instantly, that if I had gone ahead on the road of knowledge, I had on the other hand retrograded in a moral respect. I knew that there was much in my conduct and my acts which Paul would disapprove.

Disapproval from a street-singer's lips? What did that amount to? What ideas could such a person have of morality and honor? some one will say. My answer is: Paul possessed the simple and unperverted ideas that come from the sense of right, the morality of sound reason and a good heart. He had besides, during the time he resided in Pastor Wenner's house, acquired a cultivation through study, which raised him far above the ordinary street-singer.

After Paul had pressed me to his breast, I had only one desire, and that was, to talk about Hanna.

"Why have you not answered my letters?" I asked.

"From the simple reason that I have been sick," was Paul's answer.

I had drawn him with me to the fire-place. He smiled mildly, adding:

"But as you see, I am now well and am here to answer them verbally. My dear Conny, what a large and stately man you have become!"

He pressed my hand and met my inquiring glance with a look which expressed all his former tenderness, and which seemed to say: "be calm, I am just the same as ever, and will remain so however you may act toward me."

Paul and I had seated ourselves, and I then said with some effort:

"Did you come from the steamboat directly, or have you been with—with—Hanna?"

"I came from Hanna," answered Paul, laying his hand on my shoulder. "I wished to see and talk to her before we met. It is now done, Conny, I have spent two hours with her."

"Hanna is probably very angry with me! Ah, Paul!

I have much to reproach myself for, and it sometimes appears to me as if I were the cause of the old woman's death."

Paul supported his elbow on one knee, leaned his head on his hand and said:

"No, Conny, you have no part in her death. She died from a violent cold, so as far as that matter is concerned you need not trouble yourself."

"Paul, answer me frankly, have you not been grieved and offended when you thought of me?"

Paul now shaded his face entirely with his hand, so that I could not see the expression of it.

"I have been somewhat grieved; but it is not worth while to speak of it. Will you instead answer a question honestly?"

"All you can ask me."

Paul raised his head quickly and looked me steadily in the eyes:

"Do you love Hanna?"

Had Paul asked me this question half a year before, I would without hesitation have answered, yes, and believed myself to speak the truth. Now it seemed to me absurd that I should love Hanna. Hanna was his betrothed, Hanna, who had caused me to blush for myself. Impossible. So I immediately uttered a decided—no.

He drew a deep sigh; whether it was of relief or sorrow, I cannot determine.

"On my own account and Hanna's it gladdens me, Conny, but on yours it pains me," said he. "If you had loved her, your heedlessness would have been excusable. As it is, Conny, you have soiled her name, and that simply for your own pleasure. It grieves me that you could have done so."

Again Paul sighed and leaned his brow in his hand.

"Hear me, Paul," I exclaimed. "My course of action

was the result of my then lively interest in Hanna. Had she or the old woman told me that you intended to unite your fate to hers, I would immediately have drawn back."

"I believe it; but tell me, Conny, if Hanna had not loved me, if she instead had held you dear, what would then have been her lot? Would you, as a student, have engaged yourself to washer-woman Grönqvist's granddaughter?"

A hot flush covered my brow. As seriously as all that I had never thought of women, since they began to interest me. I was amused by all pretty girls, desired to be liked by them and did not devote half a thought to the future. In all that pertained to the pleasures of life, I had lived for and in the moment. It was only when it concerned my studies, my ambition, and the aim I had set before it, that I thought longer than for the day. Neither could I answer Paul's question. As he did not receive any reply, he resumed:

"Do you wish me to tell you what would have become of Hanna? Why, it would have gone with her as people now believe that it has gone."

"Paul!" exclaimed I excitedly.

"Hush, and let me finish what I was going to say. I think it is better, Conny, for me to speak the words of truth to you now, than for your conscience to do it in the future. Thus if Hanna had liked you, she would now have been what scandal says that she is—a fallen girl, and if one had then asked you: 'do you love Hanna?' you would have stared at the questioner and answered a cold, no, just as now. Hanna, however, would have been ruined. Disgrace and misery would have been what she gained, while you, forgetting your folly, would have continued the career which brought you to honor and repute. You would not have bestowed a thought upon the poor girl, and if the remembrance of her ever happened to arise in your soul, you would have shrugged your shoulders and consoled yourself by thinking: 'that folly of mine is of no more consequence than all the others that I have daily committed,' and with this you would have dispelled all remorse."

Paul again became silent. I sat there very much like a reprimanded school-boy. It was the first time in my life that I received reproaches from this brother, who had only given me love and kind words.

After a short pause Paul continued:

"I have spoken hard words to you, Conny; but I only wished to warn you. You must recollect that I spent my first youth in taverns, was in connection with the most fallen beings, saw vice without disguise and in all its abomination; and then one turns from it with loathing. Yet, any one who has learned the early life of these unhappy creatures, knows that they, too, have once been young innocent girls, who were enticed upon the road to ruin. One thus comes to the conclusion, that if gentlemen were not so unprincipled and heartless when it concerns poor men's daughters, there would not be so many degraded women. You, Conny, who think of becoming a lawyer, you cannot sit in judgment over others, if you do not try to be a just man in all respects; and one is not just, who destroys another's life. You have seen how much evil one can occasion through sheer thoughtlessness, let it be a warning to you—and now no more about that matter."

He offered me his hand and pressed mine; then he told me about his wanderings in Germany and Denmark.

The night was far advanced, when Paul rose to go. I tried to persuade him to make his home with me. He shook his head, saying:

"No, Conny, that wouldn't do, I put up at the station-house, where I have a room. It is unnecessary for you to mention our relationship to your comrades. You might possibly have something unpleasant from it. I will come here to-morrow evening at this time. We can then in all quietness see each other, while I remain here."

He went, without my being able to change his decision.

That night I walked back and forth in my room until dawn. I then formed the most earnest resolutions. Hanna should be the first, the only woman to whom I had occasioned any suffering. I would be strict in my morals, impervious to temptation, a Cato in virtue and wisdom. Reason would be my only guide through life, and feeling doomed to an eternal captivity with understanding for a keeper. It ought, so it seemed to me, to be an easy matter to become a model of honor and morality. People were constantly speaking of my uncommonly fine intellect. Well then, this would hereafter show itself in the power it exerted over all my actions.

I finally retired toward morning, after I considered myself to have completely regained my self-respect through these resolutions. It is remarkable how easy virtue appears, when one is tired and in need of sleep. A man cannot then comprehend how he ever could have yielded to temptation. If he is young and conceited besides, it is the most natural thing in the world for him to believe that he will become a saint. That he has not been it before, is only because he had not yet resolved to be it.

CHAPTER XIII.

AUNT GRÖNQVIST was buried.

I had without apprising either Paul or Hanna of it, presented myself at the cemetery, when the simple coffin, followed by Paul, the minister, and two mechanics of the old woman's acquaintance, was carried to the grave. I took my place behind all the rest. It was a tribute of respect which I considered that I owed the departed, whom I without intention, but from sheer frivolity, had so deeply wronged.

After the funeral, two weeks passed, in which Paul continued to stay in Upsala. We met every evening, when he came up to my room; between times we did not see each other. During the day he was with Hanna, helping her to turn the old woman's effects into money, and to rent the little dwelling. As soon as this was accomplished, Hanna intended to return to Stockholm.

My relationship to Paul was still a secret to my comrades. Paul might have gone away without any one finding it out, if I had not from the first evening, when I took my grand and lofty resolutions, decided otherwise. I found it incompatible with my sense of right, and why not with my pride too, that I should deny my own brother. So I had made up my mind to show Paul, when the first days of mourning for Aunt Grönqvist were past, that I was not by any means ashamed to acknowledge that we were brothers.

Paul's birth-day occurred soon after Martin-mass. I made up my mind to celebrate this day with a grand supper, to which I intended to invite all the comrades of my "society."

I had issued the invitations a whole week before. The night previous, I asked Paul to come to me the following evening a little earlier than usual.

When Paul entered, I said merrily:

"Do you know that this is your birth-day, and that you must therefore go with me to N—berg's? I have engaged a private room, and there we will, you and I, celebrate your birth-day."

Paul could not say no. We went together arm in arm. On reaching N—berg's, I led the way up to a side-room, adjoining the saloon where the supper was to be held.

My brother's attire was as usual peculiar in the highest degree. It is true there was not precisely the same inharmony now, as when he was a spindling youth and wore clothes made for an old man; but still the coat was so broad between the shoulders that it looked as if it hung on a form, the pantaloons dragged at the heels and the vest had the same irresistible tendency to leave a white space between its lower edge and the pantaloons, a lack which the long scarf in vain tried to remedy.

When we entered the private room, a black suit lay there, which I had ordered for Paul. The difficulty now was to get him to put it on, and to keep it as a present from me. Hitherto it had been impossible to induce him to accept anything from me. He was always accustomed to say:

"No, Conny, it would distress me if I had you to thank for the least thing. Self-interest could so easily be mingled with my love for you."

After I had closed the door, I said:

"Do you know, dear Paul, I have been confoundedly low-spirited for a long time? Say, will you make me happy all at once?"

"Of course I will," answered Paul, rubbing his hands; then he added with his usual careless air:

"The fact is, these last few days have been as cloudy as an autumn sky. Hanna has cried and only cried, you have looked gloomy, my violin has had to rest, like my throat and my hand-organ, which now stands silent at Jungfru Lova's in Stockholm. No, I feel that this will not do any longer. Sorrow may go to the old scratch and joy again tune its lyre. Tell me, therefore, what you wish and I will immediately do it, so that we can have a good time again."

"Bravo, Paul, you have now promised to fulfil my desire, which consists in your putting on these," I pointed to the garments. "I would like to see you well-dressed for once and you must not say no."

Paul's face clouded.

"Conny, you have cheated me into a trap," said he with a displeased expression, as he prepared to "change his skin," as they say. "But here goes for this time, still, do not repeat it, you would only wound me. It is with my clothes as with myself, one thing is not suited to the other. Habit has become my second nature, although it has from the beginning stood in direct conflict with my original disposition. Clothes made to fit my body would now incommode me as much as an orderly and regular life. The whirl of the streets, the singing at the street-corners, the applause from the people, that is something which I miss when I am away from it, notwithstanding it constituted my torment when I was a child. So with the coat I now exchange for a far better one, which, nevertheless, seems to me like a strait-jacket. My body has become out of shape, my legs crooked, under the weight of the hand-organ. It has gone the same way with my tastes and habits. They too have become awry; but now look at me, and you will see that this fine coat and these pantaloons do not befit me."

To my surprise I found that Paul was right. He appeared more crooked and knock-kneed in the elegant clothes than in those he had taken off. He looked almost ridiculous in his new costume. The result was, that I was forced to ask him to resume his old clothes, fully satisfied that these suited him best, and that his beautiful head struck one far more, when he stood there in his whole figure and outward appearance an organ-grinder.

Scarcely was Paul's toilet for the second time finished, than the voices of a swarm of merry students, who entered the saloon, met my ears.

We remained quiet in our own room, however, until I thought that they were all assembled, then I quite unexpectedly opened the door.

Before Paul knew how it happened, I had introduced my brother to my comrades and explained that it was to celebrate his birth-day that I had invited them to this supper.

Paul was so surprised and so moved, that he was completely taken aback.

They chatted, ate, drank and soon forgot to wonder what sort of a figure my brother was, a question that could be read plainly on most of their faces when I presented him.

Supper was over and the especial toast-drinking was now to begin. The first punch-bowl was carried in, and I asked the privilege of speaking.

The merry uproar ceased. Paul stood at my side.

The step earnestly considered for two weeks was now taken, and I openly acknowledged before my comrades that I was a child of the people, who only through a throw of the dice had been changed to a wealthy boy.

I was now as a student performing the same act, to

which I had once as a gymnast been forced by circumstances, with the only difference, that it was now voluntary and dictated by my affection for Paul. I had an inner need of saying before the whole world:

"This is my brother."

My story was short. I told them that they in my brother and me saw two organ-grinders, who for two years' time had wandered around Sweden to play and sing for bread. In a few words, that sprang from my heart, I described Paul's sacrifices and love for me, and with a trifle of student humor I then passed to a description of how Fortuna had thrown to me a great gain. I finished by asking those present if they did not consider it in order, that I now honored the brother, who had been more than father and mother to me.

A unanimous *yes* was the response, after which Paul's health was drank with the enthusiasm with which only students can empty a toast to the good, noble and beautiful.

Paul's answer consisted in striking up a song.

I had not heard him sing for two years, so that I, like all the rest, was struck by his rich, sonorous voice.

The remainder of the evening was taken up with toasts and singing, and then it was decided that we should go and greet the other societies. Paul withdrew into a corner and we marched off in high glee.

When I awoke the following morning, I felt pleased and satisfied with myself. As I had mentioned my past life I could now be secure and need not fear any discovery. I had had the courage to acknowledge before the world, as it behooved a brave youth, that the humble organ-grinder was my brother, and I had showed him the respect he deserved.

Quite cheerfully I sprang out of bed to dress myself and

go to the lecture. My toilet was interrupted, however, by my eyes falling on a letter that lay on my table.

It was from Paul.

"I bet anything that the owl has gone off without taking leave," thought I, as I opened the letter.

It contained a plain gold ring and the following lines:

"My dear beloved Brother: As you have done me so great an honor as that which was bestowed upon me last evening, and as I have been allowed to sing for you and your friends, I will not stay here longer.

"Thank you, Conny, for being the same dear Conny that you were in childhood. When the dark days now come, I will sing the same song, and the memory of you will make me forget the grief of the moment.

"When and where we will again meet, I do not know, but whenever and wherever it may be, I will greet you with Nordblom's song.

"The ring that is enclosed is your mother's wedding-ring. I have kept it, and did not intend to give it to you until your twenty-first birthday; but now, I beg you, Conny, to take it and wear it. When you next time see a pair of pretty eyes, then—fasten your own on your mother's ring, think of her and do not trouble yourself to talk nonsense to the poor girl.

"Write to Stockholm to thy Paul.

"P. S.—I live as usual with Jungfru Lova. Hanna wishes to be remembered to you. She is going with me to the capital, where she will stay until we can unite our fates."

With emotion I regarded the memento from my mother. I seemed to see her pale suffering face smiling upon me, as when I was a child.

A few days afterward Professor Wenner came to Upsala. He had obtained the professorship he sought; but would not begin to lecture until the spring term.

One day in the beginning of December, when I was returning from a visit to the professor, I met on the bridge a youth, at the sight of whom I involuntarily started. He seemed as surprised to meet me in Upsala, as I was to see him; but without greeting we passed each other.

The next day I learned that young Baron Casper Lodstein had come to Upsala to enter the University. He had for the last year been boarding with Magister S——n, to prepare for his examination.

The young nobleman had been particularly disinclined to attend to his studies at the gymnasium, from which he had been expelled, in consequence of some rather mean trick. With Magister S——n he had been kept very strictly. He was now in Upsala to pass the minor examination. It was not necessary for him to pass the higher one, as he intended to enter the army.

The next year I was a candidate for the law, and left Upsala to have my name entered in the Superior Court in Stockholm. I intended in course of time to become "Juris Doctor," but I would first serve some time in the court and attain the age when one can receive an appointment as judge.

Consequently I was again to change my place of residence, again bid my old teacher farewell, this time as a person of age and master of my whole property.

It was with jubilant joy that I took leave of Upsala, and I felt proud and happy in the consciousness of being free, of being rich and of having finished my college course.

I did not go directly to Stockholm, however, but first made a visit to my guardian, and spent some very agreeable weeks in his home.

At the end of September I left the parsonage. When I

stepped on board the steamer which was to take me from G——e to the capital, my attention was drawn to a lady who came up from the cabin. She wore an elegant dress and carried herself with unstudied grace. Her face was turned from me, so that I could not distinguish her features, and she went straight to a gentleman, who stood with his back to me, looking at the city, from whence we were quickly receding.

I did not hear what she said, but I caught the sound of her voice, and it seemed as though I had heard it before, but when and where was not clear to me.

With no slight impatience I waited for either her or him to turn round. Still, it was a good while before either of them changed position. Finally she seated herself and looked in the direction where I stood. I took a step toward her, on my lips trembled the name *Bertha!* but I checked myself. Taking off my hat, I advanced to her and paid my respects.

When I accosted her, the gentleman who was with her turned round. It was Herr August Lagerskog.

As a general thing one cannot meet a more disagreeable person than the husband of a beautiful woman. If he is in addition double her age and an intolerable simpleton besides, as was the case with Herr Lagerskog, then it is hard to conceal the repugnance he inspires, especially if one is only twenty and rather light-minded, as I was.

Herr Lagerskog, however, did not seem to experience any disagreeable impressions at the sight of me. He had apparently forgotten the mortification I once occasioned him, and greeted me with the greatest politeness, said a thousand fine things about the pleasure it gave him to again meet me, etc. He had heard me so well spoken of; congratulated me upon having finished my studies and attained the age when one is his own master. The man talked incessantly, his tongue went like a mill. I felt irritated by his politeness and provoked that his stream of words entirely deprived me of the pleasure of conversing with my first flame.

After Herr Lagerskog had rattled on a whole hour without ceasing, descanted upon the *beau-monde* and society life in general, fallen into ecstasies over Paris and London, and expressed his contempt for everything Swedish, he commissioned his wife to ask me to excuse him, as he was obliged to leave us. He had such a delicate constitution that he no longer dared to expose himself to the sea air. He could not endure the wind, it irritated his nerves; he could not endure the sunshine, it heated his blood, and the sea voyage had an injurious effect upon his digestion. He was greatly to be pitied, for nature had not given him such an iron constitution as his wife had—and then he sighed, took off his hat politely and cautiously, and departed.

Bertha and I then entered into conversation.

My self-love prevented me from being the least embarrassed when I was with ladies. I had as a student been very well treated by them, and I believed implicitly in my power to captivate, especially when I exerted myself to be agreeable, as in the present instance.

Whether Bertha found me so, I leave to conjecture, but one thing is certain, that we came upon a very interesting subject, that of literature, first in general, and then the Swedish in particular. I expressed myself with all the self-confidence of an Upsala student. My criticism was not a personal opinion of the matter, but a final sentence, from which there was no appeal.

Bertha let me talk. She did not interrupt me, while I unmercifully attacked one literary production after the other, and declared that it was miserable stuff, a mere rehash of old things, etc. I drew up the faults, ridiculed them, and exhausted all my wit and acrimony in depreciating works, the value of which, strictly taken, I did not understand.

At this period of my life I had acquired the false idea that censure of others' work was a proof of my own superiority. When I had thus pulled to pieces a newly issued book, which was read with much eagerness, I considered myself to have given evidence of independence, judgment, and a higher æsthetic taste than the public possessed. After I had finished my verbal criticism, which, in parenthesis, was as sharp and as unjust as those in the newspapers generally are, Bertha said with a subtle smile:

"I am surprised, Herr Fredriksson, that you can be such a hard judge. You, who are so young, ought to be milder. At your age it seems to me that merits, not faults, should strike the eye. The work you have now declared so poor that it is not worth reading, I consider one of very great value. I have read it with pleasure and derived from it much useful knowledge. It is very possible that it may possess the faults you speak of, although they escaped me, as I only perceived the beauties. But since you have expressed *your* opinion of it, perhaps you will allow me to tell you mine."

Bertha then spoke of what she liked, what she found great and beautiful in the work mentioned, and at the conclusion of her remarks, to which she simply gave the character of her own private judgment, I was a little taken down. She had during this conversation made me feel that her general culture and intelligence was so great, that it could bear comparison with any one's. Moreover, she had given me to understand, that the condemnation of what others have produced is by no means a proof of the infallibility of our own judgment, but rather lowers us, as if we spoke from envy. Finally she jested in a delicate, but to me very humiliating way, over the folly of an individual trying to make himself the absolute judge of literary productions, when the impression of them depends upon different comprehension and taste.

"To possess the right to express anything but our private opinion in such matters," said she, "we ought first to have pursued æsthetic studies and devoted our time and mental powers exclusively to literature. Then only have we acquired the culture that entitles us to pronounce upon the merits of any work, but, Herr Fredriksson, how few there are who could then occupy the judgment seat in the world of poetry and literature; it is certainly neither you nor I."

It was a sharp, but useful lesson. It had so much the more effect on me, as it was uttered by a pair of beautiful lips, and with a voice, mild and sweet as music. The natural result was, that the conversation passed over from literature to reflections upon tolerance. The hours flew quickly while we talked; the dinner-bell sounded and Herr Lagerskog, who came to conduct his wife down to the dining-saloon, interrupted the discussion. He invited me to accompany them, but as the sight of him, at the side of this uncommonly lovely woman, was repugnant to me, I declined the invitation politely, alleging that I could not possibly dine so early. They went down with the rest of the passengers, the number of which was not very great. The deck became empty, and I walked there entirely alone.

The first impression Bertha made on me had again revived, but more positive and well defined. I considered it natural that Strålkrans had been so violently in love, but more unnatural than ever, that Bertha, with her beauty, her wealth, her culture and her superiority, chose this old fool for her husband in preference to Strålkrans.

What did he possess that entitled him to such a preference? Nothing. For in his social position he was a merchant, known to have lived extravagantly and to have destroyed the greater part of his property, old and without any outer advantages, destitute of culture and intelligence, in short, destitute of everything that can attract.

While I was making these reflections, a boat had drawn up along side the steamer, and some new passengers had come on board, without my noticing it. When the steamer was again set in motion, those who had been dining came up from the cabin, and I hoped that Bertha would resume her place on deck; but to my indescribable regret and annoyance she remained down. Her husband, on the contrary, seated himself beside me, smoking his cigar and chatting like a magpie. I felt very much tempted to tell him to go to the d——l and leave me in peace; but was withheld by the thought that I would thereby for ever deprive myself of the opportunity of calling at Bertha's home and seeing her again.

Equipping myself with Job's patience, I endured listening to him and was rewarded for it; for when the cigar was consumed and he was about to go down to his stateroom, he invited me to call upon them in Stockholm.

In vain did I wait to see Bertha. Twilight succeeded the day, and still she did not make her appearance.

The moon raised its pale face over the surface of the water. We were out in the open sea and had left the islands behind us. The air was mild, as if it had been summer. The endless expanse of water lay as calm and still as if the vessel had glided over a sheet of steel. I stood leaning against the guard, contemplating the sea in its stillness. Like a restless disturber of the peace, the steamer rushed on, leaving behind it a broad foaming wake, which agitated the calmly slumbering surface.

While I stood there absorbed by this spectacle, the moon had risen higher and higher in the firmament, and the last rays of day faded out in the west.

Youth is the age of revery. A longing for I know not

what seized my mind, vague and confused images filled my soul. I had fallen into thought, or rather dreams, when a stifled exclamation, whether of pain or surprise I could not decide, met my ear, together with a hasty rustle of a silk dress and a motion as if a man had taken a few steps to hurry forward.

I stood by the wheel-house and as good as concealed behind a mass of cotton-bales that lay piled on each other.

At the exclamation and motion I turned quickly and saw Bertha, who had probably just ascended the steps, leaning against the door, as if to hold herself up. Before her stood a tall man. He had stopped a few steps from her, probably checked as he hastened forward to assist her when she reeled.

My heart beat audibly. I immediately divined who the man was. There were not two men with this form and this bearing. A few seconds elapsed, during which I saw that Bertha had great difficulty to recover from her consternation. Finally the man, whose back I persistently regarded, said:

"Excuse me, madam, for frightening you, it was not my design to occasion you any alarm through my presence. That I have done so, has occurred involuntarily; I did not know that you were here; I only came on board an hour ago."

Bertha trembled violently and was paler than death.

"You are ill," resumed he, and now stood by her side. "Allow me to lead you to the seat there. You will probably feel better, when you breathe the fresh air."

He took Bertha's hand and laid it in his arm, as he led her to the seat at the guard.

"Thanks!" faltered Bertha, sitting down.

"Are you better now?" asked he with sympathy.

"Yes, somewhat." Bertha looked at the water. "It was

so suffocating down there in the cabin that I had great need of air."

"And when you came up to get it, an adverse fate ordained that you should meet a person, whose sight was so painful to you that it called forth a cry of pain from your lips. I hoped, however, that years would mitigate your aversion."

"Herr count, I beg of you, do not talk so," said Bertha with regained self-possession. "The time which has fled does not belong to us."

"But that which *is* has shown me, that your dislike today is the same as three years ago."

"My dislike exists as little to-day as it did then. I have never detested you; but, once more, why speak of this?"

"For the simple reason that I may not always be able to avoid meeting you, as I have hitherto done. My service calls me to Stockholm, where I am obliged to remain. With the best will in the world it will not stand in my power to prevent our ways from coming together. It would distress me if I every time occasioned you pain, as has been the case to-day."

"To-day it was surprise. I did not expect to meet you."

"Thus only surprise."

It seemed to me that the count bent forward a little.

"Yes," this word was pronounced very decidedly.

"You will then see me hereafter without any disagreeable emotion?"

"I have never experienced anything of the kind," answered Bertha, but at the same time rose hastily, adding in a tone which betrayed much uneasiness:

"Herr count, if—if—you have any of your former affection left for me, then leave me, I beg of you, do it immediately. I do not wish—my—my husband to see you, it—would—"

Lagerskog's voice was heard from the cabin stairs. He asked the stewardess where his wife was.

Without clearly realizing what I did, I stepped from my hiding-place and went directly toward the stairs. Humming a student song, I rushed down them and knocked so violently against the ascending husband, that I almost sent him to the bottom again, and indeed I would not have been sorry if I had. Luckily for Herr Lagerskog's peruke and handsome false teeth, both of which would surely have run the risk of changing places, he caught hold of the railing, and after he had staggered a moment, he regained his balance. Swearing over the awkwardness of running against people in that style, he looked up at me.

I begged a thousand pardons. He was detained by the mutual compliments. When these were well over, he stood up on deck and asked me whether I had seen his wife.

"I left Fru Lagerskog just now," answered I in a loud voice. "We have been talking together a good while and admiring the beautiful moonlight."

"I am glad to hear it, yes, heartily glad to hear it," answered Lagerskog, casting a distrustful glance around the deck, evidently to discover whether any one was there besides us; but the only living being to be seen was Bertha. She remained in the same place where she had conversed with the count. Of him there was no trace. He had disappeared, but I suspected immediately that he had taken my place behind the cotton-bales.

Herr Lagerskog declared that the air was cold, that Bertha ought not to sit there any longer, and then he offered to keep her company down in the state-room, until she could fall asleep.

They went down, and I, who after my strange behavior

lacked all desire to meet my benefactor or give any explanation, followed their example.

Early the next morning we were in Stockholm. All the passengers had assembled on deck, when the steamer landed; but in vain did I look for Count Strålkrans. He was not visible. Herr Lagerskog had a great deal to attend to, in giving his servant orders about valises, dressing-cases, and God knows what. He himself was as if nailed to Bertha's side, and followed every male figure which passed them, with a searching glance. Finally he caught sight of me. Quite rejoiced over the discovery, he asked if I would do him the favor of conducting his wife to their equipage, which was waiting, while he went down in his state-room to get something that the servant could not find.

Bertha took my arm and we went ashore.

"Why did you tell my husband that you and I had conversed the whole evening?" asked she suddenly, when we had crossed the plank. "For what reason did you make up this story?"

"Have you contradicted it?" inquired I in my turn.

"No, but your question is not an answer to mine."

"Shall I give you a frank one?"

"Certainly."

"I believe that your husband is jealous of Count Strålkrans."

Bertha's cheeks became crimson. She was going to answer something, but kept silent, and I helped her into the carriage. A few moments more and the carriage drove off with the married pair, after the husband had first, in the most pressing manner, invited me to call on them.

I went on board again to look after my effects, and when I had found them, I pursued my way to the lodgings Paul had hired and put in order for me.

SECOND PERIOD.

CHAPTER I.

BROVIK was not only a large but a beautiful country-seat. It belonged to Judge Göran Liedgren.

Liedgren was a person of much repute, on account of his wealth as well as his magisterial capacity.

Brovik was spoken of as a home of magnificence, comfort and taste, and the owner of it as a man who loved the enjoyments of life as deeply as work.

Proud of what he was and of what he possessed, Liedgren did not bow his head before anybody. Son of a rich and esteemed official, whose forefathers, as far back as one could trace them, held higher or lower positions in the service of the state, he was as inflated over his origin as the most high-born nobleman.

The jurisdiction Liedgren held was very large, and he engaged as assistants no less than two and sometimes several notaries. He had two the year round.

Liedgren's house was known as one of the pleasantest. He himself had the reputation of being a distinguished jurist and a fine man. In short, all young notaries were especially anxious to get a place with him.

Judge Liedgren had been married to a wealthy girl, who in her marriage had given him a daughter, but the mother died, however, when the girl was ten years old.

It was generally believed at the wife's death that the young, stately widower would marry again, but years elapsed without his fastening his thoughts or gaze on any other woman. Eight years had gone by, and yet the departed had not received any successor. People got tired of talking about who was to be Fru Liedgren number two.

Gertrude Liedgren was now eighteen, and constituted her father's pride. He regarded her as the greatest of his treasures, and lavished upon her everything that a rich father can lavish upon his child. Gertrude was beautiful, talented and thoroughly spoiled. But she was a lovely child in all respects. Still, these are things which we ought not to speak of prematurely, and therefore we will now see what is transpiring within the walls of Brovik at the present time.

The spring sun shone into the little saloon and caressed the plants which adorned the windows.

At one of these stood a young girl, attending to the beautiful children from the floral kingdom.

"Do you know what I have been thinking of for the last few days?" said she, turning to a lady between twenty and thirty, who sat by the other window engaged with her sewing.

"Probably of the ball which is to take place at Brudgard," answered the one addressed.

"Do you really think that I would occupy my mind with anything so insignificant as a ball!" exclaimed the young girl, laughing. "Oh no, it was something far more important."

"Then it was probably your plans for a journey to Stockholm."

"Oh, you great goose! Do you actually think that that needs any consideration? If I wish to go to Stockholm in earnest this spring, I have but to express my desire, and it will be as I wish."

"Well, then it must have been about your birds, flowers or dresses."

"Am I a child, to burden my mind with such nonsense; or do you consider me such a vain simpleton that I allow the care of my toilet to take up my thoughts?"

"Yes, Gertrude, I do indeed consider you very vain."

"That sounds pleasant, and for what cause, if I may ask?" Gertrude smiled like a good and inoffensive child.

"Because you make such a fuss about your toilet. You can spend whole hours in trying on a hat or a dress; your dearest occupation is to look at yourself in the glass."

"It is astonishing how frightfully one can be calumniated," said Gertrude, laughing, "and that, because one does not wish to look like a witch, but desires to be attractive to others, to you in the first place, you naughty Bertha."

The flowers were left, and Gertrude was at Bertha's side. She seized her hand and continued:

"Even if the whole world spoils me, as you assert, you at least, form an exception; for you not only speak of my faults, but you do it in the superlative degree in the bargain, and yet, it is for you that I make myself beautiful. As a reward for it you say that I am vain."

Bertha smiled at the pretty child and declared that she could not take back her words.

"But let me hear what extraordinary thing you were thinking about?" added Bertha.

"Why, I was thinking of the new notary who is expected here to-day, and for whose benefit papa had the two rooms in the large building put in order. I cannot comprehend why he cannot stay where the former notary stayed, that is to say, in the same wing as Notary Wicker."

"Probably because he is an older man," said Bertha.

"Older, do you say? No, he seems to be quite young, only five and twenty, Wicker says."

"Well then, that arrangement probably comes from the fact that uncle stands in some relation to his family," declared Bertha.

"I have never heard papa speak of any one by that name."

"What then is the new notary called? To be sure I heard you and Wicker talking about him all last evening; but no name was mentioned."

"Oh yes, we all mentioned it, but you were so absorbed in the perusal of Dickens that you neither heard nor saw, otherwise the name of Conny Wenner would surely have reached your ears. That is the man's name; but good God, Bertha, what ails you, your cheeks are perfectly crimson? Do you know our new notary?"

"Somewhat," answered Bertha, sewing diligently.

"That is to say, very well," rejoined Gertrude. "Ah, you reserved Bertha!"

"I am not reserved," said Bertha as she looked up from her work. "I am only *slightly* acquainted with Notary Wenner."

"Why then did you blush?"

"From the simple reason that his name reminded me of events which I have not yet learned to think of with calmness."

"Of your departed husband, probably? Dearest Bertha, let the old man sleep peacefully in his grave, and do not allow the memory of his amiable qualities to agitate you. It seems to me that you had enough of him while he lived. There now, no saintly airs. I will not speak of the buried treasure, but return to Herr Wenner. How does he look? to begin with his outer man."

"He is very good looking, has a fine figure and a pair of dangerous eyes."

"Brown?" asked Gertrude.

"Dark, and of an undecided color."

"Bravo! I am pleased with his exterior. Now about his manner?"

"Easy and agreeable. Perhaps he appears too conceited, but that may be pardoned in him; the ladies have done everything to spoil him."

"That is to say, in other words, that he is stupid. A smart man ought not to allow himself to be spoiled."

"He is an uncommonly smart man, my dear Gertrude, and it is just this that he is conscious of. He considers himself superior to most people, and he is."

"Yes, in law matters perhaps," said Gertrude, "but that superiority is of no value in my eyes. So he is conceited. Well then, we will have to take him down a bit. I cannot endure conceited men."

"Believe me, Gertrude, the wisest thing for you is not to busy yourself with his education. He is a very dangerous young man."

"And dreadfully frivolous, Wicker says."

"So it is said. What I know, however, is, that with all his faults he has a very chivalrous character. If he is frivolous, he has become so through the great prosperity he has had. He has been courted and made much of wherever he has gone, and what person can resist the delight of being a favorite and of hearing himself praised? Therefore, the probability is that he has not remained insensible when people encouraged him, and that he has through this got the reputation of being irresistible."

"Ah, he is likely to afford us some fun. I suppose he thinks that he is Adonis himself."

"It is very possible that he does; but that is an indifferent matter, and believe me, it is best for you not to occupy yourself at all with either his faults or virtues."

"You thus believe that he might destroy my peace?"

"Yes. Nothing is more dangerous than when a young girl hits upon the idea of trying to correct a young man. She finishes with being mastered by him."

"Perhaps; but if any such thing had been the will of fate, she would have encountered the misfortune anyhow, even if she had never thought of his improvement, and if I am destined to fall in love with that conceited and handsome notary, I will do it, whether I occupy myself with his faults or not. But to speak frankly, I take it for granted that I will never fall in love. There is only one man who could become dangerous to me, and this man does not care at all for the undersigned."

"Who is it?"

"Sten Mauritz Strålkrans. But now I must dress myself. Papa said that he and the notary would be here before dinner. In two days the court opens, and then, God be praised, there will be life and motion at Brovik. Farewell, my angel. Shall you not change skin too? Seems to me that dress does not look quite fresh."

"I have the same opinion," replied Bertha. "Go to your toilet, however, you need at least twice as long a time as I to finish it."

"I will obey orders. But apropos, can you tell me truly, dear Bertha, whether blue or red becomes me best?"

"Blue, beyond all doubt."

"Eh bien! then blue it shall be to-day. Perhaps you have not heard that Notary Wenner almost danced the life out of a young girl at a ball. If you wish to hear the details of that sad occurrence, then talk to Wicker."

Gertrude hastened from the saloon. She flew up the stairs, covered with thick carpets, and into her room.

When Bertha was alone she put down her work and, leaning her elbows on the little table, sank into thought.

For one year Bertha had been the widow of a man who had made life very bitter to her. The last two years of

Lagerskog's life they had resided on an estate called Kungsdal, in the neighborhood of Brovik. Lagerskog had retired from business and resolved to lead a secluded life in the country. The reason of this step was, that the greater part of his step-father's property had melted away even during the old man's lifetime, and when he died there was not much of it left. Lagerskog's debts and extravagance had consumed the greater part of it. When Lagerskog, at Engberg's decease, drew the last little remainder of his wife's money, he decided to devote himself to agriculture, and for this purpose purchased Kungsdal. Still he did not know how to attend to the place, but so involved himself that, at his death, his affairs were in such a condition that it looked as though Bertha would be obliged to give up everything.

Judge Liedgren, who was related to Lagerskog through his departed wife, had, out of compassion for the young widow, taken it upon himself to straighten her affairs, and invited her in the meantime to stay with his daughter at Brovik. The young girl needed a lady in the house for company, and the judge represented the matter in such a way to Bertha as to give the invitation the appearance of a favor, and she accepted it.

Gertrude, from the beginning of her acquaintance with Bertha, when the Lagerskogs moved to the place, had conceived a lively friendship for her, which Bertha reciprocated with an elder sister's calm affection. During the year they had constantly been together, this affection had gained considerably in strength.

Bertha Lagerskog was to Gertrude an object that she admired, and the only one from whom the spoiled girl endured to hear the truth, the only one to whose judgment Gertrude conformed herself, and whose blame pained her. Gertrude's behavior changed very much under Bertha's influence. She had become less capricious, less pretentious and more mindful of herself than she had hitherto been. But we now return to Bertha.

She remained long in the same position, when the sound of carriage wheels caused her to lift up her head and rise. With hasty steps she approached the door which led out to the dining-room. The noise had ceased again, a proof that the vehicle had stopped. Bertha quickened her pace, in order to get up to her room.

At Brovik there was a long corridor, which went through the whole lower floor and divided the rooms that lay on the garden side from those that overlooked the lawn. In the middle of this corridor was the entrance, and it formed a rotunda, which was ornamented with pillars and received its light from the ceiling. At each end of the corridor was a stair-case to the upper floors, where Gertrude's, Bertha's and the judge's private suites were situated, besides a long row of guest chambers.

When Bertha came out of the large dining-room, which occupied the middle of the suite on the garden side, she found herself right opposite the front entrance.

At the instant she closed the door after her, a tall man jumped out of a light and elegant droschka.

At the sight of him Bertha withdrew behind one of the pillars. It was plain to be seen that she wished to conceal herself until he had passed through the hall or taken his way up to the second floor.

He stopped an instant, however, on the threshold and said, turning to the servant, standing by the carriage:

"Tell Mamsell Rundqvist that we will not dine until five o'clock to-day."

After uttering these words he entered the vestibule. His eyes immediately fell on the edge of Bertha's dress, which appeared from behind the pillar.

Judge Liedgren, for it was he, went toward the dining-room door, but proceeded to the left of the pillar, so that he, in this way, debarred Bertha from the opportunity of stealing to the left side of the corridor.

"Upon my honor, Bertha, I believe you are playing hide and seek," said he sportively, and at the same moment stood beside the young woman.

"I really hoped to be able to reach my room before you observed me, uncle,"* answered Bertha.

"And why were you so afraid of meeting me?"

"Simply because I had not yet made my toilet, and I know that your brow always wrinkles if we show ourselves without a certain elegance of attire."

"But this neglect I have never noticed in you."

Liedgren seized her hand and added politely: "Bertha Lagerskog, even in the simplest dress, is the most charming woman I know."

Bertha colored, her demeanor became indescribably stiff, as she drew away her hand, with the words:

"I did not think that you were in the habit of flattering."

"Again offended!" Liedgren straightened himself up. A hasty cloud passed over his brow and his tone was harsh when he added:

"I desire to say a few words to you before dinner, and as we will not dine until five o'clock perhaps you will show me the favor of returning to the saloon. There is still abundant time to dress for dinner."

Without waiting for her answer he opened the dining-room door, and indicated with a gesture that she should enter. Bertha did so, but maintained her stiff bearing.

When she passed by Liedgren he followed her with his eyes, and in his glance lay something resentful, something which showed that he was very much displeased.

Bertha went to the right into the little saloon which she

* A familiar mode of address from young people to their older friends.

had just before left. After the judge had taken off his over-coat, passed his hand through the unusually thick and bushy hair to arrange it, he followed Bertha. She stood by one of the windows when he came in.

"Please take a seat here," said Liedgren, leading her to a little sofa. He drew out an easy-chair for himself.

"Kungsdal is now sold," resumed he. "The auction took place yesterday and the estate was knocked down to Count Strålkrans." Liedgren looked fixedly at Bertha while he spoke. "The price of it was considerably increased, as there were three of us who seemed firmly resolved to become the owner of it. I suspect that the count through this had to pay higher for the pleasure of coming in possession of it than he calculated, but that is his private affair, you are through this fortunate result secured for the future."

"It would be too bad if the count had paid too much for the place," replied Bertha.

"Bah! what signifies twenty thousand rixthalers more or less in the purchase of an estate? It is not worth while speaking about that matter; but what astonished me was that Notary Wenner so persistently followed the Count's bid, until the latter, by raising the sum to twenty thousand rixthalers, silenced both Wenner and me. I knew that Wenner was a very wealthy boy, but I did not think he was so rich that he could compete with Strålkrans and me for the right of ownership to Kungsdal. What I am heartily rejoiced at, however, is that you can now be considered independent in a pecuniary respect, something which I did not dare to hope for, as real-estate is unusually low at present."

"And for this independence I have you to thank, uncle," said Bertha, offering Liedgren her hand. "I shall never forget the pains you have taken to preserve these pecuniary advantages for me, and do not think that I am ungrateful even if my manner appears so."

"I have not done more than I ought to do, and if I perchance have been so fortunate as to serve you, I have only desired in so doing that your future might not remind you too much of the past."

"You have been more than kind to me," stammered Bertha, without looking up in Liedgren's face.

The judge clasped her hand tighter in his, saying:

"And yet you are so wonderfully afraid of me. It is as if you feared to be friendly, and you draw back every time I try to approach you. I flattered myself, however, that the affection and respect I have shown you would produce a change in your manner, but I was mistaken. Tell me therefore frankly, how I shall explain your behavior?"

Bertha's face was covered with a dark flush, and her whole appearance denoted the greatest embarrassment. The experienced judge, accustomed to read in people's faces what passed within them, very well perceived that he had touched a delicate subject. Still he had resolved that she should give an answer, and did not allow the expression of painful confusion to deter him from learning the truth.

"I cannot give any explanation of my behavior," answered Bertha without looking at him.

"That is to say, you will not." Liedgren let go of her hand.

Bertha did not seem to have heard these words, but continued:

"However strange, cold and distant my manner may appear, I beg you to believe that I am deeply grateful for the kindness that has been shown me, and that I am attached to this family with a warm and sincere friendship.

"To Gertrude, yes, that I know, but you do not entertain any for me."

"Yes, uncle, I do."

"Perhaps, although I have not seen any proofs of it." The judge rose and went to the window. "It is so usual," added he, "that the more good-will a man cherishes for a person, the less he gets in return."

"So you do not believe in my gratitude?"

"I have never asked for that, never striven for it," answered Liedgren, drumming on the pane.

An instant's pause ensued, during which Bertha apparently underwent a hard struggle with herself, then she added quite calmly:

"It is impossible to be heartily grateful without also cherishing friendship for the one to whom our gratitude is due. I therefore beg you to believe in my affection."

The judge turned round quickly and cast a swift glance at Bertha.

She had risen and gone to him. He took one of her hands.

"I thank you," said he, "for having courage at this instant to overcome your shyness. If you understood me *rightly*, Bertha, you would realize that fear is entirely unnecessary."

Liedgren kissed Bertha's hand, but at this a dark flush again flew over her face, and the judge immediately dropped the little hand.

CHAPTER II.

"OH dear! so there are several gentlemen coming to dinner," said Gertrude, as she stood before the mirror in Bertha's little sitting-room. "Then I suppose I will be forced to change this muslin dress, which was put on for the new notary's sake, for my blue checked silk. Muslin will do for a notary, but for counts, barons, lieutenants, it is entirely too simple."

"Still I would advise you to keep it," said Bertha, coming out to Gertrude. "Simplicity becomes you so well."

"Do you mean to say by that, that my appearance is simple?" exclaimed Gertrude, laughing.

"Not at all; but when a girl is eighteen—"

"She ought to go in sack-cloth and ashes. I know that by heart; but at twenty-five—"

"She ought to go in a gray dress with black ornaments," interrupted Bertha, smiling.

"Yes, but good gracious, if all were as lovely as you are," exclaimed Gertrude, who just then turned to Bertha, "they could go in gray their whole lives through. It is decidedly sinful to be so beautiful. How that gray dress becomes you, and what hair you have—and what eyes! Ah, how will it go with our dinner guests? Ill, very ill, I fear. Now I hear the sound of carriages. There—my poor muslin dress will have to stay on. It is too annoying though, that I could not change it for a silk one."

Gertrude arranged her hair once more, and then Bertha and she went down in the drawing-room. The young girl placed herself by the flower-stand before one of the windows, saying:

"I will have to occupy myself with Flora's children when the gentlemen enter, it looks so poetical. In all the romances I have read, girls are dallying with flowers, doves and birds. I hope in this way to appear to advantage; but, dear Bertha, it will not do for you to creep behind that cypress. It looks as if you had chosen that place in your capacity of widow, and that is—"

Gertrude could not finish her sentence, for Liedgren entered, accompanied by Mayor D——, Judge C—— and Rector E—— from the city of S——näs.

The gentlemen greeted the two ladies. Judge C——, an uncommonly intelligent and cultivated man, immediately seated himself by Bertha. Gertrude made an ugly face when she saw the three gentlemen, all of whom were married men of full forty years of age.

A few moments afterward Notary Wicker entered, a young man, tall in stature, with a gray complexion, spectacles, sleek brown hair and ditto whiskers, high broad shoulders, and a gait in which the arms took as lively a part as the legs. After he had greeted his principal, Bertha, and the guests, he advanced with long strides to Gertrude, with whom he entered into a very animated conversation.

"Has the new notary arrived?" inquired Gertrude.

"Yes, alas," answered Wicker, sighing in a comical way.

"Why do you say alas?"

"Because that man is irresistible. As yet, no young girl, married woman or widow, has been able to see him without losing her peace of mind. I know beforehand that he will rob me of all my conquests, and I am thinking seriously of going and drowning myself."

The notary pulled out a snuff-box and took a great pinch. At that instant steps were heard in the hall. Two gentlemen entered. One was an old military man, the other a young, elegant gentleman, whose clothes were in the extreme of fashion, his shirt-bosom as fine, his boots as bright, his hands as white, and his whole appearance as completely a dandy's as possible. He carried himself with all the confidence and ease which familiarity with social life and the consciousness of one's outer and inner advantages can bestow.

He bowed first to Gertrude, as she stood nearest to him.

"My daughter, Notary Wenner," said Liedgren.

The notary's eyes slipped by Gertrude, without dwelling a single second on her blooming face, and were directed to Bertha.

"Fru Lagerskog and the notary are old acquaintances, if I am not mistaken," said Liedgren, looking at Bertha.

"Yes. I have that honor," answered the elegant notary, but to Gertrude's great joy, with some uncertainty.

When the notary, after first exchanging a few words with the judge, approached Bertha, she seemed very unlike herself. The calmness and coldness which generally pervaded her manner were not there, but it looked as though the sight of the young man had called forth some very bitter and painful recollections.

"I have hesitated whether I should dare to show myself before your eyes," said the notary, laying his hand on the back of the little sofa where Bertha sat. "Although a year has elapsed since we last met, and many changes have occurred, I feared that I would occasion you a torment through my presence, and yet I could not avoid meeting you here."

The stylish and conceited dandy, as Gertrude entitled the new-comer in her thoughts, had an appearance, while he was talking with Bertha, which was in complete contrast with the aspect he had when he bowed to Gertrude.

Conny Wenner looked at Bertha as if he begged her

with his eyes for a friendly word. While he was speaking, Bertha had entirely controlled the emotion she experienced at his entrance. Her mien was calm, her glance cold, when she with her somewhat chilling smile turned to him.

"The past, Herr notary, is like the dead, it has ceased to be. To waste words upon it, is to busy ourselves with something that does not exist."

"How shall I interpret these words?" replied Conny eagerly. "Do you really mean to say that you have forgiven me for what I have done?"

"Let that remain in oblivion. We now meet under very different conditions. That we have met before, we may as well forget."

"That is impossible."

"Impossible is not a fitting expression. When I promise forgetfulness, it is your duty not to have any memory, and if you retain it, then keep it to yourself."

Bertha smiled kindly at Conny, who bowed respectfully. At that moment, a new guest entered the saloon.

"Count Strålkrans, Fru Lagerskog," introduced the host.

The count bowed deeply. Bertha's greeting was colder than usual.

The count uttered some civilities and then went to pay his respects to Gertrude.

Dinner was served and was unusually animated. When it was over and the count led Bertha back to the saloon, he took his place beside her.

"I learn from Judge Liedgren, Fru Lagerskog, that you owned the estate which I have lately purchased. I have thus the good fortune of being your successor."

"And I hope, count, that you will think a great deal of Kungsdal, which has an exceedingly beautiful situation. I only regret that you had to pay rather too high a price for the place, according to what I am told."

"If that is so, you may blame Judge Liedgren and Notary Wenner for it. They tried to contest my right to it by constantly raising their bids; but I was determined to possess Kungsdal, and it had to become mine."

"So your will conquered?"

"It always does, madam. But allow me one question. Why did you sell Kungsdal? If the place is as beautiful as it has the reputation of being, I do not understand how its owner could abandon it, still less part with it."

"I have abandoned it because my relatives here offered me a home, and I have not kept it because my means did not admit of it."

For a while the count and Bertha conversed about the delights of country life, and then they passed over to travels.

After coffee had been passed around, Gertrude proposed a promenade.

The May afternoon was glorious, and the gentlemen accepted the proposal with avidity. The count offered Bertha his arm. Conny approached Gertrude; but she was already engaged by Notary Wicker, a circumstance which caused Conny to withdraw. The next instant, however, he was again at her side.

They directed their course to a Chinese temple which was built on a high rock, and from which they had a very extensive view and could even see the roof of Kungsdal.

"There you see your new home, Herr count!" exclaimed Gertrude, turning to Strålkrans. "If you hoisted a flag from the top of the house, and we from the temple here, we could greet each other every morning and establish a telegraph between Brovik and Kungsdal."

"If I were of Notary Wenner's age, I would avail myself of this way of expressing my respect and admiration for you every day," answered the count. "As it is, I fear that my flag would never have the pleasure of greeting yours, but would float quite solitary from the roof of Kungsdal, a sad symbol of the owner, who dwells there alone."

"Ah, that would not happen," assured Gertrude. "I would see to it that Brovik sent a greeting to Kungsdal every morning."

"In that case your kindness might make me forget my solitude to some extent."

"Solitude—and why are you solitary, count?" rejoined Gertrude. "You need only express the desire, to see yourself surrounded with guests."

"True; but even if I had the house full of them, I would still be solitary."

"Well, with friends then?"

"Yes—but those are generally very scarce."

"You are determined that we shall pity you, count!" exclaimed Gertrude, smiling. "But I have no idea of doing such a thing."

"Alas, I know that you speak the truth, and that only makes my fate still darker," said the count, with an air which indicated that he at least bore it without sinking under it.

Notary Wicker now gave the conversation another direction, and soon afterward they descended the height which led to the Chinese temple.

Conny was unusually silent. His glance frequently flitted over to Bertha, who walked by the count's side, and when the promenade was at last ended and the count took leave, in order to go to Kungsdal and survey his new country-seat, Gertrude, who was quick-sighted, had come to the conclusion that Wenner was head and ears in love with Bertha.

CHAPTER III.

IN Notary Wicker's outer room, that same evening, we find Conny stretched out in a rocking-chair, smoking his cigar and conversing with his comrade, with whom he became acquainted when court began.

"Well, dear Wicker," said Conny, "I presume that you have given the ladies a rather distorted description of my person. You have said—"

"Wait a moment," interrupted Wicker, lighting his cigar; "I have not spoken about you to more than one lady, and that was the daughter of the house."

"You are dead in love with her yourself. Well then, you have probably painted me finely."

"Ah yes, I did not spare colors when I gave her your portrait."

"Were you then afraid of having me for a rival?"

Wicker took a pinch of snuff and looked at the ceiling.

"Not far from it."

"Are you in love with the girl?"

"I will answer that question directly. But first let me know whether you have ever seen a handsomer pair of eyes?"

Conny passed his hand over his brow, muttering:

"Yes, I have."

"Then I congratulate you. This has not been the case with me. It seems to me that she is among the prettiest girls I have known."

"Perhaps, I have not observed it."

"Where the deuce were your eyes?" burst out Wicker.

"Not on your flame, at least. So you are in love, and in love with your principal's daughter. You hope to get the girl with the gold and possessions."

"I hope nothing at all. The daughter is fickle as the wind, the father fond of money and proud as a peacock; but that does not hinder me from thinking it very amusing to instil in her the conviction that you are the most conceited, the most frivolous and the vainest fool of a notary who ever tramped in a pair of patent-leather boots. I have described you as a dangerous man, a man who, about himself, had the thought: I came, I saw, I conquered."

"Thank you very much," answered Conny abstractedly.

"Gertrude also told me that she intended to rebuke your pride."

"Indeed; I am particularly obliged to you for giving her that idea, but I am afraid that I will not be so easy to educate."

Conny sprang up from the rocking-chair, adding:

"Oh, that I were what people consider me to be! a frivolous and vain dandy, who finds his happiness in looking at his image in the glass, and his enjoyment in pleasing women, how happy I would then be."

He went to the window, which stood open, and remained standing there a while. Wicker hummed:

"Fortune, come, be thou propitious!" Then he burst out:

"But, my dear Wenner, you certainly are vain and frivolous, so I do not think that you have any reason to complain of yourself in that respect."

"Possible,—let us not dispute. You see the acts, but you do not know the motives. Therefore, leave me. Let us instead speak of the persons with whom I am to live."

"Shall we begin with the old man?" asked Wicker.

"We may speak of him interminably and yet not get at the whole of him. He is like a complicated law-suit. A man is obliged to write endless reports and adjust them, before he learns what he never will learn anyhow."

"It is not worth while talking about him," said Conny. "I desire to know something about the ladies."

"About the daughter, whom you did not honor with a glance." Wicker took a pinch of snuff and looked at his companion with a mocking expression.

"You, Wicker, are then as full of the devil as ever!" exclaimed Conny rather impatiently. "You can well understand that I wish to know something about the condition of the house, and in what relation these persons stand to each other."

"All right, we will come to that directly. In the first place we have Fru Lagerskog, an excellent woman, who resides here. She is the good genius of the daughter; openly adored by the girl and secretly by the father."

"You don't say so!" exclaimed Conny. "Is the old man—"

"In love," interrupted Wicker, laughing. "Yes, sir, it looks very much like it, but I hope that none but the undersigned and the object herself suspect it. Well, well, you need not stare at me on that account. The man is only a little over forty, and he ought in all conscience to have the right to adore a woman, if he finds it pleasant."

"And she?" inquired Conny.

"She is inaccessible to all. Mild, friendly and kind to everybody, she nevertheless keeps both the judge and the notaries at a proper distance. It is impossible to get an inch nearer to her than she wishes. The only human being, man or woman, who has come upon an intimate footing with her, is Gertrude; otherwise she draws a circle around her over which none dare tread."

"Thus you believe that—"

"That father Liedgren will have to keep still and postpone his proposition indefinitely;—yes, that is my conviction."

"Well, the count then?"

"Strålkrans, you mean. There are two sides to that matter. He sees her to-day for the first time—in this house."

"What do you mean?"

"I mean a good deal, but what I mean is limited entirely to my own conclusions, and is no proof of anything."

"Let me hear your conclusions, however."

"Certainly, they run thus: Fru Lagerskog, since she came here, has in a very singular but careful way avoided meeting Count Strålkrans. Last summer he spent several weeks with Councillor U——, at Hofgard. We were all invited there, and went too, but Fru Lagerskog gave her deep mourning as an excuse and stayed at home. The councillor's family were afterward invited here, together with the count. The day before they came Fru Lagerskog went to Kungsdal and could not be persuaded to remain, in spite of the most pressing entreaties. She did not wish to appear in large companies as long as she was in deep mourning. During the winter, the judge went to Stockholm, as usual, with his daughter, for a few weeks. Fru Lagerskog accompanied them, but could not be induced to accept a single invitation. It was during these weeks that Gertrude became a little smitten with the count."

"But there is nothing in all this which leads me to think that she avoided the count."

"But it does me. Before the journey to the capital, Gertrude talked constantly about the count, that they would meet him in Stockholm, etc. In short, I will give my soul upon it, that the count and Fru Lagerskog have known each other before. That the count has been put to it in some way, on the beautiful woman's account, and that she has therefore tried to avoid him since she became a widow."

"If she is to avoid all who have been smitten with her, she will have to—"

"To avoid you in the first place," said Wicker. "Admit that that auction was ridiculous. First the old man, who was bent upon having Kungsdal, then you, who bid like one possessed, and finally the count, who bought it right before your noses. A man might have laughed himself to death. But to return to the family here, the state of affairs in the house is the following: the old man has no objection to have his daughter married, so that he, if luck favors him, may have an opportunity of getting married himself to the widow. The girl, for her part, would have no objection to become a countess, provided the widow did not stand between her and the count. The count would like nothing better than to have the widow, if you did not block the way. And you, jubilant with felicity, would marry the widow, if she were willing to have you; and I would be exceedingly glad to travel off to the altar with Gertrude, if she could be prevailed upon to accept me for her future lord and master."

Wicker ceased. Conny turned away from him, and again looked out into the silent spring night.

"Admit, Wenner, that there is substance in all this for something highly interesting," resumed Wicker. "There will be jealousy on all sides, terrible passions, boundless, unsatisfied desires, as well as an incessant running, one after the other, while each one runs away. I run after Gertrude, she after the count, the count after the widow, who is besides chased by you and the old man. If I do not succeed in marrying Gertrude, I will at least have material enough for a whole romance. And in my resentment I shall certainly plague the public by letting the offspring of my genius come out as a serial in the daily paper."

"You are welcome to do it," said Conny, "but what do you think the end will be?"

"That the count will get Gertrude and the old man the widow, while you and I will each have a long face over it. I will then rush out and swallow two bottles of champagne, after which I will seek my consolation at the parsonage, and you, you will find yours—on the stage; and now, good night."

Wicker struck Conny on the shoulder.

"Yes, it is time for us to separate," said the latter, looking at his watch.

"But before that, we will give each other the hand to camp out together as good friends and comrades, without letting envy and the like step between us," said Wicker.

"There you have my hand upon it," answered Wenner, "and now, good night."

In a few moments he walked across the lawn and took his way up to his room in the main building.

CHAPTER IV.

LETTER from Notary Conny Wenner to Paul Fredriksson:

"BROTHER: Almost two months have elapsed since I arrived here, and yet this is the first letter you have received from me.

"When our ways separated in the capital, you and Hanna went to Copenhagen, I here, and I promised to give you an account of much which was not clear to you. I promised, besides, to be the first who wrote, and yet I have made you wait eight weeks. You have probably thought about me: the volatile and foolish boy is just as he has always been, forgetful of everything except that which diverts him or flatters his ambition.

"Paul, you judge unwisely, and do not know what you are talking about. I am not volatile, not a fool who runs after pleasure, not a lunatic who stretches out his arms after the shapeless phantom which is called—flattered vanity. I am *a man* who already in his twenty-first year knows more than well what he is aiming for.

"You shake your head thoughtfully and murmur the name of Mina. Wait a moment and you will learn with how much calculation I acted, when I gave myself the appearance of being her lover. But let us proceed in order.

"Since I left the gymnasium, we have only been together for short periods. Through this transient connection you have only had the opportunity of seeing the surface of my actions, which you, without knowing the motives, considered too frivolous. You have heard about me that I was as fickle a fellow, when it concerned the fair sex, as I was commendable in my official career. Praise and blame have thus alternately reached your ears. Add to this that I have been a lion in my attire, effeminate in my habits, and gladly taken a part in social life, and it must be very hard for you to decide what sort of man I have become, especially as I have been extremely reserved for these four years, and have not cared to speak of myself. The only thing which still remained as a guide for your judgment was my unchanged affection for you. Neither time nor circumstances have effaced it.

"Still, the moment may now be at hand to let you know something more of me than the surface.

"When I turned my back upon my gay student-life and started on the journey to the place where I was to begin my career as a lawyer, an inexplicable fate ordained that I should meet the woman who for the first time led my thoughts to love.

"I had not seen her since our first acquaintance, and when we again met I was considerably changed. I had tasted of the tree of the knowledge of good and evil, been the slave of many base desires and yielded to temptations which ought not to have enticed me. I was, in short, better acquainted with the evil than with the good, and I had besides a blind faith in myself.

"I will not describe our meeting. I will only tell you, that when I took possession of my lodgings in Stockholm, I felt that her power over my soul would be decisive for all life. I was not able to visit her in her home as soon as I desired, for I was hindered from it by a letter from Professor Wenner. He had been taken ill and called me back to Upsala to bid me farewell before his death. But I arrived too late. My fatherly friend was dead and I was made his adopted son and heir.

"It was thus under the name of Wenner that I entered myself in court and was announced at the Lagerskogs'.

"They received me well. I went there often, and soon the sight of Bertha was as indispensable to me as the air I breathed. My first boyish fancy became a strong and earnest feeling. I did not love with the violence of caprice, but with the whole strength of my soul, and so reverently, that during this time I did not with a half word or a glance venture to show her that she was the soul of my existence. Her conversation became to me a revelation from a better world, and she was to me the interpreter of everything grand, beautiful and noble. The influence she exerted was such, that I could not have met her eyes, if I had known myself to be guilty of any act for which I needed to blush.

"Ideal love is a beautiful dream here on earth; but it does not last long, before it is polluted by human desires.

"Shortly after my first visit to the Lagerskogs, he began to suffer from a complaint in one knee, which kept him confined to the house and the easy-chair. Bertha was his daily and hourly companion. She did not seek any recreation, never left her home, but gladly received all those who could contribute in cheering and diverting her husband.—I was one of the fortunate few whom she was particularly delighted to see, and the oftener I came, the better.—It was thus at the side of the husband that my admiration for the wife grew and developed.

"Lagerskog was generally jealous; but this jealousy was exclusively directed to one object, and that was Strålkrans.

"You know that Strålkrans had been appointed Minister of War, the same fall I arrived at Stockholm. His name was consequently often mentioned in the papers as well as in private. But never was it uttered in Lagerskog's presence without his changing expression or indulging in some remarks about Strålkrans.—This rooted jealousy of one single person made him blind to the homage other men paid to his richly endowed wife. Even my increasing attachment escaped his attention, and he seemed to have an especial confidence in me which he did not cherish for others. This was something which Bertha also showed. She was more friendly to me than the rest, often conversed with me about my career, my life and my ambition, and seemed to entertain actual affection for me, but an affection which not even my conceit could give the name of anything but what it was.

"Women do not know what a dangerous enemy to all our fine resolutions their sympathy is.—I allowed myself to be flattered by it, was happy, and desired nothing higher than that it might always remain so.

"My ambition, which had hitherto been a bright dream of youth, became under Bertha's influence something very earnest. It developed into a positive spur to my actions, just because my love was an idyl without success or future.

"So passed the winter, and spring came.—Lagerskog could now take short walks, leaning on a cane; but notwithstanding this improvement, his physicians had advised him to take a journey to Paris, in order to consult a distinguished physician there.—I had also made up my mind to spend three months in England and France. We travelled together.—I accompanied them to Paris, spent a few weeks there, and then went to England, intending to return again to France, and in the Lagerskogs' company journey homeward. While I was in England, and did not see Bertha, my fancy grew in a formidable manner, and now for the first time it took another character and changed to a violent passion.

"My joy, when we again met in Paris, must have

betrayed me, for from that moment she was different. Her manner became colder, her demeanor stiff, and it was now impossible for me to get her to smile at me as kindly and heartily as before. Instead of this warning me to be on my guard, it tormented and irritated me. I became envious of her husband when she was friendly toward him, envious of all who received a pleasant word from her, and my state of mind was reflected in my behavior; but the only result was that Bertha entrenched herself still more behind her coldness and her pride. Under such conditions we started to return. Lagerskog was now completely recovered and had regained his good humor, that is to say, his mania for talking. His stupidity provoked me, his manner to Bertha made my blood boil, and his desire to let people understand that he had done her a great honor when he married her, made me frantic. I, who had before submitted to his follies, talked nonsense with him to keep him in good spirits, could not endure to have him open his mouth. If he only said a word, I was of a contrary opinion, and the journey home became an incessant dispute between him and me, although I saw plainly how it tormented Bertha. But what did I care for that, now that I had become jealous? In this way we arrived at Lübeck. There we went on board, to continue our way to Stockholm by water.

"We set sail from Lübeck at eight o'clock in the morning. Lagerskog, whose knee had pained him the night before, immediately went down to his state-room. Bertha stayed on deck, engaged in a conversation with a Captain Ström and his wife. I did not approach Bertha as long as she talked with them, but stood in a gloomy frame of mind and took umbrage because she could be so friendly toward others, when she was continually cold to me.

"Finally Fru Ström retired to her state-room. Then I advanced.

"'Ah,' it is well that I met you, Herr notary,' said Bertha, 'I have a few words I desire to say to you.'

"'Indeed, have you anything to talk to me about these days?' answered I, bitterly.

"'Several little matters.' At these words she fastened her eyes upon me. 'I intended to ask you to desist from constant disputes with my husband. He is an elderly man. You are quite young, and it must therefore irritate him to be opposed by you in everything. It is true, this is something to which you may be indifferent, but you will not be so, when you learn that he ought not to be excited for the sake of his health.'

"'Madam, there is something still more powerful than his health, and that is your will,' I replied. 'Say that you desire this proof of affection of me, and I promise never to oppose your husband; but do not ask me to pay any regard to him and his well-being in other respects.'

"'Yet it is this that I counted upon your doing,' said Bertha. 'You do not owe me any proof of affection, but it is incumbent upon every one to pay regard to that which is injurious to a sick person.' Bertha looked as if she had been cut out of stone.

"My answer was precipitate, was a confession. She rose to go. I seized her arm, saying:

"'Do not go, but be merciful. Speak kindly, speak encouraging and comforting words to me. You must see that you hold my peace, my whole life in your hands. Be as before, and I will go through fire for you.'

"'Yes, to-day, but to-morrow you will again cause me to repent my friendliness.'

"She again tried to rise; but my hand held her fast. At that instant two passengers went by us. Involuntarily I turned my eyes from her to see who they were. Bertha greeted one of them.

"My hand dropped hers; the person she greeted was

Count Strålkrans. The next minute she had left the deck, and the count came straight to me.

"It was the first time since we separated from him in * * * that I found myself face to face with this man, whom I had to thank for everything.

"'Allow me to ask one question,' said the count, looking at me fixedly: 'Is Fru Lagerskog's husband not on board?'

"'Yes, he is,' answered I, uncovering my head, as a subordinate always does before his superior.

"'I have been told that he was ill.'

"'He has been so, but is now better.'

"'I thank you for the information, and beg you to excuse my questions; but I am an old acquaintance of Fru Lagerskog's. My name is Strålkrans, and now you will perhaps allow me to know whom I have addressed?'

"'My name is at present Wenner, but was originally Fredriksson. Probably this name sounds strange to you, Herr count, and yet, I am indebted to you for all I possess, and all that I am.'

"My voice was unsteady when I spoke.

"'Indebted to me?' repeated the count. 'Impossible, I cannot remember that we have ever met before.'

"'Yes, in * * * about sixteen years ago,' I replied. 'Herr count, you see in me the little organ-grinder who through you was changed to a rich boy. If you have forgotten this occurrence, it is impossible for me to forget my benefactor or the great debt in which I stand to you.'

"'Ah! now I remember!' exclaimed Strålkrans in a tone of surprise. Then he contracted his brows and added almost harshly: 'I desire with all my soul that you, as well as I, may forget that we met in * * *. If I was then so fortunate as to procure you Fortuna's protection, I am glad of it for your sake; but I have on the other hand so many reasons to try to forget this period of my life, that it annoys me to be reminded of it.' He offered me his hand, adding: 'It is a pleasure for me to know that the little organ-grinder has become a man in the service of the state, and I hope that he, as such, will rightly understand the claims the community has upon him.'

"I bowed respectfully and pressed his hand with warmth. The count continued:

"'And now, Herr notary, I ask of you the promise that the world, as well as you yourself, may assume that we have met to-day for the first time. If you consider yourself to stand in any obligation to me, then prove it by keeping the promise I demand of you like a man.'

"'Your will shall be obeyed by me in all respects,' was my assurance.

"Strålkrans smiled and said in a half jesting, half serious tone:

"'You ought to thank me for not taking this assurance in too broad a sense, for then it might easily happen that your desires came in conflict with my will. Still, you have nothing to fear. One piece of advice I will give you, however; do not expose Fru Lagerskog through your importunity. People have already drawn very derogatory conclusions from the fact of your travelling with them, and do not forget that it is a woman of an uncommonly estimable character whom you make the prey of scandal. Take care that you do not become the one who injures her reputation irreparably.'

"The count raised his hat and left me.

"When Strålkrans walked away my soul was seized with an almost frantic jealousy.

"The day passed without my seeing either Bertha or Lagerskog again. The latter was sea-sick and the former invisible.

"Toward evening a lady came up on deck. In the half twilight it seemed to me that it was Bertha. She was of the same size and wore, like the latter, a gray cape. I hastened after her, exclaiming:

"'At length I have caught a glimpse of you!'

"The lady turned her head and looked at me. It was not Bertha, but a lady unknown to me and uncommonly beautiful. The look she fixed upon me was full of significance. It said that I had before me a woman who could not be mentioned in the same breath as Bertha. She gave me an answer as if what I had said had actually been to her, and then forced me to a few moments' conversation. Still, I was too much taken up by the tumult within me to long continue the miserable badinage which men employ with women for whom they do not consider it necessary to put themselves out. I therefore left the unknown and went down to take a survey of my own state-room. In the little cabin I found the count standing, smoking his cigar. He had stopped outside the door of Bertha's state-room. A host of crazy thoughts arose in my brain when I noticed that the state-room door was not quite closed. I was well aware that Lagerskog and Bertha did not occupy the same state-room. The count went up the stairs, and without considering what I did, I peeped in Bertha's state-room. It was empty. I went in. What my especial object was, I could not tell, but it seemed to me that I could not endure to live if I was not allowed to talk to her.

"I seated myself on the sofa, and leaned my head against her cape, which hung on the wall, pressing to my lips a little shawl that I had seen her wear.

"A few moments elapsed, then the door opened, and Bertha entered. When she saw me, she was going to withdraw immediately; but I grasped her by the arm and said with a suppressed and agitated voice:

"'Happen what will, you shall not go until you have heard me. Otherwise I will do that which is not right.'

"Scarcely had these words passed my lips, than the door opened and Lagerskog stood before us. Behind him I saw Captain Ström, the husband of the lady with whom Bertha had conversed.

"'What does this mean?' roared Lagerskog, without considering that he, through his heedlessness, exposed his wife to all the persons who came down from the deck.

"I had not time to say anything, for at that instant my new acquaintance peeped in, and said composedly, turning to Lagerskog:

"'It means, sir, that your wife and I have the same state-room, and I consider it very improper for you to intrude here.' Thereupon she turned to me with the words: 'How is this, sir, can you so forget yourself as to make visits in my state-room? You knew that I was on deck. I really ought to be angry with you. Now give me my shawl which lies there, and offer me your arm. We can talk much more comfortably up there on deck than down here.'

"More like a somnambulist than one awake, I took her shawl and followed her.

"Do you wish to know who this woman was that at least saved Bertha from open scandal? Why, my brother, it was the danseuse Mina Dahl.

"About the remainder of the journey there is not much to say, except that Lagerskog took his wife into his state-room. Captain Ström and his wife seemed to have resolved to watch all my motions, so did they pursue me with their eyes; and I had no other resource than to occupy myself with Mina. Through this I wished to try to mislead the passengers and give them the idea that my visit in the state-room was made to her. Still I only succeeded in part; Ström had seen me hold Bertha's hands clasped in mine, and was not slow to whisper this to a couple of my acquaintances.

"I had thus, for the second time in my life, placed an innocent and extremely estimable woman in a false light through my imprudence. From the way in which Lagerskog guarded his wife during the remainder of the journey, I saw with despair that I had made her suspected even by her husband.

"Lagerskog left the steamer at our arrival in Stockholm, without saying a word to me in farewell. He only flung an enraged glance at me in passing. Count Strålkrans went off without deigning to give me a glance. His manner was haughty, and I read in his proud face that he not only knew what had transpired, but considered my behavior ignoble.

"So ended my journey abroad.

"I had not been in Stockholm many days, before people came to me from right and left and inquired how matters stood between Fru Lagerskog and me. They told me that the strangest reports were in circulation, and that it was said that something very scandalous had occurred on board the steamer. I raved at myself and my constant weakness, which occasioned so much harm. I exerted all my power to give a different aspect to the affair, as I declared that I had gone after Mina's shawl, and in so doing fallen in collision with that crazy, jealous husband.

"In order to lend probability to my words, I became, to all appearance, Mina's declared lover. I lavished presents upon her, did everything to draw attention to her and me. Mina was so completely indifferent to me that it was a torment and not a pleasure to visit her. The only bond that existed between us was her consciousness of the fact that I had not visited the state-room on her account. She had saved Bertha, as she believed, and she made me pay for it. It was not long before people generally said that the danseuse, Mina Dahl, was Wenner's mistress; but the general report was false. She had never been, and can never become, what they asserted that she was to me. I laid myself open to such talk, because I hoped through this to save Bertha.

"Six weeks after Lagerskog's return home he removed from Stockholm to Kungsdal. That spring I also left the capital, to accompany Judge K—— to the assizes. It was at this man's house that I made acquaintance with Liedgren. I continued to reside with K—— until last fall, when I returned to Stockholm and there played the rôle of the lion of the day, all the while with my thoughts fastened upon the time, when I, according to the agreement with Liedgren, was to live with him.

"Bertha had become a widow, and I was burning with impatience to see her again. That is the main cause why I accepted Liedgren's offer.

"In May I came here to Brovik and saw Bertha. The years which lay between the time when I parted from her and our meeting have not had any power to weaken my feeling. When I stood before her, begging forgiveness for the past, I felt that she was to me dearer than ever.

"At my first appearance in my principal's house, fate so ordained that Strålkrans and I met. We had stumbled over each other shortly before, when the auction was held at Kungsdal. I had presented myself there to purchase the home which had belonged to Bertha, and if possible, through raising the price, contribute to make her pecuniary condition better. I knew that her husband left her affairs in a bad state. When the place was put up, I encountered two opponents, who were probably actuated by the same motives as I, namely Strålkrans and Liedgren. Strålkrans went victorious from the strife. The estate belonged to him.

"Eight weeks have elapsed since I made my entrance into this house. For eight weeks I have seen Bertha daily and felt that there is only one woman on earth that I can love, and this woman is she.

"Notwithstanding this I have devoted myself to another and avoided Bertha as much as possible.

"This other is a child of eighteen, my principal's daughter Gertrude. Spoiled and rather pretty, she nevertheless has no ability to interest. I seek her society only because she constantly talks about Bertha. It is generally supposed that I am attracted to Gertrude, and I would really withdraw and not be at her side so continually, if there was the slightest risk of her becoming attached to me.

"I play in this house a rôle very unusual to me, namely that of not being at all noticed by the ladies. I am entirely pressed aside by Strålkrans. When he enters everybody's interest and attention is fastened upon him, and we young men play the part of schoolboys, who are completely overlooked. If I succeed in entertaining Bertha and Gertrude with my conversation, the impression is blown away as soon as the count appears. Gertrude forgets in his society that she has found pleasure in mine, so engrossed is she by his conversation. The count on his side seems to take a lively interest in the pretty child.

"His manner toward Bertha is measured and ceremonious. Gertrude, on the contrary, he treats with so much cordiality, that it looks as though she were the one whom he had chosen to sweeten his solitude.

"And yet this man has once spoken the language of love to Bertha, and been in despair when she did not have any affection to bestow upon him.

"Inexplicable inconstancy of the human heart!

"Bertha is toward the count as toward all, calm, friendly and polite.

"Liedgren looks as though he were engaged in unravelling a complicated law-suit. He follows everybody with his eyes, encourages me in my politeness to Gertrude and does not seem quite pleased with the count's frequent visits to Brovik.

"You need not consider me too conceited, if I say that Liedgren desires a union between Gertrude and me. He has manifested this design of his too plainly for me to avoid seeing it. I only regret that I cannot meet his wishes in this respect. Were my heart free, my vanity and ambition might possibly tempt me to catch at the bait which the father throws. As it is, I neither can nor will marry his daughter, and besides, Gertrude's fancy for the count has settled the matter.

"Besides, who can tell but what Bertha, when she is obliged to realize how deeply she is loved by me, will be moved by my attachment and finally yield me an affection, the possession of which I, at this moment, would pay for with years of my life?

"It is said that women cannot resist the influence of a strong and faithful love.

"Foolish hopes, which mock my soul.

"My aim I have once for all marked out, it is, not to find happiness at a woman's side, but to become a distinguished jurist and nothing else.

"And now, Paul, try to form some sort of an image from this letter of your brother

"CONNY.

"P. S.—Many friendly greetings to Hanna. How does she accommodate herself to her fate as the wandering singer's wife?—Well, undoubtedly. Love beautifies everything, say the poets.—Amen!"

CHAPTER V.

THE August moonlight cast its mild rays over Brovik and its pleasant surroundings. By the edge of the river, which wound through the park, strolled Bertha and Gertrude, engaged in a lively conversation.

"Dear Gertrude, said Bertha, "explain your behavior to me. You say that your heart is not in the least attached to the count, that you are to-day more indifferent to him than you were at your first acquaintance, and yet you have shown yourself so interested in him."

"Has it actually appeared to you, too, as though I had been so?" asked Gertrude, stopping at the side of a little knoll.

"Yes, I have really thought that he had made a deep impression upon you."

"Is it possible, Bertha, that you have been so short-sighted? In that case I have played my part well. Sit down here," added Gertrude, throwing herself on the grass, "and I will confess. The interest I have evinced for the count has only been a mask behind which I concealed my feelings. I wished to mislead all, even myself; but now, now it is ended with my ability to act. I loathe it; and feel unhappy at seeming to be what I am not."

Gertrude burst into tears.

Bertha took Gertrude's head between her hands and said with tenderness:

"What, Gertrude, are you weeping, you, the glad, merry Gertrude, bathed in tears? What has then happened? Speak, tell me what it is that so troubles you."

"The disquietude within me is what makes me weep," whispered Gertrude, putting her arms around Bertha's waist. Leaning against her, she added with an almost inaudible voice: "Bertha, I am in love!"

"But not with the count?"

"No, no, no; I love some one else, some one that is far more worthy love than the count."

"And who could that well be?"

"Can you not guess?" Gertrude looked up in Bertha's face. It was paler than usual, probably the result of the moon's rays.

"It cannot be Wenner?" exclaimed Bertha.

"Whom else could it be?" stammered Gertrude.

"I have not suspected that for an instant," resumed Bertha. "You have been so unconstrained in your manner toward him, so little embarrassed, and have given the count such an absolute preference that it is really necessary for you to tell me that I have guessed right, for me to believe it."

"Ah, Bertha, from the first moment Wenner entered this house my heart was his. The desire to take down his self-love disappeared, and I only desired that—that—he might find me amiable."

"And yet you have often expressed yourself disapprovingly about him during these weeks, and that he appeared like a fop who lived and found his whole delight in fashionable clothes, comfortable rooms and dainty meals."

"Yes, I have said it, and perhaps thought at times that he attached too great importance to the enjoyments of wealth. But what then, these faults became in my eyes only attractive qualities. Everything about him has pleased me and contributed to make him the object of my warmest love. I hold him dearer than my father, than you, than all else on earth."

"And yet this play with the count?"

"The count has only been a means for me, through which I was enabled not to show Wenner the true nature of what I felt. I first wished to be convinced that he liked me."

"And are you now?"

"I think so at least. He has for three months daily and hourly paid me attention, when we have been together; conversed about things that entertained me, and if I expressed the slightest desire, he has hastened to gratify it. God knows, however, whether I would have had courage to speak to you now, if papa had not asked me yesterday whether I would like to have Wenner for a husband. I became terribly confused and anxious, and have since felt that I would not have any peace in my soul until I had spoken to you. Say, Bertha, do you believe that he has said anything to papa? Do you think that he has proposed?"

"No, dear Gertrude, I do not. I even fear that you have valued his politeness too highly. Think if he did not cherish any love for you, if all this has only been a tribute of respect paid to his principal's daughter."

"If that were so, there would only be two things for me to choose—either to die or to try to be loved by him."

A rustling sound was heard behind the two speakers. Bertha and Gertrude turned round hastily. Down the path came a large, stout woman. She carried a pack on her back and supported herself with a cane. Her attire consisted of a black checked skirt and jacket. Her head was covered with a large black handkerchief.

Bertha and Gertrude rose involuntarily. The woman's appearance evidently frightened them. She had in the meantime advanced, and when she saw that they were on the point of going, she lengthened her steps and soon stood quite near Bertha.

She fastened a pair of black eyes on the beautiful widow and said in a rude tone:

"Is this the way to Kungsdal?"

"No, it lies on the other side the river," answered Fru Lagerskog. "If you cross the bridge over there, you will come to the Kungsdal road; but you have a good six miles to walk."

"That is pretty far." The woman set down her pack. "Is there any house here in the neighborhood where one can stop over night? Perhaps you can direct me. You surely don't have to go six miles to your home?"

"Go to Brovik," said Gertrude, "then you will have food and shelter for the night. It is not far to the house, you only have to follow the stream straight ahead."

Without answering the woman muttered:

"Brovik, Brovik,—just so, Brovik." She sat down on the pack and went on as if talking to herself. "The d——l; well, well, we are bound to meet. Brovik, h—m, h—m!"

She got up, put the pack on her back again and continued her way, without thanking them for the information.

"That woman has a sinister look," said Gertrude, gazing anxiously after the wanderer.

"Yes, her appearance does not inspire confidence. Come, let us go home. The evening is far advanced."

"Hush, didn't you hear something!" exclaimed Gertrude, seizing hold of Bertha's arm.

A horrible, mocking laugh was indeed heard; but it died away immediately, and now the young women caught the sound of quick and firm steps, approaching.

"God be praised that some one is coming, I am just as frightened as I can be. That was a horrid laugh," exclaimed Gertrude, as she looked in the direction from whence the steps came. Notaries Wicker and Wenner advanced by the same path that the woman had taken.

Gertrude hastened toward them, declaring that they came as if sent from heaven.

CHAPTER VI.

AT the breakfast table the following morning, both the judge and his assistants were absent. A murder had been committed the night before at the station, about three miles from Brovik. The judge and the notaries had gone to court to investigate the matter.

The inspector at Brovik related the occurrence to the ladies. It was young Baron Lodstein who had been murdered. He was on his way to Westmanland. The young baron had arrived at station X—— late in the evening, accompanied by his coachman and an old servant. He had ordered horses for the following morning at eight o'clock, and then retired, after he had taken supper. In the morning, when the servant was to awake his master, he found the door bolted inside. He knocked, but without receiving any answer. Uneasy at the silence in the room, he called the landlord. They now broke open the door. The baron lay murdered in bed, and the window stood open. Although the room was on the second floor, it was plain to be seen that the murderer had chosen this way to make his escape.

The baron's money, watch and rings were gone. He had thus been robbed besides.

This shocking event engrossed everybody's mind for a few days.

Gertrude and Bertha could not help thinking of the woman they had met in the park, especially as she had not been at Brovik that evening. She had consequently not followed the direction to obtain food and shelter there.

One week after the murder, Gertrude one afternoon went to the parsonage. Bertha stayed at home alone. At noon Count Strålkrans was announced, who desired to see Fru Lagerskog.

"Admit that my coming disturbs you, madam," said the count, kissing her hand respectfully, "but I have long desired to speak to you, and therefore I took the liberty of visiting you to-day."

Bertha assured him that she would listen with pleasure to what he had to communicate.

"It is about Gertrude I wish to speak," said the count.

"What did you wish to say to me about her, Herr count?" inquired Bertha, as Strålkrans did not continue.

"Very much, and yet, very little. It depends upon the progress of our conversation. You are her only and best friend, and consequently I do not turn to the wrong person, when I address myself to you, to solicit a frank answer to a question which concerns her. Tell me, how do you think she would receive the offer of my hand?"

It is possible that Bertha was prepared for the question; but for all that it called forth a crimson flame on her cheeks.

"Do you wish an honest answer, count?" asked she.

"Of course; I have in this respect counted entirely upon your goodness."

"Then I must tell you, although with regret, that Gertrude is attached to another. Count Strålkrans will not be the man she chooses if her choice is left free."

"But yet her behavior has given me a contrary idea," replied the count.

"In that case it grieves me that I shall be the one to snatch from you so sweet an illusion."

"Madam, it is not the first time you do so," rejoined the count, and added politely: "I would rather be deprived of my lady-love by you than by any one else. It looks as though success in love did not belong to the advantages fate has bestowed upon me. I had hoped, however, that this engaging child would not play with my heart. Still, experience ought to have made me distrustful."

A pause ensued, during which the count looked at Bertha.

"There is thus no hope that Gertrude will become my wife?" resumed he. "Will you not make yourself my intercessor by telling her that my prospects of domestic felicity rest entirely in her hands?"

"If you had asked this of me a few days ago, I would have felt happy in being able to fulfil a request of yours and in some measure work for your happiness. As it is, I know what I even two days ago was in ignorance of, namely that Gertrude is in love—but not with you."

The count rose hastily from his chair and went to the window. He stayed there and bent down over the flowers, as if to smell them. Bertha pressed her hands involuntarily to her breast.

"You would thus have worked for my marriage with Gertrude with joy, if her heart had been free?" resumed the count after a while.

"Yes, God is my witness," answered Bertha seriously.

"And wherefore?"

"Because I am convinced that you love her and that you would be happy at her side."

"Happy, I—and at any one's side but yours!" exclaimed the count, turning round quickly. At this instant their eyes met. Hers had a strange light.

"Count, you love Gertrude, do you not?" said Bertha.

"And she loves Wenner."

Bertha kept silent. The count returned to his seat, saying with less calmness than he had hitherto spoken:

"*You* know *whom* she loves. Tell me, can the young girl find any happiness through him? Do you not think that she would be happier as my wife, and perhaps one day forget the love which now binds her to this man, over whose life and feelings you alone prevail?"

"Count, your affection for Gertrude must be very intense, when you, notwithstanding the consciousness that her heart belongs to another, even think of such a thing as her becoming your wife."

"*Love* can only be felt once. If we have loved truly, we are not able to do it twice. If we have played bankrupt in love, affection and respect is all that we can then give," answered the count. "Now if Gertrude had been the one whom I loved, your words would still have brought me back to the consciousness that it is not only the possession of the beloved object that we ought to strive for, but something far more,—the promotion of her happiness. Forget therefore what I have said about Gertrude; no thought of her exists any longer in my soul."

"But yet, it pains you to give her up," whispered the young widow.

"Bertha!" burst out the count, seizing her hands impetuously, but he dropped them as hastily.

A few seconds elapsed. The count broke the silence.

"Do you know any woman who is called Christina Barsk?" asked he with the most indifferent tone in the world.

At these words Bertha stared at him in affright, stammering:

"I do not know her, but the name is familiar to me. What do you know about her?"

"Not very much; but I hoped to obtain some information about her from you."

"All I can tell you, is, that this woman received a pension from my mother. After she died, I have in vain made inquiries for her, in order to pay it; but could not ascertain where she stayed, and I finally believed that she was dead. If you happen to know anything about her I entreat you to tell me."

"Madam," replied the count, "I cannot give you any information, but I beg you, for my part, not to think of her. From this day she does not exist to you. And now, thank you for this conversation; farewell!"

The count kissed Bertha's hand, and a few minutes afterward his carriage rolled away from Brovik.

CHAPTER VII.

CONNY WENNER to his brother Paul.

"BROVIK, October 20, 18—

"BROTHER:—Your letter from Copenhagen has given me great joy. I need not say that I participate in your happiness with all my soul. Hanna has always been a good and lovely woman, and at the side of such a wife happiness must bloom unavoidably.

"I do not know whether you have read anything in the Swedish newspapers about the murder at station X——. I suppose, however, that you have not. Well then, the first court I have attended since my arrival here was an extra one, held on account of this murder. The murdered man was Baron Casper Lodstein.

"A silver-inlaid knife is all that the murderer left behind him, and if the victim had not had a stab between the shoulders, one would have been tempted to believe that he had taken his own life, so impossible is it to find any trace of his assassin.

"The investigation was conducted with the zeal and sagacity which distinguishes Liedgren, but still, has not led to the slightest discovery. The only thing they ascertained, was, that at D——by Station, where Lodstein took horses for X——, an old woman with a pack on her back had come up to the carriage and asked the coachman some questions about where his master was going, etc.; and whether he intended to stop over night in X——. To these inquiries the coachman had not given any answer; but when the stable-boy harnessed the horses, she renewed them to him, and was then told that the place of destination was X——, where the fine gentleman had ordered rooms for the night. After receiving this information, she went off. A little while later the baron drove from D——by, and the coachman, stable-boy and servant, all asserted that when they rode through Grenna woods they had seen the same woman sitting behind some bushes, talking to a man dressed like a nobleman. Not a shadow has been seen of such a person, however, either at X—— or on the road there. The only place besides D——by, where a woman like the one described has been visible, is here at Brovik, where Bertha and Gertrude met a stroller who asked the way to Kungsdal. This was the same night the murder was committed.

"At Kungsdal the woman with the pack is said to have shown herself, but then disappeared, leaving no trace.—No sign of the man with whom she was talking has been found, and all that is known, is, that he was of medium height, and dressed like a nobleman. At D——by, directly after the baron's departure, a person had come and ordered horses, but when he received the answer that it would be a half hour before they could procure any, he left immediately.

"Another circumstance, in connection with this terrible occurrence which made people lose themselves in conjectures, was, that on the floor, beside the murdered man's bed, was found a white kid glove, stained with blood. They believed at first that it belonged to the departed, but when they tried it on him, it was entirely too small. The blood-stained glove was strongly perfumed, and spread around it an odor of '*Mille fleures*,' a perfume which the murdered man did not have in his dressing-case.

"This glove has had a hand, and this hand has dealt the deadly blow, according to what various marks and stains on the glove indicate. The murderer has consequently not been an ordinary malefactor.

"I will not mention the terrible suspicions that have arisen in my mind, and yet they come back continually, absurd as they appear. If the murderer were really the one I imagine, he would inevitably have been seen somewhere. It is thus only a phantasm of mine, and yet I cannot get away from it.

"After one of the examinations, Liedgren said to me and my comrade:

"'Has either of you gentlemen any knowledge of the Lodstein family conditions?—I remember that the baron, who became Count D——'s heir, was related to the count on the mother's side.'

"'Yes, he was the count's nephew,' answered Wicker.

"'Good! His uncle, Baron Fabian, is married to a Fröken D——, is he not? It is thus Fabian Lodstein who will inherit the murdered man's property?'

"'Yes, he is indeed Casper Lodstein's nearest relative,' said Wicker, looking at Liedgren.

"In their glance lay something which indicated that they also nourished some very absurd suspicions.

"The first session ended, however, without leading to any results.

"Liedgren shortly afterward took a journey to the capital.

"The evening after the day Liedgren went to Stockholm, I entered the saloon.

"Bertha was there alone. I heard Gertrude's voice from the music-room. She sang, I know not what, so confused was I at finding myself tête-à-tête with Bertha.—She responded to my somewhat awkward greeting with a more friendly smile than she was accustomed to give me.

"'It is well that you came, Herr Wenner,' said she. 'I was just thinking of something of which I desired to speak to you.'

"Here we were interrupted by Wicker and Gertrude.—

The evening was spent very pleasantly. Bertha was less stiff, Gertrude less mischievous and Wicker less sharp than usual.

"The following morning at breakfast Gertrude was absent. She had gone to the parsonage and was to stay there all day. The others were invited there in the afternoon. After breakfast Wicker immediately left the dining-room.—Bertha and I were alone. I offered her my arm and conducted her to the saloon; but was so violently agitated that I could not possibly get a word over my lips.

"Bertha seated herself by one of the windows, and pointed to a chair opposite her.

"'As I was interrupted yesterday, when I intended to tell you something that lay on my heart, you must excuse me if I now ask you to stay and hear me. I am also compelled to ask you to listen to me with patience and to reflect well upon what I am going to say.'

"'I promise it, madam.'

"Bertha looked out of the window a moment, then she said quite abruptly:

"'Is not Gertrude Liedgren an uncommonly lovely girl?'

"Gertrude's name in Bertha's mouth sounded repugnant to my ears. I had expected to hear something very different, and the impression was therefore disagreeable in the highest degree.

"'I believe that Mamsell Liedgren is what you assert her to be,' answered I.

"'Believe? Have you no opinion of your own about it?'

"'No, I have not occupied myself enough with Mamsell Gertrude to form any.'

"'Have you not occupied yourself with her, you who ever since your arrival here have been with Gertrude constantly?'

"'That is true; but it does not prove that my thoughts have been engrossed by her. I find Mamsell Liedgren's company agreeable, and that which pleases us, we do not avoid;—but it surely was not of this you wished to speak to me?'

"'Yes, Herr notary, it is just of Gertrude I intended to speak. Your whole conduct, your politeness, and, allow me to say, your marked attention, all have given me the idea that you loved her, that—'

"'Hold, madam, *you* could not have believed any such thing.'

"'And why should I not have believed it? Would it have been better for me to consider you so frivolous that you, merely to divert yourself, paid a young, attractive girl all the delicate attention which a man generally shows only the woman to whom he renders his homage? No, Herr notary, I will not think so ill of you, as that you have heedlessly played with Gertrude's feelings.'

"'But, madam, you know more than well to whom my heart is bound, you cannot be in ignorance of it. Why then assert that I have occupied myself with Mamsell Liedgren? If you wish to know why I have done so, this is the reason: She talked about you.'

"'Thus it was to afford yourself a pleasure that you appeared to be interested in Gertrude?'

"'Yes, I admit it; but what harm have I done by it? Mamsell Liedgren's interest is bound up in Count Strålkrans.'

"'Do you think so?' Bertha's eyes rested on me, and I experienced a painful feeling at this question. Before my memory appeared various glances from Gertrude's eyes; in a word, several little things which I had overlooked, but which now enlightened me all at once that I might possibly have been mistaken when I believed that she cherished warm feelings for the count.

"Bertha resumed after a short pause:

"'I read in your face that you do not believe what you have just said, and perceive that you have now *again* been guilty of a course of action, through which a woman becomes the sufferer.'

"'Madam, I do not understand you,' I stammered.

"'Do you not? Then you wish me to speak more plainly. So be it. You have succeeded in making yourself loved by Gertrude, succeeded in giving her the idea that you loved her. She has allowed her heart to be enticed from her, while you were only amusing yourself. Tell me, Herr notary, are you pleased with your conduct?'

"Bertha's words pained me. She, who knew how deeply I loved her, ought to have treated me more mercifully, I thought.

"'It is not the point whether I am pleased or displeased,' I replied. 'If it is as you say, I can only regret deeply that Mamsell Liedgren has so misunderstood my behavior, and—'

"'With this you think you have done sufficient,' interrupted Bertha.

"'At least all that I am able. I cannot love Gertrude, because I love you with all my soul. The only thing that remains to me is to withdraw.'

"'Not so hasty, Herr notary. Let us contemplate the matter a moment. Assume that I were dead, would you not be able to love Gertrude then?'

"'Perhaps, but you are living.'

"'Certainly; but I am as if dead to you; for my love you can never gain, because it belongs to another. You cannot become anything to me but what you are, a young man to whom I have rendered my good-will.'

"'I desire and hope for nothing further; but I wish,

as a free man, to possess the right to adore you in my heart.'

"'And leave Gertrude to her fate?'

"'What do you wish me to do?'

"'To transfer to her the affection that you believe yourself to cherish for me, and with her to find all the happiness you have possibly dreamed of at my side. Married to Gertrude, you will forget Bertha. If you become Gertrude's husband I will esteem and prize you; but as the destroyer of her peace, only despise you for all the evil your frivolity has produced.'

"Bertha rose, adding as she laid her hand quite lightly on my shoulder:

"'This time you can expiate your fault, see to it that you do so, and not for the second time leave a woman as the victim to your caprices.'

"The next instant she was gone.

"I felt as if stunned by a violent blow. When I recovered myself, I rushed out of the room and up to my chamber. I had much to write, and plunged immediately into work. While I was writing my mind became calmer. I reflected upon my position. Bertha was lost to me; her love I could not win, she had openly acknowledged that it belonged to another. Her respect I was able to gain; that was something.

"From these reflections I passed over to a cold calculation of the advantages of a union with Gertrude. She was an amiable girl and possessed a fine fortune, a father of great repute and influence. A match with her promised many benefits. Reason advocated it, and the resentment I felt because Bertha had given away her heart seconded reason.

"Toward evening I went to the parsonage. In returning home, I drove for Gertrude. When we came to Brovik, she had given me the promise of her hand.

"Two weeks afterward the judge was back from his Stockholm journey, and then our betrothal was celebrated.

"I am thus an engaged man and will be married next year.

"The future which lies open to me has nothing piquant and is entirely destitute of that enchantment which love lends to it; it seems to me like a long walk on a level plain. The sun shines upon it, but its rays will never burn; we will traverse it without being disturbed either by warmth or cold.

"A quiet happiness without love! Well, why not? If the felicity is not so great, I can console myself with the thought that the pangs will not be so many.

"Farewell, my brother! I lack desire to write longer. Let me hear from you soon. Greet Hanna from your faithful brother, CONNY."

CHAPTER VIII.

CHRISTMAS was over.

At Brovik they had amused themselves to their hearts' content. The Liedgrens had a new neighbor, who seemed to wish to contest the right of the wealthy judge to play the rôle of the foremost; a privilege which he, however, was not willing to resign. The result was, that one entertainment succeeded the other at the judge's stately country-seat.

The new neighbor was Baron Fabian Lodstein. He had, shortly after his nephew's death, taken possession of the Manor Wrånga, which was situated six miles from Brovik and had belonged to a person related to the Lodstein family, who had died a few days before the murder of Casper, the nearest heir of the deceased.

Baron Lodstein had immediately after his arrival to the place made a call on the judge, in order, as he said, to learn the closer details of his nephew's murder. Baron Fabian was abroad when the terrible event occurred.

Lodstein was an immensely wealthy man and knew how to appear as such. Although he did not give any large fêtes during the first winter, when the mourning for his nephew was still so fresh, he was for all that very glad to see company at Wrånga, and he entertained them in magnificent style.

Judge Liedgren, who, as a general thing, did not evince any partiality for intercourse with noblemen, had nevertheless been particularly polite to the baron and made very frequent visits to his house.

The cause of this interest was difficult to fathom, as the baron on the whole was extremely limited in his intelligence and very haughty besides. Like all mediocre minds he prided himself upon his name and his rank, something which he, in his behavior toward Liedgren, took good care not to show. He was anxious to have the judge for a friend.

With all the invitations which came from Wrånga to Brovik, Conny Wenner had not accepted a single one. This stubbornness on Conny's part Liedgren had allowed to pass unremarked. The consequence was that Gertrude did not care to visit the highborn family, when her betrothed did not do it, and Bertha also remained at home. The ladies at Brovik had thus only been at Wrånga twice, in spite of the many invitations.

It was the twenty-eighth of February. At Brovik there was always a large party on that day. All the neighbors from far and near were invited and the splendid rooms swarmed with people. Those who lived farthest away had come to dinner and were to stay at Brovik over night; the nearest neighbors did not arrive until the ball in the evening.

Among the dinner guests were Baron Lodstein and his family, as the baroness, who had very delicate health, needed to recover after the ride, in order to stand the fatigue of the ball.

The justice and sheriff of the district were also invited to dinner.

The courses were delicious, wine flowed and the company in consequence were in exceedingly high spirits. All were merry and joyous; Baron Lodstein alone remained cold and haughty. He ate little, drank still less and conversed ceremoniously with Bertha.

Dinner was over. The ladies had retired to their rooms to rest and make their toilets for the ball. The gentlemen were gathered in the judge's smoking-room, to enjoy their cigars. Liedgren and Lodstein sat on a little sofa that stood between the windows, conversing about the crops and agriculture.

In one of the window recesses sat Conny.

The sheriff, Herr Willberg, came straight toward him and seated himself on a chair opposite, saying:

"The last sessions have been especially tedious, as we have not arrived at any results in our investigations. What do you say about Pehr Mattsson's case? I, for my part, am fully and firmly convinced that he murdered his wife, and yet you will see that he will be acquitted for lack of evidence against him."

Herr Willberg, an unusually cultivated and gentlemanly sheriff, entered into a lively discourse with Conny, concerning the Mattsson affair, and after they had each expressed their opinions about it, Willberg said:

"It is well enough when we have something or other to fasten suspicion upon in a suit, but it is too provoking when a crime, like that with Lodstein, is committed without our having the slightest clue even for conjecture. I confess frankly, that I would willingly give a half year's salary if I could get track of the malefactor."

"And I can assure you that you never will get track of him," replied Conny. "Casper Lodstein's murderer does not belong to the ordinary class of criminals. A villain, who uses white kid gloves when he murders, is not easy to find, because suspicion does not dare to step so high."

"You are right, Herr notary," said Willberg. "But yet it may not be impossible. When one, like me, has set out to be a blood-hound, he must have a persistence without limit, and I assure you that I consider it a matter of honor to discover the mysterious assassin."

"But you will not succeed in reaching him," answered Conny.

"There is no place in the community so elevated that justice cannot reach the criminal. If we cannot seize the guilty person directly, we steal up to him when he least expects it."

"In that case it is fortunate that I do not fill your position," said Conny; "for I greatly fear that I would throw myself upon the criminal and show him the glove, exclaiming: 'Can you deny that this glove is yours, that your hand was covered with it when you gave the death thrust!'"

Willberg gave Conny a peculiar glance, and said with emphasis:

"To be able to act so, I ought at least to suspect some certain person as the owner of the perfumed glove."

"And this, Herr Willberg, you do not?"

Conny and Willberg looked at each other. The crafty sheriff's eyes had a queer expression.

"Another reason to congratulate myself upon not being a sheriff," said Conny.

"You have then a definite suspicion?"

"Yes, but I will keep it to myself for the present."

At that moment Baron Lodstein rose from the sofa, where he had sat talking to Liedgren. The curtains had concealed him from Conny's and Willberg's eyes; but this did not hinder their words from reaching the ears of both gentlemen.

The judge, however, had not allowed it to be perceived that he heard what was said, but continued to expatiate upon the advantages of a certain mode of clearing land.

"It seems that Baron Lodstein has been quite near us, while we were talking about his nephew," said Conny, when the baron passed by the window.

"He sat there on the sofa," answered Willberg.

"Did you know it?"

"Yes."

"And yet you led the conversation to his nephew?"

"And yet,"—repeated Willberg, laughing. "Say rather, just on that account."

A few hours afterward the ball was in full course. They had finished a galop, when Baron Lodstein approached Conny, as the latter stood leaning against his fiancée's chair, conversing with her.

The baron expressed his regret that Conny had never accompanied the judge to Wrånga. It was the first time that Lodstein had addressed our young notary. After he had spoken about the place, its natural beauty and its neighbors, he said quite abruptly:

"Your name is Wenner, sir, is it not?" Lodstein looked sharply at Conny, who bowed affirmatively.

"When I moved to Lund," resumed the baron, "there was a professor there by that name. Is he related to you?"

"I have the happiness of calling him father," answered Conny coldly, and then turned to his betrothed.

The baron went away muttering:

"Wenner, as far as I can remember, was childless. Is that young spark a bastard or—"

Here his train of thought was interrupted by Liedgren, who came to ask him to take a hand at cards.

Lodstein accepted the invitation, and said as they were on their way to the card-room:

"How nearly related is your intended son-in-law to Professor Wenner?"

"He is the professor's son."

"Ah, indeed!" said Lodstein without adding anything more. A moment later he sat at the card-table. Although usually a remarkably skilful player, the baron that evening played badly. He was absent-minded and committed one blunder after the other, and as the result of this had decided ill-luck.

But we will leave the high-born gentleman, to ascertain what is transpiring elsewhere.

They were dancing a française.

Conny had withdrawn to one of the window recesses, from which he could unobserved have a view of the dancing hall. His eyes did not follow Gertrude, however, who now danced with Notary Wicker, but were fastened on Bertha, whom he seemed to devour with his gaze.

After the dance, Gertrude hastened to her lover.

"Why did you not dance the française, dear Conny?" asked she, laying her hand on his shoulder.

"Because I did not feel like it," answered he brusquely.

"But yet you are usually so fond of dancing."

"Perhaps. This evening I am not."

"Are you ill, or are you displeased with me?" Gertrude bent forward to catch a glimpse of his face.

"I am neither, and I do not understand why you make such a fuss about my dancing or not dancing. You were engaged at any rate, and it only annoys me to have you continually ask why I do not do this or that. I do not like to be watched."

Conny turned on his heel and left her.

The young girl, it is true, had ever since she was betrothed found her lover very different from what she thought a lover ought to be, but as Conny had hitherto always been polite, attentive and friendly, Gertrude had supposed that his rather cold manner was something that belonged to his character. The idea had never occurred to her that it might come from lack of love, especially as he had never shown her any signs of bad humor. This outbreak of impatience therefore made a painful impression on her.

Gertrude, this pet of fortune, who had never known what sorrow, adversity or suffering meant, experienced such bitter grief that she almost burst into tears.

She leaned her brow against the cold window-pane, clasped her hands and whispered:

"If—if he did not like me as much as I him. Oh, my God—if—he did not love me!"

"Mamsell Liedgren, dare I remind you of the promise of this waltz?" said a voice behind her.

It was a young lieutenant. Gertrude turned to him slowly to answer the question.

While the lieutenant led Gertrude through the mazes of the waltz, Count Strålkrans took his place beside Bertha on a little sofa where she was sitting.

"If I am not mistaken," said he, "it is three months since I left the place, after being informed by you that I had nothing to hope with regard to Mamsell Gertrude, and I now find on my arrival here that you were right."

"And also that I could not have acted otherwise than I did," replied Bertha.

"With regard to me, yes; but with regard to Mamsell Liedgren and Wenner you must allow me to declare that I do not consider you to have been equally wise."

"What do you mean, count? Could I have anything to reproach myself with in my conduct toward them?"

"Not to reproach, but certainly to rectify."

"In what respect?"

"In remaining here."

Bertha looked at the speaker. His eyes rested tenderly upon her and his tone was that of a friend when he, lowering his voice, continued:

"If I were not convinced that you would thoroughly comprehend my words,. I would not venture to utter them. But I know that you will not misunderstand them, although they will throw blame upon you."

"Herr count, I did not think I deserved blame from any one, least of all from you," replied Bertha.

"Say rather, that if you deserved it, it is just from me. Still it is not of you or of me that we will this time speak, but of the newly betrothed pair. Gertrude loves her intended husband; to be convinced of it one only needs to see them together; but it is equally certain that he does not love her. I have only been here a few hours; I have already discovered their unlike positions toward each other. But this is not all. Wenner has through prompting, persuasion or calculation—or God knows what—engaged himself to Gertrude without his heart having anything to do with it. Still, this is a lack which might be remedied in time, if he did not love another to madness. I greatly fear that this other has brought about the whole engagement. She has perhaps sacrificed her own heart in so doing, with the idea of securing Gertrude's happiness; but in that event she has only made her friend a half sacrifice when she remained in the vicinity of the man who adored her. She has through her presence made it impossible for him to transfer the attachment she possesses to his fiancée. Madam, the woman, who has courage to give up a man who is dear to her, ought also to have courage to resign his love; and this you have not had. The proof of the truth of my words you can see before you. Look up, and you can have the dangerous enjoyment of reading in the eyes of Gertrude's lover that he is at this instant consumed with jealousy of me. It seems as though you did not understand the art of making sacrifices."

The count ceased. Bertha's face had become rigid. At his last words she lifted her drooping eye-lashes and glanced up. Right before her, leaning against the door-post, stood Conny. She only needed to cast a fleeting glance at him to convince herself that Strålkrans had spoken the truth. Bertha turned her eyes from Conny to the count, saying in a perfectly calm tone:

"I thank you, count, for what you have told me; I will remember your words and learn from them to act as I ought." Bertha rose and went from Strålkrans, who remained and looked after her.

"Does she love that boy or not?" muttered he. "Her course of action will contain an answer to my question."

CHAPTER IX.

IN the forenoon, two days after the ball, the judge entered Bertha's little sitting-room.

"You have desired to speak to me," said Liedgren, seating himself at her side. "If there is anything that you wish to ask of me, Bertha, I will consider myself happy if I can fulfil your request."

"It was just on this kindness of yours, uncle, that I relied," said Bertha. "I have indeed something to ask of you."

"Then it is the first time this has happened, and you need not fear a refusal," assured Liedgren obligingly. "I am burning with impatience to hear what it is."

"Something very insignificant. I desire you to release me from a promise I have given."

"A promise? I cannot guess what."

"That I should remain here until Gertrude was married."

The judge started violently and looked at Bertha, who continued:

"This desire of mine will be so much the easier for you to grant, as your sister is expected here from S——näs. She will take my place while I am gone, and Gertrude will thus not be left without a lady friend. Mamsell Liedgren is expected here next week, and then I intend to take a journey."

"Where?" asked Liedgren shortly.

"To Pastor Wenner's first, and then to my aunt who lives in Skåne."

"For what cause do you wish to take this journey *now?*" The judge looked at her searchingly.

"The cause, uncle, I beg to be allowed to keep to myself for the present. It is sufficient that I must go."

"Do you wish me to tell you the reason?" asked he.

"If you choose. But I fear that you will be mistaken."

"The reason is that you desire to spare yourself the torment of longer residing under the same roof as Wenner's fiancée. You would not eventually be able to remain the friend of one who stands between you and him." The judge spoke in a tone as if he had examined a criminal.

"Dear uncle, I predicted that you would mistake my motive; and I entreat you to let me go without making me feel through any more false guesses that you do not have the good opinion of me I considered myself to deserve. It would deeply pain me if it were altered without any cause."

The judge's face brightened, he clasped one of Bertha's hands in his.

"Thank you for these words," said he. "I shall remember them; but if they have not been utterly meaningless, I beg of you, Bertha, do not go, but stay."

"I will come back, but now I must leave. You have promised to grant my request, therefore do not make me entreat longer."

The judge opened his mouth to say something, but the door opened, and Gertrude came rushing in to apprise her father that the sheriff wished to speak to him.

With a mien which betrayed how little agreeable this call was, Liedgren left the room.

Gertrude took the seat her father had occupied, and exclaimed, as soon as they were alone:

"Bertha, I do not know what is the matter with me, but ever since the ball, it seems as though my good spirits had taken to flight. I try to keep them, but I feel that they slip from my grasp, and I am pursued as it were by heavy thoughts."

She leaned her brow in both hands and continued:

"The day before the ball I was so happy that I fancied myself the happiest mortal on earth, and now I shrink from examining that which then formed my felicity."

"What is the reason of this change?" inquired Bertha. "Something must have occasioned the inquietude which has now tormented you for two days, although you have not given it any other name to me. What thought is it that occupies your mind?"

"I dare not whisper it to myself," answered Gertrude, "still less utter it to any one else, and neither is it worth while to speak of it. In this single case, I cannot be frank with you, and to speak the truth I believe that the evil lies mainly in my imagination."

She now raised her head, looked at Bertha and smiled as she added:

"I suppose people are generally a little silly when they are in love; but who can help it? Apropos, Bertha, have you ever been in love?"

Bertha blushed.

"What woman has not some time in her life experienced what love is? I, too, have known how a woman can love."

"Then you will understand me, if I tell you how I love. It is not at all as in romances, where one suffers and strives, glows and burns; but it is as though my love were a shining sunbeam, which gives such a light to my life's landscape, that it appears more bright and beautiful. Shadows, storms and tempests do not belong there; but if the sunshine were taken away, the landscape would disappear, and only a vast, empty space remain. I have never known sorrow, never had an ungratified desire, never learned the bitterness of tears. My life has only consisted of joy and peace. Thus I cannot realize grief nor understand sorrow, and, if it reached me, would sink under it without resistance. As it is, Conny's tenderness is my felicity and my life. Take it away, and I will die."

Gertrude again leaned her head in her hands.

"This is not my conception of your character, and neither is it so," said Bertha seriously. "I am convinced that if the Lord of destiny sent you any severe trial, you would bear it with more fortitude than most persons. You have been very happy, Gertrude; but just on that account you ought to bend under misfortune, if it visits you."

"But how could I do it, I who am a spoiled child, and have never been accustomed to anything but prosperity? No, Bertha, I would die, if—" She checked herself.

"What?" asked Bertha.

"If I became really unhappy."

"But, Gertrude, when you are on the point of uniting your fate to another's, it is not of your own happiness that you must think, but of the person's whose mate you are to become; and besides, my friend, you must then place yourself so earnestly in all possible conditions that you are prepared for a less happy lot."

"I cannot do that," declared Gertrude.

"Beware, my darling, of talking so. Circumstances might show you that you are forced not only to live through adversity, but also to bear it with fortitude. It is a poor, weak creature, who cannot meet suffering and humble herself before grief. Believe me, when the days of sorrow come, you will stand upright. I know you better than you know yourself."

Bertha petted Gertrude and drew her close to her, as she continued to speak friendly and serious words.

Gertrude listened to her in silence. Finally Bertha

communicated her intention of going away. At this intelligence Gertrude began to weep aloud, just like a forsaken child. She asserted that Bertha's departure would decidedly lead to something grievous, and she accused Bertha of lack of affection, when she could so abandon her. It took Bertha several hours before she could calm her.

Gertrude had been unlike herself ever since the ball. Her naturally even disposition had become irritable and impatient. Bertha's intended journey gave occasion to an outbreak.

At the dinner-table Gertrude's eyes were red from weeping, and the judge was silent; Conny said a word now and then, and Wicker devoted himself to his food.

When dinner was over Gertrude went to her lover, saying:

"Well, Conny, will you not ask why I have wept?"

"My dear Gertrude, I really did not know that you had shed any tears," answered Conny.

"Didn't you? That is to say, you have not looked at me during the whole dinner."

Conny frowned impatiently.

"There, now you will be angry again!" exclaimed Gertrude half crying, "and yet you ought to be very, very kind to me. But lately you have been so hasty, and have shown so little cordiality, that—"

"You are excited," interrupted Conny calmly. "Sit down, Gertrude, and listen to a few words which may possibly prove to you that the faults you accuse me of proceed from you instead."

He spoke mildly, but disapprovingly of her conduct for the last few days. She had even at the ball attacked him because he did not dance, and then she had continued the same behavior, notwithstanding Conny had done all in his power to avoid giving her any occasion for this continual displeasure, which pained him, as he desired nothing so much as to gratify her wishes.

Conny spoke so finely, that when he represented the little scenes of the previous days, one could easily draw the inference that he had maintained the most exemplary behavior throughout. and that the fault, from beginning to end, had been Gertrude's alone. He also succeeded in conveying this conviction to his fiancée, and although it appeared to her that her irritable mood proceeded from his captiousness, she finished by considering herself guilty of a very great offence when she asked her betrothed why he did not dance. How could it be otherwise when he said that it was not right?

Gertrude's love was at the present period such absolute worship, that she considered Conny entirely free from faults. All that he said was law and gospel. To doubt his words, or oppose his desires, would have been the same to Gertrude as to commit a crime.

"Ah, Conny, I willingly admit that I have been very bad," said Gertrude, after her lover, with a kiss, had assured her of his forgiveness; "but that I have been so to-day will surely seem to you less strange, when you learn that Bertha intends to go away."

Conny dropped her hand and exclaimed:

"Is Bertha going!"

"You see, Conny, when even you can be so disturbed at the intelligence of it, what do you think I feel?"

"Wenner, the judge wishes to speak to you!" cried Wicker.

Conny immediately obeyed the summons.

An hour afterward the judge and Conny were seen driving off. Wicker remained at home, and tried to entertain the ladies to the best of his ability.

The next day Mamsell Augusta Liedgren arrived to pay

a visit to her brother, and, according to her habit every year, stay at Brovik several weeks.

Mamsell Liedgren was an elderly, good-looking lady, rather fleshy and very phlegmatic. She belonged to the happy few whom events go by without touching. Rich, well educated and with a quiet disposition, she had loved her brother and her parents just so much, that it never occasioned her any disquietude. When the latter died, she mourned for them a year, but without growing thin. She showed all possible respect to their memory by carefully attending to their graves. For the rest she liked comfort, a good table and a merry jest; never troubled herself with her neighbors' affairs, never talked slander and was averse to everything which roused her from a peaceful dreaming in a comfortable easy-chair. She let each and all attend to themselves, and reserved the right to avoid taking notice of anything but her own enjoyment and satisfaction.

Two days after Mamsell Augusta's arrival Liedgren and Conny returned. Each went to his own room, where each found a letter awaiting him on his writing-table.

The one to the judge was short, and ran thus:

"Dear Uncle:—Pardon me for leaving Brovik during your absence, but I could not wait for your return, and so I went as soon as Aunt Augusta arrived.—Think with friendship of your grateful and affectionate

"Bertha Lagerskog."

The judge crumpled up the letter and muttered:

"So she is gone, and that notwithstanding I had resolved that this journey should not take place."

CHAPTER X.

CONNY WENNER to Paul Fredriksson.

"BROVIK, April 20, 18—.

"BROTHER: Spring approaches, and with it the hour when we can see each other again. From your letters I find that you have for a long time rambled around in Sweden and are now staying in Gottenburg. It would be a great gratification to me to once more hear your beloved voice. Yet, what avails it to talk about such things? What you are to me you know, and assurances are superfluous between men.

"You wish to know whether I am happy as a betrothed lover and if I am firmly resolved to do everything for the happiness of her, to whom I am bound?

"Happy, Paul, when one, like me, loves another woman even to madness, and has betrothed himself merely to gain her approval? No, my brother, such conditions do not bring happiness, but only torment and wretchedness. Speak not to me of felicity; it is like talking to the blind about daylight.

"When I, without other reasons than my calculation on one hand and the desire to do what *she* considered right on the other, betrothed myself, I believed that life at Gertrude's side would pass calmly and quietly, and I hoped that I would one day be contented with my lot. I considered how much the relationship with Liedgren would facilitate my advancement, and I supposed that success in my career would console me for the defeat I suffered in my heart. Well, all that may one day be realized, but as yet I have not even the prospect of reaching this aim. I have not been able to stifle my violent feeling for Bertha, but it has only grown in strength since Gertrude and I exchanged rings. I loved Bertha more deeply than ever, just because I daily made comparisons between her and Gertrude and was daily obliged to say to myself: Bertha is lost to you. Moreover, ever since I became engaged to his daughter, Liedgren has quite openly rendered Bertha his homage.

"My soul has through this been the scene of the most infernal tortures. I was mastered by a love which I had to conceal, by a wild jealousy, which it would not do for any one to suspect, and yet I was compelled to be agreeable and affectionate toward a fiancée whom I did not love.

"Still I would have been able to go through all this with strength of will and firmness of resolution, if my betrothed had been anything but a pretty little goose, who thought that her rôle of affianced bride consisted in constantly hanging on to her lover and chattering about love as soon as we were alone, besides asking incessantly whether I loved her. During the first weeks it flattered my self-love to see myself adored. I forgot that I had the ease with which Gertrude fell in love to thank for my being persuaded by Bertha to propose. I found a diversion in beholding how Gertrude complied with my desires in all respects and never had any will but mine. But soon this lost its charm, it became monotonous. Her caresses, her boundless attachment, her desire to be with me all the time, put my blood in a ferment. She tired me out with her endearments and her talk about how happy she was and would become, etc. While she daily described her felicity, I endured the torments of hell, and a feeling of disgust seized me.

"If I had been in love with Gertrude, this eternal babble about her affection, this silly sentimentality would have killed my love, thus how much more repugnant was all this when I did not love her.

"After two months' engagement I was to that degree weary of Gertrude that I could not always control my impatience, but sometimes indulged in outbreaks which I myself disapproved, but which, however, neither bettered nor changed our position. All that I gained by it was that Gertrude really made it a study to avoid whatever she thought would displease me. She became still more tender and affectionate.

"Such was the state of affairs when a large party was given here, in honor of my fiancée's birthday.

"Before I speak of the ball and what then occurred, I must tell you something, namely that Baron Fabian Lodstein has moved to this neighborhood. He has abandoned Skåne and lives here in an estate called Wrånga.

"Since I became a man I have been spared the torment of meeting this person, whom I regard as the evil genius of our lives. It has now been impossible to avoid this connection, but still I have not been prevailed upon to accept any invitation to Wrånga. I could not avoid meeting him, however, at the house of my intended father-in-law.

"Lodstein attached no importance to me except as a betrothed lover in the family. The high-born and haughty nobleman, on the contrary, shows Liedgren a politeness which is just the opposite of his manner in general. It is evident that he is extremely anxious to stand well with the esteemed judge. He never neglects to be attentive to him on every occasion, and thus, between Liedgren and Lodstein has arisen, if not an intimate, at least a very lively intercourse.

"To the above-named ball the baron and his family were invited. A conversation between the sheriff and me, which I fear that the baron overheard, led him to observe me more particularly, so that he inquired how nearly I was related to Professor Wenner. When he asked me the question, I read in his glance that he hoped to get hold of some secret, whereby he might possibly injure me. I felt that the rich and powerful man had determined to checkmate me. I think, however, that I will not let the baron win the game this time, but that Conny Wenner is destined to avenge the harm which he has done the brothers Fredriksson.

"This with regard to the position between the baron and me.

"Now about the ball.

"Strålkrans has after an absence of three months again visited Kungsdal, which has undergone thorough repairs. The day before the ball he made a short call at the Liedgrens'. I was not at home, and did not know that he had returned to the place until I saw him appear at the ball. He was there exclusively taken up with Bertha. My jealousy, hitherto directed to Liedgren, now obtained a new and more dangerous object, and I have scarcely any recollection of the ball except the frantic agony I endured when Strålkrans was constantly at Bertha's side. Never had she appeared to me more beautiful than this evening, and if my fiancée had hitherto seemed silly, she was now more shallow-brained than ever. I could not conceal the feeling of antipathy which I felt when she plagued me with her importunity. It is incomprehensible that the womanly instinct does not tell her that it is I who ought to seek her, and not she me. In short, the ball ended with a certain tension between us; but alas it was broken entirely too soon, and I believe, by my honor, that this child, who has no idea of what a woman ought to stand, or ought not to stand, begged my forgiveness because I had been hasty to her.

"Still the impression of this was soon effaced, for she informed me that Bertha intended to leave Brovik for some time.

"Directly after this intelligence I was obliged to go with Liedgren on official business, and when we returned, Bertha was gone. She had left a note for me. The contents were such, that I felt tempted to curse the day when I engaged myself to Gertrude, while at the same time I would have begged forgiveness at Bertha's feet for being the one who drove her from the home, where she felt so happy through Gertrude's affection. But if her words filled me with repentance and bitterness over the past, they also strengthened my resolution to try to overcome my feeling, as a man of honor, and to make life as pleasant to Gertrude as possible.

"Farewell, Paul, greet Hanna and inform me of the time of your journey to Stockholm, when I shall be there to meet you.

"Your unchangeable brother,

"CONNY."

CHAPTER XI.

LETTER from Gertrude to Bertha:

"BROVIK, May 28, 18—.

"DEAR BELOVED BERTHA! You reproach me that my letters are a little inclined to be sentimental. You say that you do not recognize me. I, the joyous and merry Gertrude, have become changed, as it were, since I fastened my affection upon a man. My existence is my love; that which has no connection with it is outside my consciousness, and now that you have left me, my thoughts have become still more concentrated upon this single point.

"When you were here, I consoled myself with your presence, when I could not be with *him*, and relieved my heart by talking about him. Your affection made me forget my regret when Conny was away.

"Now that you are no longer here, everything has become so different. If my letters are sentimental it comes from the fact that I have no one who is as fond of me as you were, and with whom I can speak. I am left to myself with my overcharged heart. It seems to me that my love is so great that it has not room in my breast; I feel an extreme need of showing Conny on all occasions how I adore him, and I suffer from a consuming longing for him to tell me, on his side, that I am equally dear to him.

"You blame this, you say that the less one talks about the heart's treasures the more value they have. Perhaps you are right, although I cannot as yet realize it. Not only in words do I try to show Conny how much I love him, but in all my acts I have ceased to be capricious; I am always submissive, never quick-tempered, and at the slightest remark of his about my manner, my dress, my words or my habits, I correct that which displeases him. I have only one desire, one effort, one aim, and that is to be a pleasure to him. If I do not always succeed, I have at least made the endeavor, and I try to discover Conny's desires in his glance, so as to fulfil them before they are expressed. This, Bertha, is what a woman who loves ought to do, is it not? Caprices, oppositions and disputes cannot be in place between two persons who have resolved to live for each other. Besides, I cannot endure the least shadow of displeasure from Conny. I then feel so miserable and would be willing to sacrifice my life to dispel every trace of it, and yet his brow is often clouded, yes, oftener than before.

"The longer we have been betrothed, the more plainly I feel that there is something the matter in our connection. What it is I think I have now found out. Conny's heart remains cold, when mine is burning; his love is quiet, when mine storms; his manner is calm, when mine is enthusiastic; his words are sensible, when mine are romantic. That he loves me, I believe as certainly as in God. I would not be able to love Conny as I do, if he were not worthy my love, and he would not be, if he had proposed to me out of self-interest. Although I am now perfectly sure of his attachment, it distresses me that he never utters a word of affection, unless I force him to it.

"I have read in romances that love makes woman a heroine. I do not know whether this is true, but I do know, that if any danger threatened him, or his happiness demanded a great sacrifice, it would be my joy to make it for him.

"Now I have perhaps wearied you by talking about my

feelings, I will therefore break off abruptly, and according to your desire relate how we have spent the weeks which have elapsed since you went away; especially as you chide me for not speaking of anything in my previous letter but my inner world.

"Did I mention to you that papa and Conny came home the day after your departure? I do not remember to have done so. I therefore begin with their arrival. It was in the evening. I had not retired, but sat by my sitting-room window, looking into the moonlight night in order to catch a glimpse of Conny, as he stepped from the carriage. I heard the sound of his step when he went into his room, and felt somewhat consoled in my regret for you when I knew that he was home. The following morning I was up early. My longing to see Conny again awoke me. I was the first one who came to breakfast; but judge of my feelings when Conny did not make his appearance, and the servant informed me that Notary Wenner had started on a journey to S——näs, quite early. Papa saw that I was on the point of bursting into tears, and said:

"'Wenner has gone on business. He was in my room this morning and told me to tell you this.'

"In the forenoon papa rode away, and Wicker had to entertain us. Poor fellow, what a tedious time he had of it, with a sorrowful fiancée who was all the time listening for her lover's return, and a fat matron who in all cases took a nap in the rocking-chair.

"Two days elapsed before Conny came back. During this time papa, who is usually so pleasant and contented in his home, had been very silent and not quite satisfied with matters and things in the house. When Conny arrived, it was too late for him to come up and see me; but instead he was in the dining-room before me the next morning, and although he appeared to me much paler than usual, his embrace was so hearty and his words so friendly, that I forgot the pangs I had endured. The following day he stayed at home, but had a dreadful amount of writing to do. The moments we were together he was so kind and so handsome, and I so happy, that I even forgot my regret for you.

"A week passed and then papa and Conny again went off to court. Since then Conny has been very busy writing, or else travelling. We have only been together a few hours, but then he has been so amiable that Augusta asserts that she has never seen a more agreeable lover.

"Two weeks after you left, we were invited to Wrånga. Papa, Conny and Wicker had gone to the northern part of the district. Aunt Augusta and I went alone to the baron's. Many inquiries were made about you, and the baron said with a singular smile:

"'Fru Lagerskog did perfectly right in not remaining in the place.'

"I did not pay much attention to his words, but when we rode home, aunt took up the subject. Instead of sleeping in her corner of the carriage, as usual, she expressed herself with extreme vehemence about the baron. He had said something about you, what, she was not willing to mention, and brother Göran should know all about it.

"Papa is in Aunt Augusta's eyes as powerful as the king, and when she threatens to 'tell Göran,' the old lady is not to be played with.

"Two days afterward the Fröknarne Lodstein came on a visit to me. They chattered and gabbled about everything under the heavens, and can you believe that Eugenie Lodstein had the impudence to tell me right to my face, that her father had said that Conny was not in love with me at all, but had engaged himself for money? The impertinent girl added:

"'It must be admitted, dear Gertrude, that your betrothed has a terribly cold and indifferent manner toward you.'

"I became provoked; took Conny's part and said that it was mean to say so to me. In short, the aristocratic gossips and I separated less good friends than we were before.

"As soon as Conny came home I related the whole occurrence to him.

"'I presume, Gertrude, that you will no longer visit a family which calumniates your betrothed,' said Conny, when I finished my account. 'If you do, I have been much mistaken in your character.'

"My Conny is anyway a very high-toned man. He did not condescend to defend himself, but proved through his words that he considered himself above every accusation.

"Since then I have not seen any one from Wrånga, and never shall my foot cross their threshold.

"And now farewell, you dear, darling Bertha! Write soon, and tell me when you arrive in Stockholm. You do not know how you are missed by your own

"GERTRUDE."

CHAPTER XII.

"YOU have had a letter from Bertha to-day, have you not?" Liedgren inquired of his daughter, as he entered her room one beautiful day in the beginning of June.

"Yes, papa, I have," answered Gertrude, folding the letter which she had just finished reading.

"When is she going to Stockholm?"

"Next week."

"How long will she stay there?"

"Only a few days."

"In that case, Gertrude, I desire you to have everything in readiness for a journey to the capital. We will start the day after to-morrow."

"We!" exclaimed Gertrude, looking at her father.

"You, I and your betrothed. It seems that Conny intends to go to Stockholm anyway, and as I now have a few weeks' leisure, I think of taking a little trip to our beautiful capital. See that you are ready Wednesday morning early enough for us to be in S——näs by the time the steamboat leaves there."

The judge nodded to his daughter and went out. Gertrude's face, which at her father's entrance had been sober, brightened up and took an entirely different expression.

She was to go and meet Bertha, something which she so eagerly desired, and was to be accompanied by Conny. Oh, height of joy!

The days which elapsed before the journey, Gertrude

was so light-hearted, that she again appeared as she used to be.

Conny was in S——näs and returned to Brovik the day before the one that Liedgren had appointed for their departure. When Conny entered the room where Gertrude was, she sprang toward him, exclaiming:

"My beloved, papa and I are going to accompany you to Stockholm; think how pleasant it will be! You will get rid of travelling alone, and I—I will see Bertha again. Say, will it not be a delightful journey?"

Gertrude threw her arms around Conny's neck in the exuberance of her joy. He pushed her gently from him, saying almost coldly:

"What is it you say, are you going to Stockholm?"

Gertrude looked up at him hastily. His brow was wrinkled and his eyes had an expression which betrayed anything but glad surprise. The beaming joy which shone in every one of Gertrude's features disappeared, and her glance was dimmed by a slight mist, as she whispered:

"Ah, Conny, I believe it makes you displeased that I am going to accompany you? Tell me frankly if that is so, and I will stay at home."

There was something so truly touching in the humble tone, in the complete forgetfulness of self, which the words implied, that Conny was affected by it. Before his memory appeared all the traits of love and self-sacrifice which this favored child of fortune had so unreservedly shown him, and his conscience told him that he had not made himself deserving of it in the least respect. He clasped Gertrude to his breast, kissed her tenderly on the brow and said:

"It gives me great pleasure, Gertrude, to have you with me to the capital. If I did not immediately give indication of the joy which I felt, it proceeded from the fact that you came toward me so suddenly with the intelligence. *Forgive me*, if I have distressed you in any way."

It was the first time that Conny had uttered the word forgive to Gertrude, and her eyes now beamed with the purest joy.

Gertrude's happy state of mind continued during the whole journey. She did not annoy her lover with incessant questions about what he was thinking of or why he did not look glad, etc., but she spoke of Bertha almost the whole time and the surprise the latter would have when she was met by Gertrude in Stockholm. Conny was particularly attentive to her, was afraid that she would catch cold, and Gertrude felt like crying to heaven:

"My God, how happy I am! Now I see that he really loves me."

In this mood Gertrude arrived in the capital. Conny and the judge also seemed pleased. When they rode from Riddarholmen and across Riddarhus square, Conny's ears caught the tones of a hand-organ. He turned quickly in the direction from whence they came, and then saw an organ-grinder standing on the corner of Monk's bridge. He was singing:

"Why dost thou long for thy Fatherland!"

The carriage drove by, but not so rapidly that Conny did not have time to recognize his brother in the street-singer, and Paul his dear Conny in the fine gentleman who rode in the carriage.

The two brothers nodded to each other; but Conny did not do it imperceptibly enough for Gertrude not to observe his motion.

"Whom did you greet?" asked she immediately. Conny colored and answered brusquely:

"An acquaintance;" but after giving this answer he did

not regain his good humor. A shade of dissatisfaction remained on his face, as in his soul. He was enraged at himself for not saying: "my brother."

When they finally reached the judge's house at the beginning of Reign street, Liedgren offered Conny a room in his abode; but Conny declined the invitation, helped his fiancée and her father from the carriage, and then drove to hotel K——.

As soon as he had changed his travelling clothes he went to seek his brother's home, and not until late in the evening did he present himself to Gertrude. He found her all alone. Her father had gone out, where, she did not know; and she had employed the time in seeing that all was in order in the room that Bertha was to occupy, and adorning it with flowers. She expected Bertha every moment; but as the meeting was to be a surprise to her, the judge had expressed the desire that Gertrude should stay at home and await her arrival.

Conny seemed very much pleased at seeing Gertrude alone, and immediately introduced a serious conversation with her about true human worth. Gertrude listened to him attentively, and said in answer to his remark that only merit, never birth, ought to weigh in the judgment of an individual:

"But, Conny, there is no cultivated person who takes in contemplation anything but moral and intellectual value? What one's parents have been is immaterial on the whole, and can as little increase as deprive us of our own merit."

"This view of yours proves how little you know the world in which we live, and perhaps yourself too," said Conny. "Assume for an instant, that I were the son of a criminal,—would you then hold me as dear as now?"

"Most assuredly; what had you to do with the crime your father committed, when you yourself are a distinguished and estimable man?"

"Are you quite sure that you would be willing to acknowledge before the world that your husband's father was a convict?"

"Perfectly. In case this son were *you*, such as you now are, I would do it with an elevated brow."

"Gertrude, I fear that you over-estimate your own feelings, and that you now say so, because you consider yourself absolutely certain of never coming in such a predicament."

"I do not utter any words, Conny, but those which are dictated by my conviction. What does it concern me whose child you are? Nothing of that sort can affect my feelings; the parent's faults or virtues can confer neither shame nor greatness upon the children, as these have had no part in them."

Conny regarded his fiancée with greater interest than ever before.

"I did not believe you capable of so much independence," remarked he.

"And I, Conny, fear that there are a good many little things which you do not give me credit for, but of which I am capable nevertheless. You have been like most superior men, you have seen in me only a thoughtless child, but not a woman. I willingly admit that I am a child in much; but in my love for you I am not. In everything pertaining to that I am free and strong. The limits of my affection I have not been able to discover, and I know within myself that they do not exist. I could forgive you everything, even if I discovered that you had deceived me, that you loved another."

Gertrude had spoken with an energy unusual to her, and the truth of what she said was clearly and plainly to be read in her eyes.

"I believe you, Gertrude," said Conny, pressing her hand warmly, "and who knows but what I will have to put you to a hard test right soon? I have to reproach myself for lack of frankness toward you. Had my attention been drawn to this circumstance before to-day, I would have corrected the error long since. As it is I will not be quite satisfied with my actions until I have spoken openly with you."

"Then do it immediately," said Gertrude. "We are now alone, and it will be to me a precious recollection, if you, the first evening we are here, give me your confidence."

Gertrude put her arm around Conny's neck, adding:

"Whatever sin you may have committed, I promise you absolution."

"Even if I had committed that of not loving you?"

Gertrude sprang up from the sofa. She was deadly pale; but the next second the color returned to her cheeks, and she seated herself again at his side with a smile full of trust:

"Yes, even that,—but I know that this is a grief which God has not intended me. You have said those naughty words merely to see the effect of them."

Gertrude looked in his eyes with such firm confidence that Conny bent down and kissed her on the brow, saying:

"What I can assure you, Gertrude, is, that this at least was not *the* sin I now intended to confess, but something quite different. Do you remember that I nodded to some one when we drove across Riddarhus square?"

"Perfectly; I asked you whom you greeted."

"Well then," resumed Conny, "I answered you that it was an acquaintance, but it was somebody who stood still nearer to me, it was— "

Here Conny was interrupted abruptly by the judge, who opened the door. The next minute Gertrude was clasped in Bertha's arms.

The judge had himself been to meet Bertha at the wharf.

No confidential communications between Conny and Gertrude could be thought of that day, and neither on those following.

CHAPTER XIII.

THE days had flown rapidly, but without affording Gertrude and Conny a single tête-à-tête long enough for them to resume the interrupted conversation; and that notwithstanding Gertrude made every effort to be alone with her lover.

The judge was evidently determined to enjoy Bertha's society as much as possible, she again, who was obviously annoyed by "uncle's" importunity, seemed to be inseparable from Gertrude, who also found it very pleasant to keep company with Bertha, as Conny had so much to attend to that he was only with her a little while at a time.

Conny avoided Bertha, but did it in so skilful a manner, that no one could suspect that he was so little with his fiancée, in order to escape coming in contact with Fru Lagerskog.

Both Gertrude and Liedgren took it for granted that business occupied his time. Besides he was much sought after by old friends and acquaintances; in short, he had scarcely a moment to himself.

If Gertrude reminded him of the interrupted confidence, he said:

"My dear Gertrude, I never have you to myself. When there are no visitors here, you are out at parties and pleasure excursions. Strangers surround you from morning till night."

So passed a week. They had now only two days left to be in Stockholm.

Some councillors and assessors gave a dinner to Liedgren at Blå Porten. They were to eat and drink in honor of the distinguished friend and judge, before he left the gay capital.

Conny was present at the dinner of course. When Liedgren and he rode out to Djurgården, the former said:

"Can you explain why Lodstein seems to have a grudge against you?"

"No, unless it has its origin in a conversation between Willberg and me, which I think he overheard," answered Conny.

"Very possible," replied Liedgren; "as it is especially for the last few weeks that he was shown himself hostile to you."

"And in what way?" asked Conny calmly. "Has he said anything to you, uncle?"

"Far from it, but still he has let various things come to my ears through others. To my sister, for example, he has dropped words about you and Bertha Lagerskog which so enraged Augusta, that she assured me that she never intended to visit Wrånga again."

Liedgren looked at Conny, who could not possibly maintain his self-possession, but exclaimed with excitement:

"The wretch! Has he really dared to put Bertha's name and mine together?"

"Yes, he has, and that too in a way very derogatory to Bertha. But to try to refute a discreditable report is only to give it increased impulse. The best thing we can do, when we know it to be false, is to remain indifferent. I hope at all events to have an opportunity to silence the baron, so that he at least does not sully Bertha's name any further."

The carriage now stopped at Blå Porten, and in a few moments they joined the other guests. One of the first that Conny caught sight of was Baron Lodstein.

The dinner passed in the approved way. The merriment and wit increased according as the bottles were emptied. At length the meal was over. Part of the gentlemen seated themselves on the sofas to drink coffee with cordial and to let the food digest at their ease; others went out on the balcony to smoke and inhale the fresh air. Among the latter were Conny and some of his comrades at court. They took their places in one of the corners, smoking and talking with all the animation which young men, after having drained several glasses of wine, can throw into their conversation. In the opposite corner sat Liedgren and two of the assessors. They were also chatting in a lively manner, but not with the wild hilarity of the young men.

Right between these two groups stood Baron Lodstein, talking in a low tone with Count Strålkrans. That what the two noblemen said to each other was not of the most agreeable nature, could be seen in their faces, and Conny fancied that he caught his name and Bertha's. Their colloquy, however, was not long; for Strålkrans took his hat and left the company. He was seen slowly walking toward Rosendal.

After he went away from Lodstein, the latter remained where he was and leaned against the railing of the balcony, looking alternately at Liedgren and Conny. After a while he advanced to Liedgren, saying:

"Your daughter is well, I hope, Herr judge?"

Liedgren answered the question politely, but coldly; something which did not hinder the baron, however, from expressing himself with the most fulsome praise of Gertrude's beauty and grace.

"If Mamsell Liedgren is an amiable and lovely girl," said he, "then she has also chosen a betrothed with a very advantageous appearance. Notary Wenner,"—Lodstein made a careless motion of his head toward the side where

Conny sat,—"is really so good-looking, that his regular features ought to be the best explanation of the success he has had."

"May it not rather be his fine mind?" observed one of the assessors. "Wenner has a superior intellect and thorough culture. He is destined to rise very high."

"That is possible; but will not his birth be to him a hindrance in his advancement?" resumed the baron, taking a cigar, which he slowly lighted.

"Within the official corps, Herr baron, ability alone is taken into account. Birth plays no part there," answered Assessor K——, himself the son of a peasant.

"Understand me aright," said the baron, "I am not referring to plebeians or patricians, to the middle or upper classes, but I affirm that one ought to be the son of honest parents in order to advance in the official career."

"Even this is immaterial, if the individual himself is known as an upright man," declared Assessor K——, smiling.

"And besides," joined in Liedgren, who all this time had sat silent, "the baron cannot mean to insinuate that Wenner's birth is such that he needs to be ashamed of it?"

"I insinuate nothing, for I presume that you know as well as I who was the father of your intended son-in-law."

"Yes, Herr baron, I flatter myself that I do," replied Liedgren haughtily; but thought within himself: "What effrontery to allude to Conny's birth!"

The judge, like many others who were aware that Professor Wenner had adopted Conny, had taken it for granted that he was an illegitimate son. Out of consideration for the young man, Liedgren had never made any inquiries concerning this sensitive subject.

Beneath the balcony were heard at that moment the tones of a hand-organ, and shortly afterward a clear strong voice sang:

"Hast thou a friend, who is dear to thee," etc.

The baron leaned over the railing and looked down at the organ-grinder.

It was a tall, slight man, neatly clad, with a straw hat on his head, and an uncommonly handsome face.

"That fellow has a fine voice," said Lodstein, "and is quite good-looking. If you look at him, Herr judge, you will see that there is a singular resemblance between the organ-grinder and your intended son-in-law."

Without waiting for any answer, Lodstein raised his voice and said to Conny:

"Well, what do you think of the song, Herr notary? Doesn't that cuckoo sing quite well?"

At these words the organ-grinder looked up. His eyes fell on Conny, and thereupon his face was colored with a dark flush. The song ceased instantly. Conny, on the other hand, had risen when the baron accosted him and answered quite calmly:

"Yes, he sings so well, that I find myself called upon to go down and thank him."

Conny turned toward the stairs.

"Perhaps you will give him this money from me?" said Lodstein, handing a few coins to Conny.

"I am fully convinced that he will not receive any gift from the baron, even if it is presented by me."

Conny went down, and Liedgren, with his sharp power of observation, had discovered with surprise that there was something about that organ-grinder which only Lodstein and Conny knew.

When the latter departed, the baron informed them that he knew the organ-grinder very well, as he, the baron, had once been compelled to appear as accuser against him. The baron had many years ago lost a valuable ring, which the organ-grinder had appropriated. As something over sixteen years had elapsed since then, the baron supposed that the strolling singer had not again allowed himself to be tempted into any crime against the right of ownership, as he still went around singing.

The baron was not surprised at his not having the strictest ideas of honesty, as he was the son of a man who had committed both murder and felony. The baron presumed that the gentlemen remembered the story of a German organ-grinder, who had killed an Italian in order to get at his money.

Yes, indeed, they all recollected the occurrence. Liedgren had then accompanied Judge S——, who was the magistrate in the district where Skärparby was situated, and had thus been the secretary at the trial.

While Conny was descending the stairs, Paul had taken his hand-organ on his back and walked away; but Conny was soon beside him, and went across the plain in his company.

In the meantime the baron related the history of Paul and his father. Liedgren, however, made various corrections in the baron's account. The father had not been accused of felony and murder, but of excusable homicide.

Liedgren had just finished his statement, when Conny came back and resumed his place among his comrades, all of whom were listening with no slight interest to what the older gentlemen said.

When Baron Lodstein saw Conny, he said with a mocking smile:

"I believe that you thanked the organ-grinder so thoroughly that he took himself off. Admit that there are sometimes apparitions which are scarcely agreeable?"

"Perhaps so," answered Conny composedly. "But this

was not one of them; for it is always pleasant for me to meet *my brother*, wherever chance brings us together."

Conny said this in so firm a tone, and met the baron's wicked glance with so open an expression, that his whole demeanor gave indication that he did not consider himself obliged to blush in any way for his relationship with the organ-grinder.

Liedgren, again, had contracted his brows, and bit his lip. The words of his intended son-in-law made a disagreeable impression on him.

The baron, who had calculated that he would be the one to divulge the fact that Conny and Paul were brothers, seemed somewhat surprised at the courageous words. Still, he was not a person to be easily disconcerted, but said with a scurrilous laugh:

"I did not know that the *gentlemen* were so nearly related."

"Ah, yes, baron, you knew but too well that the singer with his hand-organ and I were children of the same father."

"You ought not to have acknowledged it so openly, however, but rather have allowed each one to retain the idea that you were the son of Professor Wenner, even if illegitimate. You would still have preserved the honor of being the organ-grinder's brother. Judge Liedgren has just informed us that your father was not arraigned for murder, but for unintentional homicide; a fact which the judge could vouch for, as he was secretary when your father received his sentence."

Conny felt as if a leaden weight had descended upon his brain, so much humiliation did he experience at hearing his father so spoken of. But yet he maintained his upright bearing and said calmly:

"Herr baron, I have never yet learned the gain of blushing over my origin, and I never will learn it—"

"And neither need you," exclaimed a voice from the door which led to the rooms. It was Count Strålkrans. He went to Conny and slapped him familiarly on the shoulder, adding:

"I believe, upon my honor, that it was the baron's intention to tempt your patience; but in that case you have stood the test like a man, and I fear that it is the baron himself who has suffered the hardest defeat. It is always mortifying when one does not come off victorious from an assault, but is beaten with his own weapons. I pity you, Baron Lodstein," continued he, turning to the latter. Thereupon he exclaimed quite gayly to the rest of the gentlemen: "See here, my friends, two punch-bowls are awaiting us inside, which we must empty in honor of Judge Liedgren, our esteemed guest. It is really necessary to wash down the baron's stupidities with some glasses."

Lodstein cast an enraged glance at Strålkrans, but remained silent. He was as if dumfounded at the latter's course.

Liedgren walked cold and straight past the baron as well as Conny and the count. In the proud man's soul the scene had left such wounds, that they could not be so easily healed. The baron had actually succeeded in attacking one of his most vulnerable points, and if Liedgren could not readily forgive him for it, it was also evident that he would not be able to forget that Conny had been the cause of it all.

At last the toasts were over. Liedgren and two of the assessors rode together to the city. Count Strålkrans offered Conny a seat in his carriage. The count, who had hitherto maintained a proud, reserved manner toward Conny, had after the occurrence on the balcony entirely changed his demeanor.

CHAPTER XIV.

THE night was far advanced when Conny reached his home, but notwithstanding that he found Liedgren there.

The judge's face was stern. Conny saw at the first glance that he had come to hold a trial.

"I have desired to see you this evening, *Herr notary*, in order to speak out my mind," said Liedgren coldly. "It is high time that we understood each other. I, for my part, have not very much to say, it limits itself to the simple declaration that I will not have for my son-in-law a man who has so little idea of what his duty demands, that he engages himself to a girl of good repute, without first informing her father of his true family relations and giving him a chance to decide whether he wishes to have the son of a murderer for his daughter's husband. You have acted, sir, like a man without honor and principle, when you exposed my respected name to scandal and derision. You have behaved as if you had no heart in your breast, when this heart did not command you to mention honestly who you were, and for such a person I have only contempt. You ought to have realized that Göran Liedgren himself ought to have had the privilege of deciding whether he wished to be related to an organ-grinder and an accused thief. Even if I could have so far forgotten the respect for my name as to give you my daughter, although conscious of your real origin, it would have been impossible for me to make her the wife of an adventurer, who, like any other impostor, gained my consent through false means. I now see that the connection with me was a great benefit to you, but you must excuse me, if I cannot serve your selfish and ambitious interests. The engagement between you and Gertrude is broken. It only remains to you to send her the ring and to take back the one which you have given. And now, I have said all that I have to say."

The judge rose. While he was speaking, Conny had stood with head erect and the paleness of marble on his brow. He did not make the least show of interrupting Liedgren, but allowed him to utter the harsh and humiliating words unhindered. It was evident that Conny had resolved to drink the bitter cup of paternal disgrace and undeserved shame to the bottom. When the judge rose, Conny took a step toward him, saying with a voice as cold and calm as if it had treated, not of him, but of a lawsuit:

"As a judge, acquainted with the requirements of justice, you ought to acknowledge, Herr Liedgren, that as the accusation against me has been pronounced, I have the right to defend myself. I shall be as brief as possible, and then our ways may part. When I was adopted by Professor Wenner as his son, he had informed me in an epistle, that he desired that my father's crime through this act might be buried in oblivion. He demanded of me, in case I considered myself bound to him by any ties of gratitude, that I should avoid reviving the sad memories which were attached to my father. I was, through adoption, the professor's son, his heir, and the world had nothing further to do with the man who had given me life. This, Herr judge, was my foster-father's desire. He held the conviction that a man's integrity, his ability, knowledge and intelligence was that which decided his worth, and not his family connections. That he gave me his so highly respected name was the best proof of it. He did it, because he wished to save me from suffering in the future from an undeserved, but inherited disgrace, through the persecutions of a certain high-born gentleman. From the instant I was Professor Wenner's adopted son, I imposed it upon myself to obey his will, and I have therefore maintained silence about my parents. But had you, when I requested your daughter's hand, asked me a single question on this subject, I would have given you a candid answer. You did not interrogate me, and I considered you, the widely celebrated judge and the man so highly spoken of for his enlightened views, too free from prejudice to pay regard to anything but personal merit. I supposed that it would be an indifferent matter who had given me life, if I myself were only a good man. That I have made myself known as such, I think I can conclude from the fact that you offered me a place with you. That I, even at the University, enjoyed the respect of my comrades, both for application and integrity, I believe you are aware. Against my personal character there is thus no remark. Why then am I called to account for my father's faults? I acknowledge, Herr judge, that I committed a mistake, and a very great one besides, when I requested your daughter's hand; this you have now punished, and I will to-morrow return the betrothal ring. You are spared the evil of coming in relationship with an accused thief, as you expressed yourself, but if you by this epithet mean my brother you are in error, and I wish that we both, you, Herr judge, and I, were as honorable, conscientious and noble persons as the humble street-singer. If Baron Lodstein has been pleased to call him a thief, it may happen in the future that he calls you a venal judge. And now, Herr judge, I have nothing more to add."

Conny drew aside. Liedgren looked at him as if he was astonished at his daring.

"And you consider yourself to have acted in complete accordance with the laws of honor, when you left my daughter and me in ignorance of whose child you were?" asked Liedgren.

"If my father had been alive and confined at Langholmen, I would then have considered it my duty to inform you and Gertrude of it. But he was dead; the grave concealed him and his crime, and it is always bitter to speak of the evil a departed relative has done. It is possible that I ought to have considered you and Gertrude less enlightened than I did; it is also possible that it would have been more correct for me to tell you all, I will not contradict it; but that my silence did not proceed from the moral cowardice of feeling ashamed because I was born one of the unfortunate children of the community, although circumstances spared me this fate, is something which I believe I have proven through my behavior to-day."

"Your behavior to-day!" exclaimed Liedgren angrily. "That sounds as if you accounted it an honor."

"I hope at least that you do, judge," replied Conny proudly.

"Yes, if I were crazy; but as a sane man, I cannot regard your conduct otherwise than as an outbreak of folly. You present yourself among reputable men, and yet you have the audacity to leave this company for the sake of running down to an organ-grinder and talking to him, as well as proclaiming to all present that he is your brother. If you really have so little respect for yourself, for the corps to which you belong, and your comrades, you ought not to have forgotten, however, that the scandal you occasioned also reached me. Out of consideration for me you ought to have avoided proclaiming relationship with a street-singer."

"And let Baron Lodstein do it instead," said Conny. "Would the so-called scandal have then been less great? Would I have played a better rôle if I had kept a cowardly silence and allowed him to say before all assembled: that street-singer is the brother of Notary Wenner?"

"But why the deuce did you run down to the organ-grinder, and through this give the baron the opportunity to relate your father's history?" retorted the judge with heat.

"My father's history he would have related whether I stayed or not. The reason why I went down to my brother I would not be able to make comprehensible to you, if I tried, for it was an act dictated by the heart. When Baron Lodstein asked me what I thought of the song, I had only one thing clear to me, and that was to show this man with a high-sounding name that the poor organ-grinder whom he wrongfully accused of theft was not a brother that I was ashamed of, but a man whom I before the whole world acknowledged as a child of the same father. When I left the company, to hasten down, I felt that the murderer's sons were true gentlemen; but that the rich nobleman, on the contrary, was a rascal. I knew that if honor and conscience were really held as they ought to be held, the baron would have been turned out of the company. Now, Herr judge, we have certainly nothing further to say to each other. To-morrow I will call on your daughter, and in two days leave the capital."

Conny again drew aside, and Liedgren said, as he advanced to the door:

"It is unnecessary to apprise Gertrude of the reason why the engagement is broken. You can allege whatever cause you find most suitable."

"I do not find anything more suitable than the real one. You have to-day taught me that a man ought not to conceal the truth. I will bear the lesson in mind."

The judge looked at Conny, exclaiming:

"You will perhaps array my daughter against me?"

"How could that be done? You have, in your own opinion, acted right in not daring to confide your daughter to a murderer's son. Probably Gertrude will in this respect think the same as her father. She will feel pleased to avoid being the sister-in-law of a street-singer. I am fully convinced that the truth will be the best cure for her love. People cannot love a man they despise, and they cannot respect a man who has so low an origin as I, if he were ever so excellent a person."

The judge left, and Conny threw himself down on a sofa, with his hands pressed hard against his brow. The cup of humiliation is always bitter to drain.

CHAPTER XV.

GERTRUDE, the following morning, had just finished her toilet, when her maid entered to say that Notary Wenner desired to see her.

Gertrude was agreeably surprised that Conny came so early. She hurried out in the saloon to receive him with open arms; but Conny averted the embrace, as he said:

"The reasons which brought me here are such, that I cannot accept the greeting intended for me. I have come, Gertrude, to return this, and to ask mine back."

Conny handed her the betrothal ring.

Gertrude did not utter any exclamation, did not burst out in tears or lamentations, made no inquiries or reproaches; she did not faint, she did not drop down on a chair, but she remained standing as if paralyzed. Every drop of blood had fled from her cheeks and lips. She looked as though she had died and yet lived. She did not take the proffered ring, did not open her lips to speak, but stood there perfectly motionless.

"Gertrude," exclaimed Conny, frightened by her appearance, and seizing one of her hands, "what is the matter?"

She hastily drew away her hand and said with evident effort:

"How was it, do you break the engagement?"

At these words uttered by herself, the blood rushed up to her face, which was suffused with as dark a flush as it had been snow-white the instant before.

"Yes, I must."

"And why?"

Gertrude drew her breath as if she had been near suffocating. She was not able to hold herself up, but sank down on a chair.

"Because a union between us is no longer possible.—Had I on our arrival here been allowed to tell you what I was on the point of saying, you would perhaps have broken our connection yourself. Fate has ordered otherwise, and therefore I am forced to do it. When I asked for your hand, I committed a crime against you and my own sense of right, for I asked for it without loving you."

A shudder passed through Gertrude's frame. Conny continued:

"When we came here, I was awakened to the full consciousness of the injustice of my course of action. It was my brother's voice that recalled me to what was due you. My honor then commanded me to immediately acknowledge to you my birth and the unfortunate inheritance which had fallen to my lot, and then ask you whether you, in spite of this and my heart's lack of love, wished to become my wife. This, Gertrude, was my intention, when I commenced the conversation we had the first evening of our stay here. We were interrupted. I postponed the intended declaration, and to-day, I am forced by circumstances to break my engagement."

"And what are those circumstances?" asked Gertrude with an inaudible voice.

"One of them is the fact which was made known to all present at the dinner yesterday, that I am the son of an organ-grinder, who in an outbreak of passion had the misfortune to kill a man. Besides, I have a brother who is a street-singer. This brother I love with my whole soul and can never be induced to deny him. I wished to mention this to you alone; but chance revealed it to a whole company. And now, Gertrude, we must part. I know your proud father; even if he, out of love for you, would submit to accept as his son one whose father he heard sentenced to death, this humiliation would rankle in his mind, and I—I could not bear the consciousness of it, even if I loved you to madness."

"How much more impossible, then, when you do not love me at all," whispered Gertrude. She slowly drew the ring from her finger, and added with energy:

"Take back this ring, which no power in the world, except the conviction that you did not love me, could have induced me to return you. At the same moment you say that your heart never belonged to me, truth forces me to tell you that my heart will beat for you unto death. If you had loved me, I would have become your wife, even if the whole world had abandoned and rejected you. There is no place in the community so lowly, no lot so humble, which I would not have gladly shared with you, if I had been rich enough to possess your love. You have said that I did not possess it, may we then separate. But before you go, never to return, tell me, what prompted you to request my hand, when your heart was cold?"

"The hope of finding at your side a happiness which love had refused me," answered Conny. "I had loved, loved without being loved in return, and I then sought a friend, who, in the journey through life, might make me forget what I had suffered."

"And this friend I was intended to become? You had thus only a luke-warm affection to give in exchange for my fervent and devoted attachment. Still, that is past." She rose and offered him her hand, saying, almost in a whisper:

"Farewell, my own beloved! May the good God make you as happy as I desire! I bless you for the season of felicity which has fled."

"Gertrude!" exclaimed Conny, pressing her hand with emotion to his lips.

Gertrude hastily drew it away, and the next minute she was out of the room.

It was several seconds before Conny could come to himself. If the father had wounded his pride, then the daughter had truly humiliated him in his own sight.

Conny had gone to Liedgren's house with resentment and bitterness in his heart; he went away from it with repentance. The young girl's farewell words had contained such a high degree of love and forgetfulness of self, that Conny felt something resembling shame over his behavior.

In every person's life there is a turning point, when the character takes an entirely different direction from what it has previously had.—This was the case with Gertrude. The broken engagement formed one of those events which exerted a powerful influence upon the development of her soul and gave it a definite shape.

Gertrude, who had never known what a deep pain, an acute sorrow or a crushing misfortune meant; whose way had gone on roses, illumined by the sunshine of prosperity, and who had not even conceived of the possibility of there being any thorns, or that a hard blow could befall her heart,—she had taken it for granted that at the first visitation of sorrow she would sink down and die.

And now, now Gertrude had been reached by the bitterest grief that she could experience.—She had received the crushing blow without reeling, without a sigh or a tear escaping her.

Gertrude stopped inside the door, which she had closed after her when she left Conny, and leaned against it to catch the last sound of his steps. When they died away, she sank down on the threshold and remained lying there. The colorless lips moved, as if she had breathed a prayer.

Now was heard the sound of another door opening, and

some one approached. Gertrude rose hastily. It was Bertha.

"How is it, Gertrude?" asked Bertha. "You are so pale. Has anything unpleasant happened between you and Conny?"

Gertrude extended the ringless finger toward her with the words:

"Conny and I are no longer betrothed!"

Bertha stared at Gertrude. The latter continued:

"Sometime I will tell you all, not now; for I cannot speak of it. Still I will have courage to do so before long. If you will inform my father of what has transpired, you will spare me a trial. It is not I, but Conny, that has broken the engagement."

She pressed Bertha's hand and went to shut herself up in her room.

The young widow's appearance betrayed the greatest distress and anxiety when she looked after Gertrude. She then entered the saloon, which had just been the scene of the interview between Conny and Gertrude. The judge now stood there. When he saw Bertha, he went toward her, saying:

"Have you seen Gertrude, Bertha, and how does she take it?"

"So you know what has happened?"

"Yes, perfectly, as it was I who broke the engagement, or rather, forced Wenner to do it."

"But, uncle, what has Wenner done that could induce you to heap this suffering upon Gertrude's head?"

"What has he done?" replied the judge irately. "He has deceived me, when he proposed to my daughter, without first saying that he was the son of a condemned criminal and the brother of a strolling organ-grinder, who had also been accused of theft. Now, I ask you on your conscience, ought a man with such an origin and such family connections become the son-in-law of Göran Liedgren, and is he not a shameless scoundrel, who deserves to be turned out of every honorable family, when he dares to try to come in it without first saying: 'do you wish to be related to a criminal's son?' "

"I cannot comprehend what his origin has to do with the matter," replied Bertha. "Wenner himself has neither stolen, nor committed murder; he is generally known to be a young man of fine attainments and uncommon culture. He is also respected for his upright character, and this, according to my opinion, ought to be sufficient to make him worthy the hand of any estimable girl whatsoever."

"Romantic ideas, my dear Bertha. The children of crime have received such an inheritance that they ought to realize themselves that they cannot become members of reputable families.—The disgrace they have inherited is punished for the third and fourth generation; and honor and conscience enjoin them not to make any one else a participant of it."

"What do you mean by that, uncle?" said Bertha with agitation.

"That one who knows that there is disgrace or crime attached to his parents' name ought to beware of entailing the shame upon an innocent person. The marriage between a dishonored man's son or daughter and a person who has a good name will always be a curse to the latter, because she or he will have to share a thousand mortifying humiliations. You say that Wenner enjoys public respect for his ability and uprightness, and I admit that you are right; but what avails it if he is ever so excellent a young man, the stain which his father has given him will always remain, and with it follows a secret fear that the son will one day, sooner or later, show through some act that he is of the same blood as the condemned criminal. Wenner has a fine mind, has had a good education, and through this has acquired the power to control and govern the ebullitions of his ruder passions; but if any circumstance should arise, when they are wrought up, there is always danger of his yielding to faults which would brand his whole life. In short, it shall never be said of me, that I have given my daughter to a man who is an upstart and who only through a happy chance has been removed from the lowest strata of society to one which he never ought to occupy. It is a downright mockery of the law and its representatives that a murderer's son should occupy the seat of justice."

Bertha had changed color incessantly, while Liedgren was speaking. When he finished, she said:

"How is it possible that so enlightened a man as you can reason so one-sidedly, as that the children ought to suffer for the sin of the parents? What part have they in it?"

"A very great one. If you had as much experience as I of how the descendants of criminals inherit their vices and crimes, you would not speak as you now do, but would, like me, withdraw from all close connection with them. Education and habit, it is true, are able to mitigate and modify the inherited propensities, but I cannot think of such a thing as entrusting my daughter's happiness and future in the hands of a brother of a street-singer accused of theft."

"But yet, something still worse might have happened to you!" exclaimed Bertha firmly, "and that it has not occurred, you have circumstances alone to thank."

"What do you mean, Bertha?" asked the judge, giving her a sharp glance.

"I mean that about a week ago you offered a woman your hand and your heart."

"True, and I asked her to consider the matter until the day before our departure."

"But she answered immediately, however, that she did not need any time for consideration, that she could not become your wife. Had she not already made up her mind, this conversation would have decided her answer. She has now learned that she must *never* marry, even if she were attached to a man with her warmest feelings."

"I do not understand you, Bertha. What has my proposal to you to do with Wenner? He is certainly not the cause of the refusal you gave me, or could report have spoken the truth in asserting that—"

"I do not desire to know what report asserts," said Bertha proudly, "because I only intend to ask: Do you know the origin of the woman to whom you offered your hand? Do you really know whether her parents were better than Wenner's, and whether she like him has not a disgrace for a paternal inheritance?"

"I know that her father was uncle to Lagerskog and thus distantly related to my wife."

"But that does not hinder my poor father from having spent three years in—" Bertha laid her hand on Liedgren's arm and whispered some words in his ear.

The judge turned pale and made a motion as if the words had burned him. He looked at the young widow with a doubting glance, but the expression of her face was such that it corroborated but too much the sad truth of her words.

"Well then," resumed Bertha, "am I, his daughter, less worthy of respect and affection on that account? I do not think so. And yet, you would to-day hesitate to offer me your name. Am I any worse after this acknowledgment than before it? Do I not possess the same virtues as before I uttered it? And if so, they ought to weigh something. If virtue and human worth alone weigh, then, uncle, the judgment over Wenner is unjust, and you have sacrificed your child's peace and happiness to a prejudice. If Wenner cannot become Gertrude's husband, because his father has committed a murder, then I cannot remain in your house as Gertrude's friend. If we are to let prejudices rule us, they must be applied with consistency. I am thus fully prepared to have you forbid Gertrude all connection with me, as a person unworthy of her. To spare us both the humiliation of hearing this expressed, I will await your decision in my room. Until I receive it, we will not see each other again."

An hour later a little note was handed Bertha from the judge. It ran thus:

"The lesson which you gave me, Bertha, was sharp, and perhaps also just. I will not reflect upon it now. All that I have to say for the moment is: You will not become my wife; this you have positively declared. So be it; yet do not think that what you have revealed to me makes me bear this refusal with better grace, but be assured that it does not affect my affection in any respect. The proof of this, is, that I ask you to remain with Gertrude. She needs your friendship to console her for the loss she has sustained, and you will surely not wish to revenge upon her the mistake which you consider to have been committed by

"GÖRAN LIEDGREN."

CHAPTER XVI.

WHILE all this took place in Liedgren's house, Count Strålkrans was seen walking up Reign street to St. John's place, where he went in through the gate to a little red wooden house on the corner of the streets mentioned.

The court-yard was large, and on the threshold of one of the little crooked houses sat a man covered with rags, engaged in putting perches in a bird-cage. Beside him stood a larger cage, filled with little unhappy feathered captives, who flopped around frightened and fluttering, everywhere beating against the bars of the prison.

When the count entered, the man looked up and eyed the fine gentleman askance.

"Does any one live here by the name of Fredriksson?" inquired the count.

The bird-fancier closed one eye as he answered:

"I suppose the gentleman means the organ-grinder prince, Paul? Yes, the cuckoo lives there." The man pointed to the little corner house.

The count entered a small, freshly scoured entry, with fine sand and juniper strewn around the surbase. The entrance itself gave indication that the house was presided over by an orderly woman hand. Strålkrans knocked at the door, and in a few seconds it was opened. Before the high-born gentleman stood a young, pretty woman, with a child in her arms. Her attire was simple, but extremely neat. The large white apron and the little ruffle around the neck, which fell down on the dark, homespun dress, gave to her person something so attractive, that the eye rested on her with especial delight.

"Is Fredriksson at home?" asked the count.

"No, my husband has just gone away this morning," answered the young wife, dropping a curtsey.

"That is too bad; I wished to see him," said the count, who, instead of allowing himself to be dismissed by this intelligence, stepped into the dwelling. He looked around the large corner room. The three windows were filled with flower-pots and adorned with white curtains. The furniture was plain, it is true, but there was a stamp of tidiness and home comfort over the whole, which made a favorable impression.

Hanna, Paul's wife, looked surprised at the count, who had stepped in so unceremoniously.

"My name is Strålkrans," said the count, "and as I cannot see your husband, perhaps you will allow me to tell you what I intended to say to him, or rather, beg you to answer some questions.'

"If I can, I will, most certainly." Hanna placed a chair for the stranger.

"Is it from necessity that your husband continues to go around with a hand-organ?" asked the count.

"It is his livelihood," answered Hanna without constraint. "He has never done anything else, and he has earned his bread in this way ever since childhood."

"Has he no saved-up means, or anything else to live on? I have been told that he has a rich brother; does the latter do nothing for him?"

"My husband has a little money saved up, but we do not wish to touch it, because it is intended for our old age," responded the young woman. "It is true that his brother is both a rich and respected man and that he would willingly give Paul half of his property, if my husband would accept it. But Paul has once for all refused all gifts from his brother. He likes him too much to wish to have anything but his affection. Paul is grieved if his brother even speaks of giving him anything, so it is not Conny's fault that Paul does not share his money. Besides, what could my husband do with it? He couldn't anyhow refrain from going around the country with his hand-organ, it has become second nature with him. When he has given it up for a time he longs for his wanderings, and why then should he not continue them? We have our income, are cheerful and happy, without abundance and without need."

There was something in Hanna's tone and appearance which spoke of true contentment.

"But has it never occurred to Paul that his capacity of organ-grinder gives him the character of an adventurer, and that his brother may possibly have unpleasant consequences from it?"

"Ah, Herr count, if he had ever thought of any such thing, he would assuredly have immediately ceased singing in the streets. Far higher than his own comfort, me and the child, he places the affection for his brother. But who could ever suspect that the organ-grinder and Notary Wenner were brothers! We tell it to nobody. Conny has never, since he entered court, been able to prevail on Paul to visit him. Paul always says: people would wonder what the street-singer had to do with the notary. It is no one's business that we are brothers, that is a matter which we can keep to ourselves."

"Are you then sure that there are no persons who are aware of the relationship and might use it to lower Wenner? I consider him besides a man who would not deny his brother, however unpleasant the consequences might be which he would draw upon himself through this acknowledgment."

"Yes, you are certainly right, Herr count," replied Hanna with animation, "and it was just this which induced Paul to go away to-day. He said that he would be gone until Conny had left the capital, which ought to occur to-morrow."

"Was there anything especial that prompted your husband to this step?"

"Yes indeed, there was. Conny, yesterday, left a large company to speak to Paul, and that too, although there was a baron in the company by the name of Lodstein, whom Paul believed to have knowledge that he and Conny were brothers. He had not intended to go to Djurgården that day; but in the morning a boy came here from Blå Porten and told Paul that some gentlemen, who were to dine there, desired to hear him sing, and they promised to pay him, if he came there with his hand-organ. Paul went, but had no sooner begun to sing than he saw that baron and afterward his brother. Paul immediately suspected that some snare had been laid, and that they had lured him there, in order to humiliate Conny. He took his hand-organ and left, but had not walked many steps before Conny came after him. Paul begged Conny several times not to go with him, as he feared that the baron had guessed that Conny was his brother, but Conny answered: 'Well, what then, do you think I make any secret of it? No, my dear Paul. When I separate from you, I intend to tell the whole company up there that you are my brother.' These words of Conny's troubled Paul, and he said when he came home: 'I am going away for a few days, for otherwise I will be the cause of annoyance to Conny. All are not like him, and most people will withdraw from him, when they learn that he is my brother.'"

"Would you like to have your husband abandon his itinerant life?" asked the count, after a moment's silence.

"Ah, yes. I would much prefer it if he had another vocation, but I love him so well, and know that he would not be happy otherwise, therefore I am satisfied as it is."

"Still I would have liked to make him a proposition,

namely, to become chorister in the country. There is such a place vacant in a community where my large estates are situated. If Fredriksson were disposed to accept this occupation, I would see that he obtained it. His fine voice could then be turned to account. Now I desire you to inform him of my proposition. Tell him also, that if he loves his brother, you and his child, he ought to sacrifice his itinerant habits and try to reconcile himself to a regular life. He will then have a future, and as a married man he ought to think of securing a steady position in life."

"But, Herr count, I do not wish Paul to lay such bonds upon himself for our sake. Ah, he would not thrive if he were obliged to give up his present way of life."

"If you do not wish him to do it for you and your child, you will not refuse, when I tell you that his appearance at Blå Porten will probably result in the engagement between Wenner and Mamsell Liedgren being broken. You do not know what prejudices people have against all persons who travel about and gain their living by amusing others. Wenner will never be induced to deny his brother, and this brother, on the other hand, will always, if he does not give up the life calling he now follows, have a disastrous effect on his future. And again, your little son will sometime grow up, and you certainly cannot wish to have him become what his father is. Not one among a hundred can keep his soul so free from the contamination of vice, when he is obliged, like Paul, to live among the populace of the streets. If you wish to make your son a useful man, then use your influence and persuade your husband to accept my offer. Farewell."

The count rose and gave the young woman his hand, as he added:

"I will come back in a week. Your husband will only be away a few days. But what you must promise me, is, that nothing shall be mentioned to his brother, until Paul has given a decided answer. May all be well with you."

Hanna curtseyed and expressed her thanks at length for the count's goodness, after which the latter took his departure.

Strålkrans thought, when he walked away:

"As yet I do not know whether Bertha loves Wenner or not, or whether report spoke the truth, when it asserted that she did. But be this as it may, it shall never be said of me that my jealousy hindered me from acting so that I felt satisfied with myself. Lodstein has resolved to injure Wenner, I, to counteract his work. This I consider my duty, as both Wenner and his brother, through that unlucky gain at the gambling-table, have drawn upon themselves the baron's hatred. If Wenner possesses the happiness which I have striven for in vain, this can never exert any influence upon my actions."

After the count left the organ-grinder's home, Hanna opened a door leading to a little room, next to the large one.

"Dear Aunt Lova," cried she to an old woman who was in there, and in whom we recognize our old acquaintance Jungfru Lova, "do you know what aristocratic company I have had?"

"Yes, indeed, I have heard every word, and I tell you what it is, Hanna, if you do not make a man of your strolling husband this time, we will never be friends. Only think, to be a respected chorister in the country, with a homestead and good-repute! I should think that was something worth while, and a little better than to roam around the streets, and bawl with the hand-organ. If you don't speak plainly to Paul, I will, for a stop shall be put to this sort of life, I promise you."

"But, aunt, Paul is such an orderly and good man that—"

"That he is anyhow only a miserable organ-grinder. Yes, indeed, that is just the way it is; but you see the matter is now settled, he shall become a chorister just as sure as my name is Lova."

Hanna smiled at her aunt and begged her not to meddle in the matter, but allow her to speak to Paul.

Late that evening Conny visited his brother's home, and then learned that Paul had gone away. Hanna said that she did not know when Paul would come back.

Conny had a long private conference with Jungfru Lova about a yearly allowance which he made for his nephew, so that the boy might have a good education. He confided the letter of agreement to Lova, who was to give it to Hanna, together with a sum of money for unforeseen needs, after he had left Stockholm.

When Conny was about to go, Hanna said:

"You look sad, Conny, has anything happened?"

She thought of the count's words about the betrothal.

"Oh, no, I do not feel quite well," said Conny, and took leave.

"Are you going to-morrow, as you said to Paul?" inquired Hanna, when he stood at the door.

"I think not. We will see each other again before I leave Stockholm."

Conny went.

Two days afterward Paul returned, late in the evening. He walked quite merrily to his home with the dear hand-organ on his back. When he entered the court-yard the bird-fancier sat outside his door.

"Good gracious, is the organ-grinder prince home already!" exclaimed he, at the sight of Paul. "Why have you been in such a devilish hurry this time; perhaps you think, you crowing cuckoo, that your wife has been crying for you? She hasn't by a long shot. An aristocratic gentleman has been here and consoled her. One must be as blind as an owl in the day-time, and stupid as a sparrow, not to calculate where the organ-grinder gets his money from. Well, well, it pays better to have a pretty wife than a cage full of birds. Ha, ha, ha."

Paul stopped when the bird-fancier hailed him. He had at the insults against Hanna put down the hand-organ; and when the ragamuffin uttered his mocking laugh, Paul stood before him.

"See here, Nilsson," said he with suppressed anger, "you may exhaust your malice and envy upon me, but do not open your bill to say an evil word about my wife, for then you may get such a rap over your mouth, that you will never forget it."

"Oh, the d——l, it would be too much honor if you should condescend to put your delicate paw on my dirty skin. Or do you think, you screech-owl, that I am frightened by such words from you? No, sir, I care no more for it than the screaming of birds, and therefore I will tell you that your wife, before you married her, was in Upsala a—"

Nilsson could not finish, for Paul's hand fell with an energetic blow on his mouth, and there was great danger of this being followed by a dozen others, had not a voice just then exclaimed:

"What, Paul, I believe you allow that scoundrel to excite you!"

Paul turned round, and Conny stood there.

"Come, and waste neither words nor blows upon that low fellow; it is of no use," added Conny, as he took hold of Paul's arm and drew him away.

The bird-fancier, who had been accustomed to have Paul endure all his attacks and abuse quite patiently, without ever showing his resentment, had been perfectly dumfounded by the violent blow. Like most mean persons, Nilsson was only bold and courageous toward those who did not defend themselves, but sneaking and cowardly, when he had a pair of strong fists before him. Paul's blow had therefore completely silenced him, until he saw Paul and Conny receding. Then he called after the former:

"You will have to pay up for that blow, d——n me, and in a way that will send you to the d——l!"

Conny and Paul had proceeded directly to the house, without paying any attention to his words; and Hanna welcomed her husband with beaming eyes. At the same moment she put her arms around his neck, a man, who through the half open gate, which Conny had forgotten to close, had witnessed the latter part of the scene between Nilsson and Paul, entered the yard and went to the bird-fancier.

"Have you birds to sell?" asked he, looking at the man's face, distorted with rage.

"Of course I have," snarled Nilsson, and added, muttering to himself: "If I can do anything to that rascal, then—"

"You will not keep from it," interrupted the stranger. "All right, let us go in your house, and I may perhaps be able to help you with that matter."

END OF THE SECOND PERIOD.

THIRD PERIOD.

CHAPTER I.

HERE are periods in our life with which we do not willingly occupy our thoughts. Such a period was that which lay between my arrival in Stockholm and the breaking of my engagement.

The impression of being declared unworthy to obtain an honest man's daughter for a wife, because I was the son of a criminal, at first left no room for any feeling but wounded pride. Howsoever I examined my life, I found nothing, when I compared it with that of other young men, which entitled Gertrude's father to act as he had done. I had made myself known all through for capability and integrity. There was no deed which could be said to have cast the least shadow upon my honor, and yet Liedgren had declared that I could not become his son-in-law. The only thing which might have made me unworthy of it, my love for Bertha, he had no knowledge of, and even if he had divined it, this would not have affected his consent to give me his daughter, when I requested her hand. It was thus prejudice, and only prejudice, which caused this break.

When Liedgren left me, wounded self-love alone prevailed. Under the influence of this and governed by my resentment, I seized the pen and wrote to Bertha, whom in my excited condition I accused of being the cause of the evil. It seemed to me that *she* ought to have known the man to whose daughter she as good as forced me to propose, and that it was her duty to inform me of his arrogance. I had actually succeeded in convincing myself that I had every right to regard Bertha and Gertrude as those who had drawn these humiliations upon me; accordingly I wrote the following letter to Bertha:

"MADAM! You can now triumph and be satisfied, for through you I have experienced all the agony that a human being can endure. I have loved you without hope. Still you could not even grant me the poor joy of adoring you as a free man, but you enjoined it upon me to bind myself to another, alleging that I disturbed the poor girl's peace. I obeyed you, because I have never yet allowed any one to appeal to my sense of duty in vain. I consequently proceeded without any hesitation to devote my life to this girl, whom I never loved. Thus I have nothing to reproach myself for.

"Now to you, who led me into this connection. How have you acted? Like a heartless egotist. You wished to be rid of a person whose homage displeased you, and you threw him quite recklessly into a closer connection with Gertrude's father. What mattered it to you, if he in his arrogance affronted me in such a manner that a whole life would not be able to expiate the insult, if you only escaped a love to which you could not respond! Well then, madam, this is the gain of your course of action. If Gertrude had been loved by me as deeply as I once loved you, I would nevertheless, after the father's behavior toward me a few hours ago, have been forced to detest her. How then do you think my feelings are now, when I never cherished love for her? Why, they are so bitter, that they can only be compared to those I have for you, the cause of all the humiliations which have been heaped upon me. You have conquered, Bertha; for to-day you are as hateful to me as the woman whom you made my fiancée.

"If I once, in the outbreak of an unrestrained passion, was so unfortunate as to compromise you against my will, you have now been revenged, as Gertrude's father has declared me unworthy to marry his daughter. Now, farewell, and congratulate yourself upon having paid me back for the evil which I once involuntarily occasioned you. When you read these lines, I will have returned Gertrude the ring which bound her to

"CONNY WENNER."

The contents of this letter best prove what an insignificant rôle reason then played in my perturbed soul; for had its voice been heard, when I wrote down these inconsiderate words, they would probably never have been written.

After I had sealed this edifying epistle, I went to Gertrude, to, under the influence of the same feeling which dictated the letter, break the engagement. I gave Liedgren's servant the letter to Bertha to carry up to her, and then took my way to the saloon. My desire was that Bertha should read the letter while I returned Gertrude her ring. My conversation with the latter, however, was very different from what I had supposed.

I had expected first tears and accusations, then a proud contempt, when she learned that I was a child of low origin. But I left this girl, whose betrothed I had been for half a year without knowing what a noble heart she possessed, with a warmer affection than I had ever felt for her. I therefore experienced something resembling shame over all my selfishness, and I returned to my lodgings and shut myself up in my room, in order to reflect upon my past life, examine my actions and try to mark out my future.

I had spent the whole day without seeing or receiving anybody, when the servant knocked at my door and handed me a letter. Without looking at it I threw it on the table; for I had recognized Liedgren's servant and supposed that it was from Bertha. The letter had to lie there a good while before I opened and read it. At length I resolved to do so, but with a peculiar repugnance, as I had wished, after my return from Gertrude, that I had never written to Bertha.

Just as I broke the seal, my eyes fell on the address. It was not to me, but there stood in Bertha's handwriting: "Count Mauritz Strålkrans." The servant had made a mistake with the letter, or else given me the count's instead of that which was intended for me, and now I had opened the count's letter. My honor and my delicacy commanded me to immediately seal and send it to the right owner, but a feeling of bitter envy seized me.

This *favorite of birth*, who enjoyed all the advantages I lacked, perhaps also possessed that of being beloved by the woman whom I adored.

The injustice of our inheriting honor or dishonor, as we inherit wealth or poverty from our parents, was keenly realized, and I felt a deep animosity toward this man from whom I had never received anything but that which had been a blessing to me. I forgot that he had appeared as my defender, when I as a child was abused because I was a murderer's son. I forgot that his lips had been the first that expressed sympathy for me on account of my unfortunate paternal inheritance, and I had only the recollection that he belonged to the privileged class of nobility. I drew parallels between the count and me, and I could not comprehend why he should stand above me, yet he did. Had he a better brain, superior knowledge or higher ideas of honor and duty than I? My self-love answered no, and yet, through his rank, his wealth and his social conditions, he had risen to the position of councillor. If I worked with the greatest zeal my whole life through, displayed the greatest capability and made myself known as the most distinguished man in my profession, I would for all that never occupy a position corresponding to his, never gain the respect, through my own merits, which was rendered him unconditionally.

"Has this man then been so irreproachable in his morals?" thought I. "No, he has been a gambler and ruined himself. He has at one time led a very dissipated life, although he again became a rich man through the property left him by his high-born relatives. I have never been a gambler, never been dissipated, and yet people dare to insult me, while they bow before the count.

While I so reasoned, I forgot that the same gambling, which had once swallowed up the count's fortune, had made me rich. I only sought for the shadows in the life of the man to whom I owed gratitude.

Human egotism is a poor adviser. While I was nursing my wrath over social injustice, my envy whispered to me to take cognizance of the contents of this letter. I opened it. Bertha wrote:

"Count Strålkrans:—My hope that fate would spare me the bitter grief of once more causing you sorrow, you have baffled. It is the second time that you speak the words of love to me, the second time that you place your future in my hands, and for the second time I am forced to disappoint you.

"Do not feel aggrieved. I shall not now, as the former time, recklessly push you from me; I shall open my heart to you, and you will understand and respect my reasons, when I say to you that our destinies *cannot* be united.

"From the first time of our acquaintance, I have loved

you. I was then a child and a stranger in the land and the family where I was educated, and in need of an affection, which I lacked. You gave it to me and became to me *all.* That the feeling which then bound me to you was something that never ought to have arisen in my soul, something which would heap sorrow and suffering upon you and me, I did not then understand; but circumstances were to open my eyes. We parted. When we again met, I was fully conscious how I ought to act. I had made a crushing discovery. It concerned my father, and enlightened me that he in his younger years had committed some crime, which, like a dark stain, clung to his past life and cast a shadow upon his honor. He had since then changed his name, in order to escape public contempt and persecution, and he had tried, through strictness toward himself, activity and usefulness, to gain a respect which a youthful offence had caused him to lose. He was kind toward his dependents, merciful to the poor, and so conscientious, that not even malice had anything to say against him. But notwithstanding all this, strange reports were circulated about him, although people knew nothing of his past life.

"There were only two persons who, in the land-owner Engberg, recognized a man who had been punished by the law. These two were my departed husband, and the woman Christina Barsk. The last-named received from my father a yearly allowance, as a payment for her silence; the former demanded his daughter's hand, as the only price for which he would keep mute.

"When I saw you again, I had already endured all the misery which these discoveries of a necessity occasioned, and I knew that my father's honor and reputation rested entirely in Lagerskog's hands. It was my duty to sacrifice myself, so as to save my father. Neither did I hesitate to do it, and in order to make it easier for you to forget me, I was firmly resolved to leave you in ignorance that I obeyed the voice of duty at the expense of my heart.

"You left me with hard words and bitterness. I did not call you back; neither did I die of grief, although it seemed to me that I ought to cease to live, when you went away. We saw each other only twice during my marriage. One year after I became a widow we met. Your manner and whole behavior led me to suppose that you had forgotten the fancy which bound you to me. But, count, years had not changed my feeling, it belonged to you. I hoped, however, that I would never be tempted to tell you this, never be obliged to answer you as I must now do, that the criminal's daughter cannot become the wife of the noble Count Strålkrans.

"I will not and cannot tell you what my father did, but you will understand me when I declare that no love nor any suffering could induce me to give a hand, to which is attached the curse of disgrace, to one whom I love and admire with my whole soul. I have to-day learned how cruel people are toward the children of parents whom society has branded. I do not wish the time to come when you would think, with a feeling of fear, of a woman who by a single word can inform the world that I am the daughter of a convict. You shall never through me have to engraft so unworthy a shoot upon your noble family-tree.

"If I had been the daughter of an ever so poor and humble man, known for his integrity, I would without hesitation have obeyed the voice of my heart. As it is, honor and conscience command me to stifle it.

"Count, endeavor to understand me; try not to feel vexed at me, but allow the woman, to whom you have to-day offered your hand, to remain your friend. We, the children of parents who have left us to atone for their misdeeds, ought to beware of drawing others into the circle of shame and disgrace which surrounds us; we have been born for sacrifices; we must through good deeds and forgetfulness of ourselves try to pay the debt they left behind. It would be wrong to complain because the retribution falls back upon the children. The thought that a single offence brings a whole series of sufferings with it, not only to us, but to our descendants, must stand as a shield between us and temptation. Those who cast this shield aside and deviate from their duty have doomed their family to penance.

"As your friend, I desire to live and die; but your wife, I cannot become. It would pain me if you could not give me your friendship. That you may forgive the sorrow which I occasion you, is the prayer of

"BERTHA."

I, who at the least attack against me for my father's crime, felt wounded, humiliated and irritated, experienced at the perusal of Bertha's letter a complete revolution in my soul. I began to regard our social prejudices from an entirely different standpoint, and to judge of my own position in life with less self-illusion than I had hitherto done.

That night, like the preceding, slumber fled from my couch, and I spent it in reviewing the past.

I resolved to go to Strålkrans, give him the letter and acknowledge that I had learned much since I opened it.

I was dressing myself in the morning, when a messenger from the count presented himself with a letter. It was to me, written by Gertrude. Beside the seal the count had written: "This letter I found on my arrival late last evening, on my table. It has been left in my room by mistake. If one to me has strayed to you, Herr notary, then send it back by the messenger."

I gave the man the answer that I would call on the count in an hour's time. Then I opened Gertrude's letter, somewhat puzzled at her writing to me after the break that had taken place. What could she now have to say? The first object that met my eyes when I took it from the envelope was my letter to Bertha. It lay enclosed in one from Gertrude. "Could Bertha have asked Gertrude to return it?" thought I, as I unfolded the latter's letter and read:

"CONNY: The enclosed letter was intended for Bertha, but it has never come to her hands, for I have read it. She has no knowledge of its existence and I hope she never will have. May it remain as if it had never been written. Allow me, as your friend, to add these words: it is seldom other persons that we ought to accuse for our sufferings, but naturally ourselves. If we examine our own acts, we will find in them the cause of our misfortunes.

"It is not necessary for me to say more. You have probably gained so much calmness by this time, that you will not call Bertha to account for trying to secure my happiness. This happiness was not in accordance with your taste, and therefore it was destroyed; but on the ruins of it we can raise a new structure, stronger and better than that which fell, I mean friendship. You are surprised at this proposal from the daughter of the man who has so deeply wronged you.

"Ah, do not be surprised, but take my hand, which is to-day offered you in friendship. It is offered you from a sincere heart. Why should you detest me? My only fault has been that I loved you, and this I would have done even if you had been born in a prison. I would have liked to be Bertha, to possess your love; but I will die content, if you will remember me without bitterness and, before we part for ever, let me know by a few words that you without ill-will think of GERTRUDE."

With emotion I raised Gertrude's letter to my lips, and had she stood before me I would have thrown myself at her feet and acknowledged that I considered myself unworthy her love and friendship.

But two days previous Gertrude was in my opinion a child, upon whom I looked down with a certain superiority, and now she stood so high above me in magnanimity and greatness of soul, that I felt keenly how worthless I was in comparison with the young girl.

Gertrude had taken such a revenge, that she had placed herself between me and any other woman, for where in life would I find this disinterested and forgiving love?

I wrote in reply these words:

"At this moment it stands plainly before my soul that if I had two lives, I ought to use one to atone for what I have done to Gertrude, and the other to make myself worthy her friendship. At Gertrude's feet is the right place for CONNY."

CHAPTER II.

MY visit to the count was perhaps the most humiliating to my pride of anything I had undergone. I had to acknowledge to him a deed which gave evidence of lack of delicacy.

When I mentioned that I, after the seal had been broken by chance, read the letter, Strålkrans sprang up, seized me by the arm and exclaimed:

"Sir, have you actually dared to read *her* letter to me?"

"Yes, Herr count, I have indeed forgotten myself so far."

For an instant I believed that he intended to throw me out of the door. But the next minute he let go of my arm and seated himself in an easy-chair, muttering something which I could not hear.

Some seconds elapsed, then he looked up, and said with a firm and serious voice:

"You have entered upon a wrong road, if you think you can gain success in life through a blind submission to your passions. Such a weakness sullies a man's honor as a matter of course; for as yet the slaves of passion have never created happiness and success, either for themselves or others. What avail intelligence and culture, if they are not able to guide us, so that we act in all respects and on all occasions as honor commands? Hand me Fru Lagerskog's letter, and I will try to forget that you have violated the requirements of delicacy."

The blood burned like fire in my veins at these words, but they were deserved, and instead of exciting my anger, they called forth my shame. I also had courage to tell the count the motives which actuated me. He listened to me while he stared at Bertha's open letter, and when I finished, he reached me his hand, with the words:

"Envy of others' advantages is a bitter enemy to our peace and always leads to the degradation of our better nature. But that which is done, Herr notary, cannot be altered, and therefore we will speak no more about it. You have, however, now given me the right to give you some advice. I will use it. When a man, like you, has resolved to gain a name, a position in life and the respect of his fellow-beings, so as to conquer the prejudices which are attached to his birth, he must firmly and earnestly make up his mind to banish all paltry and selfish desires which have only the pleasure of the moment in view. He must not sacrifice the future for a fleeting enjoyment. He must not begin, as you have done, by exposing women and trifling with their peace, but devote himself to useful occupations and strive for self-command. There is no one so humble, whose birth is so disreputable, whose parents have been so base, that he cannot through capability, culture and elevated deeds, gain respect and make the world forget his origin. People are far less slaves to their prejudices than we believe, if we only take good care to fulfil the requirements of honor and conscience in every respect. The fault generally lies with the individual, who does not realize that he has roused prejudice against him through his own acts, and then he complains about injustice. You have done so, you have been absolutely wrong in not telling Liedgren when you asked for his daughter's hand: so and so was my father. If you had done that, you would have left him free to decide how much your origin weighed in the balance of prejudice, and you would then have escaped the trials which befel you. As it was, your conduct appeared as if you had tried to gain Liedgren's daughter by unfair means and by concealing yourself behind your foster-father's name, and therefore you received his affront. Consequently you have no one to blame but yourself for what has happened. Take a retrospect of your life and you will find that you have never been assailed by any prejudice against your origin, when you yourself fearlessly acknowledged whose child you were. Such an acknowledgment silences calumny, and people render their respect unreservedly to merit, even if it has had a criminal for progenitor. You have devoted yourself to the legal profession. Well then, first sit in judgment over your own soul, and do not allow false accusations against others to serve you as an excuse, when you are to consider your own mistakes. And now, my young friend, we must separate. I do not yet know the contents of this letter, and I desire to learn right soon what you already know. You are welcome to come again, if I can serve you with any advice, and you can henceforth regard me as your friend."

The count offered me his hand, I pressed it with warmth and gratitude.

Chance so ordained that I, after my conversation with the count, met with my former principal, Judge K——. He inquired when my wedding was to take place, and when he learned that the engagement was broken, he immediately offered me a place with him. I accepted the offer, and two days afterward went with him to M——.

I was now to begin my life anew.

As soon as I arrived at my place of destination, I plunged into work. I no longer appeared as the lion of the day, but I devoted my time and my whole attention to my vocation, and tried to identify myself in every way with my calling as a lawyer. K—— found me much changed, and as he often said, to my advantage. "It is now evident," he asserted, "that you embrace your new calling with true interest."

Some time elapsed without my getting any letter from Paul. I had only received one since my departure from Stockholm, and then he promised to write soon and inform me of a change which he contemplated for the future. But no further letter came, although I immediately wrote a reply to him. One day in September I received the following epistle from Wicker.

"My honored Brother! What a deuced amount of work you must have to do there in M——, as you have not had time to scribble a few lines in answer to my last letter. I for my part think that you ought to be particularly interested in knowing how events roll on here.—When I last wrote, the old man had not returned, as you may remember. He arrived here a week after my letter was despatched. He came home all alone, with an appearance as if he had been in company with the devil's 'Fru mamma.' Directly afterward the court sat. I will say in passing that it was a tremendous one. The old man had got it into his noddle that I united two individuals in my person, and consequently ought to work for two. I put in with all my might, but it was beyond me. I had to procure help; but that matter did not seem to affect the old man. He was silent as a fish and let me write ahead as much as I could. He looked fierce and glum on the seat of justice. I have never seen him so before. We work-horses hailed the end of the session with joy, but on the last day of court, we received a new case for our entertainment. The old scratch, or rather, the Stockholm police, had got hold of a poor wretch of an organ-grinder, with whom had been found Baron Casper Lodstein's watch, various articles of jewelry and some silver boxes from the murdered man's dressing-case. The latter had the baron's coat-of-arms on them. All these things the rascal had concealed in his hand-organ, and there they would probably have remained for some time to come, had not the police happened to make a visit to the organ-grinder's home and there discovered the treasure. The organ-grinder was seized unceremoniously and sent here. We thus had the pleasure of receiving him at our bar of justice. I cannot comprehend what ailed the old man, when the organ-grinder was brought in and required to tell his name, but he became as white as a sheet and for a few seconds, even agitated; but in a trice he was again composed, and with unshaken calmness he asked the usual questions.

"The person at last suspected and accused of the Lodstein murder is a tall, slight man, thirty-three years old, with a handsome head. He is called Paul Fredriksson, and has such an intrepid bearing, that one is tempted to immediately declare him innocent of all complicity in the dark deed. His answers were decided, and not once could he be caught in any double meaning. He said that he was completely ignorant of how the articles found in the hand-organ had come there, and he declared that he had not been in these parts for many years. He had never had any knowledge of the baron's journeyings or of anything that concerned the deceased. Everything in the appearance and behavior of the accused indicated innocence and a free conscience, but as he could not account for the articles being in his possession or explain in a satisfactory manner how he, an organ-grinder, had gained so large a sum of money as that which was found in his home when he was arrested, he had to remain in custody until further investigation could be made.

"The session was just over when Fru Lagerskog and Gertrude returned to Brovik. The following morning, the sheriff, who, during the whole trial, had been as furious as a mad dog, was to make a transfer of the prisoner, against whom besides was found the grave circumstance that he, as a youth, had been accused of the theft of a ring, which he had taken from Fabian Lodstein, but had then been acquitted for lack of proof. It looks as if the organ-grinder was perfectly possessed to steal from Baron Lodstein, although he has not otherwise been known for dishonesty.

"The sheriff, who is usually so zealous in prosecuting thieves and villains, was on this occasion unable to conceal his vexation at all proofs against the organ-grinder.

"That evening when we returned home, we gathered as usual in the saloon. I rushed ahead with the intelligence that they had got hold of an organ-grinder, who was regarded as Lodstein's murderer, or at least suspected as one who had been an accomplice in the murder. Gertrude asked me the name of the accused, and when I mentioned it, her cheeks became snow-white. By the way, your former fiancée, during the weeks she has been absent, has undergone a very essential change. Whether it is to her advantage or not, I leave to conjecture; but she is no longer like herself. She looks as if she had become ten years older and more sensible. She never indulges in any comical caprices and freaks, never utters any foolish jest; but maintains a dignity and a seriousness which are quite matronly. The condition between her and her papa appears somewhat strained. She does not throw herself on his neck as before, and he no longer pats the round cheeks, but they keep themselves at a proper distance from each other.

"But we will now return to the organ-grinder. Gertrude asked me all sorts of questions about how he deported himself during the trial, when he was to be taken to prison, etc. After I had given her all the information I could, she left me abruptly, and did not honor me with another word for the whole evening.

"The widow, I mean Fru Bertha, is just as she has always been: beautiful and stiff.

"I could be tempted to wager my stately beard that something has transpired between her and the old man. Whether the latter has got it through his head that Bertha has no desire to pair her youth's summer with his manhood's autumn, I do not know positively; but there is one thing certain, the haughty man no longer seeks her society. She is polite, but cold as a frozen fish.

"Now I come to the best part of the whole story:

"The morning after the ladies' return to Brovik, Mamsell Gertrude was missing. She had gone to S——näs, it was said, for something which she had forgotten. The old man and I had too much else to think of to busy ourselves with what led Gertrude to go to the city. At dinner Liedgren asked Bertha if she knew *what* Gertrude had forgotten that required her to go after it herself. Late that evening Gertrude came home, and that too, with her eyes red from weeping and an appearance which indicated that she had not found what she sought. I stood in the dining-room by one of the windows when she entered. She did not see me, but took her way to the saloon where Bertha sat.

"'Where have you been?' I heard the latter ask with anxiety.

"'In S——näs with the arrested Paul,' answered Gertrude. 'I have spent several hours talking to him. He is completely innocent; that I knew before, is he not the brother—' Of whom, I never learned; for the old man came in and greeted his daughter, without asking her any questions.

"In a fortnight there will be another session, and then the investigation with the organ-grinder will be continued. Our sheriff travels around the country as if he were in pursuit of Beelzebub's emissaries. Whenever he gets sight of me, he grinds his teeth with rage, muttering:

"'If I do not succeed in getting hold of the real villain and in having him convicted of the murder, I will shoot myself in vexation. But it is as if the devil himself was determined to protect *him!*'

"What him he means the birds alone know; I know it as little as I can comprehend why Gertrude started off to the prison. But not enough with all this folly, the day after her journey to S——näs she wrote to Count Strålkrans. I was privately commissioned to post the letter for her, which, when interpreted, signified that her dear papa was not to have any knowledge of it.

"Three days after the letter was mailed, the count's equipage drove up. He then came rushing into the room where the old man and I were working. After a long consultation, the result of which I did not learn, the count went away as quickly as he had come. The next day the organ-grinder's wife and child were lodged at Kungsdal.

"After the count's appearance, Willberg seemed to have regained a part of his reason, and now behaved pretty nearly like a sane man. He is now in a hot chase after the woman with the pack, who was in the neighborhood at the time the crime was committed. If he keeps on he will certainly ferret her out, and I am sure I have no objection.

"And now, I will take a pinch of snuff and confide you to the divine protection of justice, as well as hope that you have sufficient power left in your right hand, in spite of all report writing, to let me know how time has treated you, or you it, and what you are about. I can assure you that I have not the slightest inclination to be your successor with the beautiful Gertrude. That I once took a fancy to her must decidedly be a mistake; God preserve me from girls who have been engaged. She can certainly go in peace, without being disturbed by your honest friend

"WICKER."

To speak of the impression which this letter made, is superfluous. My resolution was instantly taken. I must go to Paul and assist him, but in such a way as to effect something.

It was of no use for me to wait upon him with my condolence, but I must procure information and try to get at the truth.

In the first place, my way led to Stockholm. But before I had time to carry out this decision, another letter arrived in Wicker's hand-writing. I opened it with impatience; but came near dropping it, when I found that only the address was written by my comrade; the contents by Gertrude.

"My friend," wrote she; "as I know that you may perhaps learn by this day's post that your brother has been arrested, I will hasten to calm you with the intelligence that Count Strålkrans has promised to do all in his power to assist Paul, so that his innocence shall be brought to light. I have been to your brother and talked with him. He is perfectly secure in the consciousness of not being a participant in the crime of which he is accused. The only thing which disquiets him, is, that your name may in some way be mixed in the suit, or that the public may learn that he is your brother. He has therefore avoided accounting for the sum of money which was found in his home at the time of the arrest, because you seem to have given this money to his wife's aunt.

"Count Strålkrans has had Hanna and Paul's little son brought to Kungsdal. At the next session we all hope that his innocence will be fully proved, and he himself acquitted. I have this morning been to Kungsdal and seen Hanna. She was very much depressed. Once more, Conny, be assured that all that can be done for Paul will be done by GERTRUDE."

Of this girl I had once written that she excited my disgust, that she wearied me. Oh, what crazy words!

It was one afternoon in the middle of September, when I arrived at the capital. I went directly from the steamer to my brother's former home, after I had first seen that my trunk was sent to the hotel where I generally put up during my stay in Stockholm. When I came to the end of Reign street, it was almost dark. A pair of street lamps, mourning deeply over their solitude, as it seemed, fluttered faintly at the corners, and gave just enough light for people barely to find their way. The street was almost deserted, and only one poor wretch, whose home was probably on the so-called new road, shuffled before me with a pair of wooden shoes. I could with difficulty distinguish the contour of the figure, which I regarded with the attention that one bestows upon a solitary pedestrian in an empty street. After straining my sight, I perceived that the figure carried something in his hand, and when he finally reached one of the small flickering lamps, I saw that it was a bird-cage.

A vivid recollection of the bird-fancier whom Paul had given a blow in the face, when the latter vilified Hanna, and the threat the rascal uttered, flashed across my mind.

The man, who noticed that some one came after him, stopped and turned round. We were not many steps from the lamp, whose dim light illumined his face. A single glance was sufficient to convince me that I was not mistaken. It was indeed the bird-fancier who had been my brother's neighbor. When the latter cast his eyes on me, he seemed perfectly reassured, and continued his way quite at his ease. I followed him, but in such a manner that he could not suppose this to be my intention. On arriving at the corner of St. John's place and Reign street, he went very properly into the house opposite the gate. I walked ahead on the new road, so as to give him time to get fairly in, before I visited my man. About a quarter of an hour after I had seen him disappear through the gate, I entered, passed by the entrance of Paul's abode and now stood outside the door of the shanty where the bird-fancier lived. I knocked, as I called out:

"Does any one live here who has birds to sell?"

In an instant the door opened, and the red-haired fellow's tricky face grinned at me, lighted by a tallow dip, which he held raised above his head, so as to see better. I asked him if he had any canary birds. He told me to walk in, after he had first surveyed my outer person. I wished to purchase a pair of birds, and he led me to a large cage, where he had some. I pretended to regard the little creatures with the greatest interest, made him take them out of the cage, and inquired whether they were tame and good singers, etc. He praised them up very much and asked a pretty high price for them, as he had probably come to the conclusion that I was an amateur and that he might make a good bargain. I higgled about the terms and finally chose two pair. He was to bring them to me the next morning, and received from me the money to buy a cage. The birds I did not pay for, but he should get the money for them when he came. After the bargain was made and I was about to go, I said, as if I had just then thought of it:

"Doesn't an organ-grinder live here in this row?"

"He did live here," said the bird-fancier with a repulsive smile, as he squinted at me with his half-tipsy eyes, "but now the police have provided a room for him, so that he can get rid of paying any rent."

"The police," repeated I, "what then had the poor satan done?"

"Oh, not so much; it was only suspected that he had stabbed a baron to death. At least he had something to do with the affair and took his share of the pillage; for you see, they found in Paul's house a whole lot of things that had belonged to the murdered man. He hadn't calculated that they would find all these valuables; but so it goes, when one tries to be a nabob among poor wretches. Organ-grinder Paul has had his nose pulled for—"

"So he was a bad fellow?" interrupted I.

"Worse than that, for he was a stuck-up jackanapes, who never could ask one to take a sup or a glass of beer, and thought himself too good to go with his equals into a tavern. But you see, it may now happen that others think themselves too good to keep company with him."

The bird-fancier had an ugly look when he said this, and the suspicion, which from the beginning had arisen in my mind, that he had some part in my brother's arrest, was now strengthened. My resolution was accordingly taken to try to ferret out the truth through this wretch, who was probably as cowardly as he was wicked. But in order not to excite any suspicions then, I put an end to the conference.

My plan was made. When I got him on my own ground, I would try to discover from what reason the police had made a visitation to my brother. I hoped that if I could learn this I might also ascertain who had smuggled the murdered man's things into my brother's keeping. If I only obtained some clue, it might lead to the discovery of the crime. It is true, I could have obtained this information through the hirelings of the police; but I did not wish to be seen, until I could appear as one who had procured sufficient proof of Paul's innocence.

If the accusation was instigated by the person I supposed, then Paul's enemy was so powerful and probably so vigilant, that the greatest caution was demanded in order to succeed. The only means which I considered myself to possess was to join the bird-fancier's interests to mine, and through him, arrive at the facts.

I accordingly took my departure; but returned two hours later, when I stole to Paul's former abode and knocked at the door. In a few minutes it was opened by Aunt Lova, who held a light in her hand. She opened her mouth for an exclamation, but I pushed her into the room and closed the door behind us.

From Lova I obtained the full account of Paul's arrest.

The police had presented themselves in Paul's house late one evening and asked him a multitude of questions about his whereabouts at the time the murder was committed.

When Paul said that he was then in Copenhagen, they were not willing to believe it, because they had been told that he was seen in the neighborhood of X——.

After the inquiries followed the search, and Paul had quite calmly allowed them to proceed, when, to his great consternation, they found in his possession various trinkets and things which had belonged to Casper Lodstein. Paul was arrested. Lova finished her narrative with the words:

"I am fully convinced that the bird-fancier, the rascal, has his claws in the matter; for I happened to go out in the entry, where the hand-organ stood, quite late the evening before, and then I saw the loafer sneaking away from here. I immediately thought: What deviltry is he up to now, and what can he have to do in the entry? He has always had a spite against Paul, and it is no one but he that has done it."

"But," objected I, "how could the things stolen from the murdered man get into the bird-fancier's hands? It would not have been possible, unless he was an accomplice in the murder."

Lova kept silent a moment, and then said:

"No, he had nothing to do with the murder. To be sure he is wicked, but he does not kill. There is some other solution to the whole matter, although I cannot get at it. I believe that they have persuaded him to put these things in Paul's hand-organ, so that the true criminal should not be discovered, and Nilsson, who is envious of Paul, has taken upon himself the commission."

"Who could have persuaded him?" asked I.

"That is more than I can tell," replied Lova. "You, Herr notary, who have made such things your business, ought to be able to find out that; and I'll tell you what it is, you must spare no pains to unravel the mystery and inform the judge first and foremost where the money came from, else I will do it myself, in spite of Paul's prohibition."

Lova and I did not separate until late in the night. The following morning the bird-fancier presented himself, according to orders, in my abode; but he looked at me with an inquiring and distrustful mien, as if he had tried to remember whether he had seen me before or not. I feigned the most complete indifference, and deported myself in the beginning as if I was exclusively interested in the birds. When I had talked about them quite a while, I went behind him suddenly and locked the door, after which I said in a changed tone:

"Do you know who I am?"

The fellow stared at me in dismay and tried to recall to mind when and where he had seen me. I continued:

"It is I who have taken it upon myself to get track of

Baron Lodstein's real murderer, and I now wish to know how you came in possession of the things you succeeded in smuggling into Paul's hand-organ? That you are the one who put them there, I have evidence, and it is no use for you to say anything but the truth. Did you have anything to do with the murder, or are you the assassin?"

The bird-fancier's yellow complexion had changed to an ashy gray. He was taken by surprise and evidently had no courage to speak of. He stammered with trepidation:

"I am entirely innocent. I know nothing about the murder."

"Then how came you to have the murdered man's things, which you put in Fredriksson's hand-organ the night before he was arrested?"

I spoke with confidence and decision, and added that if he did not immediately confess all, I would have him arrested on the spot, and summon the witness who had seen him put the things in the hand-organ. The only thing that could help him was a truthful explanation of how great a part he had in the murder. My manner was such, that I only seemed interested in the discovery of the murderer, but did not pay any regard to Paul. When I showed myself firmly persuaded that the bird-fancier was implicated in the murder, the declaration finally escaped him that he had no knowledge of it, but that he had received the things which he smuggled into Paul's hand-organ from a strange man. All attempts to obtain any further information about the person who had given him the charge, were fruitless, as the bird-fancier himself knew nothing about him, except that he had come to his house twice, the first time after Paul struck Nilsson in the face, and the stranger had at this visit proposed to Nilsson to take revenge on Paul for the blow the latter had given him. The man had finally promised Nilsson a good compensation, if he could smuggle some articles and a gold watch into the hand-organ. I now asked him if he thought he could recognize the man, if he saw him. The bird-fancier scratched his eye and gave me the answer:

"I guess he didn't mean that I should see his face; but you see, I didn't drop him from sight until I had caught a glimpse of it, for I had no desire to risk my hide, without knowing how I could get at his."

I pass over the further examination with the bird-fancier. The next day he and I were on the way to Kungsdal.

It was late in the afternoon when we arrived there.

The conversation between Strålkrans and me was long. I communicated the discoveries I had made, and after we had consulted about the best use to make of them, I bade the count good night, and a servant conducted me to my sleeping apartment.

Nilsson had been entrusted to the inspector, who was enjoined to keep a watchful eye upon him.

Strålkrans placed at my disposal two rooms which he usually occupied, and took for his own accommodation an apartment in another part of the house. The rooms which I had were situated by themselves in the east end of the building.

The recent events and the conversation with the count had been such, that they did not leave any peace in my soul. When I now entered these rooms, where I, after a fatiguing journey, was to seek rest, I did not feel at all disposed for it. After the servant left, I walked to and fro in the inner room for a long time, reflecting upon how insufficient all the evidence I had gained was, and how impossible it was for me to find the criminal on these grounds. I might succeed in getting so far that Paul was not called to any account for the articles found in his possession; but this was a trifling advantage. He would for the second time stand in the false light of having been acquitted only for lack of proof, and I had sworn that Paul should receive a complete justification.

Tired from walking, I finally threw myself, dressed as I was, on the bed, and closed my eyes. I was just on the point of falling asleep, when a peculiar sound, as if some one had crept from under the bed, caused me to quickly open my eyes. At the same instant the light was extinguished and I was enveloped in darkness.

I started up; but was thrown back again on the bed and experienced a violent pain in one shoulder. I had received a stab. The instinct of self-preservation made me forgetful of pain, and I succeeded in getting hold of my assailant's right arm; but before this, however, he had given me another stab. I wrenched the knife from his hand, and flung it from me, after which a struggle ensued between us. We seemed to be equal in strength; but I possessed greater agility. I finally got him under me on the floor, so that I had my knee on his breast; but he then gave me a blow on the temple, which almost made me tumble backward. The danger which threatened was such, that without any hesitation I dealt him several hard blows, which I aimed at his head.

At the last his grasp loosened, and his arms fell powerless. I was immediately on my feet and at the dressing-table to strike a light. The next second the room was illumined.

On the floor lay a man outstretched, senseless and covered with blood. I let the light fall on his face, but started back. I had recognized the features; they belonged to Janne.

I sprang to the bell-cord to ring, but it was cut.

Janne, who had been stunned by the blows, might revive any instant. I hastened to the window and opened it, calling to the servants for help, as I knew by the blows that I had received, and the stabs, which had caused great loss of blood, that I would inevitably be worsted in a fresh encounter. Scarcely had I thrown up the window and raised my first cry, before it seemed to me that I was flung head-long out of it by a pair of strong arms.

When I again opened my eyes, the room was full of people, and I lay on the bed. They were busy binding up my wounds. One was in the shoulder, the other, a long gash in the breast. Among those that surrounded me I looked in vain for the count's and Janne's faces. Finally I inquired after the latter, and received the answer that they had taken him in custody. As my wounds were not of a dangerous nature, I was, thanks to the count's and Hanna's care, so far recovered in two days' time that I could leave my bed.

CHAPTER III.

JANNE had also needed this time to recover from the violent blows which he had received in his head and face during our battle.

Court began again.

The trial was conducted with much zeal. It could be seen that Liedgren was extremely interested in the case, especially as the bird-fancier, after being confronted with Janne, declared that it was he who had commissioned Nilsson to put Casper Lodstein's valuables in Paul's hand-organ.

Baron Lodstein, in whose service Janne said that he had been for many years, was also obliged to present himself at court, where he testified that he, the baron, had no knowledge of Janne's early life, or what part of Sweden he was from; but, that he had taken him in his employ ten years ago, and Janne during this time had so conducted himself that the baron was satisfied with him. Lodstein supposed that Janne had been led by some private desire for revenge, when he concealed himself in the count's apartments; for that he had done it to steal was not likely. As far as the bird-fancier's assertion was concerned, that Janne had given him the murdered Casper's trinkets, the baron considered it a fabrication, as Janne was with him in Copenhagen when his nephew was murdered.

It was utterly impossible to induce Janne to explain the reason why he had concealed himself in the count's room or why he had attempted to murder me. He announced at the beginning of the trial that he did not intend to answer any questions, and he kept his word.

The first day passed, without yielding any results, and as it was an extra session, there was no other case on the docket: the next day it would be continued. Strålkrans and I returned to Kungsdal in the afternoon. Just as our carriage drove up in the yard, a droschka stopped before the right wing. A lady jumped out and went in the house. I recognized Gertrude. The count and I had sat silent during the whole ride from the court-house. At the sight of Gertrude, I turned my head involuntarily and looked at him. He smiled and said:

"Scarcely a day passes in which she does not visit your brother's wife. If any woman has proven herself to have a truly elevated character, it is that girl."

The carriage drove up to the large steps, and we alighted. I had a burning desire to see Gertrude, and for an instant I felt tempted to go down to Hanna, so as to meet her; but the next minute I overcame this desire and remained faithful to my resolution not to bring her ways and mine together of free will.

It was through me, although indirectly, that Paul had been subjected to all these new persecutions; it was consequently my duty to deliver him from the undeserved suffering that had befallen him.

Strålkrans and I spent that evening conversing about various things. I perceived very well that a peculiar shade of depression pervaded my noble protector's demeanor, although he tried to conceal it behind the mask of politeness. I believed that I divined the cause, but I did not dare to utter a single word in allusion to it. When we separated late in the evening, I entered my sleeping apartment in a state of mind as if I realized more keenly than ever that the Supreme Being did not allow us to struggle in vain with injustice and prejudice, but that it was for our benefit, and I believed more firmly than ever in the victory of truth.

The whole of my past life appeared before my soul's eye, and after I had gone through it, my thought stopped at these two women, whose influence had taken such a deep hold upon my life. One I had loved, and that so madly, that I had been blind to the other's uncommonly elevated character. I thought with regret of Gertrude, and I desired to remove the hindrances which raised themselves in the way of Bertha's happiness.

My mind did not dwell long, however, upon these objects, but it was soon directed to that which I considered more important; my efforts to arrive at the truth with regard to Casper Lodstein's murder.

Just as I, after the day's exertions, prepared to retire, some one knocked quite softly on the outer door. I took a light and went to open it. Before me stood an old woman, with a face so dark and wild, that it resembled a fury's.

She was dressed in a shabby skirt and jacket, and wore on her head a large black handkerchief, which looked very much like a pall, under which straggled gray elf-locks.

I had not seen these features since childhood, and time had marked its ravages upon them. Nevertheless I recognized Black Stina.

She looked at me a few seconds and then said:

"Is it you who have testified against Janne?"

"Yes," answered I, curious to learn what she especially wanted, and therefore added: "but what have you to do with that matter?"

"Do not speak so loud," muttered she, giving me a timorous look. "Let me in, and I will tell you something, but I must be on my way before the day dawns, for that hound, the sheriff, has been after me for a long time. But

I am not one to let the devil's allies catch me, if I can help it."

She entered the room and closed the door behind her, saying in a low tone:

"I come from that wretch, the baron. He was not willing to help Janne, but you see, he will have to pay up for that now."

She rubbed her forehead, and her gaze strayed with a singular expression around the room. Then she seated herself on a chair by the door and resumed:

"You are Paul's brother, you cannot bear the baron and you must save Janne. Yes, yes, you will do it, for otherwise it will be Paul who will be left in the lurch."

I promised her that if Janne could be saved, I would try to do it. After she had obtained this assurance, she began a very dismal narrative, of which I will give a brief statement.

It went far back and commenced with the time when Barsk was a private in the same regiment of which Lodstein was second lieutenant. In order to have a clear idea of the course of events, an account of the Lodstein family conditions must precede.

Fabian Lodstein's father had been married twice. By the first marriage he had a son, the heir to the Lodstein property. This son was Casper's father. The second time he married, it was to a widow, with whose beauty and amiable character he fell in love. Her name was Carlon. Through her he became step-father to a daughter and a son. The first-named was ten years old, and the latter nine, when the mother entered into the marriage with Lodstein.

By this marriage the baron obtained the son Fabian. The three half-brothers were brought up together. Between Fabian and the heir a deep hatred arose, which proceeded mainly from Fabian's side. Oscar Carlon, the eldest of the three half-brothers, was the one who constantly played peace-maker, and therefore became loved by both. He himself was especially attached to Fabian, who, all of ten years younger than Oscar, was the mother's favorite. Oscar's predilection for Fabian probably had its chief cause in the circumstance that the mother most loved the youngest son, and Oscar, again, adored his mother. Everything that was dear to her became sacred to him. In addition to this, Oscar's step-father had been very kind and liberal both to Oscar and his sister, who, when quite young, married a lieutenant Lagerskog. A few years after his sister's marriage Oscar became "Auditeur" in one of the regiments of the Guard. A few years more, and Fabian was second lieutenant in the same regiment. Simultaneously with this, Barsk enlisted, in order to escape being called to account for some minor offences which he had committed.

Auditeur Carlon was generally spoken of as a genial, agreeable comrade and an upright young man. Fabian Lodstein, on the other hand, was soon known as a madcap. He was a reckless gambler, an extreme debauchee, proud and arrogant toward all who stood under him, and with the false idea of his position in life, that he, as Baron Lodstein, could do much that was not allowable in others. Barsk had all the baron's vices, although in a more unpolished form; but as he besides was smart and good looking, he was employed by the lieutenant as a messenger, attendant, etc., always executing his commissions to the satisfaction of his superior.

Oscar had also treated the recreant soldier with especial good-will, in the hope of making something of him. He was besides the young auditeur's attendant and all in all.

Fabian had been lieutenant only two years and become of age, when the old Baron Lodstein fell ill and died. On his death-bed he enjoined Oscar to be a father to Fabian and to guard against his staining his noble name with any unworthy or frivolous act. Oscar gave his step-father, to whom he considered himself to stand in a great debt of gratitude, the required promise, fully determined to sacrifice everything rather than break it.

After the old baron's death, the oldest of his sons became sole owner of the whole property. The widow and the younger sons received from the heir only a yearly allowance, which was by no means superabundant.

The year after the baron's decease, Oscar engaged himself to a wealthy and lovely girl. They had not been betrothed many weeks, however, when a disastrous event occurred in the regiment. A large sum of money had disappeared from the treasury. The circumstances were such, that either Fabian Lodstein or Auditeur Carlon must inevitably be suspected. The only one who knew anything positively, as he had been an eye-witness when the theft was committed, was Barsk, but he kept silent for the time being, in order to see how things would shape themselves and what advantage he could derive by speaking or saying nothing. The result of the investigation was that Auditeur Oscar Carlon was arrested. The case created great excitement, and it terminated with Carlon being doomed to imprisonment.

When he had been taken to the place where he was to do penance for his crime, Barsk went to Fabian quite early one morning, and declared that it now depended upon him whether the true thief should be revealed, as Barsk could take his oath that he had seen the baron commit the theft with his own eyes. Besides he had a letter in his possession, which Carlon had written to Fabian the day before he was sent to prison. This letter, Barsk, who on that occasion visited his former protector, had been charged to deliver to Baron Fabian. But he had instead opened and read it. The contents comprised a serious warning to Fabian to beware for the future of every deviation from the right, as he could not always escape the consequences of it by having some one else to assume the crime and suffer the penalty, as Oscar had done.

Barsk demanded money of Fabian for his silence, and the young baron was obliged to pay him, so as not to be accused.

The next year Barsk committed such misdemeanors in the regiment that he was expelled from it. After visiting Fabian and obtaining money, he went to the country, where he made acquaintance with Stina, the daughter of a rag-man of gypsy origin, who lived in Skärparby. He married the rag-man's daughter, and through the step-father became involved in a large robbery, for which he was sentenced to several years' imprisonment. Fate ordained that he was taken to the same place where the former auditeur, Carlon, was confined; but they only remained under the same roof a few days, when Carlon, through his elder step-brother's aid, gained an opportunity to escape. It was so managed that the flight was not discovered until the fugitive was placed in security. Everything was prepared by the elder Lodstein, and through a passport with a strange name, Carlon left Sweden.

In Lübeck Oscar met his former fiancée. When he was arrested, he had sent her back the ring, and then in spite of her eager desire, refused to receive her in prison. Now they met. Oscar wished to withdraw, but she kept him with the positive declaration that she was determined to accompany him, with or without his will.

In Berlin they were married, after which they continued to live abroad for three years. Then the young wife, who had become mother to a daughter by the name of Bertha, was seized with so violent a home-sickness, that her life was in danger. Oscar then resolved to risk the attempt of returning to Sweden, under his assumed name Engberg, and of settling down in some remote province. For this object he purchased the estate Engsgård, and we find in him Bertha's father.

Baroness Lodstein was now dead.

In the meantime Barsk's term of imprisonment had expired; he had regained his freedom and become so thoroughly corrupted in his soul, that he finished by committing a deliberate murder. After this crime he succeeded in eluding detection for several months. While the officers of justice were on his track, he came to Engsgård, where he met Oscar and recognized in him Auditeur Carlon, the escaped convict. Barsk succeeded, by threatening to accuse Carlon, in inducing him to pay him a large sum of money, and to bind himself besides to send a yearly pension to Barsk's wife, if he should die.

Barsk was shortly afterward captured and executed. He had told Stina the whole story about Fabian and Oscar, and given her the letter which the latter had written.

Oscar assigned a yearly annuity to Stina, according to his promise, as long as she lived and maintained silence.

Years went by. Stina received her allowance regularly, and when Oscar died, there was a clause in his will, that Bertha's husband, Lagerskog, should pay a yearly pension to Stina Barsk.

Lagerskog, who was Oscar's nephew, was aware that his uncle had committed a theft and escaped from prison, and when he learned through his mother, on her death-bed, that Carlon, under the name of Engberg and as a wealthy man, lived in Sweden, he looked him up and compelled him, as the price of his silence, to promise that Lagerskog should have his daughter, Bertha, if she was willing to become his wife.

This of the Lodstein conditions. Now to Janne, and how he became Lodstein's servant.

When Janne was dismissed from Professor Wenner's and came to the capital, he met his mother in Stockholm. Stina had then heard that Lodstein resided there, and with the knowledge of the old history, she went to Fabian, in order to force him to give her money, something of which she was always in need. She gained her point; but when she came home with it Janne considered that his mother had received entirely too little and decided to go to the baron himself and have a plain talk with him.

The result of the visit was that Janne was taken into Lodstein's service. The latter had formed a very correct judgment of Janne at their first interview, and regarded him as a man, who, if bound to Lodstein by self-interest, would be useful to him. No conscientious scruples would ever trouble Janne when his advantage beckoned to him.

The master and servant were well suited to each other, and years elapsed, during which Janne, through Lodstein's liberality, as well as less justifiable means, scraped together a nice little sum. The baron observed that his servant was not of the honest sort; but he acted as if he saw nothing, so as to make Janne more confident and if possible get a firm hold upon him.

Shortly before Casper Lodstein took the journey to Westmanland, he was on a visit to his uncle. While he stayed there a large sum of money and a valuable jewelled pin disappeared.

Casper made a great stir about it and demanded the assistance of the sheriff to recover the stolen property. Baron Fabian, however, had prevented this, and without accusing Janne, directed his nephew's suspicions to him. In short, Casper went to Janne and found the money and pin; but then Fabian appeared and hindered the affair from being carried into court. Still Casper had assured Janne that he would bear him in mind.

When Janne's drawers were searched, several other articles of jewelry, which he had stolen, were found there, and Fabian now considered that he had him in his power.

After Casper Lodstein left his uncle to go to Westmanland, Fabian, accompanied by Janne, went to Denmark. Their course, however, led to the same regions which Casper visited; but it was so arranged that the baron and Janne were dressed alike and gave themselves the appearance of being a pair of travelling merchants. Janne's mother, whom the son met in Stockholm, was going to Kungsdal to draw her pension, and received instructions to inquire at every station where Casper was to stay over night. In the woods at D——by, Stina informed Fabian that Casper would remain in X—— until the next morning.

Stina in the meantime went there herself. She suspected that the baron had some private reason why he wished to know his nephew's stopping-places, and resolved to find it out, so as to have another hold upon the rich man, if it was necessary.

The night was far advanced, when Stina saw a man steal into the station. She was just going to creep to the entrance, in order to await the moment when he came out again, when she saw another figure, with noiseless steps, approach and stop under one of the windows. She was not mistaken, it was Janne. A few minutes elapsed, then a stifled shriek was heard, and all became silent again. A few minutes more, and the window, under which Janne had taken his post, was opened. A man swung himself out of it, and holding to the sill, slipped down, so that he gained a foot-hold on Janne's shoulders, after which both retreated as rapidly as they had come.

Stina had recognized Baron Lodstein in the person who

came out through the window. She then continued her way to Kungsdal, where she saw the count instead of Lagerskog, of whose death she was not aware. When she supposed that she would have to lose the money which she expected to receive from Lagerskog, and learned that he was dead, some threatening words escaped her, which Strålkrans believed to be directed toward Bertha. He gave her the sum of money which she said that she was in the habit of getting from Lagerskog, and promised to provide for her, but on the condition, that she did not show herself in that region. She had the right to seek the count in Stockholm, but not at Kungsdal. When Stina went away, she chose the most out-of-the-way routes, so as to avoid the main road. She succeeded in baffling all pursuit. On reaching the capital she procured new clothes and stayed in one of the most remote parts of the city. From the count she received a sufficient support to enable her to live free from care, if she had chosen to do so, but her habits were not such as to admit of it. She kept quiet, it is true, because Janne had warned her of the search that was being made for the woman who had shown herself at X——; but she led the same low life that she had always led, and kept the money in order to one day give Janne a little capital, which put with the amount he had saved up, ought to make him a rich man. Janne had at one of the few meetings with his mother, shortly before Paul's arrest, declared that he only meant to remain in the baron's service half a year, as he expected to have enough by that time to buy a country-place and become his own master.

After this meeting, the baron and Janne left the capital quite suddenly. A short time afterward Paul was arrested. When the latter was called before the bar, the search for Stina was continued with increased vigor. The Stockholm police were notified that she was in the city. She left it and took her way to Wrånga, to tell the baron that he must protect her, or else she would denounce him as his nephew's murderer. She had taken a roundabout course, so as not to be seized or give the hirelings of justice any clue. The same day Janne stood before the court she had arrived at Wrånga, but the baron, who did not wish it to appear that he knew the suspected woman, had her driven from the place. She went away, but with the firm determination to come again in the evening, when it was dark. For this purpose she betook herself to a secret ale-house. Here she learned that a servant of the baron's had been arrested, because he had murdered the baron's nephew, and that it was a Notary Wenner who had discovered that the servant was the murderer.

It was easy for Stina to ascertain where I was staying, and she made up her mind to seek me and tell me who the real murderer was.

When she finished her account, she said:

"The glove that was found in the dead man's room will fit the baron, if you only try it on; and now that you know the whole story, you must save Janne."

I promised that he at least should not suffer punishment for more evil than he had actually committed, and then Stina took her departure, saying that she would see to it that I kept my word.

The first thing I did, although it was late at night, was to go to Strålkrans. He had already retired; but notwithstanding that I entered his room.

I communicated to him in a few words what a new shape the case had taken, and that at last, the suspicion, which I had long nourished that Casper Lodstein's murderer was none other than his uncle, was confirmed. I also informed the count that Bertha's father, out of love for his mother, respect for his step-father's name and affection for his half-brother, had assumed a crime of which he was completely innocent, and that Bertha was consequently no longer obliged to blush for her father.

The count had listened to me with a mingled expression of sorrow and joy. When I finished, he said:

"Glad as it makes me to bring Bertha the consolation that her father was the noblest and most unselfish of men, it is bitter to know that a man with such a name as that of Lodstein, can be guilty of such a crime and degrade himself so deeply. How can they now, without attracting too much notice, free the innocent and yet avoid exposing the actual criminal to scandal?"

"Avoid," rejoined I, "how could that be done? To-morrow morning the high-born scoundrel will be accused of the murder, and the whole world will know whose hand it was that wore the bloodstained glove."

"What, Herr notary, do you mean—"

"To appear as the one who demands a close investigation concerning the baron's stay in Denmark, during the time the murder was committed. There is a voice within me, Herr count, which says that I will succeed in having the criminal convicted of the murder."

"I do not doubt it," replied the count, "but notwithstanding, I say you must not do it, you must allow me to act. The innocent shall be acquitted, without the Lodstein name being branded and the Swedish nobility disgraced."

"Herr count," exclaimed I, "would this man be the object of your intercession, if he belonged to the same class as my brother, would you then step between him and the law? You say: do not drag him before the bar, do not expose him to scandal or call down such a disgrace upon the Swedish nobility. Is then aristocracy a shield, behind which one can commit crime without being molested for it? No, count, the nobleman and the plebeian are alike before the judge, and if you consider it just for the law to punish a criminal belonging to the people, the same law also holds good for the nobleman."

"You are right," answered the count, "and I would not meddle in the matter, if the murderer belonged to any of the lower classes, but I would then let the law take its course, because the disgrace would not fall back on a whole caste. I would act in the same way with regard to Lodstein, if one of the noblest families in the Swedish nobility would not suffer an open disgrace, not only here in Sweden, but before the whole civilized world."

"Wait a moment, Herr count," I interposed, "and reflect that before the law there are no considerations. There rank disappears and we have only before us the guilty or not guilty. If the criminal occupies a high social position, he is so much the more guilty, because culture, enlightenment and refined habits, ought to stand as guards between him and temptation. If the murder of Casper Lodstein had been committed by a starved-out wretch, sunk in misery, who, driven by the desperation of want, hoped to save himself from need through this step, then there would have been some palliating circumstances, but as it is—there are none. Lodstein has been driven to this dastardly act simply and solely by a base greed. He wished to be changed from a wealthy man to a millionaire, and therefore became a murderer.—But not enough with this, he allows an innocent person to be suspected, accused and imprisoned, in order to save himself. How shocking you would consider all this, if you had read an account of it, and yet, count, you hesitate to have the aristocratic criminal brought to justice. His rank and his social position, far from shielding him, only make him doubly culpable.—Consequently either no one ought to be called to account before the tribunal, or all. If the law should ever be rigorously enforced, it is just when a man of the class to which the baron belongs, transgresses against it."

"Yes, if its penalty could be inflicted without the shadow of it falling upon several heads besides the criminal's," said the count; "I can assure you that I deem Lodstein more worthy of punishment than any one else, but I have before my eyes something which is of still more importance than the punishment of the individual, namely, the influence which such an example must exert upon our community. In every land where an aristocratic or a cultured class exists, this ought, as a matter of course, to represent the moral principle of the nation; it is the cultivated classes who must form the people's model and exert a moral influence upon them. Well then, if this is a truth, we must on the other hand admit that in the countries where the higher classes have been demoralized, the people have also become so. If the people are accustomed to see one criminal act after the other committed by the most prominent men of the land, they become contaminated by their vice. When human beings cannot entertain respect for those who stand above them, they do nothing for their own advancement, either in a moral or an intellectual point of view. Add to this, that the rude masses always regard each and all who are more happily lotted with envy, and consequently embrace with avidity every opportunity to draw them down, and you ought to understand that the exposure of a criminal from the higher circles has a ruinous effect upon the multitude, who reason thus: When these rich and high-born men murder and steal, they cannot expect us, the children of poverty, to act better than they. In this way, crime becomes something which does not excite abhorrence."

"I do not share your opinion in this respect," rejoined I, "it is my firm belief that the people, who see that neither rank, wealth nor culture is able to shield a crime, but that each and all, rich and poor, high and low, are alike before the law, will deeply revere and respect the law, and hold it in such sanctity, that they, less than others, will be guilty of any offence; for '*a country is built by law.*' On the other hand, if the people see that the rich, the high-born, go free, that justice is vigilant only when it concerns the children of poverty, or the lower classes, then this engenders contempt for the law, hatred toward the judges and detestation of the injustice of such a course. They do not obey a power which they despise.—Therefore speak not to me of sparing Baron Lodstein. Were I even his brother, I would still, with the proof which I now possess, appear as his accuser."

"Is this your final word?" asked Strålkrans.

"Yes, by my honor. There is no power that can induce me to change my resolution. I would despise myself, if I allowed myself to be influenced."

"All right, do your duty and I will not neglect to do mine. At the same time that I acknowledge you to be right and admit that you act in complete accordance with the sense of justice, I will on my side try to save the honor of the Swedish nobility. To-morrow we will see each other again."

The count offered me his hand, and I returned to my room.

The first intelligence that reached me the next morning was that the sheriff had got hold of the woman, whom he had so long been pursuing. He had found her lying in the road in a fainting fit. She was taken into custody, although very ill.

At the examination of Janne and the bird-fancier Nilsson, such testimony was gained, that Liedgren declared that Paul must be released at once.

Janne had probably during the night taken a new view of his position, and, through his mother's statement to the sheriff about the murder of Casper Lodstein, come to the conclusion that the best way to save himself from serious consequences would be to inform against the baron, as the latter had not done anything for Janne, but had only tried to place himself beyond suspicion. In short, he now confessed that he had helped the baron, when the latter in X—— came out from his nephew's window; but said besides, that he had no knowledge, either then or before the murder, of any such thing. After it was discovered that Baron Casper was killed, Janne had felt pretty sure who the assassin was, but did not wish to denounce his master. He also acknowledged, when Nilsson positively declared that Janne was the one who had prompted him to put the valuables in Paul's hand-organ, that he, Janne, had done it at the baron's instigation, because his master had promised him a large recompense if Paul could be implicated in the dark deed. The only thing of which they could not induce Janne to give any explanation was the reason why he had concealed himself in my sleeping apartment and attacked me.

The trial was suspended for the day and would be continued the following, when the baron was summoned to appear, at the risk of being taken by force.

After I had returned to Kungsdal from the court, the count came to me. He looked agitated. He handed me a letter in silence.

I glanced through it. It was written in a trembling and almost illegible handwriting, and ran thus:

"HERR COUNT: Only God and you know of what the conversation which you had with my husband last night treated, and only He and you know what the paper contained which you compelled him to sign in the presence of a witness. I only know what followed, and may the Almighty in his justice punish you. A few hours after your departure, or early in the morning, the report of a pistol was heard from my husband's room, and when I rushed in, I found him weltering in his blood. He had shot himself through the head. You, who have killed him, are also the first whom I apprise of it. You have made me a widow. AURORE LODSTEIN."

"So he is dead!" exclaimed I, looking at the count.

"Yes, nothing else remained to him, unless he wished to end on the scaffold," replied he.

With the baron's death and Paul's acquittal my interest in the criminal suit was over.

The count had directly after my departure that night gone to Lodstein and made it clear to him that the only course for him to pursue was to flee immediately; but before this, however, he must sign a paper, in which Paul was exonerated from all complicity in the murder. The baron had at first refused to give Paul this justification, but then the count had declared that if Lodstein did not do it, he would appear as a witness and testify that the baron was not in Copenhagen when the murder was committed. The count's testimony in conjunction with Stina's and Janne's, together with the circumstance that the glove must fit Lodstein, and that the count, upon closer examination, recognized the dagger as one which Lodstein had purchased when they were both in London a few years before, would inevitably prove that he was Casper's assassin. The count had said besides that the baron had only two alternatives, either to acknowledge Paul's innocence in writing and then take to flight, or submit to having the count appear against him as a witness. The baron accordingly signed the paper, and then ordered his coachman to harness up. The departure was hindered, however, by the sheriff, who appeared at Wrånga directly after the count left.

Sheriff Willberg informed the baron that if he attempted to leave the place, he, Willberg, would detain him in the name of the law, as such grave evidence was found, that the sheriff, as accuser, intended to insist upon the baron's arrest.

It was probably this that decided the baron to take the desperate step and thus put an end to all investigation.

After Paul's liberation and the conclusion of Janne's trial, I returned to my principal, Judge K——, and this, without having seen either Gertrude or Bertha. Only at court had I and Liedgren met.

Paul, with his wife and child, was to stay at Kungsdal over the winter, and in May go to Skåne, where Paul was to enter upon his position as chorister in Wigelsjö parish, in which the Strålkrans estates were situated.

Before my departure I spent a few days with Paul. He had entirely forgotten the sufferings he had undergone, in order to sing praises to Gertrude, and it seemed very hard for him to forgive me for what I had once written about her during our engagement.

In the writing signed by Lodstein, Paul had also been declared innocent of the theft of the ring. Thus, my youthful dream was realized, that I should be the one to free Paul from the shadow which Lodstein had cast upon him.

CHAPTER IV.

TWO years elapsed after these events, during which I steadily devoted my time and all my interest to my official duties.

I had without a sigh of regret received the intelligence of Bertha and Strålkrans' marriage. My love for Bertha had died out the same day that the engagement between Gertrude and me was broken.

The next year after Lodstein's death, I was appointed judge of one of the northern provinces of Sweden, and through this became a near neighbor to Pastor Wenner, my former guardian. I had not visited my old friends for many years, so that it gave me true joy to see them again.

It was at mid-summer time that I went to R——tuna parsonage, to pay them a visit and present myself as judge of the district.

The month of June was in all its beauty. However little inclined I generally was to be romantic, I could not refrain from being overcome by a peculiar feeling of melancholy, when I drove through the wood, where I for the first time saw Bertha and Strålkrans. They were now happy, and past sufferings were forgotten. They possessed in each other's love all that life could yield of felicity. I, on the contrary, had during the last years devoted my mental powers so exclusively to my judicial career, that I scarcely thought of my individual happiness. The heart's voice had been silenced and only ambition was allowed to speak. But when I now all alone passed through this region, which revived the recollections of my youthful years, my heart was seized with an intense longing for domestic bliss and love.

It was the first time that I felt desolate at the thought of remaining alone, and I desired a hearth of my own and a wife to cherish.

While I, leaning back in a corner of the carriage, allowed these somewhat soft and to me strange feelings to take possession of me, the driver had fallen asleep. The horses went step by step. Suddenly they lifted up their heads and neighed. I was aroused from my fancies and the peasant boy from his slumber.

He seized hold of the reins, smacked his lips, cracked the whip and the nags quickened their pace. Just as we came to the bend of the road, at the same place where I first saw Bertha, two persons on horseback came dashing down the road, one on each side of the carriage. Their speed was such, that I could not make any observations until they were quite a distance ahead of the vehicle. I then perceived that it was a lady and a gentleman. This was all, however, for they disappeared at the turn, without my catching a glimpse of their faces.

"Who were those persons?" I asked the driver.

"I cannot tell exactly, but I guess it was his grace, the count," answered he.

"What count?"

"Why, the one who owns Engsgård, of course. They say he is married to the old proprietor's daughter. He has just bought Engsgård of Pehr Olsson, who bought it of the old man. They are now going to stay there in the summer, as I have heard, although they have many other country-seats elsewhere, which they live in between times."

"And the count, what is he called?"

"Strålkrans. You must know it, sir, for they say he

has been in the government, and stands well with the king."

A half hour later my carriage stopped at the parsonage. Lotta, now a woman of thirty, as cheerful and hearty as ever, was the first of the inmates who bade me welcome. Aunt Juliana, more wrinkled and thinner than before, also smiled a welcome to me, and "Herr judge," as they merrily called me, was led in triumph to the saloon.

My official dignity, my seriousness and my reserve, were all blown away by the friendliness and cordiality which here greeted me.

I had decided to spend mid-summer at the parsonage, and when I after a day's stay there had begun to feel at home, I resolved to make a call at the count's. I desired to see Bertha again at the side of the man who under all vicissitudes had shown himself so magnanimous toward the organ-grinder's sons.

It was early in the afternoon when I drove off in the pastor's newly-painted chaise. I did not ride up to the house, however, but left the horse and chaise at the porter's lodge and went up to the mansion on foot. At the entrance a servant met me. I inquired if the count was at home, to which he gave an affirmative answer, and then hastened to apprise his master of my visit, after showing me into a large, handsome drawing-room on the first floor. The room seemed to be the family's gathering place. At one of the windows stood a work-table, upon which lay a piece of embroidery and some sewing things. A handkerchief that had fallen on the floor announced that the person who had sat there had quite recently left her place. Before the middle window was another table, covered with sketches and drawing materials, and at the third window, farthest away, was an easy-chair with its book-stand. A piano and a large centre-table with books on it showed that they here spent the hours, when they read, worked or had music.

I had with a peculiarly uneasy feeling entered this room, where I was to meet the object of my now extinguished love. I would see her again with the man who possessed her heart, and I was not quite sure what impression this would make upon me.

When the servant left me, I went to the work-table. I took up the embroidery and looked at it. Bertha's hands had probably just touched it. After I had held it in mine quite a while with a certain emotion, I bent down to pick up the handkerchief, but just as I raised up, I heard the rustle of a dress and turned round hastily. I was perfectly certain that it was Bertha. I was mistaken, it was—Gertrude.

When I turned, she stopped, amazed at the sight of me; but she recovered herself immediately, came toward me and said:

"The person whom I least of all expected to meet here, was Conny Wenner." She extended her hand, adding, with captivating cordiality: "but if it was an unexpected meeting, it was none the less pleasant to meet a *friend* again." She laid a certain emphasis upon the word "friend," as if she wished through this word to free me from all constraint and place us both in a natural position toward each other.

I seized the outstretched hand and assured her, in less steady accents than hers, that no meeting could be more agreeable to me.

Still I must acknowledge that notwithstanding I was so accustomed to society, I was anything but at my ease in this interview. It was impossible for me to assume the unembarrassed tone which Gertrude succeeded in preserving, and this vexed me. It would have flattered my self-love far more, if she had been confused, and I the one who had given a more free and easy stamp to our unexpected tête-à-tête; but Gertrude had not granted me this advantage. She began immediately to converse upon indifferent subjects; informed me that Strålkrans and Bertha were out for a walk, that they would soon return, and invited me to take a seat while I waited for them. She seated herself at the work-table and took the embroidery, which I had held in my hands a few minutes before, in the supposition that it was Bertha's.

Gertrude asked me when I came to the place; how long I intended to stay there, etc.; and mentioned that she would be with Bertha until the beginning of July, when she intended to return to Brovik.

During the first half hour Gertrude carried on the conversation almost alone. My answers were brief, and I could not refrain from letting my eyes rest steadily on the head bent down over the work. From the moment she took her embroidery, Gertrude had not once lifted her eyes from it, but continued to sew diligently.

It was over three years since I had last seen Gertrude Liedgren. Had these years actually produced such a change as I fancied she had undergone, or did I now see her with other eyes than then? The answer would be hard to give. What I positively know, is, that the more I regarded the young girl, the more beautiful she appeared to me. As Gertrude sat there, she was to my mind the type of a charming and lovely woman, and when I remembered how she had conducted herself, what a good angel she had been to Paul and Hanna, how she had forgotten and forgiven the harm I did her, I experienced a desire to fall at her feet and thank her. But there was within me a voice which whispered:

"If her love had been strong and deep, she could not have consoled herself as easily as she had done." Gratitude was silenced, contrition for my former course of action was forced into the back-ground, and I finally regained my usual bearing. When she finished speaking of her stay at Engsgård, I was freed from my constraint, and I said after a short pause:

"My first words, when I saw you again, Gertrude, ought to have expressed the great obligation which I feel for the goodness that has been shown my brother, but the whole weight of my debt fell upon me, when I stood before one I had once so deeply wronged, and therefore my lips remained closed. Yet, do not think that I can ever forget how magnanimously and nobly you have acted toward a man who did not deserve anything but ill-will and contempt."

Gertrude's cheeks became somewhat warmer, while I spoke, but when I ceased, she looked up and fastened her eyes upon me. I once answered Wicker, that I had not observed whether they were beautiful or not; but if I had not done it before, I did it now.

"Why should I feel ill-will toward *you?*" said Gertrude; "and why should Conny at the sight of me feel any burden of gratitude? You have not occasioned me any harm, at which I can reasonably feel resentment, and I have not done you any good, for which you need to thank me. We owe nothing to each other, but can meet as a pair of old acquaintances and good friends. Why need we remind ourselves of anything that lies behind the present time?"

"We need not, if we are able to forget it, but we cannot banish or escape memory, it comes to us without our seeking it."

"Dear Conny, in that way memory would be very much like an apparition, which pursues us to our torment."

Gertrude resumed her work and added:

"I for my part believe that we can do whatever we will to do; thus if we will to forget, we can forget."

"According to that theory we would be free to love or hate just as we pleased; to cease or begin it, whenever we chose, and in that case our feelings would not amount to much."

"Very true. Neither do I think that they do amount to much," returned Gertrude, laughing. "We allow imagination to over-rate them and believe in their strength ourselves, until we quite unexpectedly discover that they are not so dangerous as we supposed them to be."

"Is it from your own experience that you speak so?" asked I, within myself offended at her words.

"Yes, certainly, else I would not dare to express myself so decidedly. Of others than myself I would not venture to pronounce any judgment."

I do not know what folly trembled on my lips, but fortunately for me, it was not uttered, for at that instant, a young man in uniform entered the saloon. He greeted Gertrude familiarly and was introduced by her as her cousin Lieutenant Liedgren.

Male cousins have always been my detestation. They are the most tantalizing beings one can see at the side of a young, lovely girl. The individual now introduced seemed to me more hateful than any I had hitherto met. He kissed Gertrude's hand, greeted me with a presumptuous glance and seated himself beside her. As he drew his chair quite near Gertrude's, he began to talk about the weather and wind, about hunting and fishing. But to my joy, he was not allowed to continue long, for Gertrude interrupted him abruptly and turned to me. In a little while the count and countess came in.

I stood before Bertha as calm as if I had never cherished for her anything but a brother's affection; my heart did not beat a single degree more quickly and I did not experience any regret at seeing her Strålkrans' wife.

The evening was spent very pleasantly. Gertrude conversed on all subjects with an ease which struck me with surprise, and expressed herself well. I thought:

"Why was she not this attractive woman when we were betrothed? Then it would not have been so easy for me to give back the ring."

When I returned to the parsonage, I had only one object in my thoughts, and that was Gertrude.

The count had asked me to renew the visit quite soon, as I was now going to be one of their nearest neighbors.

The whole night Gertrude's image pursued me, and when I woke the following day, I experienced something resembling grief at the thought that Gertrude and I could not be anything to each other but what we now were. Friends, it is true, but that was to me entirely too little.

During the time I stayed at the parsonage, I visited Engsgård daily. Gertrude and I rode on horseback together. We talked about Paul, and I entertained myself by relating to Gertrude various circumstances in his life and mine, when we roamed about in Denmark and Germany as a pair of organ-grinders. I had regained my former habit of taking the lead in conversation, and this to her cousin the lieutenant's vexation, as he had to play the rôle of mute, something which I rejoiced at with heart and soul. To be sure, Gertrude often tried to draw her cousin in, but I was not at all inclined to allow it. Therefore I only chose such subjects as he could not discuss.

Gertrude had spent a year abroad. I had also been in London and Paris, but her cousin, on the contrary, had never put his nose outside of Sweden's boundaries; so, when we spoke of foreign lands, he was obliged to keep silence. Besides I enjoyed speaking of my childhood and the time I ground the hand-organ, in his society.

There was a peculiar pleasure in seeing how the lieutenant, the son of parents of high standing, nursed in prejudices against the masses, cast contemptuous glances at me, when I jokingly described our adventurous life, and yet the haughty knight was obliged to show me, as *judge*, all the respect which a civil officer has the right to exact.

If there had been a time when I never alluded to my origin, then I had made it my pride, after the scene between Liedgren and me, to speak of it quite freely.

It is true I had never been so weak as to feel ashamed because I was the organ-grinder's son, but only because this organ-grinder had been a murderer. This was the reason why I never liked to mention anything about my early life at the beginning of my official career. Fate, however, had taken upon itself to teach me that one gains nothing by trying to conceal that which cannot be covered.

It is unnecessary to describe how I day by day became more and more enamored with my former fiancée.

When the month of July came, and with it her pending departure, I felt that life without Gertrude was valueless to me, and that there was only one woman on earth with whom I could be happy, and this woman was Gertrude.

I loved her with my whole soul, but between her and me stood the proud father and my wounded self-love.

The day was fixed for Gertrude's journey.

Two days previous, directly after dinner, I rode to Engsgård to see and talk to her one evening more.

When I arrived there, the servant told me that the count and countess had gone out, but that Mamsell Liedgren was in the garden.

I bent my steps to Gertrude's favorite spot, and found her there. When she turned toward me her face bore traces of tears.

She had wept.—Wherefore?—I had a certain feeling of

joy at the discovery of these signs of sorrow in her usually so calm features.

What I said I cannot recall, but that I told her everything I had resolved to keep to myself, is what I remember. I spoke with all the animation, all the warmth and intensity, which overcharged feeling can call forth. I told her that she was now revenged, as I loved her with my whole soul, and that notwithstanding I knew that she never could become mine. I begged to be allowed, as a consolation, to take with me the assurance that the feeling she had once cherished for me was not dead, but that she still had a spark of tenderness left for one whose whole peace she had taken.

There was no change of color on Gertrude's cheeks, while I opened my heart to her. When I finished, she looked up at me. A tear glistened in her eye, when she answered:

"Conny, God has heard my prayer. I have implored Him for your love, I have not implored in vain, and I shall go away from you happy and grateful in the consciousness of being loved by you. I have now received the highest happiness which life can render me. Until death my heart will beat only for you."

She gave me both her hands. I seized them passionately; but at the same instant I raised them to my lips steps were heard, and a servant approached, saying:

"Judge Liedgren has just come."

Gertrude and I rose hastily; we exchanged a glance. Gertrude extended her hand once more, whispering:

"Farewell, beloved!"

"For ever," added I, and pressed it convulsively.

A few minutes afterward I threw myself on my horse and rode away, away from her whom I loved and resolved never to see again.

When I reached home, I shut myself up in my room,

where I spent several so bitter hours, that I can scarcely imagine anything more bitter.

The evening was far advanced, when my servant knocked at the door, crying:

"A gentleman is down in the saloon, and wishes to see you immediately."

My desire would have been to send that gentleman where the pepper grows; but well recollecting that I was the judge of the province I went, although with reluctance, to hear what he could want of me at this late hour. I entered the saloon.

With his back turned to the door and contemplating the prospect, stood my guest. At the sound of my steps he turned round, and I recognized Gertrude's *father*.

The blood rushed to my head. All the humiliation which this man had occasioned me stood before my mind, and my deeply wounded pride came in activity. My salutation was stiff, and probably my tone would have been cold and haughty, if he had given me the word, but he said before I had time to utter anything:

"You are surprised, *Herr judge*, to receive a visit from me after what has occurred between us; but I will immediately explain it. I have come to make you reparation for the affront which I once gave you. I was unjust *then;* and I hope that you will not be unjust *now*, by refusing to accept the hand which I extend to you in reconciliation. I have wronged you,—forget it. I have wounded you,—forgive it, and be content when I through this step prove to you how high you stand in my esteem."

He ceased and offered me his hand. This hand belonged to Gertrude's father. I seized it without an instant's hesitation.

"Herr judge," said I, pressing his hand, "I thank you for the words you have uttered; they comprise the most complete reparation, and I am proud to have received it."

"If that is so," resumed Liedgren, "you will not refuse to accept Gertrude as your wife. I was the one who caused the engagement to be broken; it is thus incumbent upon me to join what I, out of arrogance, have sundered, and what you, out of pride, would never have tried to reunite. You love my daughter, she has told me so, and she—she has had no thought or feeling for any one but you, since you succeeded in winning her heart. Well then, Conny Wenner, will you become my son-in-law?"

The answer was already given by my heart—my lips only confirmed the verdict which feeling pronounced.

At Engsgård Gertrude and I, for the second time, exchanged rings; but with what different emotions did I clasp my fiancée to my breast, compared to the former time? Now she was all to me, then she was nothing.

Three months afterward our wedding was celebrated at Brovik. Among the guests who occupied the place of honor were the bridegroom's brother, Chorister Paul Fredriksson, and his wife. They had come from Skåne, to be present at "the festival of joy," as Paul expressed himself.

My father-in-law himself had invited Paul and Hanna.

Count Stralkråns had begged the favor of being to me in a father's place that day; and Bertha was the one who placed the crown on the bride.

Paul remained at Brovik a whole week. To my inexpressible satisfaction, I learned through Hanna that he thrived well in his new condition and had almost entirely overcome the regret for his wandering life.

I had been married three years when I obtained complete jurisdiction.

Ten years afterward I became counsellor at law. My ambition had now attained its aim. I felt proud and happy at being allowed to share this success with a wife like Gertrude, who every year we lived together became more indispensable to my life. I had now come as far as was possible on the path of distinction, and all Paul's dreams, of what his little Conny might in time become, were realized. So nothing further remains to relate about the *organ-grinder's son.*

Before I lay down my pen, however, I will mention that Janne ended his life as a convict. Black Stina died a few weeks after he was arrested.

Janne had acknowledged during the trial that he stole into my sleeping-apartment to murder me in the night, because he feared that I would bring him into trouble, after my meeting with the bird-fancier Nilsson.

Paul lived happy and contented with his Hanna, as a well-to-do chorister in the country.

Liedgren never had cause to repent that he took the brother of a former street-singer for a son-in-law.

THE END.

SELECTED LIST OF BOOKS

PUBLISHED BY

PORTER & COATES,

No. 822 Chestnut Street,

PHILADELPHIA.

The Books in this List, unless otherwise specified, are bound in Cloth.

☞ All of our Publications mailed, post-paid, on receipt of price. ☜

SELECTED LIST OF BOOKS

PUBLISHED BY

PORTER & COATES,

No. 822 Chestnut Street,

PHILADELPHIA.

ALEXANDER WILSON AND CHARLES LUCIEN BONAPARTE.

AMERICAN ORNITHOLOGY; OR, THE NATURAL HISTORY OF THE BIRDS OF THE UNITED STATES. Illustrated with Plates engraved and colored from original Drawings taken from Nature. By ALEXANDER WILSON. With a life of the author, by GEORGE ORD, F.R.S. With Continuation, by CHARLES LUCIEN BONAPARTE (Prince of Musignano). 3 vols., imperial 8vo., with a folio volume of carefully colored plates embracing nearly 400 figures of birds mostly life size. Elegantly bound in cloth, extra gilt top, $97.00; half Turkey morocco, gilt edges, $110.00.

THE SAME, complete in 5 vols., 3 of letter-press and 2 vols. quarto of plates. Cloth, extra, gilt top, $97.00; half Turkey, gilt edges, $110.00.

A new and magnificent edition of this world-renowned work, printed from new stereotype plates, on the finest laid paper, and bound in the best manner. The plates are printed from the original plates, engraved by Lawson, "the first ornithological engraver of our age," and are carefully colored, after the author's own copies. The superiority of this work for accuracy of description and naturalness of drawing, has long been acknowledged. Daniel Webster speaks of it in the highest terms, saying that of the salt water birds, mentioned in Wilson, "he had shot every one, and compared them with his delineations and descriptions, and IN EVERY CASE found them PERFECTLY ACCURATE TO NATURE." And the *London Quarterly Review* characterized it as "an admirable work, unequaled by any publication in the old world, for accurate delineations and just description." A moment's comparison of this work with any other on the same subject, will convince the most skeptical of its great superiority. One of its chief values being, that the birds are mostly of the size of life, enabling any one to easily recognize them in nature; and, at the low price it is now offered, should be in every public and private library of any pretentions.

"With an enthusiasm never excelled, this extraordinary man penetrated through the vast territories of the United States, undeterred by forests or swamps, for the sole purpose of describing the native birds."—*Lord Brougham, Architecture of Birds.*

"Wilson contemplated nature as she really is, not as she is represented in books: he sought her in her sanctuaries;—the shore, the mountain, the forest, were alternately his study, and there he drank the pure stream of knowledge at the fountain head."—*Swainson.*

"With regard to the literary merit of his American Ornithology, passages occur in the prefaces and descriptions which, for elegance of language, graceful ease, and graphic power, can scarcely be surpassed."—*Encyclopedia Brittanica, Vol. XXI.*

EDWARD GIBBON.

THE DECLINE AND FALL OF THE ROMAN EMPIRE. With Notes by Rev. H. H. Milman. To which is added a complete Index. 6 vols. crown 8vo, with a steel portrait. Cloth, extra, per set, $9.00; sheep, library style, per set, $10.50; half calf, gilt, per set, $18.00.

"Gibbon, the architect of a bridge over the dark gulf which separates ancient from modern times, whose vivid genius has tinged with brilliant colors the greatest historical work in existence."—*Alison.*

DAVID HUME.

THE HISTORY OF ENGLAND, FROM THE INVASION OF JULIUS CÆSAR, TO THE ABDICATION OF JAMES THE SECOND, 1688. A new Edition, with the author's last corrections and improvements. To which is prefixed a short account of his life, written by himself. With steel portrait. 6 vols. crown 8vo, cloth, extra, per set, $9.00; sheep, library style, per set, $10.50; half calf, gilt, per set, $18.00.

"Considered as a calm and philosophic narrative, the history of Hume will remain as a standard model for every future age. His just and profound reflections, the inimitable clearness and impartiality with which he has summed up the arguments on both sides on the most momentous questions which have agitated England, as well as the general simplicity, uniform clearness, and occasional pathos of his story, must for ever command the admiration of mankind. In vain we are told that he is often inaccurate, sometimes partial; in vain are successive attacks published on detached parts of his narrative, by party zeal or antiquarian research: his reputation is undiminished: successive editions issuing from the press attest the continued sale of his work; and it continues its majestic course through the sea of time, like a mighty three-decker, which never even condescends to notice the javelins darted at its sides, from the hostile canoes which from time to time seek to impede its progress."—*Alison's Essays.*

THOMAS BABINGTON MACAULAY.

THE HISTORY OF ENGLAND FROM THE ACCESSION OF JAMES II. Standard Edition, with an Index. 5 vols. crown 8vo, with a steel portrait. Cloth, extra, per set, $7.50; sheep, library style, per set, $8.75; half calf, gilt, $15.00.

"With the rest of the world, we come with our homage to Macaulay. Steady, strong and uniform, the stream of his thought continues to flow: and, without effort, or without outward sign of it, he keeps his place as the first living (1856) writer of English prose. * * * On whatever side we look at this book, whether the style of it or the matter of it, is alike astonishing. The style is faultlessly luminous: every word is in its right place; every sentence is exquisitely balanced; the current never flags. Homer, according to the Roman poet, may be sometimes languid; Mr. Macaulay is always bright, sparkling, attractive."—*Westminster Review*, April, 1856.

DUCHESS OF ORLEANS.

MEMOIR OF THE DUCHESS OF ORLEANS. By the MARQUESS DE H——, together with Biographical Souvenirs and Original Letters. Translated from the French, by Prof. G. H. DE SCHUBERT. One volume, with a portrait on steel, 12mo, pp. 391. $1.50.

"The materials of this volume consist of a memoir by the Marquis de H——, which is an interesting narrative of the varied and peculiar fortunes of the subject, and a collection of souvenirs and original letters by Professor Schubert, of Germany, who was the family tutor of the Duchess of Orleans. The work derives not a little interest from the character of the Duchess, which was equally remarkable for loveliness and heroism, especially during her troubled career after the abdication of Louis Philippe. The translation shows fidelity and considerable skill, and will be regarded as a valuable accession to biographical reading."—*Harper's Magazine.*

SIR WALTER SCOTT.

WAVERLEY NOVELS. Complete in 23 vols. Illustrated. Toned paper. Price per vol., *Globe Edition:* cloth, extra, $1.25; half calf, gilt, $2.75. *Standard Library Edition:* cloth, extra, gilt tops, bev. boards, $1.50; half calf, gilt, $3.00; half mor., gilt tops, $3.50.

Waverley.
Guy Mannering.
Antiquary.
Rob Roy.
Black Dwarf, and Old Mortality.
Heart of Mid-Lothian.
Bride of Lammermoor, and A Legend of Montrose.
Ivanhoe.
Monastery.
Abbot.
Kenilworth.
Pirate.
Fortunes of Nigel.
Peveril of the Peak
Quentin Durward.
St. Ronan's Well.
Redgauntlet.
The Betrothed, and the Talisman.
Woodstock.
Fair Maid of Perth.
Anne of Geierstein.
Count Robert of Paris, and Castle Dangerous.
Chronicles of the Canongate.

This is the best edition for the library or for general use published. Its convenient size, the extreme legibility of the type, which is larger than is used in any other edition, either English or American, its spirited illustrations, quality of the paper and binding, and the general execution of the presswork, must commend it at once to every one.

TALES OF A GRANDFATHER. Uniform with the "Waverley Novels." Illustrated. 4 vols. Toned paper. Price per vol., *Globe Edition:* cloth extra, $1.25; half calf, gilt, $2.75. *Standard Library Edition:* cloth extra, gilt tops, bev. boards, $1.50; half morocco, gilt tops, $3.00; half calf, gilt, $3.50.

The only edition containing the Fourth Series, "Tales from French History."

IVANHOE. A Romance. Youth's Favorite Edition. Illustrated. Crown 8vo. $1.50.

LADY OF THE LAKE. With twenty-five engravings on wood, from designs by Birket Foster and John Gilbert. 16mo. Bev. boards, $1.50; half calf, gilt, $3.00; full Turkey mor. antique, $4.00.

LIFE OF SIR WALTER SCOTT, with remarks upon his Writings, by Francis Turner Palgrave; an Essay on Scott, by David Masson, M.A., and Dryburgh Abbey; a Poem, by Charles Swain. 12mo. Illuminated cover, 30 cents. With fine portrait on steel, cloth, extra, 60 cents.

"Relates the events in the life of the illustrious novelist in an agreeable style, with an unpretending, but singularly acute, criticism of his writings."—*New York Tribune.*

"A centennial offering of large worth. The biography is brief but comprehensive, while the remarks upon his writings which crop out every here and there, are marked by great judgment and keen appreciation."—*Philadelphia Inquirer.*

"One of the ablest reviews of Scott's life and works that has ever been written. It is very able and very just."—*New York Evening Mail.*

THE BEAUTIES OF WAVERLEY. Selections of the most striking passages from the Waverley Novels. With forty-five fine steel engravings. Elegantly printed on fine paper, and bound in the most tasty style. A new and perennial gift book. One volume, crown 8vo. Cloth, full gilt, extra, $5.00; morocco, bevelled boards, antique, $8.00.

RUFUS W. GRISWOLD, D.D.

THE PROSE WRITERS OF AMERICA. With a Survey of the Intellectual History, Condition, and Prospects of the Country. New edition, thoroughly revised and completed to the present time, with a supplementary Essay on the Present Intellectual Condition and Prospects of the Country. By Prof. JOHN H. DILLINGHAM, A.M. With seven portraits on steel and vignette title. Imperial 8vo. Cloth, extra, gilt top, bevelled boards, $5.00; sheep, marbled edges, library style, $6.00; half calf, $7.50; full Turkey morocco, $10.00.

"We are glad to possess in this form, portions of many authors whose entire works we should never own, and if we did should probably never find time to read. We confess our obligations to the author for the personal information concerning them which he has collected in the memoirs prefixed to their writings. These are written in a manner creditable to the research, ability, and kindness of the author."—*William Cullen Bryant.*

"An important and interesting contribution to our national literature. The range of authors is very wide; the biographical notices full and interesting. I am surprised that the author has been able to collect so many particulars in this way. The selections appear to me to be made with discrimination, and the criticisms show a sound taste and a correct appreciation of the qualities of the writers, as well as I can judge."—*William H. Prescott, the Historian.*

"Can be cordially recommended for its sterling qualities, and the handsome style in which it has been gotten up by the publishers makes it particularly worthy of the notice of those who wish to make a Christmas present that will be appreciated by the recipient."—*Philadelphia Evening Telegraph.*

"Is really a desirable acquisition to any library, and, indeed, a library could scarcely be called complete without it."—*Marshall (Mich.) Times.*

GEMS FROM THE AMERICAN POETS. With brief biographical notices. With a fine engraving on steel. 32mo, cloth, 60 cents; illuminated sides, 90 cents; Turkey mor., extra, $1.50.

FREDERIC H. HEDGE, D.D.

THE PROSE WRITERS OF GERMANY. With Introductions, Biographical Notices, and Translations. With six portraits on steel and engraved title. Imperial 8vo. Cloth, extra, gilt top, bevelled boards, $5.00; sheep, marbled edges, library style, $6.00; half calf, gilt, $7.50; full Turkey morocco, $10.00.

"There is no book accessible to the English or American reader which can furnish so comprehensive and symmetrical a view of German literature to the unitiated: and those already conversant with some of the German classics will find here valuable and edifying extracts from works to which very few in this country can gain access."—*Prof. A. P. Peabody, in North American Review.*

"It is universally recognised as one of the best collections of specimens of German literature in the English language. It has been prepared on the plan of giving a limited selection of authors, with large extracts from their works. The translations from the editor's own pen are singularly vigorous, and in the accomplishment of his task, he has had the co-operation of several American scholars."—*New York Tribune.*

"A new and beautiful edition of a work of sterling merit. Compilations are good even in our own language, for so great is the multitude of books that few have leisure to read a tithe of them. But to the great stores of literature in foreign tongues, only those skilled in them have access. The treasures of German literature are inaccessible to most American readers. It is, therefore, no common addition to our information and pleasure, to have put before us well selected passages of the best works of the most celebrated German authors. This is done with the most excellent judgment in this volume. The reader of it will here form some acquaintance with the principal German classics, and that acquaintance he may improve by a further perusal of those which he finds most to his taste. Enough, however, s given to furnish an ample specimen of the style and method of each writer. Many complete pieces are furnished. Among those to whom considerable space is accorded, are Kant, Lessing, Herder, Goethe, Schiller, the Schlegels, Richter, Heine; with these are many others of celebrity."—*Age, Philadelphia.*

HENRY WADSWORTH LONGFELLOW.

THE POETS AND POETRY OF EUROPE. A New and Revised Edition, with the addition of 137 pages of entirely new matter, *never before published*, making it one of the most elegant and complete works extant. With Introduction, Biographical Notices, and Translations, from the earliest period to the present time. By Prof. HENRY WADSWORTH LONGFELLOW. Illustrated with engravings on steel and engraved title. Imperial 8vo. Cloth, extra gilt top, beveled boards, $6; sheep, marbled edges, library style, $7.50; half calf, gilt, $9; Turkey morocco, $12.

"In all this there is great clearness and precision; the details dear to the student of a particular literature or literary epoch, but, confusing to the average culture, are sacrificed to the fullness with which the principal and important features are brought out. Whenever it is possible, the criticism is founded upon the opinions of each writer's countrymen, and in all cases it appears to us that the best authorities are consulted; and one of the best is Mr. Longfellow himself, who speaks his own mind only too sparingly. His work is often merely that of an editor, but he does it with that taste, sympathy and good sense, which his whole literary life embodies in such degree, that we feel anything else to be impossible with him, and gives it thus the finest value of original production. The labor involved in the preparation of such a volume as this, will by no means appear to the general reader it delights, and to whom we venture to suggest grateful consideration of the vast acquaintance with authors and authorities, the tacit service of comparison and selection implied by the abundance and the succinctness with which every topic is treated. We will not say that here is all the general reader need know of the poets and poetry of Europe, but we assure him that he cannot do better than possess himself of all the information here given, and that he could no where else find it so availably and so agreeably presented, and with so little that he need not know. To this new edition Mr. Longfellow has added a supplement of 137 pages, devoted to such poets as have recently won distinction, and to the poets whom recent study has brought into notice anew. The poems in this supplement are marked by that greater fidelity and regard to the originals which no one has done half so much to urge upon translators as Mr. Longfellow himself, in the high example of his 'Dante.' Here are his own exquisite translations from German, French, Italian, and Spanish; here is one version, most sympathetically tender and spirited, by Mr. Lowell; here is a part of Faust in Bayard Taylor's conscientious and admirable English; here are some songs from Heine, by Leland; here are Mrs. Wister's charming pieces from De Musset; here are Bryant's Specimens of modern Spanish poetry; here are Rosetti's beautiful versions from the earliest Italian poets, and here are abundant extracts from the latest. The supplement, in fact, lays before the reader the freshest and best poetry of all Europe, and worthily completes the work. It is not easy to give a just idea of its merits and graces, but those who already know it will not need a lecture from us upon it, and to those who do not we can but heartily commend it."—*Atlantic Monthly, January*, 1871.

"This edition has been revised and enlarged by the author, and contains his best touches and corrections to his labors. But they have stood the test of criticism. Their accuracy and felicity have been acknowledged by the best scholars in Europe. The attainments of Mr. Longfellow as a linguist have been recognized by those best qualified to judge them in each sphere of his labors. . . . In it is given, in a convenient form, a summary of the poetic literature of Europe which is not to be found elsewhere."—*The Age, Philadelphia.*

"It is now a better book than ever, the Professor having added an appendix and supplement, the latter dated 1870, containing a very precious list of newer poetical translations. . . . The supplement is very choice and interesting, and absolutely rejuvenates the work. Here we have specimens from Bayard Taylor's translation of Faust, not yet received in complete book form, a charming passage from King Rene's Daughter, &c., &c. The whole volume is an acquisition to our letters, and to that disposition of literary curiosity, an honorable distinction of the American people, which has made such a difficult work, so well done, necessary."—*The Evening Bulletin, Philadelphia.*

DEAN STANLEY.

SERMONS PREACHED during his Tour in the East. With Notices of some of the Localities visited. Published by arrangement with the author. New edition. With plan and diagram. 12mo, cloth extra, $1.50.

Dean Stanley's Sermons are famous, as finished specimens of pulpit oratory, and the fourteen comprised in this volume are pre-eminently characteristic of their distinguished author. They are specially interesting for the very graphic description of the various localities visited during the tour in the course of which they were delivered.

Three of these sermons were preached in Egypt, on the Nile, and in the great hall of the Temple of Karnak; four were preached in Palestine, in the harbor of Jaffa, at Jacob's Well, at Nazareth, and by the Sea of Galilee; three more were preached in Syria, on Mt. Hermon, in the Temple of Baalbec, and under the cedars of Lebanon; three were preached upon the Mediterranean, with the fresh impressions of Ephesus, Patmos, and Malta, &c. These circumstances of composition and delivery would give interest even to ordinary discourses. But these are not ordinary. The thought is simple, but very free and very wide. It is not merely illustrative of the scenes and the history, but it is excellent counsel, both practical and spiritual, to the principal listeners."—*North American Review for July*, 1863.

REV. TREADWELL WALDEN.

THE HISTORY OF OUR ENGLISH BIBLE AND ITS SEVEN ANCESTORS. An Historical Plea for Revision. 16mo, tinted paper. Cloth extra, $1.25.

"In itself a story of profound interest, the ripe and elegant scholarship of the author gives it many additional charms; and it is specially welcome now, when our version of the Holy Book is to take another step forward, and assume that additional completeness necessary for a new age."—*Christian Union (Rev. Henry Ward Beecher, Editor).*

"We cordially commend it to the attention of our students and ministers, as a summary of useful and highly interesting information, even if they do not agree with the author on every point."—*United Presbyterian, Pittsburgh.*

"In this neatly printed little volume, Mr. Walden has gathered information concerning our English Bible, which everybody ought to possess, but which is not easy of access."—*Old School Presbyterian, St. Louis.*

"The book is extremely interesting, and will not fail to carry fresh information to very many readers."—*Watchman and Reflector (Baptist).*

"The work exhibits great research and scholarship, and is written in a clear and graceful style."—*Lutheran Observer.*

"A very Christian and scholarly effort."—*Methodist Protestant, Baltimore.*

"An admirable popular account of the successive steps in the growth of the English version of the Bible, from the first attempt by Wickliffe down to the final revision in the reign of King James."—*Sunday-School Times.*

THOMAS A'KEMPIS.

OF THE IMITATION OF CHRIST. Four books. New Edition, beautifully printed on toned paper. 18mo, cloth, extra, 50 cts.; cloth, extra, beveled boards, red edges, gilt stamp on side, 75 cents; cloth, extra, beveled boards, gilt edges, gilt stamp on side, $1.00; full Turkey morocco, antique, gilt edges, $2.50; full calf, antique, $2.50.

WILLIAM SHAKSPEARE.

COMPLETE WORKS. Dramatic and Poetical, with the "Epistle Dedicatorie," and the Address prefixed to the edition of 1623, a Sketch of the Life of the Poet, by ALEXANDER CHALMERS, A. M., and Glossarial and other Notes and References. Edited by GEORGE LONG DUYCKINK. With nine full-page steel Illustrations, a superb portrait on steel, from the celebrated Droeshout picture, and beautiful engraved title, on steel. 976 pages. Imperial 8vo. Cloth, extra, gilt back, $3.75; sheep, library style, $4.50.

FINE EDITION OF THE ABOVE, on extra calendered paper, with the addition of a History of the Early Drama and Stage to the time of Shakspeare, a full and comprehensive Life, by J. PAYNE COLLIER, A.M., Shakspeare's Will, critical and historical Introductions to each play, and thirty-five full-page tinted engravings, from designs by Nicholson, a superb portrait on steel from the celebrated Droeshout picture, and beautiful engraved title on steel. Imperial 8vo. 1084 pages. Half calf, gilt, $8.75; full Turkey morocco, $10.00.

POEMS AND SONNETS. With a fine engraving on steel. 32mo. Cloth, 60 cts.; illuminated side, 90 cts.; Turkey morocco, $1.50.

THOMAS PERCY, D.D., Bishop of Dromore.

RELIQUES OF ANCIENT ENGLISH POETRY: consisting of Old Heroic Ballads, Songs, and other pieces of the earlier poets, with some of later date, not included in any other edition. To which is now added a Supplement of many Curious Historical and Narrative Ballads, reprinted from rare copies, with a copious glossary and notes. New edition, uniform with the above. 558 pp. Imperial 8vo. Two steel plates. Fine cloth, bev. bds., gilt, $3.75; sheep, library style, $4.50; full Turkey morocco, $10.00.

"But, above all, I then first became acquainted with Bishop Percy's Reliques of Ancient Poetry. . . . . I remember well the spot where I read these volumes for the first time. It was beneath a huge plantanus tree, in the ruins of what had been intended for an old-fashioned arbor, in the *garden* I have mentioned. The summer day sped around so fast, that notwithstanding the sharp appetite of thirteen, I forgot the hour of dinner, was sought for with anxiety, and was still found entranced in my intellectual banquet. To read and to remember was in this instance the same thing, and henceforth I overwhelmed my schoolfellows, and all who would hearken to me, with tragical recitations from the ballads of Bishop Percy. The first time I could scrape a few shillings together, which were not common occurrences with me, I bought unto myself a copy of these beloved volumes, nor do I believe I ever read a book half so frequently, or with half the enthusiasm."—*Memoirs of his early Life, by Sir Walter Scott prefixed to Lockhart's Life of Scott.*

LORD BYRON.

COMPLETE WORKS. Prose and Poetry. With five engravings on steel. Imp. 8vo. Sheep, library style, $4.50; Turkey morocco, antique, $10.00.

"If the finest poetry be that which leaves the deepest impression on the minds of its readers,—and this is not the worst test of its excellence,—Lord Byron, we think, must be allowed to take precedence of all his distinguished contemporaries. 'Words that breathe, and thoughts that burn,' are not merely ornaments, but the common staple of his poetry; and he is not inspired or impressive only in some happy passages, but through the whole body and tissue of his composition."—*Lord Jeffrey, Edinburgh Review.*

THE MORAL AND BEAUTIFUL IN THE POEMS OF LORD BYRON. Edited by REV. WALTER COLTON. 32mo. Cloth, 60 cts.; illuminated side, 90 cts.; Turkey morocco, $1.50.

THOMAS HOOD.

COMPLETE WORKS. Prose and Poetry. Illustrated. 5 vols., crown 8vo, tinted paper. Cloth, extra, per vol., $1.75; half calf, gilt, per vol., $3.50; half morocco, antique, per vol., $3.25.

"This very good edition of a favorite author has the advantage of being lower in price and neater in appearance than any other yet published in this country."—*The Press, Philadelphia.*

POETICAL WORKS. 2 vols., crown 8vo, tinted paper. Cloth, extra, per vol., $1.75; half calf, gilt, per vol., $3.50; half morocco, gilt top, per vol., $3.50.

SELECT POETICAL WORKS. With a fine engraving on steel. 32mo. Cloth, 60 cents; illuminated side, 90 cents; Turkey morocco, $1.50.

"Hood's verse, whether serious or comic,—whether serene, like a cloudless autumn evening, or sparkling with puns like a frosty January midnight with stars,—was ever pregnant with materials for thought. . . . . Like every author distinguished for true comic humor, there was a deep vein of melancholy pathos running through his mirth; and even when his sun shone brightly, its light seemed often reflected as if only over the rim of a cloud.—*D. M. Moir.*

UP THE RHINE. Crown 8vo, tinted paper. Cloth, extra, $1.75; half calf, gilt, $3.50; half morocco, antique, $3.25.

HOOD'S COMICALITIES. A Series of Comical Pictures from Hood. Containing 200 illustrations, by Thomas Hood. Fully equal to Leech's and Cruikshank's admirable drawings. Oblong quarto. Half morocco, extra, $4.00.

JOHN MILTON.

COMPLETE WORKS. Standard Edition. With a Life of the Author, by Rev. John Mitford. 2 vols., crown 8vo, laid and tinted paper, largest type, $4.00. Library edition, with engravings on steel, 1 vol., 8vo, sheep, library style, $4.50; Turkey morocco, antique, $10.00.

ROBERT BURNS.

COTTER'S SATURDAY NIGHT. Elegantly illustrated with fifty engravings from drawings by Chapman. Engraved by Filmer. Beautifully printed by Ashmead, on the finest tinted plate paper. 4to, cloth extra, bev. boards, $4.50; Turkey morocco, antique, $9.00.

This noblest poem of "the greatest poet that ever sprang from the bosom of the people" until the issue of this edition had never been detached from the collected works of Burns, to receive the adornments of art which have been so bountifully and lovingly bestowed on Gray's "Elegy," Goldsmith's "Deserted Village," Coleridge's "Ancient Mariner," Thomson's "Seasons," and other kindred treasures of English verse. The poem itself is a classic, and the beauty and appropriateness of the illustrations to be found in this edition, place it far ahead of any other.

EDWARD, EARL OF DERBY.

THE ILIAD OF HOMER RENDERED INTO ENGLISH BLANK VERSE. From the ninth London edition, with all the author's latest revisions and corrections. With a Biographical Sketch of Lord Derby, by R. SHELTON MACKENZIE, D.C.L., LL.D. Two volumes, crown 8vo, on laid and tinted paper, gilt top, beveled boards, cloth extra, $4.00.

"It must equally be considered a splendid performance; and for the present we have no hesitation in saying that it is by far the best representation of Homer's Iliad in the English language."—*London Times.*

"The merits of Lord Derby's translation may be summed up it one word; it is eminently attractive; it is instinct with life; it may be read with fervent interest; it is immeasurably nearer than Pope to the text of the original. . . . It will not only be read, but read over again and again. . . . . Lord Derby has given to England a version far more closely allied to the original, and superior to any that has yet been attempted in the blank verse of our language."—*Edinburg Review.*

"As often as we return from even the best of them (other translations) to the translation before us, we find ourselves in a purer atmosphere of taste. We find more spirit, more tact in avoiding either trivial or conceited phrases, and, altogether, a presence of merits, and an absence of defects, which continues, as we read, to lengthen more and more the distance between Lord Derby and the foremost of his competitors."—*London Quarterly Review.*

"While the versification of Lord Derby is such as Pope himself would have admired, his Iliad is in all other essentials superior to that of his great rival. It is the Iliad we would place in the hands of English readers as the truest counterpart of the original, the nearest existing approach to a reproduction of that original's matchless feature."—*London Saturday Review.*

REV. JOHN KEBLE.

THE CHRISTIAN YEAR: Thoughts in verse for the Sundays and Holidays throughout the Year. 16mo, Cloth, red line, beautifully printed, $1.50; Turkey morocco, antique, gilt edges, $3.50.

"In this volume old Herbert would have recognized a kindred spirit, and Walton would have gone on a pilgrimage to make acquaintance with the author."—*London Quarterly Review.*

"These and many other thoughts and feelings concerning the 'vision and the faculty divine,' when employed on divine subjects, have arisen in our hearts, on reading—which we have often done with delight—The Christian Year, so full of Christian poetry of the purest character. Mr. Keble is a poet whom Cowper himself would have loved; for in him piety inspires genius, and fancy and feeling are celestialized by religion. We peruse his book in a tone and temper of spirit similar to that which is breathed on us by some calm day in spring, when

'Heaven and earth do make one imagery,'

and all that imagery is serene and still,—cheerful in the main, yet with a touch and tinge of melancholy which makes all the blended bliss and beauty at once more endearing and profound. We should no more think of criticizing such poetry than criticizing the clear blue skies, the soft green earth, the 'liquid lapse' of an unpolluted stream, that

'Doth make sweet music with the enamell'd stones,
Giving a gentle kiss to every flower
It overtaketh on its pilgrimage.'

Beauty is there,—purity and peace: as we look and listen we partake of the universal calm, and feel in nature the presence of Him from whom it emanated."—*Recreations of Christopher North, (John Wilson).*

CHARLES FENNO HOFFMAN.

COMPLETE POETICAL WORKS. Edited by his nephew, EDWARD FENNO HOFFMAN. New Library Edition, containing several poems never before published. With a new portrait on steel by Whitechurch, from a painting by Inman. Beautifully printed on laid and tinted paper. 16mo, cloth, extra, beveled boards, gilt top, $1.75.

CUMMINGTON, MASS., Aug. 5, 1873.

MY DEAR SIR:—I congratulate you on the completion of the task which you have undertaken of collecting the poetical productions of your uncle, Charles Fenno Hoffman, whom, while he lived in New York, I was proud to reckon among my friends, and whose kindly and generous temper and genial manners won the attachment of all who knew him. His poems bear the impress of his noble character. They are the thoughts of a man of eminent poetic sensibilities, who delights to sing of whatever moves the human heart—the domestic affections, patriotic reminiscences, the traditions of ancient loves and wars, and the ties of nature and friendship. These thoughts are expressed in musical versification with the embellishments of a ready fancy. The friends of your uncle have reason to thank you for presenting them in this manner the moral and intellectual image of him whom they have had such reason to esteem.

I am, sir, very truly yours,

WM. CULLEN BRYANT.

MRS. ELIZABETH F. ELLET.

PIONEER WOMEN OF THE WEST. One volume, 12mo, pp. 434. Illustrated, cloth extra, $1.50.

The history of the wives and mothers who ventured into the Western wilds, and bore their part in the struggles and labors of the early pioneers, is sketched in this work. The materials were collected from the records of private families, and the recollections of individuals who passed through the experiences of frontier and forest life. Descriptions of the domestic life and manners of the pioneers, and illustrative anecdotes, have been woven into the memoirs of prominent women, and notice has been taken of such political events as had an influence on the condition of the country.

"The biographies contain fine descriptions, enlivened with anecdotes of the domestic life and manners of those pioneer matrons, and are worthy of a perusal."—*The Watchman and Reflector (Baptist).*

"This volume is devoted to the history of the wives and mothers who bore a part in the struggles of the early pioneers in the Western wilds. Mrs. Ellet is familiar with this branch of the American annals. She has given much time to research on this subject. Her inquiries have been attended with remarkable success. Gathering a rich fund of local anecdote and tradition, furnished with interesting details by the descendants and the acquaintances of her subjects, and in many cases visiting the scenes of their adventures, she has obtained abundant materials for an attractive work, and has wrought them up with evident ability and good taste. Her volume, though full of interest to all classes of readers, is especially adapted for circulation at the Great West."—*Harper's Magazine.*

AGNES STRICKLAND.

STORIES FROM HISTORY. 12mo, illustrated, cloth extra, black and gold. Price, $1.25.

TRUE STORIES FROM ANCIENT HISTORY. Chronologically arranged from the Creation of the World to the Death of Charlemagne. 12mo, illustrated, cloth extra, black and gold. $1.25.

STORIES FROM MODERN HISTORY. 12mo, illustrated, cloth extra, black and gold. $1.25.

STORIES FROM ENGLISH HISTORY. 12mo, illustrated, cloth extra, black and gold. $1.25.

"Miss Strickland has performed her task with taste and ability."—*London Atheneum.*

THE LEADERS OF FRANCE; OR, THE MEN OF THE THIRD REPUBLIC. Biographical, Historical and Character Sketches. 12mo, satin cloth, black and gold, $1.75.

CONTENTS.—M. Thiers; Marshal MacMahon; M. Gambetta; M. Grevy; M. Barthelemy St. Hilaire; M. Rouher; The Duc de Broglie; M. Dufaure; M. Alexandre Dumas; The Duc D'Audiffret Pasquier; M. Ernest Picard; General Faidherbe; Bishop Dupanloup; M. Louis Veuillot; The Duc D'Aumale; M. Emile de Girardin; Father Hyacinthe; M. M. Erckmann-Chatrian; M. Henri Rochefort; M. Edmond About; M. Casimir Perier; M. Jules Simon; M. Victorien Sardou; Admiral Pothuau; M. Louis Blanc; M. Victor Hugo.

"These essays are the work of no 'prentice hand. They show not only a mastery of analytic and picturesque description, but an intimate acquaintance with the literature, the politics, and even the gossip of France and England during the past half century. * * * * Whoever wants instruction in the living politics and letters of France, cannot get it under a more rational or fascinating tutor than the unknown author of *The Men of the Third Republic.*"—*The Christian Union, N. Y.*

"A collected republication of the very brilliant and well informed sketches which excited much attention and speculation on their appearance in the *Daily News*, and led men to ask whether there could be on the English press two men with opportunity and ability like those of the author of "The Member for Paris." Here are five-and-twenty sketches of notabilities who, since Sedan, have been prominent in French affairs, from M. Thiers and Jules Simon to Alexandre Dumas, Louis Blanc, and Victor Hugo; while the account of such less-known politicians as Gambetta, Grevy, Rouher, Dufaure, Rochefort, Girardin, will be interesting from the freshness of their information. Such brilliant and sagacious sketches as those of Thiers, Louis Blanc, and Jules Simon will be read very eagerly. So with the characterizations of literary celebrities like Dumas, M. M. Erckmann-Chatrian, Edmond About, and Victor Hugo. The charm and value of most of these sketches are, that they are histories as well as portraits. It argues well for France that novels like those of M. M. Erckmann-Chatrian are superseding those of Dumas and Paul DeKock, and penetrating every village."—*British Quarterly Review* (*the highest authority in England*).

Rev. WM. BACON STEVENS, Bishop of Penna.

SUNDAY AT HOME. A Manual of Home Service, intended for those who are occasionally hindered from attending the House of God. With Sermons and a Selection of Hymns. 12mo, cloth, extra, $1.50; cloth, extra, beveled boards, red edges, $2.00.

HOUSEHOLD WORSHIP. Partly responsive. A book of Family Prayers. By a Layman With an Introduction by REV. DANIEL MARCH, author of "Night Scenes in the Bible," &c. 12mo, cloth, extra, $1.25; cloth, extra, beveled boards, red edges, $1.75.

JOHN BUNYAN.

THE PILGRIM'S PROGRESS, FROM THIS WORLD TO THAT WHICH IS TO COME. With four beautiful illustrations, printed in colors. Large type. 16mo. Cloth, extra, $1.25; morocco, $3.00; Turkey, antique, $4.00.

"There is no book in our literature on which we could so readily stake the fame of the old unpolluted English language; no book which shows so well how rich that language is in its own proper wealth, and how little it has been improved by all that it has borrowed. . . . . We are not afraid to say that, though there were many clever men in England during the latter half of the seventeenth century, there were only two great creative minds. One of these minds produced the Paradise Lost, the other, the Pilgrim's Progress."—*Lord Macaulay.*

JANE R. SOMMERS.

HEAVENWARD LED; or, The Two Bequests. 12mo, paper, $1.25. Cloth extra, $1.75.

"It is really an excellent work."—*Germantown Telegraph.*

"This story is one of good society, is graphically told, and a sound moral is inculcated."—*Rutland Herald.*

"Artless in style and simple in plot, it is a pure and beautiful story, and richly merits a place in every Sunday-school library in the country."—*Toledo Commercial.*

"After a careful perusal we strongly recommend the work as one worthy of a place on the centre-table of every Christian family in the land. The story is well written, couched in beautiful language, and shows how much good may be done by those who take an interest in religious matters."—*Banner of the Church, Atlanta, Ga.*

LOUIS ENAULT.

THE PUPIL OF THE LEGION OF HONOR. Translated from the French by Mrs. Charles Pendleton Tutt. 8vo, paper, $1.00; cloth, $1.50.

"This is a translation from the French of a very fresh, quietly written, and interesting story, as unlike the average modern French novel as any thing can well be. There is perhaps somewhat more sentiment than Americans will care for, but the skill with which the story is told will more than atone for that."—*San Francisco Daily Record.*

"A very clear and natural, though rather un-Gallican story. A novel without a hero, unless M. De Verteins, who puts in a tardy appearance in time to marry Jeanne Derville, say at page one hundred and fifty, or thereabouts, it is a remarkably fresh, vivid story, nevertheless—the more vivid, perhaps, from the fact that, with the exception of Miss Derville herself, who is a sort of female John Halifax, it is not at all overwrought, and has none of the spectacularity so common in modern Gallic romance. Biographical in tone, and written in the manner of 'John Halifax,' it details the struggles of a young girl, Miss Derville, with exceeding minuteness, and considerable subjective power. The translation is well executed."—*Home Journal, New York.*

OLIVER GOLDSMITH.

THE DESERTED VILLAGE. A Poem. Exquisitely illustrated with thirty designs by George Thomas and Birket Foster. Elegantly printed in square 16mo, on the finest calendered paper. Cloth, gilt, extra, $1.50; morocco, antique, gilt edges, $2.50.

"There is no poem in the English language more universally popular than the Deserted Village. Its best passages are learned in youth, and never quit the memory."—*Chambers's Encyclopedia of English Literature.*

"'The Deserted Village' has an endearing locality, and introduces us to beings with whom the imagination contracts an intimate friendship. Fiction in poetry is not the reverse of truth, but her soft and enchanted resemblance; and this ideal beauty of nature has been seldom united with so much sober fidelity, as in the groups and scenery of the 'Deserted Village.'"—*Thomas Campbell.*

GEORGE CRUIKSHANK.

THE LOVING BALLAD OF LORD BATEMAN. Humorously illustrated by George Cruikshank. Sq. 16mo, boards, 25 cents.

YE BOOK OF SENSE. A new comic book. A companion to Book of Nonsense. With thirty-two illustrations. Oblong 8vo, boards, 50 cents; cloth, with plates colored, gilt, $1.00.

CHARLES KNIGHT.

HALF HOURS WITH THE BEST AUTHORS. With Short Biographical and Critical Notices. Elegantly printed on the finest paper. With fine steel portraits. 6 vols., crown 8vo. cloth, bev. boards, gilt tops, $9.00; half calf, gilt, $18.00; half morocco, gilt tops, $18,00; or bound in 3 vols., thick crown 8vo, fine English cloth, bev. boards, gilt tops, per set, $7.50; half calf, gilt, $12.00.

Selecting some choice passage of the best standard authors, of sufficient length to occupy half an hour in its perusal, there is here food for thought for every day in the year; so that if the purchaser will devote but one half-hour each day to its appropriate selection, he will read through these six volumes in one year, and in such a leisurely manner that the noblest thoughts of many of the greatest minds will be firmly implanted in his mind forever. For every Sunday there is a suitable selection from some of the most eminent writers in sacred literature. We venture to say, if the editor's idea is carried out, the reader will possess more information and a better knowledge of the English classics at the end of the year than he would by five years of desultory reading. The *variety* of reading is so great that no one will ever tire of these volumes. It is a library in itself.

MISS JANE PORTER.

The two following are new stereotype editions, in large, clear type, with initial letters, head and tail pieces, &c. The illustrations were designed expressly for this edition, and engraved in the highest style of art.

THE SCOTTISH CHIEFS. Illustrated by F. O. C. Darley. Crown 8vo, 748 pp. Fine English cloth, gilt. Price, $1.50; half calf, gilt, $3.50.

"Sir Walter Scott, in a conversation with King George IV, in the library at Carlton House, admitted that 'The Scottish Chiefs' suggested his 'Waverly Novels.'"—*Allibone's Dictionary of Authors.*

"This is a new and by far the best edition of a national romance which has been as much read and admired as almost any of Scott's or Dickens' novels. It is low-priced, well printed, and handsomely bound. Thousands of readers will be glad to go over this stirring tale once more."—*Philadelphia Press.*

REGINA MARIA ROCHE.

THE CHILDREN OF THE ABBEY. Illustrated by F. O. C. DARLEY. Uniform with "The Scottish Chiefs." Crown 8vo, 646 pp. Fine English cloth, gilt. Price, $1.50; half calf, gilt, $3.50.

"This classic is more neatly published in the new edition than we have ever seen it. It was long a standard, and had more favor than 'Thaddeus of Warsaw,' and it deserved better. It takes a new lease of existence now, and we almost envy those who read it for the first time."—*North American,* Philadelphia.

ROBERT McCLURE, M.D., V.S.

THE AMERICAN GENTLEMAN'S STABLE GUIDE. Containing a Familiar Description of the American Stable; the most approved Method of Feeding, Grooming, and General Management of Horses; together with Directions for the Care of Carriages, Harness, &c. Expressly adapted for the owners of equipages and fine horses. Cloth extra, illustrated. $1.50.

A handy manual, giving to the owner of a horse just the information of a practical nature that he often feels the need of, and by an author who thoroughly understands what he is writing about, and what is needed by every gentleman.

"Such a treatise has been needed for years, and we think this volume will supply the want. The illustrations are very good and timely."—*Pittsburgh Daily Gazette.*

JOHN J. THOMAS.

THE AMERICAN FRUIT CULTURIST. Containing Practical Directions for the Propagation and Culture of Fruit Trees in the Nursery, Orchard, and Garden. With Descriptions of the Principal American and Foreign Varieties cultivated in the United States. Second edition. Illustrated with 480 accurate figures. Crown 8vo. Cloth extra, bev. bds., gilt back. $3.00.

We have read hundreds of criticisms on this book, and they unanimously pronounce it the most *thorough, practical*, and *comprehensive* work published. The engravings are not copies of old cuts from other books, but are mainly original with the author.

J. H. WALSH, F.R.C.S. ("Stonehenge.")

THE HORSE IN THE STABLE AND THE FIELD; his Management in Health and Disease. From the last London edition, with copious Notes and Additions, by ROBERT MCCLURE, M.D., V.S., author of "Diseases in the American Stable, Field, and Farm-yard," with an Essay on the American Trotting Horse, and suggestions on the Breeding and Training of Trotters, by ELLWOOD HARVEY, M.D. With 80 engravings, and full-page engravings from photographs from life. Crown 8vo. Cloth, extra, bev. bds. $2.50.

"This Americanizing of 'Stonehenge' gives us the best piece of Horse Literature of the season. Old horsemen need not be told who 'Stonehenge' is in the British Books, or that he is the highest authority in turf and veterinary affairs. Add to these the labors of such American writers as Dr. McClure and Dr. Harvey, with new portraits of some of our most popular living horses, and we have a book that no American horseman can afford to be without."—*Ohio Farmer*, Cleveland, April 24, 1869.

"It sustains its claim to be the only work which has brought together in a single volume, and in clear, concise, and comprehensive language, adequate information on the various subjects of which it treats."—*Harper's Magazine*, July, 1869.

THADDEUS NORRIS.

AMERICAN FISH CULTURE. Giving all the details of Artificial Breeding and Rearing of Trout, Salmon, Shad, and other Fishes. 12mo, illustrated. $1.75.

"'Norris's American Fish Culture' published in this city by Porter & Coates, is passing around the world as a standard. Mr. Norris's authority will be quoted beside the tributaries of the Ganges, as already by those of the Hudson, the Humber, and the Thames. The English publishers of the book are Sampson Low, Son & Co.; and a late number of the *Athenæum*, after an attentive review of Mr. Norris's methods, concludes thus: 'Mr. Norris has rendered good service to the important subject of fish-culture by the present publication; and, although his book goes over ground (or water rather) occupied to a great extent by English writers on fish culture, it contains several particulars respecting this art as practised in the United States, which are valuable, and may be turned to profitable account by our pisciculturists.'"—*Philadelphia Evening Bulletin.*

THE AMERICAN ANGLER'S BOOK. Embracing the Natural History of Sporting Fish, and the Art of Taking Them. With Instructions in Fly Fishing, Fly Making, and Rod Making; and Directions for Fish Breeding. To which is added Dies Piscatoriæ; describing noted fishing places, and the pleasure of solitary fly fishing. New edition, with a supplement, containing a Description of Salmon Rivers, Inland Trout Fishing, &c. Illustrated with eighty engravings. 8vo, cloth extra. $5.50.

"Mr. Norris has produced the best book on Angling that has been published in our time. If other authors would follow Mr. Norris's example, and not write upon a subject until they had practically mastered it, we should have fewer and better works. *His* volume will live. It is thoroughly instructive, good-tempered, and genial."—*Philadelphia Press.*

HIRAM WOODRUFF.

HIRAM WOODRUFF ON THE TROTTING-HORSE OF AMERICA: HOW TO TRAIN AND DRIVE HIM. With Reminiscences of the Trotting-Turf. The Results of the Author's Forty Years' Experience and Unequalled Skill in Training and Driving, together with a Store of Interesting Matter concerning Celebrated American Horses. Edited by CHARLES J. FOSTER, of "Wilkes's Spirit of the Times." New edition, with Supplement, bringing it down to 1873. Illustrated with Steel-plate portrait of HIRAM WOODRUFF, and full page engravings from Photographs from Life, and Sketches of "Lady Thorne," "Goldsmith Maid," "Mac," "Flora Temple," &c., &c. 12mo, cloth, extra, $2.25; half calf, gilt, $4.00.

"The estimation in which we hold it is well known to our readers. We believe it to be *the most practical and instructive book that ever was published concerning the trotting horse;* and those who own or take care of horses of other descriptions may buy and read it with a great deal of profit."—*Wilkes's Spirit of the Times.*

"Hiram Woodruff was the great trainer of his day; but, by his unsullied integrity and unequalled capacity, he rose above his profession. No man could ever say of him that he had his price. Indeed, it is the universal testimony of all who knew him,—friends and foes,—that his integrity was absolutely unassailable. *It is a book for which every man who owns a horse ought to subscribe. The information which it contains is worth ten times its cost.*" —*Mr. Bonner's New York Ledger.*

"*This is a masterly treatise by the master of his profession,*—the ripened product of forty years' experience in handling, training, riding, and driving the trotting horse. There is no book like it in any language on the subject of which it treats. It is accepted as authority by the owners of racing trotters, and of fast roadsters. Its publication has been hailed by gentlemen as critically appreciative as Robert Bonner, and by trainers and drivers as distinguished as Sam Hoagland, Dan Mace, and Dan Pfifer. The book is unquestionably one of great value. For in America and England the development of the horse has long been considered second only in importance to the development of man. This work contains the results of forty years' uninterrupted labor in bringing the trotter up to the highest speed and greatest endurance of which he is capable. Before we read it we had seen with curious surprise very hearty commendation of it and eulogy of its author in the leading Presbyterian, Baptist, and Methodist journals. No wonder, for Hiram Woodruff's system is based on the law of love."—*New York Tribune.*

"We have a decided distaste for everything connected with horse-racing, and when the "Trotting Horse of America" was put into our hands the book dropped of its own weight on to the table. Ashamed of this prejudice, we took it up, and soon found ourselves reading at full pace about the way colts should be raised, and horses trained, and racers cared for, and the breed improved. . . . . In reading the book we were struck with the analogy between the scientific treatment of the horse and the best treatment of the human being. . . . . What a pity parents and teachers would not learn wisdom from the horse-trainer!"—*The (N. Y.) Liberal Christian (Unitarian).*

"One may read and study this book with profit, for it was written by a man who loved the horse, knew his peculiarities, and from the experience of years utters words of wisdom as to the best way of training and driving the noblest animal ever given to man for service. *The advice, the suggestions, the rules given in the book are invaluable.* If we owned a "stable," we would make our grooms study it; if we were a Vermont farmer, each son should have a copy, for, while it is specially devoted to trotting horses, the work contains valuable information for every man who owns or drives a horse."—*Boston Watchman and Reflector, (Baptist).*

"The record of his experience and suggestions constitutes, therefore, a valuable accession to our knowledge, and will prove to be of *standard authority among the most skilful.* The graphic style of his descriptions, the vivid pictures he draws of the breeding and education of his favorites, and the reminiscences he recalls of incidents on the turf, form a work of great merit. . . . Those who are desirous to form an accurate idea of the characteristics of the trotting horse, for their benefit as riders or drivers, *cannot find any other work in our language so replete with useful information,* interesting hints, and readable anecdotes. Hiram Woodruff is now dead, and it will be many a year before we shall look upon his equal in his line of business."—*The Nation.*

THE INSTRUCTIVE GAME OF MYTHOLOGY, with descriptive and biographical sketches on every card. Price, 50 cents.

THE INSTRUCTIVE GAME OF POPULAR QUOTATIONS, with descriptive, biographical and character sketches on every card. Price, 50 cents.

These games are uniform with "The Instructive Games of Authors and Poets," brought out last year. They are printed on the finest card-board, with colored backs, and are put up in either a handsome cloth case or a beautifully illuminated case as desired.

J. R. SYPHER.

THE YOUNG AMERICA SPEAKER. Designed for the use of the younger classes in Schools, Lyceums, Temperance Societies, &c. Containing selections in Prose, Poetry and Dialogue; in style, sentiment and expression, suited to the minds and spirits of the youth of the present day. 16mo, half bound, 75 cents.

"This little volume contains unexceptional selections of Prose, Poetry and Dialogue. The selections evidence extensive reading, good taste, and some experience with the predelictions of young declaimers."—*New Orleans Picayune.*

"An important and interesting addition to our school literature. The pieces presented in the work are well selected, and they have this advantage—each piece is short, and will not too seriously strain the faculties of any student. Being short, a greater variety is presented than in most speakers now before the public."—*Banner of the Church, Atlanta, Ga.*

THE AMERICAN POPULAR SPEAKER. Designed for the use of Schools, Lyceums, Temperance Societies, &c., &c. 12mo, half bound, 384 pp., $1.50.

"Admirably adapted to the purposes of declamation. We recognize many of the old standard pieces which boys have declaimed since our remembrance, with many also which we have not found in other similar compilations. The book is not encumbered with a multiplicity of rules and directions which serve to confuse and hinder the students rather than to help them; but a few, simple, practical directions are given which are admirable, and all that are needed. We commend the volume to the attention of teachers and students as one of high merit."—*Portland Evening Argus.*

"Excellent selections of prose and poetry and dialogues. The subjects embrace every conceivable want for school declamations with concise practical instructions for the speaker."—*New Bedford Evening Standard.*

MME. MARIE SOPHIE SCHWARTZ.

THE SON OF THE ORGAN GRINDER. A Novel. Translated from the Swedish by SELMA BORG and MARIE A. BROWN. With a portrait and sketch of Mme. Schwartz. 1 vol., 12mo. Cloth, $1.50; paper, $1.

This volume recommences the publication of the works of this brilliant and popular writer, and is considered equal to the best of her works yet translated.

MME. EMILE DE GIRARDIN, MM. THEOPHILE GAUTIER, JULES SANDEAU, and MERY.

THE CROSS OF BERNY; OR, IRENE'S LOVERS. A Novel. Translated from the French. 1 vol., 12mo. Cloth, $1.50; paper, $1.

"The Cross of Berny" is a brilliant literary tourney of four famous writers, and is pronounced by a former literary editor of *The Christian Union* to be the most powerful, witty, and interesting foreign novel translated since "On the Heights."

HENRY T. COATES.

THE COMPREHENSIVE SPEAKER. Designed for the use of Schools, Academies, Lyceums, &c. Carefully selected from the best authors, with Notes. Large 12mo, 672 pages, half bound, cloth sides, $1.75.

PHILADELPHIA, *April* 18, 1872.

I consider your "Comprehensive Speaker" to be one of the most valuable contributions to the literary apparatus of schools, academies, and lyceums ever published. But its usefulness is not limited to these institutions: it is an excellent family-table book, and should be in every private as well as in every public collection.

In carrying your readers through various departments of literature, from "gay to grave, from lively to severe," you have evinced much taste and judgment, as well as great industry. That the sale of so good a book should be large I should be sorry to doubt.

S. AUSTIN ALLIBONE,
Author of Allibone's Dictionary of Authors.

'It contains a judicious selection of pieces from the best authors, omitting all of doubtful morality, of a sectarian or political character, and of transient literary value. Great care has been taken in the selection of extracts to give the genuine text of the author without the errors in quotation and punctuation which are such a frequent blemish in this class of school books. A large proportion of the contents are from American authors, furnishing the materials for a comparative survey of our native literature."—*The New York Daily Tribune.*

"It is an excellent selection of pieces for declamation and reading."—*The Nation, New York.*

"On careful examination, we do not hesitate to characterize it as the BEST compilation of its class that has ever come under our notice. The merits of this large and varied collection are numerous. Hackneyed pieces have been carefully excluded, and political and sectarian pieces are not to be found in its pages. There are, of course, some humorous passages, in prose and verse, but none that are immoral or vulgar."—*The Philadelphia Press.*

"We cannot too highly commend the felicitous manner in which the compiler has accomplished his work. It is valuable as a volume for general reading as well. It seems to us wholly good, with nothing to add or change—a difficult achievement in view of the number of "Speakers" already in existence."—*Ohio State Journal, Columbus, Ohio.*

"The instructions are simple and practical, most admirably adapted to the student's use. Mr. Coates has shown in the preparation of this work a wide range of scholarship and rare good taste. The book is worthy of a grand success."—*Watchman and Reflector, Boston, (Baptist).*

"We need only say of this book that it is a remarkably rich collection of excerpts from the very best specimens of English prose and poetry, selected with singularly good taste and judgment. Its influence, as a familiar school-book, cannot be but very elevating."—*The Advance, Chicago.*

THE LATEST AND MOST IMPROVED GAMES.

THE INSTRUCTIVE GAME OF AUTHORS. Containing on each card the leading characters in the books named, the history of the author or the leading events mentioned in the books named, thus familiarizing one with each writer, by attracting the attention to some special persons or prominent incidents. Also, containing short biographical notices, in handsome cloth case. 50 cents.

THE INSTRUCTIVE GAME OF POETS. Uniform with the above in style. Cloth case. 50 cents.

JAMES HOGG, the Ettrick Shepherd.

THE MOUNTAIN BARD AND FOREST MINSTREL. Legendary Songs and Ballads. With two fine engravings on steel. 32mo, cloth, 60 cents; illuminated side, 90 cents; Turkey mor., $1.50.

"He is a poet, in the highest acceptation of the name."—*Lord Jeffrey.*

PERCY BYSSHE SHELLEY.

POETICAL WORKS. With a fine engraving on steel. 32mo, cloth, 60 cents; illuminated side, 90 cents; Turkey mor., $1.50.

ROBERT BLOOMFIELD.

THE FARMER'S BOY, and other Poems. Illustrated with a fine engraving on steel. 32mo, cloth, 60 cents; illuminated side, 90 cents; Turkey morocco, $1.50.

"Few compositions in the English language have been so generally admired as the Farmer's Boy. Those who agreed in but little else in literary matters, were unanimous in the commendation of the poetical powers displayed by the peasant and journeyman mechanic."—*Allibone's Dictionary Authors.*

ROBERT BURNS.

POETICAL WORKS. With a fine engraving on steel. 32mo, cloth, 60 cents; illuminated side, 90 cents; Turkey mor., $1.50.

"Burns is by far the greatest poet that ever sprang from the bosom of the people, and lived and died in an humble condition. Indeed, no country in the world but Scotland could have produced such a man; and he will be forever regarded as the glorious representative of the genius of his country. He was born a poet if ever man was."—*Prof. Wilson's Essay on Burns.*

WILLIAM DODD, LL.D.

THE BEAUTIES OF SHAKSPEARE. From the last London edition, with large additions, and the author's latest corrections. With two fine engravings on steel. Fine edition, on toned paper, with carmine border. Square 24mo. Cloth, gilt edges, $1.50; Turkey, $3.00; 32mo, cloth, 60 cts.; illuminated side, 90 cts.; Turkey morocco, $1.50.

This republication of a book so universally and deservedly popular as Dodd's Beauties, makes it peculiarly valuable as a gift book.

THOMAS HOOD.

POETICAL WORKS. With a fine engraving on steel. 32mo. Cloth, 60 cts.; illuminated side, 90 cts.; Turkey morocco, $1.50.

"Hood's verse, whether serious or comic,—whether serene, like a cloudless autumn evening, or sparkling with puns like a frosty January midnight with stars,—was ever pregnant with materials for thought. . . . . Like every author distinguished for true comic humor, there was a deep vein of melancholy pathos running through his mirth; and even when his sun shone brightly, its light seemed often reflected as if only over the rim of a cloud.—*D. M. Moir.*

THOMAS MOORE.

THE MORAL AND BEAUTIFUL FROM THE POEMS OF. Edited by REV. WALTER COLTON, author of "Deck and Port," &c., &c. With a fine engraving on steel. 32mo. Cloth, 60 cts.; illuminated sides, 90 cts.; Turkey morocco, $1.50.

"The combinations of his wit are wonderful. Quick, subtle, and varied, ever suggesting new thoughts or images, or unexpected turns of expression—now drawing resources from classical literature or of the ancient fathers—now diving into the human heart, and now skimming the fields of fancy—the wit or imagination of Moore (for they are compounded together), is a true Ariel, 'a creature of the elements,' that is ever buoyant and full of life and spirit."—*Chambers's Eng. Lit.*

ALFRED HOWARD.

THE BEAUTIES OF CHESTERFIELD. Consisting of Selections from the Works of Lord Chesterfield. 18mo, illustrated. Cloth extra, black and gold, $1.25.

CHARLES CALEB COLTON.

LACON; or, Many Things in Few Words Addressed to Those Who Think. Revised edition, with a life of the author. Globe edition, 16mo, cloth extra, $1.25.

"It is one of the most excellent collections of apothegms in the language."—*Allibone's Dictionary of Authors.*

COL. GEORGE CHESNEY.

THE BATTLE OF DORKING, AND GERMAN CONQUEST OF ENGLAND IN 1875; or, Reminiscences of a Volunteer. By an Eyewitness, in 1925. Reprinted from Blackwood's Magazine. 12mo, 64 pp., 30 cents; cloth, 50 cents.

"Everybody is talking about it, and everybody is quite right. We do not know that we ever saw anything better in any magazine, or any better example of the *vraisemblance* which a skilled artist can produce by a variety of minute touches. * * * * * The writer of this paper, living about 1925, gives his son an account of his adventures as a Volunteer during the invasion of England fifty years before, and so powerful is the narrative, so intensely real the impression it produces, that the coolest disbeliever in panics cannot read it without a flush of annoyance, or close it without the thought that after all, as the world now stands, some such day of humiliation for England is at least possible. The suggested condition precedent of invasion, the destruction of the fleet by torpedoes attached by a new invention to our ships, has attracted many minds; and with the destruction of the regulars, the helplessness of the brave but half organized Volunteers, and the absence of arrangement, make up a picture which, fanciful as it is, we seem, as we read it, almost to have seen. It describes so exactly what we all feel that, under the circumstances, Englishmen, if refused time to organize, would probably do."—*Spectator* (*London.*)

"The extraordinary force and naturalness of the picture of the calamity itself, its consistency throughout, from the bits of the last *Times* leader, read by the unhappy volunteer in the City, to the description of the conduct of the Germans in the fatal Battle of Dorking, and in the occupation of the English homes which follows, seem to us as natural in its touches as can well be conceived."—*Pall Mall Gazette.*

"The Britons are stirred up by it as they have been by no one magazine article of this generation. The 'Fight at Dame Europa's School' did not hit the bull's eye of English feeling more squarely than this clever shot from old Maga. . . . . The verisimilitude is wonderful. We have read nothing like it outside of Robinson Crusoe."—*Journal of Commerce* (*New York.*)

THE SECOND ARMADA. A Chapter of Future History. Being a Reply to the Above. 12mo, paper covers. 10 cents.

The story of the German Conquest has produced a sensation both in America and England, having run into eight editions in this country in less than one month. The "London Times" of June 22d contained their version of the famous battle, with a totally different result however, and also had a long editorial on the two versions. This is given also with the reply.

"An intensely interesting little book, and must be read to be appreciated."—*Providence Gazette.*

OLIVER BUNCE.

ROMANCE OF THE REVOLUTION. Being true Stories of the Thrilling Adventures, Romantic Incidents, Hair-breadth Escapes and Heroic Exploits of the Days of '76. Laid paper, with six illustrations. 16mo, cloth, extra, $1.50.

While the principal events of the history of our glorious Revolution are known to every intelligent American, much remains to be disclosed of the inner history of the war, and the motives and patriotism of the people. There were deeds of individual daring, heroism worthy of the proudest days of Greece and Rome, dashing and hazardous enterprises, and hardships bravely borne, performed by subalterns and private soldiers in the grand army of heroes, which should never be forgotten. To collect and preserve the sketches of these almost forgotten passages of the war, as they originally appeared in the newspapers and private letters of that stirring period, and the stories told by scarred veterans round the blazing hearth-stone; these legends of the past; has been the object of this work, and the publishers are confident that none will rise from its perusal without acknowledging that "Truth is stranger than fiction," and with a deeper feeling of reverence for the heroes of the days of '76

"A collection of anecdotes and traditions relating to the War of Independence, which presents in a brilliant light chivalrous adventures called forth by the struggles of the early patriots for the freedom of their country. If some of the incidents here recorded have rather an apocryphal air, they yet serve to illustrate the spirit of the time, and present the truth more vividly to the imagination than the more formal pages of history. The volume is eminently adapted to popular reading."—*Harper's Magazine.*

CECIL B. HARTLEY.

LIFE OF THE EMPRESS JOSEPHINE, Wife of Napoleon I. With a fine Portrait on Steel. 16mo. Printed on fine laid paper. Cloth, extra, $1.50.

"Her career and her character were alike remarkable; surrounded by the demoralizations of the French Court, she was a Roman matron in stern rectitude, with a pre-eminent fidelity to a sensitive conscience; and blended comprehensive genius with a warm heart and a noble personal presence. She was the peer of Napoleon, and in some respects his superior. Her executive force was less, but her foresight was greater. It is to her that the index finger of history points, as an example of female grandeur. Napoleon got a divorce from her because he wished his seed to inherit the French Crown. The son born of his Hapsburg marriage died crownless, while the grandson of Josephine now wears the purple of France—this is more than poetic justice. * * * In the book before us, the story of her life is told in a simple, classic style, and possesses a fascination rarely met with in biography."—*Chicago Evening Journal.*

MRS. ANNA JAMESON.

LIVES OF CELEBRATED FEMALE SOVEREIGNS AND ILLUSTRIOUS WOMEN. Edited by Mary E. Hewitt. With four portraits on steel. 16mo, beautifully printed on laid paper. Cloth, extra, $1.50.

The celebrated Mrs. Jameson, who wields a powerful, ready, and pleasant pen, has taken hold of some of the leading events in the brilliant lives of some of the most world-noted women, and depicted them in very attractive colors. It is a lovely book for young ladies, and will give them a taste for history.

W. S. GILBERT.

THE BAB BALLADS; or, Much Sound and Little Sense. With 113 illustrations by the author. Square 12mo., cloth, bev. gilt edges, $1.75.

These Ballads, first published in periodicals, rapidly achieved a whimsical popularity, which soon demanded their publication in a collected form. Much of this is due to the series of inexpressibly funny drawings by the author, who is happy in being artist enough to interpret his own humor in these admirable sketches: we pity the man who cannot appreciate and enjoy them. The Ballads will rank with the best of Thackeray, Bon Gaultier, or Ingoldsby. Let every one who in these dull times has the blues, procure a copy as the cheapest remedy. While it is a nearly perfect *fac simile* of the English copy, it is only half the price.

"Everybody likes, occasionally, a little sensible nonsense. 'Mother Goose' is enjoyed in childhood, and something similar, but more advanced, is needed to provoke a smile on a wearied face in later years. This volume of comic poems answers such a purpose; some of them have a sly moral, while others are simply amusing from their supreme absurdity. The mirth is aided by the author's original cuts, which are quite in keeping with the poetry."—*Advance*, Chicago, the Great Religious Weekly.

C. M. METZ.

DRAWING-BOOK OF THE HUMAN FIGURE. With many Examples from the best Studies of the Old Masters, beautifully engraved in the first style of the art. Folio, half morocco, antique, $7.50.

H. B. STAUNTON.

THE AMERICAN CHESS PLAYER'S HANDBOOK. Teaching the Rudiments of the Game, and giving an analysis of all the recognized openings, amplified by appropriate games actually played by Morphy, Horwitz, Anderssen, Staunton, Paulson, Montgomery, Meek, and others. From the work of Staunton. Illustrated. 16mo, cloth, extra, bev. bds. $1.25.

"Among the great wants of students of this noble game of chess has been a handbook which should occupy a middle ground between the large and expensive work of Staunton and the ten cent guides with which the country is flooded. This want is happily supplied by the present volume. It is an abridgment of Staunton's work, and contains full accounts and descriptions of the common openings and defences, besides a large number of illustrative games and several endings and problems. It is a book which will be decidedly useful to all beginners in the game, and interesting to those who are already proficient in it."—*Peoria Transcript.*

"Will prove an invaluable guide for the admirers of the great and strategic game of chess. It should be in the hands of every chess-player."—*Galesburg Republican.*

"It is the best manual for the beginner with which we are acquainted,—exceedingly clear and intelligible."—*New Orleans Picayune.*

SARAH E. SCOTT.

EVERY-DAY COOKERY, FOR EVERY FAMILY. Containing nearly 1000 Receipts adapted to moderate incomes, and comprising the best and most economical methods of roasting, boiling, broiling and stewing all kinds of meat, fish, poultry, game and vegetables; simple and inexpensive instructions for making pies, puddings, tarts, and all other pastry; how to pickle and preserve fruits and vegetables; suitable cookery for invalids and children; food in season, and how to choose it; the best ways to make domestic wines and syrups, and ample receipts for bread, cake, soups, gravies, sauces, desserts, jellies, brandied fruits, soaps, perfumes, &c., &c., and full directions for carving. Illustrated. 16mo., cloth. Price, $1,25.

OTTO MÜLLER.

CHARLOTTE ACKERMAN. A Theatrical Romance, founded upon interesting facts in the life of a young artist of the last century. Translated from the German, by Mrs. Chapman Coleman and her Daughters, the translators of the Mulbach Novels. Paper, $1.00; cloth, $1.50.

"The author of this romance has acquired a solid reputation in Germany, and it is evident, from this translation, that it is deserved."—*San Francisco Daily Record.*

T. S. ARTHUR.

IDLE HANDS, AND OTHER STORIES. A new volume by this popular author. With six exquisite full-page cuts, engraved by Lauderbach. Square 8vo. Cloth, full gilt, $2.00.

"The most popular of all our American writers on domestic subjects."—*Godey's Lady's Book.*

"In the princely mansions of the Atlantic merchants, and in the rude log cabins of the backwoodsmen, the name of Arthur is equally known and cherished as a friend of virtue."—*Graham's Magazine.*

"As a writer of short moral stories and sketches, Mr. Arthur has probably no superior in this country. There is no mistaking the lesson intended to be taught. Thousands of young readers will hail the advent of this book with genuine joy."—*Indianapolis Evening News.*

"The name of T. S. Arthur is so well known as a charming writer for juveniles as well as for adults, that to commend this selection of beautiful and instructive stories, so tastefully gotten up by the enterprising publishers, would be but to put pencil and paint to finished work."—*Central Baptist, St. Louis.*

"The paper and printing are superb, and the binding, which allows the margin to be wide, is in the best style of green and gold. It is a book for the holidays."—*Worcester (Mass.) Daily Spy.*

FRIENDLY HANDS AND KINDLY WORDS. Stories illustrative of the Law of Kindness, the Power of Perseverance, and the Advantages of Little Helps. Eight fine illustrations by H. K. Browne, John Absolom, and the brothers Dalziel. 16mo, cloth, extra, 75 cents.

SMALL BEGINNINGS; OR, THE WAY TO GET ON. Beautifully illustrated with eight fine drawings by H. K. Browne, John Absolom and the brothers Dalziel. 16mo, cloth, extra, 75 cents.

THE ART OF DOING OUR BEST: As seen in the Lives and Stories ofs ome thorough Workers. Eight fine illustrations by H. K. Browne, John Absolom, and the brothers Dalziel. 16mo, cloth, extra, 75 cents.

YE BOOK OF SENSE. A new comic book. A Companion to Lear's celebrated Book of Nonsense. With thirty-two illustrations, brightly colored, Oblong 8vo, boards, $1.00; cloth, extra gilt, $1.50.

MISS H. B. McKEEVER,

Author of "The Flounced Robe, and What it Cost," Edith's Ministry," Woodcliffe," "Silver Threads," &c., &c.

These stories have the merit of being entertaining, instructive, and really much superior to the common run of Juveniles. The Springfield *Republican*, which is competent authority, pronounces them the best and handsomest Juvenile Books of the season."—*Lyons Republican.*

"Miss McKeever always writes with point and meaning, and in a manner to gain and hold the attention."—*Sunday-School Times.*

ELEANOR'S THREE BIRTHDAYS. "Charity seeketh not her own." Illustrated. 16mo., 295 pp., $1.00.

MARY LESLIE'S TRIALS. "Is not easily provoked." Illustrated. 16mo., $1.00.

LUCY FORRESTER'S TRIUMPHS. "Thinketh no evil, believeth all things, hopeth all things." Illustrated. 16mo. Price, $1.00.

R. M. BALLANTYNE.

New and beautiful editions of these world-renowned books, second only to those of Cooper and Marryatt, and better than those of Mayne Reid, in the pictures presented to the reader of wild life among the Indians, the hairbreadth escapes and fierce delights of a hunters' life, and the perils of "Life on the Ocean Wave." Ballantyne's name is well known to every intelligent boy of spirit. Leading the reader into the jungles and forests of Africa, sweeping over the vast expanse of our western prairies, "fast in the ice" of the Polar regions, or coasting the shores of sunny climes, he ever presents new and enchanting pictures of adventure or beauty to enchain the attention, absorb the interest, excite the feelings, and always at the same time instructing the reader.

THE GORILLA HUNTERS. A Tale of the Wilds of Africa. 16mo, illustrated, cloth, extra, $1.25.

"Thoroughly at home on subjects of adventure. Like all his stories for boys, thrilling in interest and abounding in incidents of every kind."—*The Quiver, London.*

THE DOG CRUSOE. A Tale of the Western Prairies. 16mo, illustrated, cloth, extra, $1.25.

"This is another of Mr. Ballantyne's excellent stories for the young. They are all well written, full of romantic incidents, and are of no doubtful moral tendency; on the contrary, they are invariably found to embody sentiments of true piety, manliness and virtue."—*Inverness Advertiser.*

GASCOYNE, THE SANDAL-WOOD TRADER. A Tale of the Pacific. 16mo, illustrated, cloth, extra, $1.25.

"'Gascoyne' will rivet the attention of every one, whether old or young, who pursues it."—*Edinburgh Courant.*

FREAKS ON THE FELLS; or, Three Months' Rustication. And why I did not become a Sailor. Illustrated, 16mo, cloth, extra, $1.25.

"Mr. Ballantyne's name on the title-page of a book, has for some years been a guaranty to buyers that the volume is cheap at its price."—*London Athenæum.*

THE WILD MAN OF THE WEST. A Tale of the Rocky Mountains. 16mo. Illustrated, cloth, extra, $1.25.

This is generally considered the best of Mr. Ballantyne's famous narratives of Indian warfare and border life. In this field he is second only to Cooper.

SHIFTING WINDS. A Story of the Sea. Cloth, extra, illustrated. $1.25.

R. M. BALLANTYNE—Second Series.

"Indulgent fathers and good uncles will look a long time before they will find books more interesting or instructive for boys than these. In the four volumes the author introduces his young readers to the wonders of the Arctic regions, the wild hunting-grounds of the Hudson's Bay Company, the rugged coast and midnight sun of Norway, and the exciting chase of the monsters of the deep on the pathless fields of the ocean. He is quite at home among the scenes he describes, and has the faculty of taking the boys along with him in his narrative, and making them feel at home in his company. His object is to give information and to inculcate sound principles of virtue, and he mingles enough of fancy with the fact and the moral lesson to make both more impressive and the more sure to be remembered. The boy who reads these volumes at the time when his mind is most susceptible to the stirring scenes of peril and adventure, will cultivate a taste for more complete and elaborate works of travel and discovery, in mature years."—*Rev. Daniel March, D.D.*

FIGHTING THE WHALES; or, Doings and Dangers on a Fishing Cruise. With four full-page Illustrations. 18mo., Illustrated, 75 cents.

AWAY IN THE WILDERNESS; or, Life Among the Red Indians and Fur-Traders of North America. 18mo., Illustrated, Cloth, extra, 75 cents.

It is one of the most delightful books this famed author has written. Whilst describing the exciting adventures of Indian life, he conveys new and attractive information about the far north portion of our continent.

Seldom, if ever, has there been a better description of life in the lands of the Hudson's Bay Company, than is found in this little work.

FAST IN THE ICE; or, Adventures in the Polar Regions. 18mo. Illustrated. Cloth, extra, 75 cents.

"Is attractive and useful. There is no more practical way of communicating elementary information than that which has been adopted in this series. When we see contained in 144 small pages, as in "Fast in the Ice," such information as men of fair education should possess about icebergs, Northern lights, Esquimaux, musk-oxen, bears, walruses, etc., together with all the ordinary incidents of an Arctic voyage, woven into a clear connected narrative, we must admit that a good work has been done, and that the author deserves the gratitnde of young people of all classes."—*London Athenæum.*

CHASING THE SUN; or, Rambles in Norway. 18mo. Illustrated. Cloth, extra, 75 cents.

Describing a country almost new to us, the author tells of many strange natural curiosities, of the manners and customs of the people, and the curious modes of travel and conveyance.

ANNE BOWMAN.

THE BEAR HUNTERS OF THE ROCKY MOUNTAINS. 16mo. Illustrated. Cloth, extra, $1.25.

A story of trapper life in the Rocky Mountains. A better insight of real life in these uncivilized wilds is gained from books like this than from scores of the dry details of travellers.

ADVENTURES IN CANADA; or, Life in the Woods. 16mo. Illustrated. Cloth, $1.25.

This is not a mere work of fiction, but the true narrative of a bright boy who roughed it in the bush when Canada, the home of adventure and sporting, was much wilder than it is now. The boys, especially, will be charmed with the adventures with Indians, bears, and wolves, the racoon hunts and duck shooting; while the older class of readers will be drawn to it by its charming description of the scenery, and condition of what may, before long, become a part of the United States.

FOSTER'S TRANSLATION.

THE THOUSAND AND ONE NIGHTS; or, The Arabian Nights' Entertainment. A new edition. With eight full-page illustrations. Large 12mo, cloth, extra, $1.50.

"More widely diffused among the nations of the earth than any other product of the human mind. While it is read or recited to crowds of eager listeners in the Arab coffee-houses of Asia and Africa, it is just as eagerly perused on the banks of the Tagus, the Tiber, the Seine, the Thames, the Hudson, the Mississippi, and the Ganges. . . . While there are children on earth to love, so long will the 'Arabian Nights' be loved."—*Appleton's American Encyclopedia, article "Arabian Nights."*

D. W. BELISLE.

THE AMERICAN FAMILY ROBINSON; or, The Adventures of a Family lost in the Great Desert of the West. 16mo. Illustrated. Cloth, extra, $1.25.

DANIEL DE FOE.

THE LIFE AND ADVENTURES OF ROBINSON CRUSOE. Including a Memoir of the Author, and an Essay on his Writings. Large 12mo. Illustrated. Cloth, extra. Price, $1.50.

Carefully printed from new stereotype plates, with large, clear, open type, this is the best, as well as the cheapest, edition of this charming work published.

"Perhaps there exists no work, either of instruction or entertainment, in the English language, which has been more generally read and more universally admired, than 'The Life and Adventures of Robinson Crusoe.' It is difficult to say in what the charm consists, by which persons of all classes and denominations are thus fascinated; yet the majority of readers will recollect it as among the first works that awakened and interested their youthful attention, and feel, even in advanced life and in the maturity of their understanding, that there are still associated with Robinson Crusoe the sentiments peculiar to that period, when all is bright, which the experience of after-life tends only to darken and destroy."—*Sir Walter Scott.*

JEAN RODOLPHE WYSS.

THE SWISS FAMILY ROBINSON; or, The Adventures of a Father, Mother, and four Sons, on a Desert Island. Two parts, complete in one volume. Illustrated. Large 12mo. Cloth, extra, Price, $1.50.

GRIMM.

POPULAR GERMAN TALES AND HOUSEHOLD STORIES. Collected by the Brothers Grimm. With nearly 200 illustrations by Edward H. Wehnert. Complete in one volume. New edition. Fine English cloth, bev. bds., full gilt back and side stamp, $2.50; half calf, gilt, $4.50.

The stories in these volumes are world-renowned, and they will continue to be read, as they long have been, in different languages, and to charm and delight not only the young, but many readers in mature life who love the recollections of childhood and its innocent diversions.

COUNTESS DE SEGUR.

FRENCH FAIRY TALES. Translated by Mrs. Coleman and her daughters. With ten full-page illustrations, by Gustave Dore and Jules Didier. 16mo, price, $1.50.

The Countess de Segur, the authoress of this charming work, and the mother of the wife of the French ambassador at Florence, the brilliant Baroness Malaret, is a Russian lady, and a daughter of the heroic Prince Rostopchin, who ordered the burning of Moscow, when Napoleon captured that devoted city.

"Not many of the fairy stories written for children are so admirably contrived or so charmingly written as these."—*Worcester Daily Spy.*

HARRY CASTLEMON.

THE SPORTSMAN'S CLUB IN THE SADDLE. This is the first of the new Series of Six. The new volumes of this series will follow from time to time as rapidly as possible. Illustrated, 16mo, cloth, extra, black and gold, $1.25.

"The 'Sportsman's Club in the Saddle' is a splendid book for boys."—*Daily Journal, Newburgh, N. Y.*

"This story, we are quite certain, will please the boys immensely; it is full of amusing and exciting incidents."—*Worcester Daily Spy.*

"This is the first of the 'Sportsman's Club Series' by one of the most popular authors of Juvenile books. The boys who love dogs and guns will enjoy this volume."—*Democrat, St. Louis.*

"A delightful writer is Castlemon. Has seen everything and remembers what he has seen. Describes scenes with great spirit, while all his volumes are full of incident and excitement. The author has a nice sense of the wants of boyhood, and produces such stories as give entire satisfaction to the future rulers of the republic."—*Albany Evening Post.*

"Mr. Castlemon is the author of several series of fascinating books for boys, and the present volume but adds to its reputation."—*Morning Herald, Utica, N. Y.*

"A spirited and lively sketch of the huntsman's sports. It is replete with exciting adventure wrought into the form of an animated story, and the young will follow its entertaining pages with unflagging interest."—*Albany Evening Journal.*

THE GUNBOAT SERIES. 6 vols., 16mo, illustrated. Cloth, black and gold, $7.50.

Frank the Young Naturalist.
Frank in the Woods.
Frank on the Lower Mississippi.
Frank on a Gunboat.
Frank before Vicksburg.
Frank on the Prairie.

THE ROCKY MOUNTAIN SERIES. 3 vols., 16mo, illustrated. Cloth, black and gold, $3.75.

Frank among the Rancheros.
Frank at Don Carlos' Rancho.
Frank in the Mountains.

THE GO-AHEAD SERIES. 3 vols., 16mo, illustrated. Cloth, black and gold, $4.50.

Go Ahead; or, The Fisher Boy's Motto.
No Moss; or, The Career of a Rolling Stone.
Tom Newcombe

JULIA McNAIR WRIGHT.

A MILLION TOO MUCH. A Temperance Tale. By Mrs. Julia McNair Wright, author of "Priest and Nun," "Almost a Nun," "New York Ned," "John and Demijohn," &c. 12mo. Fine cloth, $1.50.

"It is a valuable acquisition to the temperance literature of the day, probably the best work of the kind ever published, as it deals with absolute facts. It is really a wonderful book, and those who would work effectively in staying the tide of intemperance, would do well to circulate it."—*Bloomington Daily Leader.*

"It is infinitely better than stories of the kind generally are."—*Philadelphia Inquirer.*

"This story is one of the best pieces of temperance advocacy we have seen. Its scenes are graphic; its progress only too natural, and its conclusion a powerful warning. It is less of a tract than many of the same kind of tales, and merits attention for the freshness and force of its delineations."—*The Age, Philadelphia.*

"A first class temperance story. The career of one born with appetite for drink and with the means to gratify every wish is depicted with vigorous and rapid strokes in a well told story. * * We recommend this book for Sunday-school libraries."—"*The Pacific,*" *San Francisco.*

MARGARET HOSMER.

Author of "Cherry, the Missionary," "Grandma Merritt's Stories," "The Voyage of the White Falcon," &c., &c.

LITTLE ROSIE'S FIRST PLAY DAYS. Illustrated. 18mo., 160 pp., 75 cents.

LITTLE ROSIE'S CHRISTMAS TIMES. Illustrated. 18mo., 160 pp., 75 cents.

LITTLE ROSIE IN THE COUNTRY. Illustrated. 18mo., 160 pp. 75 cents.

"Very nice children's books, indeed, and we only wish that we had more space to say so, and more time to say it in. Any present-giving fathers, mothers, uncles, aunts, brothers, or sisters, who have a care for the little people, may safely order these for home consumption."—*The Hartford Churchman.*

"A charming series of stories for the younger class of readers, full of interesting incidents and good moral and religious instruction, brought down to the comprehension of a child in such a way as to produce a salutary impression. They are calculated also to teach parents how to keep children employed in what is pleasant and useful, thus superseding the necessity of imposing so many restraints to keep them from evil. This is apt to be the great fault in the management of children. They are given nothing innocent and useful with which to employ their active, restless minds, and then parents wonder that they need be always in mischief. Rosie's mother better comprehended the wants of a child, and forestalled temptations to end by incentives to good."—*Springfield Daily Union.*

UNDER THE HOLLY; or, Christmas at Hopeton Grange. A Book for Girls. By MRS. HOSMER and MISS ——. 12mo. Illustrated. Cloth, extra, $1.50.

"And this we can and do most confidently recommend to parents who are faithfully striving to provide only wholesome food for the intellectual appetite of their children. The tone of the book is pure and healthful, the style easy and graceful, and the incidents are such as to give pleasure without at all kindling the passion for exciting fiction, which is so rampant among the young people of our day."—*Maryland Church Record.*

"This is entitled, 'A Book for Girls,' but it would interest the youth of either sex. It is a succession of tales told at the Christmas season. We can recommend them all for their interest and moral. It is for 'children of a larger growth,' not a mere story-book for the little ones."—*Philadelphia Daily Age.*

LENNY, THE ORPHAN; or, Trials and Triumphs. Illustrated, by Faber. 16mo. Price, $1.25.

"A story book of an orphan boy, who is thrown loose upon the world by a conflagration, in which his mother and only surviving parent is burnt. The varieties of experience, both sorrowful and happy, through which the boy passes, are wrought up into a story of no little power, and yet are such as often occur in actual life. The religious teachings of the book are good, and penetrate the entire structure of the story. We recommend it cordially to a place in the Sunday-school library."—*Sunday-School Times*, Philadelphia.

"The author of this book has written some of the best Sunday-school books which have recently been issued from the press of the American Sunday School Union. The volume before us portrays the trials of a little boy, who loses his mother in early life, and is subjected to the intrigues of a designing person, from which he obtains a happy deliverance. The story is well planned and written, and its moral and religious lessons are good."—*Weekly Freedman*, New Brunswick, N. J.

BARONESS MARTINEAU DES CHESNEZ.

LADY GREEN SATIN, AND HER MAID ROSETTE. Translated from the French. Illustrated. 1 vol., 12mo. Cloth, black and gold, $1.50.

This will be one of the most charming juveniles published this fall, both inside and outside.

HECTOR MALOT.

ROMAIN KALBRIS: HIS ADVENTURES ON SEA AND SHORE. Translated from the French by Mrs. JULIA MCNAIR WRIGHT, authoress of "Priest and Nun," "A Million Too Much," etc. Illustrated with 47 original French designs, by Emile Bayard, engraved in the handsomest style. 1 vol., 12mo. Cloth, black and gold, $2.50.

This will be the handsomest juvenile of the season, and is confidently recommended to the trade.

CAROLINE H. B. LAING.

THE SEVEN KINGS OF THE SEVEN HILLS. A Popular Ancient History of Rome, designed for Children. 16mo, illustrated, $1.

"A very attractive and well-told rendering of the fables of early Roman history. Everybody needs to know these stories, and this book will serve a good end in introducing them to children."—*The Nation, New York.*

"The early history of Rome is treated by the accomplished authoress of this work in a manner adapted to the comprehension and tastes of juvenile readers, without attempting to draw too sharp a line between the results of critical research and legendary fictions. Her little volume is highly entertaining, the language is chaste and graphic, and the narrative abounds with striking incidents."—*New York Tribune.*

THE HEROES OF THE SEVEN HILLS. A sequel to "The Seven Kings of the Seven Hills." A Child's History of Ancient Rome. 1 vol., 16mo. Illustrated. Cloth, black and gold, $1.

This little book, and the one to which it is a sequel, supply a want which has long been felt. The reception accorded the first one guarantees popularity to the coming volume.

MRS. S. C. HALLOWELL.

BEC'S BEDTIME, and other Stories from *The Christian Union.* 1 vol., 12mo. Illustrated. Cloth, black and gold, $1.50.

Mrs. Hallowell is well known as one of the most popular contributors to *The Christian Union*, and as a writer for children has a high standing.

VICTOR HUGO.

GAVROCHE, THE GAMIN OF PARIS. From "Les Miserables," by Victor Hugo. Translated and adapted by M. C. PYLE. A charming story. 16mo, cloth, black and gilt, $1.

"This story is a charming episode in Victor Hugo's famous book, 'Les Miserables.' It is a very touching and strongly drawn picture of Parisian life. The hero is a 'Gamin,' or street boy of Paris, who lives a vagabond life, and takes a precocious part in events of the great capital."—*The Age, Philadelphia.*

PAUL KONEWKA.

THE CATASTROPHE OF THE HALL. Illustrated with original drawings in Silhouette by the late Paul Konewka, in his most characteristic manner. Beautifully printed on tinted paper. Quarto. Boards, $1.00;

"A rhymed tale about three kittens, Beauty, Monkey and Dot, illustrated with silhouettes, by the late Paul Konewka, so spirited and so funny, that the children who read will be apt to agree with the boy on the title-page in being 'particularly glad that God *did* cats.'"—*New York Daily Tribune.*

MISCELLANEOUS.

THE LIBRARY; or, What Books to Read, and How to Buy them. A few practical hints, by an old Bookbuyer. 16mo, paper cover, 10 cents per copy; $8.00 per hundred.

Everybody has felt the want of a reliable guide in selecting books for their library. In this little manual, the author has endeavored first, in a preliminary essay, to point out how to read books to the best advantage, and how to buy them; second, what books to buy, by giving lists of some fifteen hundred volumes of standard works, such as are *necessary* to every well-selected library; these are given with the number of volumes, the best and different editions, and the prices. It thus forms a complete and intelligent guide, as to what is best to buy first, such as every person of any pretensions to literary taste should possess.

THOUGHTS OF PEACE; or, Strong Hope and Consolation for the Bearer of the Cross. From the last London edition. Beautifully printed on tinted paper, with carmine border. Square 16mo. Fine English cloth, bevelled boards, red edges, $1.50.

"Remarkable as the assertion is, that very many of the best works are the product of the chastened and afflicted in society, it is nevertheless true that the world is greatly enriched by the presence of invalid gifted minds in all ages. This delightful little volume is the product of one who has felt the acuteness of disease, and it illustrates the experience of one who has long been an invalid. The Scriptural texts, and poetic suggestions, evince a rich acquaintance with the scriptures and the poets. The book is beautifully printed on tinted paper, red line border, and richly bound. Many would prize it as a gift book."—*Pittsburg Gazette.*

"This is a reprint from the latest London edition, and is a beautiful little work, both in style of typography and binding, and in the sentiments judiciously selected and collated from the Sacred Scriptures and poets. It comprises three hundred and sixty-five of the most soul-comforting and inspiring texts of the Bible—one for each day of the year. Following each text is a short selection from some hymn, or sacred poem of corresponding sentiment. No better souvenir could be given to one having experienced some of life's sorrows—and who has not!—and who has learned to look for consolation to Holy Writ."—*Mauch Chunk Gazette.*

PAPA'S BOOK OF ANIMALS. Wild and Tame. Chiefly from the writings of Rev. J. G. Wood and Thos. Bingley. With sixteen large and spirited drawings, by H. C. Bispham. Small 4to., fine English cloth, gilt, bev. bds. Price, $1.25.

SLOVENLY PETER; or, Cheerful Stories and Funny Pictures for Good Little Folks. With nearly two hundred engravings. Beautifully colored. Printed on heavy paper. Large 4to. Cloth, bevelled boards, extra, $1.75.

A new edition of this charming book, a standard among juveniles. Surely lessons of stern morality and humanity were never more pleasantly and effectually taught than in this book.

NORTHERN LIGHTS. Tales from Swedish and Finnish authors. Collected and translated by SELMA BORG and MARIE A. BROWN, the translators of the Schwartz Novels. 1 vol., 12mo. Illustrated. Cloth, black and gold, $1.50.

This collection of Northern Tales is full of beauty, and for imagination and poetic expression excels the far-famed tales of Hans Christian Andersen.

STANDARD FAIRY TALES. Containing Aladdin, Cinderella, Beauty and the Beast, Jack the Giant Killer, Red Riding Hood, Tom Thumb, Puss in Boots, and numerous other Favorites of the Nursery. Beautifully illustrated with eight full page engravings after designs by GUSTAV DORÉ and GEORGE CRUIKSHANK. 12mo, cloth, extra, black and gold, $1.50.

ADVENTURES BY LAND AND SEA. Perils, Hardships, and Escapes; taken from the most famous travels. 1 vol. Small 4to. Profusely illustrated. Cloth, black and gold, and illuminated side. $2.

PERILOUS INCIDENTS IN THE LIVES OF SAILORS AND TRAVELLERS. Small 4to. Profusely illustrated. Cloth, black and gold, and illuminated side. $2.

These are companion volumes, and will be great favorites for the holiday season.

M. C. PYLE.

MINNA IN WONDERLAND, AND ROLAND AND HIS FRIENDS. A charming new juvenile. Beautifully illustrated. Cloth, black and gold, 75 cents.

ROSE VALLEY LIBRARY. 6 vols. 32mo. Illustrated. In neat box. Per vol., 25 cents.

Robinson Crusoe.
Eva Bruen.
Willie and Ned.
Discontented Tom.
Edith Locke.
Ben Benson.

ALADDIN; or, The Wonderful Lamp. With fifteen large and beautiful illustrations, by F. O. C. Darley. Small 4to, fine English cloth, gilt, bev. bds., $1.50.

THE HAPPY CHILD'S PICTURES OF ANIMALS AND BIRDS. 4to. Illustrated with large colored pictures from drawings of animals and birds, by Harrison Wier. Fancy boards. Price 45 cents.

MOTHER GOOSE'S COMPLETE EDITION OF HER RHYMES, CHIMES, AND MELODIES. 128 pp., profusely illustrated, colored, square 12mo. Fancy boards, 60 cents; cloth, gilt, 75 cts.

LETTER WRITERS.

THE GENTLEMAN'S LETTER-WRITER. Bound in boards, cloth back. 139 pp. Price, 35 cents.

THE LADY'S LETTER-WRITER. Bound in boards, cloth back. 139 pp. Price, 35 cents,

THE COMPLETE LETTER-WRITER. For the use of Ladies and Gentlemen; containing both the above bound in one volume. 273 pp. Cloth, gilt. Price, 75 cents.

www.ingramcontent.com/pod-product-compliance
Lightning Source LLC
LaVergne TN
LVHW020117110826
845151LV00001B/184

* 9 7 8 1 4 2 5 5 4 2 5 5 9 *